Rules for a Perfect Life

NIAMH GREENE

PENGUIN
IRELAND

PENGUIN IRELAND

Published by the Penguin Group
Penguin Ireland, 25 St Stephen's Green, Dublin 2, Ireland
(a division of Penguin Books Ltd)
Penguin Books Ltd, 80 Strand, London WC2R ORL, England
Penguin Group (USA) Inc., 375 Hudson Street, New York, New York 10014, USA
Penguin Group (Australia), 250 Camberwell Road,
Camberwell, Victoria 3124, Australia (a division of Pearson Australia Group Pty Ltd)
Penguin Group (Canada), 90 Eglinton Avenue East, Suite 700, Toronto, Ontario, Canada M4P 2Y3
(a division of Pearson Penguin Canada Inc.)
Penguin Books India Pvt Ltd, 11 Community Centre, Panchsheel Park, New Delhi – 110 017, India
Penguin Group (NZ), 67 Apollo Drive, Rosedale, North Shore 0632, New Zealand
(a division of Pearson New Zealand Ltd)
Penguin Books (South Africa) (Pty) Ltd, 24 Sturdee Avenue, Rosebank, Johannesburg 2196, South Africa
Penguin Books Ltd, Registered Offices: 80 Strand, London WC2R ORL, England

www.penguin.com

First published 2010

1

Copyright © Niamh Greene, 2010

The moral right of the author has been asserted

Set in 13.5/16pt Garamond
Typeset by Palimpsest Book Production Limited, Grangemouth, Stirlingshire
Printed in Great Britain by Clays Ltd, St Ives plc

A CIP catalogue record for this book is available from the British Library

ISBN: 978-1-844-88201-4

www.greenpenguin.co.uk

'They say that nobody is perfect. Then they tell you practice makes perfect. I wish they'd make up their minds.'

Winston Churchill

Preface

It was the yellow jelly-baby that finally did it. I hadn't felt right about Robert for a long time before then, of course, longer than I'd dared to admit to anyone, but in the end it was a harmless little yellow jelly-baby that crystallized it all in my mind.

For months, I'd tried to convince myself that everything was fine between us. All couples went through bad patches, it was perfectly normal, especially when you'd been together as long as Robert and I had. Even my sister Theresa, who lives a charmed life in England with her doting husband Malcolm and their angelic twins, once confided that she went through a phase of hating the very *sight* of her husband. It happened a short while after the twins' arrival – poor Theresa had endured not one, but two forceps deliveries and then had the added indignity of suffering a prolapsed womb as well, all because of 'that pervert', as she took to calling Malcolm back then.

The trouble was that Malcolm had promised her faithfully that he'd insist on an emergency C-section when the time came, emergency or not. But when the time *did* come, he never delivered on that promise. Instead he stood by, wringing his useless manicured hands helplessly as the ob-gyn – who had an unnatural preference (in Theresa's opinion) for natural births when possible – went and butchered her on the delivery table! Then he had the audacity to go and faint when the first twin, its skull a strange, alien cone shape because of the forceps, was dragged kicking and screaming from her body.

I

When she was feeling rational, Theresa said she knew that what she'd suffered probably wasn't Malcolm's fault as *such*, but still she sometimes used to lie in bed at night plotting how she might kill him. She'd once read of a man who'd strangled his wife while she lay snoring and later said he'd done it in his sleep and known nothing about it. He claimed straight-faced to the judge and jury that he was unconscious the whole time – and the amazing thing was that he'd got away with it! They actually believed him when he said he'd had no idea he was choking the life from the poor soul and that he was now racked with guilt and remorse and on seventeen kinds of pills to get over the incident.

Theresa confessed to me that she'd started to like the sound of this plan – it seemed so simple and yet so plausible. She didn't think it would be that hard to pull off either – she was an active member of her community theatre group and she'd had excellent experience playing a grieving widow in *Fiddler on the Roof*. She'd even had rave reviews in the local paper. Best of all, a legal precedent had already been established in a court of law – she could do it, of that she was sure. And if she ended up on seventeen different kinds of medication after-wards, so be it. She reckoned it might be her fate.

Theresa said it was only when the doctor diagnosed severe post-natal depression and put her on the little blue pills that she realized how close she'd come to toppling over the edge of her perfect life. It had been craziness – all of it – and just so long as she kept taking the tablets she could see that.

All this gave me a glimmer of hope, until I remembered that Robert and I didn't actually have any children, so there was no post-natal depression to blame for how I felt. Besides, post-natal depression or not, Theresa really *did* have very good reason to hate Malcolm because he *was* a pervert – he'd tried it on with me two Christmases before. He'd said it was an accident, of course, but I knew he'd dropped the roast potatoes on the floor on purpose just so he could look up my skirt.

And so I spent endless nights listening to the rise and fall of Robert's infuriating breathing and wondering what to do. Mostly I did my best to try to ignore how I felt and plodded along with life, clocking in and out of work every day at Hanly and Company estate agents, hoping things would change. After all, the whole world was feeling unsettled and off-kilter, what with the global economic collapse; it wasn't as if I was the only one. Robert, an architect, was feeling it too, I could tell. He spent almost every night reading unemployment statistics and muttering to himself that everyone's heads were on the chopping block and there was no hope left.

We would be OK, though, I knew that. We'd have to be – we were childhood sweethearts and it was definitely against the childhood-sweetheart charter to break up. Even the thought of it made me feel sick in ways I'd never known possible. I couldn't contemplate a split – I wouldn't. This weirdness had to be a phase, something to be got through. It was to be endured and then discussed later, much later, when we were madly in love again and could admit to each other that we'd been through a sticky patch. We'd probably laugh about it all when we were an old married couple. Because that was what the next logical step would be: marriage. It was what everyone expected – a big white wedding. That was what two people in love did. They didn't go splitting up when they were perfect for each other.

But the truth was, I was starting to think I didn't love Robert any more. How could I when almost everything he did irritated me – from the way he woke, stretching his jaws wide so they cracked noisily, then snorting violently through his tweezed, hair-free nostrils, to the way he fell asleep, his breathing getting heavier and heavier with each tiny little snore? I often felt I wanted to lean across and hold the pillow firmly against his drooling mouth, just to finally shut him up. I'd even started to keep a list of reasons why I should leave him: I couldn't stand seeing his toothbrush beside mine in the bathroom every morning; I hated the way he poured his milk so carefully on to his cornflakes; I thought I might ram the *Irish Times* down his throat if he muttered the phrase 'economic meltdown' just one more time.

I kept the list buried in my best Prada handbag and added to it, on and off, for months. But I never did anything about it because, after all, I wasn't perfect either. And, besides, this was all some horrible mistake. So what if there was no excitement left in our relationship? Robert had always been naturally cautious; it wasn't as if I didn't know that. His idea of excitement was watching three episodes of *Grand Designs* back to back. He wasn't the type to take off on mad adventures at whim – no bungee-jumping or African safaris for him. No, he was steady, reliable and utterly predictable, and that was how I had always liked it. Until, that was, everything he did and said began to either bore me rigid or grate on my nerves beyond belief. I hated myself for feeling that way. Robert was a good man, a nice person. None of it was his fault. But as time marched on, I found it harder and harder to keep pretending that things were right between us.

The straw that broke the camel's back happened one innocuous Tuesday night, as these things often do. We were sitting at either end of the sofa: I was channel-surfing and he was working on some complicated architectural design on his PC. Feeling completely disillusioned with work, the gloomy economic climate and the way my hair was never going to be as shiny as Cheryl Cole's, I'd bought a jumbo bag of jelly-babies on the way home and was happily munching my way through the entire pack. I didn't even feel too guilty about this

4

because jelly-babies are, as everyone knows, fat-free and therefore practically good for you.

The first time Robert leaned across and took one without asking, I bit my lip and said nothing. After all, we were a couple – a couple of many years' standing, not some fly-by-night pair; we were *supposed* to share. In fact, I knew somewhere deep inside that I should have actively *wanted* to share with Robert. I should have been bending over backwards, trying to ply him with jelly-babies. Generously stuffing him with the things was what I *should* have been doing, yet there I was clutching the pack with the fierce territoriality of a truculent two-year-old. My teeth were set in grim determination: I wasn't going to give any of them up without a very long, hard-fought battle and possibly a full-on tantrum.

Robert, of course, was oblivious to my annoyance, which, in my irrational rage, didn't surprise me one little bit – he was mainly oblivious to all his flaws. For example, I couldn't understand how he didn't know that flossing several times a day was a peculiar and unsavoury habit, but he seemed to think it was perfectly reasonable to whip the minty string from his person, even in public, and do the business in full view of anyone who might be passing. It was no wonder he saw nothing wrong with freely dipping his hand into and out of the bag on my lap with not so much as a by-your-leave, just as he had always done. My temper was at boiling point by the time he went to pluck a fourth, and when he popped that yellow jelly-baby into his mouth, something inside me snapped.

Suddenly I knew. I just *knew* with blinding certainty that I couldn't stay with him any longer. Because if I didn't go, I'd spend the next twenty years regretting it. I might even end up doing time for murder – I'd never been anywhere near as good an actress as Theresa – and I definitely wouldn't have coped in one of those women's prisons. I'd seen *Bad Girls* on TV, I knew what would happen: some butch inmate, hair bleached with toilet cleaner, would want to be my pimp and if I didn't agree I'd get my fingernails pulled out one by one. I wouldn't last five minutes.

In that moment, as Robert chewed unknowingly, his wet lips slapping noisily off each other, I made up my mind once and for all: I was leaving him. That yellow jelly-baby had finally broken our relationship in two and there was no going back.

Rule One: *Be professional*

Six months later

'Maggie, there's something about you this morning,' Dom says, as I struggle to take off my coat and face another miserable day at Hanly and Company estate agents. 'You look . . . different.'

'There's nothing different about me, Dom,' I reply. Except that maybe I have somehow put a stone of fat on each bingo wing since I last wore this blasted coat. Why else would it have such a vice-like grip on my fleshy biceps? It's taking a sweaty battle to get out of the thing, just like it did to wedge myself into it in the first place.

'No, no, there *is* something,' he goes on, undeterred, as I try to wrestle myself free. 'I just can't put my finger on it . . . Now, don't tell me, let me figure it out for myself . . . Is it your boots? New, are they?'

I pretend I can't hear him as I finally wrench my arms out of my coat, fling it in the general direction of the stand and collapse, panting, at my desk. Playing the I-can't-hear-you game is a tactic my sister Theresa always uses when the twins act up. Whenever they throw themselves on the floor and scream blue bloody murder, which they both often do for a wide variety of reasons – ranging from their Cheerios not being round enough to their strawberry jam not being red enough – Theresa simply pretends to go temporarily deaf. Of course, this means she often has to pretend to be deaf for most of the week. But, then, it's a well-known fact that ignoring a naughty child and not engaging until its behaviour improves is the best policy. And Dom is a big baby who can't behave himself at the best of times, so I reckon the same rules may well apply.

'No, maybe it's not your boots,' he muses, changing tack. 'Is it your skin then – have you put on fake tan? Is that it?'

He's not giving up. Maybe I should set up a naughty step and make him sit on it. That might work. Theresa swears by that ploy – if the ignoring is ignored, that is. Mind you, Theresa often sits on the naughty step herself, for a sneaky fag and a bit of peace and quiet – sometimes she says it's the only thing that gets her through the day, that and the little blue pills.

'I'm ignoring you,' I say loudly, switching on my computer. I'll stick to the ignoring for a while – consistency is key.

'No . . . it's not the skin.' He puts a hand under his chin and drums his fingers against his cheek, pretending to be thinking deeply. 'What could it be? Let me think, let me think . . .'

I roll my eyes – I know exactly where this is headed.

'Could it be . . . could it possibly be . . . the hair?' He smirks.

'Oh, grow up,' I growl, and he dissolves into hysterical laughter at his little joke. OK, so I may have overdone the hairspray this morning but only because I overslept and didn't have time for a shower. Trust him to notice – he's such a metrosexual. He even keeps a pot of hair wax in his top drawer in case of any styling emergencies.

I take a quick glance at myself in the mirror I always keep on my desk so I can do a daily check that I don't have half my lunch stuck in my teeth. The situation is worse than I'd thought: I'd tried to sweep up my mop and do a not-trying-too-hard beehive but it looks nothing like as chic as I'd thought it did. It looks as if a very hairy, very dead animal is squatting on my head and rigor mortis has already set in. It's a disaster. It's all that Cheryl Cole's fault, giving people false hope that they can ever look anything like her. It's never going to happen, no matter how much hairspray I use.

'Can I touch it?' Dom splutters now, guffawing. 'You know – to see if it moves?'

'At least I *have* hair, *Dominic*,' I retort, 'unlike you . . .' I search for the perfect word to wound him '. . . baldy.'

'Ouch!' He clasps his heart, as if I've done him a serious injury, and I try not to laugh. I've managed to get two direct hits there. One: Dom's touchy about his hair – ever since he found it's receding he's spent ages examining his head every day to check for follical retreat. Two: Dom's real name is Dominic but he prefers to be called Dom because he thinks it sounds hotter. He likes to believe he's a bit of a stud – he swaggers around in too-tight trousers, jutting his crotch at anything with a pulse and calling himself a sex god. He even drinks his coffee from a special mug that has 'Stud Muffin' stencilled on the side – or it had until I did a bit of a job with the Tippex and changed the inscription to 'Trouser Snake'.

I see it as my responsibility to remind Dom that it's far from a Stud Muffin he is. Very, very far. To be a stud you have to partake in regular sex with many women and his record in that department is pretty dismal. Of course, he *claims* to have sex all the time – at least three times a week with willing females who, he says, fall all over him at the seedy nightclubs he likes to frequent – but there's very little evidence that it's true. Granted, he does go to an awful lot of trouble to come up with fictitious names for all the gorgeous girls who apparently find him irresistible, but I have yet to see any actual evidence of his legendary sexual magnetism or success with the 'laydees', as he calls them. For example, none of these conquests ever come into the office looking for him and he never gets any mysterious calls from husky-voiced women either. In fact, he never gets any calls at all, except from his mother telling him she's finished his ironing and he can come round for his dinner. Dom is a classic poster child for a mummy's boy and proud of it, a fact I like to tease him endlessly about – or I did until I met his mother. She was a bit scary.

'You've hurt me, Maggie.' He pulls a sad, wounded face. 'You've hurt me deep.'

'Oh, shut up, you muppet.' I laugh, pulling a face back. 'You started it.'

I know Dom's not the least bit hurt by my jibe. Our mutual slagging is like a little tradition between us now. It began on the first day I started work in Hanly's five years ago and has more or less continued unabated since then. I walk in, Dom comments on what I wear, how I look – and even occasionally how I smell – I tell him to go ride himself and then we get on with our day. In a strange way, it's a comforting ritual and one that I cherish in these dark, uncertain times when no one knows what's around the next corner. Unemployment, weird flu and possible Armageddon are what the papers say we all have in store, so insulting each other is something Dom and I can rely on, even if the whole world is apparently falling off some cosmic cliff. Besides, I don't take any of the jibes he flings at me seriously because I know that behind the banter Dom's actually a sweet guy who'd do anything to help anyone in trouble. Not that I'll ever let him know I think that, of course – his head is big enough as it is.

I turn back to my computer, a feeling of dread consuming me. It's bound to be another awful day, trying to fill in eight hours pretending to be busy. I used to love working here, but since the property market went bust, an estate agent's office is not the laugh a minute it used to be. In the good old days, people tossed money around like it was going out of fashion and you didn't even have to try to sell a property because it sold itself. A few short years ago, punters were lining up, begging you to sell them just about anything, but now that boom has turned to bust, buyers are scarcer than hens' teeth and you practically have to throw in convertible sports cars to get so much as a sniff of interest in anything. And that is exactly what some sellers are doing, they're so desperate. Cars, boats, plasma TVs – you name it, they'll include it if it means getting a quicker sale. Last week one vendor even offered to hand over a time-share in his Marbella penthouse just to offload an investment flat he'd bought in the city centre.

I've seen it all since the market imploded and unfortunately, most of the time, even these tactics have no impact: people just aren't buying and even the lure of free stuff won't persuade them to part with their cash. Meanwhile, anyone who *does* want to buy is being refused finance by the banks. Dom and I have spent many hours viciously dissecting these bankers and fantasizing about what we might do to punish them for refusing prospective buyers' mortgages. It's a fun game, deciding which torture devices we could employ (the water wheel is my particular favourite) – and, more importantly, it helps to pass the time.

Passing the time has become the main focus of my day in past months because, instead of actually selling anything, I now spend most of it filing properties over and over again. Dom is determined to look on the bright side – but, then, as I always tell him, he makes it his business to be stupidly optimistic. Now, instead of enjoying the buzz of selling, he focuses on getting his kicks in other ways – mostly by sexually harassing anyone who ventures into the office, including the postman. In fairness the postman, a nice middle-aged man called Nigel, who has seven children, a wife and two girlfriends, takes it in good spirit.

Meanwhile Dermot, our boss, spends almost every day staring

blankly into space. He has sunk into a severe depression since the market collapsed. Even Dom can't cheer him up by sending him snippets from porn sites. Nothing can raise a smile – although Dom keeps trying his best. His theory is that Dermot needs to see busty platinum blondes frolicking with each other now more than ever. He maintains he's only trying to help, but we both know it's not working because Dermot is still hollow-eyed with worry and stress over the business. I can't say I blame him – like so many businesses out there the company is in serious trouble. We have eighty-nine unsold properties on the market, and ninety-nine places to let. Nothing is moving and, thanks to the economic downturn, nothing is likely to anytime soon. We are – to use a highly technical estate agent's term – screwed.

'So . . . how are you *really*?' Dom asks coyly, sliding over to me on his swivel chair. 'Meet anyone nice over the weekend, did you?'

It's the same line he's been using every Monday morning since I broke up with Robert. He's convinced I need to get out and play the field before I become a born-again virgin and forget how to do it at all. He doesn't want to hear that I've been home alone, watching reruns of *Friends*. (I still occasionally like to fantasize that I'm Jennifer Aniston in series four – when she had the straight blonde hair extensions and the washboard stomach.) But I *like* staying in: the apartment that Dermot rents to me as part of my package is so cosy. It's in a complex he invested in with a local developer and it was a Godsend when I left Robert. Dermot charges me next to nothing for it, which I'm grateful for: trying to pay full rent on a salary that's no longer bulked up with commission would be impossible.

'My weekend was fine,' I say.

'Come on – don't hold back the details. You met some bloke

out on the town and exhausted him with dirty sex, right?' Dom suggests, winking at me. 'Do you need a strong coffee to help you stay awake?'

'No thanks,' I deadpan. 'I think I'll manage.'

Coffee is the last thing I want. My stomach is already queasy from the anxiety of not knowing what today will bring. I'm not sure I can stand one more hour of pretending to be busy, or filing every property we have yet again.

'Aren't you going to ask me how *my* weekend was?' Dom says, pouting. He's desperate to get to the juicy stuff – his own dirty-stop-out exploits.

'How was your weekend, Dom?' I enquire obediently.

Dom likes to tell me about his fictitious conquests every Monday morning and usually I try to ignore him. Because I've nothing urgent to get to immediately, though, I'm willing to indulge him for a bit now. I could do with cheering up and a story about one of his highly unlikely liaisons may just work.

'Well,' he slides closer, 'you're not the only one who had a dirty weekend, if you know what I mean.' He puffs out his chest. 'I'm pretty whacked myself.'

'Really?' I say, trying to look totally disinterested.

'Yeah.' He leans across the desk to tell me more. 'I met this Australian bird on Saturday night. She was a real goer.'

'Let me guess – she was an air stewardess, right?' I say.

'Yeah – how did you know that?' Dom misses the sarcasm in my voice.

'Let me think, Dom. Could it possibly be because almost every woman you allegedly sleep with is an air stewardess?'

He grins at me, delighted with himself. He firmly believes he's a legend – I blame his mother for inflating his ego.

'The trolley-dollies love me, Maggie – what can I say? Maybe it's because I take them to amazing heights – gettit?' He roars with laughter at his tried and trusted joke.

God bless him, but Dom also thinks he's some sort of comedian. He reckons he could give Graham Norton a run for his money if he really wanted to.

'Go on,' I sigh.

'Oh, OK.' He looks disappointed by my neutral reaction to what he thinks is his brilliant wit. But he recovers pretty quickly. 'So, anyway, we're in bed and you'll never guess what she asked me.'

He grins broadly at me again, and I try not to grin back. I don't want to encourage him too much, even if I am just a teeny bit interested. His tales, although completely fabricated, are usually hilarious. Not that I would ever tell him so, of course.

'Let me see . . . Did she want you to go Down Under?'

'Eh?' He misses my joke and I decide not to attempt to explain it to him.

'I don't know what she asked you,' I say. 'Do tell me.'

'OK. Well, she only asked me to pretend to be Crocodile Dundee!'

'Crocodile Dundee?'

'Yeah. Like, the movie? You know – he lives in the outback and wrestles wild crocodiles?'

'Yeah, I remember that movie.' God, how does he make this stuff up?

'So, she has this hat, right? You know, like Crocodile Dundee wears?'

'A wallaby hat?'

'That's the one!' He beams. 'So I put that on and I start to feel the part, you know?'

'Not really, but go on.'

The thought of Dom wearing a wallaby hat and nothing else is pretty disturbing. I try to erase the image from my mind.

'Anyway, I'm there wrestling with a pillow, pretending it's a man-eating croc.'

'You were pretending a pillow was a man-eating croc?'

'Yeah – I was improvising, you know, to spice things up.'

'Right.'

'So, there I am, letting the pillow have it – shouting at it and telling it its days were numbered – when this bird goes crazy.'

'She goes crazy?'

'Yeah, she starts moaning and groaning – it was really wild.'

'And then what happened?' I'm waiting for the punch line. Had a troupe of air stewardesses leaped from the wardrobe and performed safety manoeuvres in the nude, perhaps?

'Well, we did it, of course.' Dom looks confused.

'So, that's it? That's your big story? You pretended to be Crocodile Dundee and you had sex with an air stewardess?'

'Well, yeah.' He beams at me. 'Isn't it fantastic? I can barely walk this morning – she almost freaking killed me!'

'And that's it?'

He looks disappointed that I'm not more impressed.

'Yeah, that's it. Why – what did *you* do?'

'I don't know what you mean.' I certainly don't want to go there.

'Well, obviously you had a much wilder weekend than I did.' Dom seems devastated by the idea that he's not the most sexually adventurous male on the planet. He likes to think that he's King of the Wild Sexual Exploits – it's why he gets his back waxed every four weeks in Ultimate Wax Off. He denies it, of course – but I know the truth. I've caught him coming out of the salon more than once.

'No, I didn't,' I mutter, fiddling nervously with my computer keyboard.

'No, go on, tell me. Or let me guess . . .' He starts to cheer up a bit. 'Did you play Tarzan and Jane with some dark stranger, maybe?'

I concentrate on my computer screen.

'Aha!' Dom jabs the air between us with his index finger. 'If ever there was a guilty look that's it! I've hit the nail on the head, haven't I?'

'Don't be ridiculous.' In spite of my best efforts, I feel heat rise to my face. Of course, it's the one morning I didn't have time to use the special green concealer – the one that covers broken veins and hides high cheek colour.

'Oh, Maggie, you're blushing! God, what did you get up to? It must have been X-rated! You didn't tape it by any chance, did you?' He sounds positively excited.

The phone goes and I pick it up gratefully before I have to answer him. 'Hanly and Company, how can I help you?' I say, injecting as much enthusiasm into my voice as possible. This may be the only call I get today so it's vital I sound friendly and approachable. Not that it will matter, of course – the market is dead so sounding friendly and approachable probably won't make any difference one way or the other.

'This is Rita Hyde-Smythe.'

The voice on the line is clipped and businesslike and my heart drops to my toes, waving hello to my spasming stomach on the way down. Rita Hyde-Smythe is the greatest bitch in the city, possibly the entire country. She's been trying to sell her hideous mansion for months now, to no avail, and to say she's not happy about it is a serious understatement. It was built at the height of the Celtic Tiger and is the most repulsive display of ostentatious wealth I've ever seen. And that's saying something because there's a lot of temples to bad taste out there.

Rita's nine bathrooms are decked out with gold-plated taps, she has hand-cut marble work surfaces in her one-off custom-designed kitchen and, as she likes to remind me every time we speak, there are solid mahogany floors throughout. Dom now calls her Solid Mahogany Hyde-Smythe, among other things.

Rita paid a snotty interior designer a vulgar amount of money to achieve what she believes is the ultimate in luxury, but the trouble is that all this 'glamour' has failed to attract even one bid from the buying public. There have been viewings, but the opulent interiors coupled with the enormous price tag have failed to attract even one offer. Rita feels this is all my fault, and she's not afraid to tell me so. She calls me frequently to berate me because she believes I haven't arranged enough viewings. I haven't marketed her ugly mansion properly. I haven't followed up potential buyers effectively. The sole reason her house is still on the market is apparently due to my incompetence and nothing to do with the fact that her taste in furnishings is horrific and the house is overpriced by at least half a million euro. If Rita had her way, I would be traipsing up and down the street with a sandwich board strapped to my back, advertising her property twenty-four hours a day. Even then she probably wouldn't be happy because Rita is a breed of Celtic cub who just doesn't understand why she can't get what she wants – she always has before.

I silently curse myself for being so eager to answer this call. Why didn't I let Dom take it? He's much better at handling Rita than I am – mostly because she falls for his charm every single time. What she doesn't know is that while he's sweet-talking her and reassuring her that her exquisite property will be sold very soon indeed, he is also sticking his fingers down his throat and making vomit gestures to me.

'Good morning, Rita,' I say, trying to sound professional.

'Is that Mary?'

'Maggie,' I correct her.

Rita never gets my name right. I know she does it on purpose to wrong-foot me.

'Have we had any enquiries about River House?' she asks coldly, getting straight to the point. Rita doesn't do pleasantries. She also likes to talk in the 'royal we' – as in, 'we haven't been trying hard enough' or 'we need to do better'.

'Let me double check for you, Rita,' I reply, as politely as I can. 'I'll pull out the file. Just give me a second.' I put her on hold before she can protest and try to think.

I'm playing for time. I know full well that there hasn't been a single enquiry since we last spoke before the weekend. Rita knows that too, because if there had been even a glimmer of hope I would have called and told her straight away. I wonder if now is the time to take the bull by the horns, insist she pare back on the lavish interiors and slash the asking price. We might have a few bites then. And we have to do something about the name too, that's critical: even though it's called River House, her stately pile is nowhere near a river. The nearest water – a paltry stream that dries up in summer – is at least ten miles away, something that the handful of prospective buyers who have viewed the property in the past few months have felt enormously aggrieved about. The only reason it's called River House is because Rita thought it sounded grand. She even had a limestone slab specially hand carved with the name and placed at her customized electric gates.

I wish I had the courage to say all this to Rita but I know if I do she'll hit the roof – again – and I'm really not in the mood to listen to her histrionics this morning. It's not as if she really needs to sell the property anyway: she inherited millions from her uncle when he died so she doesn't even have a mortgage. She's in a much better position than some of the other vendors desperate to get rid of houses they can no longer afford. Maybe if I try to tell her delicately – drop just a few hints – she might react better.

I flip the file open and immediately spot a Post-it note at the top of the page. I can hardly believe it – it looks like Dom took a call about the property on Friday when I was out. His scrawl is barely legible, so I can't make out what it says, but my heart leaps with hope. Maybe things are looking up. Maybe someone wants to view it. Dom is on the other line and I can't risk keeping Rita on hold for much longer – I have no time to quiz him about the query. I'll have to bluff, tell her there's been an enquiry and get the details from Dom later.

'Rita?' I depress the hold button.

'Yes, I'm waiting. I must say I don't care too much for being put on hold. If you were a true professional you'd know the exact state of affairs regarding River House without having to consult any file.'

I resist the urge to slam down the phone on her. She really is a battleaxe.

'It seems there's been some interest in the property,' I go on, willing myself not to snarl. 'According to the file, we received a call about it on Friday.'

'Really?' Rita perks up. 'Why didn't you contact me immediately? I should have been informed!'

'Well, I didn't know about it. I just need to talk to –'

Before I can finish, she interrupts me rudely: 'I don't want to listen to any of your excuses, Mary. I *am* paying you to handle all River House affairs, am I not? This breakdown in communication is *most* unsatisfactory.' Her voice is icy.

'I was away on business, Rita,' I say, trying to remain calm. 'Dom took the call, so I just have to get the details from him.'

'I see.' Her voice is less clipped – she has a soft spot for Dom, that's for sure.

'I'll investigate and get back to you ASAP.'

'Make sure you do, Mary,' she sniffs haughtily. 'Otherwise I may have to take my business elsewhere. I'm very unhappy with this level of service – we expect better.'

She hangs up and I slam the receiver back into its cradle.

'The name is MAGGIE, you stupid cow!' I shout at the phone.

'Maggie, why so excited?' Dom arches an eyebrow at me. 'Not that I'm complaining. I love nothing better than to see you get hot and sweaty.'

'Shut up, Dom, or I'll sue you for sexual harassment,' I snap grumpily. Solid Mahogany has managed to put me in an even worse mood than before.

'I look forward to it, darling. Or, if you prefer, we can just play Courthouse? I'll be the judge and you can be the very bad girl – how about it? Now, I'm not saying it would be as hot as playing Tarzan and Jane but I'd do my best.'

He licks his lips cheekily and I can't help but laugh in spite of my bad humour.

'Maggie, Dom.' Right then, Dermot appears in front of us, his face ghostly white. He's been getting progressively sicker-looking for the past few weeks – but he looks really deathly today.

'Are you all right, Dermot?' Dom asks.

'Not really,' Dermot says, his voice raw. 'Actually, I need to talk to you both. Can you come into my office, please?'

He promptly disappears without another word. Dom and I glance at each other anxiously before we rise silently from our seats. I try not to let the panic in my chest overcome me but I know this is probably it. Dermot doesn't make a habit of calling us into his office and, from the expression on his face, he's not about to offer us performance bonuses and company cars.

'Chin up, Maggie,' Dom whispers, grasping my hand in his. 'Maybe it's not what you think. And even if it is, it's not the end of the world.'

I smile at him and nod, but I feel as if I'm floating above

my body, looking down. If Dermot is calling us in to tell us our jobs have gone it *is* the end of my world as I know it.

I've already left the man everyone else insists is the love of my life. Mum and Dad were so devastated when I finally told them that they had to go to Marbella for a holiday to recover. How will they take this news? And then there's Theresa. I've spent months listening to her harp on and on about how I've made a huge mistake in leaving Robert – she says he's 'a fine catch' and definitely irreplaceable, especially at my advancing age. I never used to think thirty-two was so bad, but then again I hadn't known that it's apparently the exact age when any decent man ceases to look at you. Theresa wasted no time informing me of this fact – she says it's why she's hung on to Malcolm for dear life, even though he abandoned her in her darkest hour.

Now not only am I going to be manless, I'm going to be jobless too. It's utterly tragic – which technically means that I'm a tragic heroine. Funnily enough, not even that thought is enough to cheer me up as I stumble blindly into Dermot's office to hear my fate.

Rule Two: *Always have a Plan B*

'I'm really sorry, but it looks like I'll have to let you both go.' Dermot's face is ashen. He's explained to us, as if we weren't already painfully aware, that the collapse of the property market means that Hanly and Company is in serious financial trouble and that it no longer makes sense to keep us here when he could easily do the pitiful amount of work involved himself.

'It's all my fault,' he goes on, his voice cracking. 'If only I hadn't invested in that damn apartment complex I might have been able to get through this. But I'm screwed now – the developer's talking about handing back the keys to the bank. I've lost my money, I can barely hang on to the business and I'm ruining your lives as well. Christ, it's the pits.'

He buries his head in his hands, distraught, and my heart constricts. How will he cope without us? He won't be able to deal with clients shouting down the phone at him. I'll have to find the answering-machine for him before I leave so he can screen the worst of the calls. Where *is* that thing? I think I shoved it under the stairs the last time Dom left all those rude messages on the tape. I'll have to dig it out.

It suddenly strikes me that I may be in shock – isn't this what people do when they're in shock? Focus on insignificant details, like where they might have put the answering-machine?

'Whoa there, steady on, Dermot. You're not ruining our lives.' Dom pats Dermot on the arm. I know this physical gesture of support goes against his better judgement – Dom doesn't believe in being overly demonstrative to his own sex:

he told me it once led to a very awkward encounter in the toilets of Sheeba nightclub with a man in a pair of very tight leather trousers. 'Every cloud has a silver lining. This little setback could be just what we all need to reassess where we're headed.'

I smile gratefully at Dom for trying to make Dermot feel better. He's lying, of course. This cloud has no silver lining – it's an utter disaster – but there's no point in telling Dermot that, and it's kind of Dom not to rub salt in his wounds. Dermot doesn't need to hear that he's responsible for ruining our life plans: he's upset enough as it is.

I try to assess how I feel now that the 'what if' has become a 'for sure'. It's almost as if I'm floating above my own body – as if this isn't really happening to me at all. It's not an unpleasant sensation: it sort of reminds me of the time I smoked weed with the cool gang at the back of the school football pitch when I was fifteen. It turned out that I'd actually been smoking a tobacco roll-up and I made a right fool of myself because I told everyone I felt all spacey and out of it. That was when Patty O'Houlihan laughed and said they'd only been winding me up. It was so embarrassing.

I never admitted any of that to Mum or Dad. What will they say when I tell them this? They're still devastated about me and Robert splitting up so this will send them over the edge. I'm sure when I was growing up they didn't think I'd be such a disaster zone.

'It could?' Dermot raises his head from his hands and looks at Dom hopefully.

He's as vulnerable as a small child. It's so sad to see him this way. He's always been soft-hearted – which is probably another reason why he didn't capitalize on bigger property deals when others wouldn't have thought twice. He only invested in the apartment block when everyone else was getting out of the market. Now he looks like a broken man. As well as his unhealthy pallor, his eyes are bloodshot and he's lost weight too – his cuddly jowls have all but disappeared. I suddenly realize I can't remember the last time I saw him eating one of the BLTs he loves so much – in fact, I can't remember the last time I even saw him nibble a biscuit. He's clearly been too stressed to eat.

Unlike me. Theresa says the fact that I overeat when I'm under pressure is a symptom of some unresolved psychological issue: she maintains I'm subconsciously trying to eat my pain away. Theresa loves to read self-help books – she often says she might become a psychotherapist once the twins are older and less dependent on her for everything – after all, if she can retain so much knowledge about emotional baggage when they won't even let her wee in peace, who knows what she could achieve? I know the thought often keeps her going when one of them poops on the hall rug for the umpteenth time in a week.

'Sure it could!' Dom says brightly. 'This blip could be our golden opportunity!'

It's weird, but he sounds almost . . . sincerely cheerful. I'm quite impressed. If I didn't know better I might start to believe his pep talk myself. Obviously lying about all the women in his life has made him quite the expert.

'Yes. I, for one, refuse to be broken by all this financial misery,' Dom goes on, smiling broadly. 'I already know what I'm going to do.'

'You do?' I turn to look at him and realize he *is* serious – he's not mucking around. He *does* think this could be some sort of opportunity.

'Yup,' he announces. 'I'm going to Australia!'

He grins at both of us, thrilled with himself.

'Australia?' I repeat, dumbstruck. This is the first I've heard of it – how come he never told me? 'Why Australia?'

Suddenly I'm a little bit annoyed. He should have confided in me. It was almost – almost sneaky of him not to. Maybe then I would have made some concrete plans too, instead of just vaguely hoping that everything would turn out OK.

'It's not *why*, my gorgeous Maggie. It's *why not?* I've always wanted to go and now's the perfect opportunity. My cousin Pierce says there's still work over there and I know from experience that the Aussie birds are little crackers. Pierce says threesomes are ten a penny and he's no James Bond, so can you imagine how well I'll do?' Dom rubs his hands together, beaming at the idea.

'I can't believe you're thinking with *that*,' I dart a disdainful look at Dom's crotch, 'at a time like this.'

Why is everything always about sex with him? It's unnatural. Maybe he has some sort of real problem. His outrageous stories are funny, but if even half of them are true he could be a proper sex addict.

'Maggie, Maggie, Maggie,' Dom shakes his head in mock seriousness, 'you know I *pride* myself on thinking through *this*.' He glances at his zip and grinds his hips in my direction, grinning, just in case I missed his point. It's his signature move, one he practises endlessly in front of the full-length mirror in his bedroom. He says it's far more effective when he isn't wearing anything. Thankfully I've never seen that version.

'Well, I think you're mad,' I say stiffly. 'Barking mad.'

I'm really put out that he hasn't mentioned his grand plan to me before now. Somehow I had just presumed that he hadn't thought things through – that he'd flounder if the worst happened, just like me. Hearing otherwise has thrown me.

'In fact,' I go on, unable to stop myself, 'I read in the papers last weekend that there are no jobs in property in Oz either so you're fooling yourself if you think you're going to land some big number. It'll never happen.'

Technically, all this is untrue. I've never read anything of the sort but Dom won't know that. He never reads any papers – not unless they feature page-three girls, that is. I feel a little guilty for lying but for some reason the thought that Dom has a life plan in place now that disaster has struck is extremely unnerving. Dom is a fly-by-night, a messer. He never plans for anything. He lives from day to day, minute to minute – so how come he seems to have thought through this scenario? It doesn't add up.

'Maybe so,' Dom smiles enigmatically at me, 'but who says I'll stay in this business? Who says I won't do something completely different?'

'Like what?' I retort. 'You're not qualified to do anything else. Not that you were ever qualified to work here either, of course.' I make a face at him.

'Maggie, why so negative?' He tuts. 'It's a very unattractive trait in such an attractive girl.'

'I think you're right to go,' Dermot pipes up suddenly.

His voice takes me by surprise – I'd almost forgotten he was in the room, I was so busy being annoyed at Dom for his stupid optimism.

'See?' Dom winks at me. 'This man has the right attitude. Tell us more, Dermot!'

'Well . . . I always wanted to travel,' Dermot muses slowly, 'but I never made the time. I was always too busy with this place.' He gestures helplessly round his office. 'Now it's too late.' He looks forlornly at his desk, where stacks of files jostle for space. Dermot has his own special filing system that no one else has ever been able to interpret. His office is like a bomb site but if he wants a memo he can usually find it in less than thirty seconds. His unique method of organized chaos seems to work just perfectly for him.

'Dermot, my friend,' Dom counsels, moving to stand behind him and pat his shoulder, man to man, 'it's never too late.'

'Nah, my time has passed,' Dermot laments. 'I'm far too old to be off gallivanting round the globe. And now I couldn't afford it, even if I wanted to. I've worked all my life and it's amounted to a big fat nothing. I can't believe I'm such a failure.'

His voice breaks and I feel tears well in my eyes – it's awful to see him like this. 'Don't be so hard on yourself, Dermot,' I choke.

He looks so devastated – I know he really is heartbroken that things have turned out this way.

'I guess I did my best,' he shakes his head again, 'but I must be the only estate agent in Ireland not to have made any serious money during the Celtic Tiger years. What kind of a gobshite does that make me?'

I wince. Dermot never uses bad language – never.

'Now I won't even have enough to fund my retirement,' he says. 'It's going to involve far less luxury than Yvonne had bargained for. God knows how she's going to react when she finds out the truth.'

'You mean she doesn't already know?' Dom asks, glancing at me to gauge my reaction.

I try to keep my face neutral to hide any surprise that may be registering, but the truth is, the fact that he hasn't told her is not that much of a shock. Yvonne is Dermot's second wife. They married exactly three years after his first wife, Marie, died of breast cancer and Dermot has always treated her like some sort of princess. He's showered her with gifts and money since the day they met. My personal theory is that he's been trying to make up for the frugal existence he and Marie had – they reared three children and put them through college but they never treated themselves. Marie died without ever enjoying any of the perks of wealth, and I'm convinced that Dermot is so racked by irrational guilt about all she missed out on that he's been trying to make up for it ever since. He still never spends anything on himself, but Yvonne has been living a cosseted existence since she met him. Telling her that the business has collapsed and her gilded life is about to come to an abrupt end will be very difficult.

'Not exactly,' Dermot admits sheepishly. 'She's aware that things have been . . . tighter than usual. But I haven't been able to bring myself to tell her everything. I didn't know how she'd take it.'

'Give Yvonne some credit,' I say. 'She didn't marry you for your money.'

Dom raises his eyes at me behind Dermot's back but I try not to react. We've always agreed from the very beginning that Yvonne is a proper gold-digger. Anytime she breezes into the office she's wearing the latest designer creations and carrying a must-have It bag with a superior sneer to match. This change in circumstances is going to devastate her and Dermot is right to be worried: if funds dry up she may well decide to walk and take her collection of gorgeous handbags with her. Poor Dermot would be gutted if that happened – he actually seems to love her, not that I can understand why. She's shallow, manipulative and charmless. She isn't even that good-looking – take away the hair extensions, fake tan and inflated boobs and she'd be really ordinary. Dom's theory is that she gives Dermot so much kinky sex that he's willing to look past all that – but then again, he has a sexually related theory for almost everything.

'She had her heart set on an indoor pool,' Dermot says mournfully. 'She'll never get that now.'

'Did I mention I'll have a pool in Oz?' Dom interrupts. 'And a Jacuzzi – that's where all the threesomes happen, Pierce says.'

'Dom!' I shoot him a look to shut him up. 'Pools are vastly overrated, Dermot,' I go on. And they play havoc with fake-tan addiction, I want to add but I stop myself just in time. There's no point in making it worse – Dermot will find out soon enough that Yvonne's loyalties lie firmly with her Platinum Visa.

'Try telling Yvonne that,' Dermot replies, forlorn. 'She has expensive tastes. If I can't provide for her the way she expects I don't know what will happen. She could leave me.'

'Oh, stop being so melodramatic,' I say briskly. I have to get his mind off things somehow or he'll end up crying on his desk. 'She'll never leave you – she's mad about you.'

This is another barefaced lie. I don't think Yvonne loves Dermot – I think she loves what she thought he had. Now that that's all gone she probably won't be able to pretend any more.

Dom makes another face at me, but I continue regardless. It would be useless telling Dermot that his wife is a twenty-four-carat bitch who will dump him like lightning for a new model once she discovers how bad things really are.

'Do you think so?' Dermot sniffs, and I know he's trying to pull himself together.

'Of course she is,' I confirm, 'and why wouldn't she be? You're not half bad.'

Dermot smiles a watery smile at me, the first since we entered his office. I know I'm safe half flirting with him like this – he's old enough to be my father after all.

'I have some money for you both.' He clears his throat to

compose himself and passes two envelopes to us. 'It's not as much as I would have hoped to give you, but it might help a bit.'

'Thanks, boss,' Dom says, and I bite my lip so I won't cry.

I know Dermot will have done his best by us. The scary thing is this money is going to have to last me until I can find a new job. Not that there's much hope of that any time soon because no one is hiring. The newspapers are full of features about the terrible situation that thousands of people have found themselves in. Five hundred hopeful applicants turned up for a cashier position in a city-centre supermarket the other day. The terrifying thing is I don't even know how to operate a digital cash register – I wouldn't have stood a chance.

I take the cheque from Dermot and lean in to give him a hug.

'Will you be OK, Maggie? What will you do?'

He looks so anguished again that I can't tell him the truth. That I have no idea what to do next. I don't have Robert to rely on any more. I'm all on my own in more ways than one. Maybe Theresa was right. Maybe I should have stuck with him.

I try to push this thought from my mind. We weren't meant for each other, not really, and there's no point in pretending otherwise now just because I might soon be destitute. Even if it is tempting, just for a split second.

'I'm not sure yet,' I answer vaguely.

'Maybe she'll come to Oz with me?' Dom jokes, and I swat him with my redundancy envelope.

'No chance, baldy,' I say. 'What are *you* going to do now, Dermot?'

'I'm not sure.' He runs a hand through his hair and looks pained. 'Batten down the hatches, I guess. Stay here, man the office and hope things improve. I only wish there was enough business to keep you and Dom on. You two were the best employees I ever had – by a mile.' His voice breaks.

'Ah, now, Dermot, save all that mush for the reference letter!' Dom tries to jolly him along. 'Anyway, I think we all know there was very little work involved – sure weren't people knocking down the door to buy? All we had to do was hand them a pen to sign on the dotted line!'

Dermot laughs darkly. 'You're right – those were the days. Do you think it will ever get any better?' He sounds suddenly desperate. 'Do you think things will improve?'

I've never seen Dermot like this. Usually he's supremely confident. Never cocky, he was never that – not like some of the estate agents who creamed the market when the going was good – but he was always quietly assured. Now, in the face of financial ruin, he's an emotional wreck.

'Of course it will, Dermot.' I do my best to reassure him. 'Things will be on the up again soon, everyone knows that. You'll be hiring us back before you know it.'

'Yes, maybe you're right,' he murmurs, smiling weakly at us, and I realize with a shock that Dermot has aged at least a decade in the last six months. His eyes are haunted with worry and his hair is greyer than ever round the temples. The stress has really taken its toll on him.

I stuff the cheque into my pocket. 'Now pull yourself together,' I say. 'It's time for Plan B.'

'Plan B?' Dom's face brightens.

'That's right,' I say. 'Plan B. Let's go for a drink to cheer ourselves up.'

'That's the spirit, Maggie!' Dom whoops, and Dermot manages a chuckle.

We've always gone with Plan B whenever anything tricky has come up – like when Solid Mahogany Hyde-Smythe has thrown a massive wobbler. We've sunk a lot of pints over that pain in the arse.

'Ah, I don't know,' Dermot mumbles. 'I've a lot to do here.'

He gestures feebly at some paperwork. 'You two go on – have one for me.'

'Dermot,' Dom says, 'I don't think there's anything too urgent that can't wait till later – do you?'

'Well, I have stuff to do . . .' Dermot says, but I know he's tempted – I can see it in his eyes.

'Ah, go on, one little drink won't hurt. Just the one.' Dom is very good at wheedling – it's apparently how he manages to get so many women into bed: he annoys them into agreeing.

'Oh, all right so.' Dermot laughs weakly, then hauls himself up from behind the desk. 'You're a terrible lad.'

'Good man!' Dom cheers aloud. 'I'll just get my coat.'

He sprints out of Dermot's office and it's then that Dermot grabs my hand. 'Maggie, I'm so, so sorry,' he says, his eyes moist.

'Ah, Dermot, it'll be OK.'

'No, I'm not sure you understand . . .'

What's not to understand? I don't have a job any more, that's crystal clear.

'It's about the flat.'

'The flat?'

'Yes . . . If the developer is handing back the keys to the bank, I'll have to ask you to move out.' He swallows, choking back emotion.

'Oh.' My voice is a squeak. I hadn't thought of that.

'You can come and stay with Yvonne and me for a while, you know, until you get yourself sorted. Yvonne would probably love the female company – you two could talk about stuff . . . shoes, maybe . . .' His voice trails away uncertainly.

My head swims as the gravity of the situation hits me full force: I have no job. Working here is all I know – it's not as if I have a heap of other talents I can fall back on to earn an income. I've never even waitressed. Not that there's a need for waitresses now that the restaurant industry is on its knees too.

And now I have nowhere to live either. I'm going to be bunking in with my ex-boss. I'm going to be talking shoes with his gold-digger wife. Oh, God.

A wave of real fear overtakes me and I feel sick. What if I can't find work? What if I spend the rest of my life on the dole? I've got to face facts – no one's hiring estate agents. No one's hiring anyone, anywhere.

'Maggie?' Dermot's features are creased with concern.

'Don't worry about me, Dermot,' I say, taking a deep breath and fixing a fake smile to my face. 'I'll figure something out. Now, let's go for that drink.'

His face crumples in relief. It's a weight off his shoulders that he doesn't have to worry too much about me. He's grateful I have some sort of plan for survival.

I throw my bag over my shoulder and link my arm through his, trying to quell the fear rising in my chest. Dermot may think I'll be OK, but the reality is I don't have a plan at all. In fact, I have absolutely no idea what I'm going to do.

Rule Three: *Nourish your soul*

'This could be the best news ever,' Claire says.

'And you think that because?' I take a sip of my wine and try to figure out how losing my job and my home could be a good thing. It certainly doesn't feel that way.

'Because this gives you the freedom to pursue your dreams – you know, reclaim your inner self,' she replies confidently.

'Right.' I grip my glass, a wave of irritation washing over me. If she bangs on about this inner-me stuff again I may just lose it. I love Claire dearly – she's my best friend – but she lost her high-powered job with a hedge fund a few weeks ago and she's been on a spiritual voyage of discovery to 'find her core self' ever since. It was funny to begin with, but now it's becoming very, very boring.

Not for the first time I wonder about getting her and my sister Theresa together – they could have a self-help fest. Maybe with them both off my back, I could just wallow in anxiety in peace, like I want to.

'I'm not convinced you were ever that happy in Hanly's anyway,' Claire says meaningfully. 'I think it stifled your creative side.'

'I *was* happy there,' I sigh, 'perfectly happy.'

'No, you were perfectly *settled*. There's a difference. A very big difference.'

'What are you talking about?' These days, trying to decipher what Claire means is a full-time job.

'I mean, you showed up every day, you clocked in, you clocked out, but what were you really getting from it all?'

'Um, the highest residential sales in the office?'

Dom tried and failed to beat my sales record a million times and Claire is aware of this: why is she acting as if she's somehow forgotten? She knows how good I was at my job. I surpassed targets, I set records. That was before the market collapsed, of course. After that it didn't matter how good I was: all my sales skills were irrelevant when the property boom ended.

'Besides that? Besides all the sales, what were you actually *achieving?*'

'That's all that really counted, Claire. Commission was always based on sales, you know that.'

'OK.' She pauses. 'Let's look at this problem from a different angle. I've been reading a brilliant book recently – there was a chapter dedicated to this precise phenomenon, so I know exactly what I'm talking about.'

'Right,' I sigh.

Claire is able to quote chapter and verse from dozens of self-help books – it's as if that's all she does at the moment. The ball-breaking she used to indulge in, just for fun, is ancient history. Now it's all loving your fellow man and random acts of kindness.

'So . . . you were earning commission,' she says seriously, as if she's trying to solve some sort of riddle and never shafted half her staff to serve her own professional purposes without a second's thought.

'Yes.'

Shedloads of commission when times were good – which, to be fair, seems a long, long time ago now.

'And . . .' she continues slowly '. . . what did that commission *give* you?'

'Duh, Claire! The ability to buy stuff, of course!' What is she missing here? She knows I always spend all my disposable income . . . and maybe a little – OK, a lot – more every month. Consumerism is the cornerstone of my existence, for God's sake. It has been ever since I used to work as a teenager in the corner shop every Saturday.

Miserable Stinky O'Connor paid me just fifty pence an hour to stand behind the counter and deal with all the grubby kids who piled in to spend their pocket money on sweets every week. The abuse I had to take from those children was mind-boggling – they called me every name under the sun if I didn't get them their Wham bars fast enough or if their fizzy cola bottles were too sour. Working in Stinky's was hell and the only way I could get through the day was by promising to buy myself something with my wages – usually fluorescent socks or *Jackie* magazine. That was until I discovered handbags, of course.

I think about my handbag collection now. It's nothing like as vast as Yvonne's mammoth one – Dermot's wife should have a PhD in shopping – but it's tipping along nicely all the same. I have a Mulberry tote and a Lanvin clutch. I even have a baby Paddington with its coveted chunky padlock. The Holy Grail, Chanel, has been out of my grasp so far, but that hasn't stopped me fantasizing about owning an iconic 2.55. It occurs to me that this dream will never materialize now that I'll have to stop acquiring unnecessary luxury items. I probably won't even be able to buy a Chanel knock-off. After all, I'm unemployed. Not to talk of homeless. The thought makes my heart pound so hard in my chest I feel dizzy.

'So,' Claire is still talking, 'you liked buying stacks of stuff?'

'Of course – what woman in her right mind doesn't? It's hardwired into our genes.'

I take another sip of my wine and mentally try to close the door on Chanel, which is very difficult when I can still visualize myself sweeping into a five-star hotel with a piece of quilted perfection under my arm.

'Aha!' Claire takes a swig of her mineral water and nods vigorously, as if she's made some sort of psychological break-through. I tried to convince her to have a wine, but she wouldn't hear of it – she's very strict about alcohol intake now. She keeps harping on about her body being a temple and all that crap.

'What's your point, Claire?'

'My point is – stuff can't make you happy.'

Has she lost the plot? Of course it can. My bags make me very happy on a daily basis. 'I beg to disagree,' I say.

I know by saying 'I beg to disagree' I sound like something from the eighteenth century, but Claire is bringing out that side of me. It's not a side I like.

'OK. You have lots of bags,' she says, as if she's almost reading my mind. 'But how does that fulfil you?'

'They make me feel good. They accessorize my outfits.' Has she completely forgotten how designer stuff can alter your mood? *Her* Chanel handbag is her prized possession. Or it used to be, until she started all this spiritual mumbo-jumbo. I look at her now and wonder where that bag is. She doesn't have it with her – today she's carrying something that looks suspiciously like she may have bought it in a charity shop. And not a cool charity shop where you might see Kate Moss rummaging round either. Some place where everything is mouldy and moth-eaten.

The bag is a patchwork concoction, with beading and – horrors – tiny little mirrored tiles stitched to the edges. It's absolutely hideous, and if Claire was in her right mind she'd shove it into the pub fire that's glowing nicely in the grate beside us. The old Claire wouldn't have used that bag to put her dirty laundry in. Then again, the old Claire wouldn't have appeared in public without at least six inches of slap on her face – and from where I'm sitting her skin looks completely devoid of makeup. I'm not sure she's wearing bronzer, which usually she even wears to bed.

'OK, you look nice. But do all these material goods do anything for your soul?'

'My soul?' I wonder if she'd consider donating her Chanel to me. After all, it looks like she's taken a completely different style direction. I'd probably be doing her a huge favour if I offered to take it.

'Yes, your soul,' she says, and I snap back to the present. 'Do those bags and other possessions nourish your inner self?'

I think about that for a minute. OK, they may not exactly balance my *chi* or whatever Claire is talking about, but they make me feel great about myself and that has to count for something. There's nothing like holding a perfect handbag – it's like toting a work of art around with you. At least, that's how I've always managed to convince myself that the extortionate price tags have been worth every penny. Besides, exclusive bags are heirlooms – I'm not buying them for myself so much as passing them on to the next generation. My unborn daughter will thank me for my foresight one day, I know it.

'Well, they nourish *something*,' I say defiantly. 'I feel brilliant when I carry them.'

I don't mention that I've felt increasingly uncomfortable flaunting them recently, though, what with the recession. Since the whole world began its economic downslide, it's seemed a bit crass to cart designer bags around. Now it looks like I might have to sell them all anyway, just to pay the bills. Why didn't I ever save for a rainy day? Why?

Claire cocks an eyebrow at me, as if to imply that what I've just said is shallow and completely inappropriate, considering the financial crisis the world is facing. She's become so politically correct since she lost her job and started believing crystals could heal. Just as I'm thinking that, she takes one from her bag and presses it into my hand. 'Here, take this, keep it close, it'll help,' she says, a weird I-am-wise expression pasted on her face. Claire's been very keen on looking and acting wise recently – it's unnerving: she used to specialize in snarling when she worked in the hedge fund. Snarling and decking people. She once discovered that a colleague had hacked into her email account and she lamped him – he was out cold, slap bang in the middle of the third floor. Now she's gone all other-worldly. And what is it with the weird sing-song voice? She almost sounds like one of those self-hypnosis tapes that help you stop smoking.

I'm starting to wonder if Claire and I have anything in common any more. Maybe I should have called Lisa instead. She still loves to shop. And she'd be happy to tell me my life was screwed, without insisting I give up my precious Prada handbag.

'Let's talk about Robert for a minute,' Claire says now, munching a prune from the packet that's stuffed surreptitiously into her pocket. She's already told me in very graphic detail how, combined with her increased intake of roughage, prunes have significantly improved her bowel habits and that if I followed her lead I'd have tons more energy and my skin would lose its grey tinge. I could even see her wincing when I devoured my bag of cheese and onion – I'm almost sure she muttered something derogatory about trans-fats under her breath.

The prunes are really off-putting. If the barman knew what she was doing would he confiscate them? It does say that only food purchased in the bar can be eaten here. Maybe I should give him a wink and a nod. It might be worth it just to get rid of them – even the sight of her chewing is turning my stomach.

'What does Robert have to do with anything?' I really don't want to talk about him.

'Well, you broke up with him because he wasn't your soul-mate, right?'

Claire used to scoff at the notion of soul-mates. Anytime she even *heard* the expression she'd fume that the theory was complete rubbish and anyone who believed there was just one person out there for them was deranged. Now she seems to be taking the concept seriously – so much about her has changed that it's hard to keep track.

'Yeah,' I agree. At least she hasn't mentioned the jelly-baby thing. Not like Theresa. She's happily beaten me over the head with that for the past few months. Theresa can't fathom how anyone could ever leave a perfectly good specimen of a man over a jelly-baby, of all things. She thinks what I did was ludicrous – especially after all she's been through with Malcolm. She reckons that until I have a couple of forceps deliveries and a husband who couldn't change a nappy if his life depended on it I won't know what hardship is.

'Yes, and that was the right decision,' Claire goes on. 'You need to strip your life back to improve it – look at me, I've never been happier!'

She's getting into her stride: her eyes have gone a bit glassy. I just hope she doesn't try to tell me she's been taken over by some celestial being like she did a few weeks back. Now, that *was* embarrassing.

I take a long hard look at Claire, as she asked me to. Her previously blow-dried, glossy mane of hair is now scraped back into a very unflattering ponytail – the kind of ponytail that sarky gossip magazines would call a Croydon face-lift. I can tell from the tiny grey springy hairs at her temples that she hasn't seen the inside of a hairdresser's salon for quite some time. She's wearing a scruffy hoody top that she wouldn't have worn to bed when she was a hedge-fund manager. Less than three months ago she would have sneered at someone like her in a pub. All in all, she's in a bit of a state and nothing like her normal groomed and pristine self. Ironically, she seems to have no clue she looks so strange – or if she does she doesn't care.

She pops another prune into her mouth, just as I'm trying to figure out where I've seen that hoody before. Did she use to wear it to the gym, maybe? It looks so familiar . . .

'Losing my job was the best thing that ever happened to me,' Claire goes on. 'It really is amazing how the higher power works. I mean, I didn't even believe in any higher power until I was fired and I started to find myself. I'd been living half a life. At last I can see what really matters – do you understand?'

'I'm not sure I do, no.' I don't want to be rude, but I have no idea what she's talking about. How can being made redundant be a positive thing? Is there something about it that I'm missing? Some up-side I haven't figured out yet? Because all I can visualize is me sitting slumped in a chair, endlessly searching the newspapers for a job of any description. That's if I ever find somewhere to live.

Claire is still talking. 'I mean, if I hadn't lost my job, I never would have discovered my real passions. You need to get your priorities right, Maggie – it's now or never. Let's face it, you're not getting any younger, are you?'

That's a bit harsh. I'm not telling her she needs to get her hair seen to, am I? And I certainly don't need reminding that I'm not a teenager any more – I can tell that just by looking in the mirror every morning. 'I'm not over the hill yet,' I say, feeling defensive.

'Yes, I know, sorry, I didn't mean it like that. But the clock *is* ticking. If you want to change your life, now is the time. I mean, when we were younger did you imagine that you'd end up an estate agent?' She pops another prune into her mouth and rolls it around with her tongue.

'Probably not,' I say. Does anyone ever dream of becoming an estate agent, though? It doesn't exactly feature highly on the list of most popular careers – it's not up there with pop star or actress.

'What about your art?' she asks. 'You always wanted to be an artist when we were at school. You were really good, Maggie. Maybe now's the perfect opportunity to go back to it.'

I swirl my wine and think about this. It's true I loved to paint, but it's not like I could have done it for a living. It was only ever a pipe dream – one I buried a long time ago, along with my burning ambition to marry Jon Bon Jovi. That plan didn't work out either.

Suddenly it comes to me. I know where I've seen that shabby hoody she's wearing before. It looks suspiciously like the one she used as a blanket for her toy poodle. What was that dog's name? Charlie, that's it. Claire sent poor Charlie to the pound when he refused to be house-trained. He used to piddle all over her hand-woven rugs, no matter how hard she tried to teach him to go outside. The final straw was when he did his number twos in her precious Balenciaga handbag. Is it possible that Claire is actually wearing her dog's *bed*? I shake my head to get rid of the image of Charlie the poodle chewing insanely on the hoody. Are those tiny little toothmarks I can see on the neckline?

'Maggie?' Claire says. 'Did you hear what I said? Maybe now's the time to explore what you really want from life. It's not too late.'

'Eh?' I tear my eyes away from her neck and try to concentrate on what she's saying.

'I think you should pursue your art. You used to be so good – why not give it another chance?'

'Artists don't make much money, Claire,' I say. 'And unfortunately I need to keep earning so I can live. Rent isn't cheap, you know.'

'But would you like to paint?'

'Yes, maybe in an ideal world. If I won the lottery, I'd spend every day painting. But it's not like that's ever going to happen.'

'But you *want* to do it?'

'Claire,' I sigh, getting impatient, 'I've just lost my job. I have about five euro to my name and nowhere to live. Painting is the last thing on my mind.'

'But if you found somewhere cheap to rent, took a sabbatical for a few months, then you could dip your toes back in . . .' Claire sounds positively enthusiastic about this idea – she's read one too many self-help books.

'Even if I wanted to, it's not as if there are tons of cheap places to rent, is it?' I reply. 'Especially not now I'm unemployed. And, before you suggest it, I'm not going to move back in with Mum and Dad.'

The term buzzes round my head, bouncing off my skull. I'm unemployed. *Unemployed.* God, I never really believed this would happen to me. What if I can't get another job? How am I going to live?

'Maybe there's nowhere cheap in the city, no,' Claire looks at me carefully, 'but have you ever thought about moving to the country? Everything's much better value there.'

'The *country*? Are you mad?' I snort into my wine.

I've been on quite a few pampering weekends in grand country hotels. The spa treatments are always nice enough but forty-eight hours is the maximum I can stand before I start to yearn for the hustle and bustle of the city. Living permanently in the middle of nowhere is unthinkable.

'It could be the perfect solution to your problem,' Claire goes on. 'The pay-off Dermot gave you would last much longer there. You could take some time out, decide what you want to do next, maybe even paint. Who knows what might happen? We only live once, Maggie – life isn't a dress rehearsal, you know.'

She has *definitely* been reading too many of those motivational books. I'm hooking her up with Theresa for sure – they can indulge in their self-help heaven together and leave me out of it. 'No offence, Claire, but that's crazy talk.'

'Why? It's what I'm doing.'

'Eh? What are you talking about?'

She looks at me levelly, then takes a deep breath. 'I've decided to retrain as a holistic therapist and move to the country.'

I splutter my white wine across the table, narrowly missing splatting her in the eye. A trickle of Chardonnay runs down her cheek instead. 'You're *what*?' Claire is going to become a holistic therapist and live in the country? That's insane! Claire has a serious addiction to caffeine. She smokes. She thinks water is for sissies. Or she did until she started this whole detoxing thing. I thought that was just a phase. I fully expected her to snap out of it soon.

'Yes,' she says, dabbing the dripping wine from her face with the sleeve of her shabby hoody. 'I've been feeling so fulfilled since I started this journey that I want to move to the next level.'

Oh, God. She really is talking like a lunatic. Is this what happens when you lose your job? This could be my fate too. I'll be wearing dog-chewed clothes and carrying crystals soon – it's inevitable.

'I don't want to get sucked back into the rat-race. I realize what's important now – and it's not money or possessions. So that's why, before I retrain, I'm going to spend some time in an ashram.'

'An *ashram*?'

I gulp down my wine and signal to the barman that I want another. I'll need something to fortify me for this news. First Dom announces he's off to Oz. Now Claire says she's going to an ashram and then moving to the country. What next?

Will Dermot pop out of the woodwork and tell me that Yvonne is really a man? Mind you, that wouldn't surprise me too much – her upper arms are far too toned.

'It's a hermitage – where you can practise yoga and meditation.'

'I know what an ashram is. I just never thought . . .' I'm stumbling over my words.

'What? That I'd want to go to one?'

'Well, yes,' I admit.

'But I do, Maggie – I can't wait! This is going to be properly life changing.'

'Right.' I can't sound enthusiastic, I just can't.

'Aren't you excited for me?' A cloud of concern crosses Claire's face.

'Um, I guess so. If that's what you want to do. It's just that I never thought that going to an ashram would be your sort of thing.' What I don't say is that this hare-brained scheme sounds like the type of plan Claire would have laughed at only a few short months ago – didn't she use to say that yoga was a useless waste of time?

'Well, neither did I, but that was before . . .'

Claire's voice trails away while she tries to compose herself. I think I see a tear glinting in her eye and Claire *never* cries. She's been known to thump people who cry in public. She whacked me once when we were watching a sad movie and I broke down as the heroine died in a freak tragic accident. The bruise lasted for well over a week. I look into my wine glass and silently wish the ground would open up and swallow me whole. That would be much better than seeing Claire dissolve into snotty emotion.

'Sorry,' she sniffs, 'the journey to your core self can be so emotionally draining. Anyway,' her voice steadies, 'once I get back from India, I can get stuck into country life – start afresh.'

Maybe she's on drugs – that may be why she's acting so strangely. Perhaps she's hooked on some sort of over-the-counter painkiller. She did have an awful lot of paracetamol lying round in her flat last time I was there. The addiction could have started after she had her veneers done. I'll have to talk her out of this nonsense – that's the only thing to do.

'An ashram is one thing, Claire,' I say slowly. 'That's only a short-term move. But is relocating to the country such a good idea? It's a very big step. Can't you set up as a holistic therapist somewhere in town?' Or go back to the hedge fund, my inner voice screams.

'I've always wanted to live in the country, Maggie. It's now or never. Life's too short not to go for what you want. And this is what I want, I know that. I've even found the perfect place to rent on-line. It's called Rose Cottage.' She pulls a printout from her patchwork bag and passes it across the table to me. 'I know it sounds corny, but I always had a dream of living in a little cottage, with roses growing round the door. This place is perfect. I get a really good feeling about it . . . I can see myself there – do you know what I mean?'

'Sort of.' I drain my wine. I've heard this sort of thing from clients – they see photos of their dream home in a property prospectus and before you know it they've imagined their entire life there. It rarely works out that way, though – not once they step through the front door and realize that the whiff of curry will never leave the carpets or the front room will always be cold and dark, no matter how many lamps they plug in. First impressions can be very misleading.

I cast my eye over the photos. I have to admit, it does look gorgeous. It's a tiny stone cottage, with sparkling whitewash on the exterior walls and a duck-egg blue half-door. There are even roses creeping round the frame. The windows look like original working sash, and the garden is really pretty, with pink hydrangeas and what looks like an apple tree by the gate. The place couldn't be any cuter, but all is probably not what it seems. The way the shots are taken, it looks exactly like something from the front of a twee chocolate box, but I know all the old tricks so I'm cautious.

'This thing could face a main road,' I say. 'Usually if a property is photographed up close, like this one is, they're trying to hide the fact that the front gate opens on to a motorway.'

'It doesn't.' Claire grins. 'It's in the middle of nowhere – near a village called Glacken.'

'There might be a waste-treatment plant next door.'

'No,' she laughs giddily, 'it's surrounded by acres of fields.'

'Neighbours from hell?'

'The nearest neighbour is the main house – that's where the landlord lives.'

I strain to see anything amiss in this idyllic photograph. There must be something wrong. Maybe they've used Photoshop to erase all the imperfections.

'You can stop looking for negatives. It's perfect, Maggie.'

'It can't be.' I still don't believe her. Nothing is ever as perfect as it first appears. 'Those roof tiles could be asbestos.'

'They look like they've been replaced recently, though.'

'There's obviously no heating, then.'

'Don't be silly. Of course there is.'

'There must be *something*.' I'm not giving up.

'There's not. It's all in really good nick and the rent is negotiable if the tenant gives a hand at the big house for a few hours a week.'

'Aha!' I shout. 'I knew it! What does that mean?' Giving a hand at the big house? It sounds dubious in the extreme – what kind of a dodgy operation is this landlord running? I've heard about those wild swinging parties in country manors.

'I don't know exactly,' Claire says. 'Brush the ponies, walk

47

the hounds, shepherd sheep, whatever it is they do in the country all day, I suppose. Sounds like paradise to me.'

'Right.' The landlord wants help with the farm animals in exchange for a rent reduction. I rearrange my features so that Claire won't see what I've been thinking – obviously I've spent far too much time in Dom's company: his depraved mind has rubbed off on me.

'Yeah, I've wasted so much time in that damn hedge fund, feeling miserable in uncomfortable heels and pencil skirts. Now I'll be free to express myself in a way I never thought possible.'

She gathers her hideous patchwork handbag to her bosom and hugs it joyfully. If this is Claire expressing herself, we're in serious trouble. But if the photos are to be believed, then she's right about one thing: this place *does* look like paradise, the perfect escape from the city grind. If you were into that sort of thing, which I'm not. I'm a city girl through and through and I always will be.

'So, can you see yourself living there for a while?' Claire's eyes gleam.

'*Me?* What do I have to do with it?'

'Think about it, Maggie. I'm going to the ashram for three months, but I could sign the lease now and you could live in the cottage while I'm in India. It's ideal for both of us – you could watch the place for me while I'm away and take a breather from the city at the same time. It'd be the perfect opportunity to chill out for a bit and decide what your next step is going to be. What do you have to lose?'

I look at the photos. The place *is* nice – she's right about that. Maybe some time out would do me good. After all, I haven't had a proper break since Robert and I split up. I could just relax for a while before I try to get another job – a few months probably wouldn't make any difference either way.

Maybe I could even think about changing career direction . . . look into doing a few retraining courses myself.

'You don't have to stay for ever – you can go straight back to the city when I'm finished in the ashram, if you want. There's no commitment, Maggie – and, of course, I'd cover the rent. You'd be doing me a massive favour.'

I have to move out of Dermot's investment flat ASAP and I don't exactly have anywhere else to go. Besides, if Claire pays the rent then my redundancy money will last much longer – there'll be far less pressure to rush out and get a job, any job, to pay the bills.

'Just come with me to see it and then think about it, that's all I ask,' Claire wheedles.

'OK,' I murmur. 'If you really want me to.'

I suppose I may as well go along for the ride – it's not like I have much else to do. And going to see the cottage can't hurt, even if it comes to nothing. The truth is, once Claire sees the place she'll probably run back to the city with her tail between her legs anyway. She'll change her mind about this country plan when she realizes that her quaint cottage doesn't have a power shower or a climate-controlled heat-recovery system – I'd bet my last pay cheque on it.

Rule Four: *If you can't be the sun, don't be a cloud*

'Go through the third crossroads,' the deep voice at the other end of the line bellows, 'and then keep an eye out for the lime kiln.'

I'm on the phone to Edward Kirwan, landlord of Rose Cottage, getting new directions to the house. We've become lost in the middle of nowhere on the drive down – all because Claire insisted on disabling the sat-nav in her BMW. She used to live and die by that electronic device, but now she maintains that it's an unnecessary distraction and we're perfectly capable of finding the way ourselves. Turns out she has seriously over-estimated our map-reading skills.

'The third crossroads, did you say?' I repeat, just to make sure I haven't misheard him. There's a lot of noise in the background and it's hard to make out exactly what he's saying.

'That's right,' he shouts, above the din. 'Then take the second right after the lime kiln.'

I strain to hear him – the racket is intensifying. I can hear some sort of weird wailing noise. Could it be a wild animal? It's incredibly loud whatever it is.

'Do you know what a lime kiln is?' I ask Claire, suddenly hoping she has a change of heart and decides that living in a country cottage would be hell. From the noise at the other end of the phone it certainly *sounds* like it is. I should have put this call on loudspeaker so she could hear for herself. I wonder if I could manage to do just that without cutting him off.

'Yes!' Claire nods, beaming. She's in a fantastic mood and

has been since we left the city. Her heart is set on this cottage – she's spent the journey so far telling me that it has everything she's ever dreamed of in a home: charm, character and an open fireplace where she can burn smelly turf and 'contemplate her life'. Considering she had a gas fire in her apartment and she'd always thought open fires were a messy inconvenience, this change of heart is staggering. Claire used to love high-end appliances – she got a Nespresso machine a full year before anyone else. Her apartment is a shrine to polished granite surfaces. But now she says she prefers the shabby-chic look. She says she loves lime plaster (whatever that is) and flagstones and she doesn't care if the cottage doesn't have a Miele dishwasher. In fact, she says she's looking forward to getting Cath Kidston rubber gloves. She's even claiming that washing up is a very soothing exercise – I have trouble believing that, especially since I know she hasn't washed up in at least twenty years, not since she used to do it for her mother to earn some extra pocket money. Even then, the way I remember it, she used to moan all the way through.

'Hang on, I'll just check if June can meet you there,' the landlord says now, sounding even more hassled. 'I'm having a little . . . domestic difficulty here.'

The noise has abated – maybe that was some sort of interference on the line.

'He's going to check if his wife can meet us there,' I whisper to Claire, who's still smiling serenely as she negotiates the narrow country roads with care. She hasn't grumbled once, even while her precious BMW ground through dozens of potholes. I know she's trying to be at one with nature and pretend that none of it bothers her.

Suddenly I hear rustling in the background. And more yelling. Someone shouts, 'Take that *off* your head, Polly,' then there's a crash and the unmistakable wail of a child who has just come a cropper. That definitely wasn't interference on the line. There's mayhem going on there.

'Christ almighty!' a voice swears. 'Polly, for goodness' sake, will you take that bucket *off* your head!'

I wince. It sounds like World War Three has broken out. 'Er, I can call back if you like?' I offer tentatively. I'm not sure if he's even at the other end any more but it seems like chaos there – which doesn't bode well for the cottage. In general, landlords who lead chaotic lives have properties that are disorganized and badly maintained. The same is true of landlords who are dishevelled in appearance: the shabbier they are, usually the shabbier their property is. There are exceptions to the rule, of course. I once had a landlord who dressed from head to toe in stinking sweatpants and never seemed to wash but her rental was immaculate. She'd even installed an internal vacuuming system. I can't help but wonder how she's faring in this market, when rents have dropped and there are so many properties available. Now that prospective tenants have the pick of hundreds of properties, the tables have finally turned.

'No, no, just give me a minute,' the voice pants. He's obviously running with the phone. 'I can't find June – she must be in the garden.'

'I'll call back,' I say, rolling my eyes at Claire. 'He's a total idiot,' I mouth to her.

'Hang on,' she mouths back, winking cheerfully at me.

'Look, someone will be there to meet you, OK? I just don't know who.'

Then the receiver rattles back into its cradle before I can say any more.

'Talk about disorganized!' I huff, snapping my mobile shut.

'It'll be fine, Maggie, chill out.' Claire has been telling me to chill out a lot recently – it seems to be her new philosophy. She also keeps telling me to stop sweating the small stuff, which is even more disconcerting because that was exactly what she did for years.

'Listen, Claire, I don't want to burst your bubble,' I say, 'but this Edward is a complete flake – I don't know what was going on in the background but it sounded chaotic. *And* he made a right mess of giving directions to the cottage. I mean, telling us to go through some random crossroads and then look for a lime kiln, whatever the hell that is. It's madness – that kind of thing just isn't on.'

'I think that's how it works down here,' Claire says. 'It's not like there are street names we can follow. Anyway, we know where it is now, so all's well that ends well.'

'Yes, well, a good landlord should be far more organized,' I mutter. 'What if you get a leak in the middle of the night? If he's not on the ball it could be a disaster. His attitude just doesn't bode well.'

'You shouldn't be so quick to judge people, Maggie,' Claire says. 'Live and let live, that's my new motto. It's amazing how calming it can be when you take that approach to life.'

'That's funny,' I say. 'Your old motto used to be "Everyone is an arsehole until proven otherwise."'

'Anyway, I like this country approach to things,' Claire says stoutly, ignoring me. 'It's quirky.'

'You don't like quirky,' I remind her.

Claire thinks that anyone who has more than one body piercing is socially unacceptable. I once got a blonde streak in my fringe and she was appalled. Claire does not do quirky. She does strait-laced. At least, she used to. Now she does patchwork quilted handbags and unplucked eyebrows.

'I'm learning to *love* quirky,' she protests. 'Besides, I like taking the scenic route – it's fun! It's just like the road trip we took to Las Vegas.'

We did that legendary trip across California back in 1999,

when we were young, free and single. We travelled to San Francisco, Napa Valley and Yosemite Park, but Vegas had been the highlight. I'll never forget driving through the desert, spotting the twinkling lights in the distance and whooping and hollering with glee. We'd only planned to stay in the Luxor Hotel for two nights, but we were there for four. Just strolling through the foyer was incredible – we felt like we'd been transported back to ancient Egypt.

And the buzz in the place was amazing. Within an hour we'd become addicted to the slot machines and the free cocktails. We never mastered any of the more sophisticated games – like blackjack or poker – we never wanted to: the slots were exciting enough for us, and when we got bored with pouring buckets of money into them, we'd wander over to the high rollers and watch them casually throw thousands of dollars' worth of chips on to a table, like it meant nothing at all. Then there was the shopping. God, I loved that place – even thinking about it makes me feel all nostalgic and gooey.

'How is driving to a shack in the middle of nowhere like our road trip to Vegas?' I grin at her.

'Maggie,' she mock-tuts, 'Rose Cottage isn't a shack, it's *quaint*. And doesn't this trip remind you of driving to Vegas, just a little?'

'We don't have an open-top car,' I point out, laughing.

We'd hired an amazing red convertible in California – we had the roof down constantly so we could soak up the glorious sun. We spent most of the journey pretending to be Thelma and Louise. It really was brilliant fun.

'That's true,' she admits. 'But I do have the *Thelma and Louise* soundtrack on CD!' With a flick, music booms round the car.

'Do you remember the all-you-can-eat buffets?' I say, thinking about the spectacular spreads we used to have. When they said 'all you can eat', they really meant it. I'd never seen such monstrous displays of food in my life. heaven.

'Oh, yeah, they were amazing, weren't they?' Claire's eyes go misty at the memory. Before that holiday she used to pride herself on having a tiny portion of toast, no butter, for breakfast but even she couldn't resist the Vegas food – she really let herself go. She put on seven pounds from the buffets alone.

'Yeah, they were.' I nod. 'Do you remember the muffins?'

'Seventeen different types? Oh. My. God. *Amazing.*'

'What about . . . the pancakes?'

She knows exactly what I'm talking about and we both burst out laughing.

One morning, Claire had been wobbling towards our table with a stack of pancakes so high I could barely see her face. It was her second trip to the pancake stand – she'd already eaten a huge pile but couldn't stop herself going back for more. She was setting her plate on the table when the server appeared and asked if we wanted a coffee refill. Spotting Claire's oversize stack he'd done a double take, then asked, 'Y'all want extra syrup?'

For some reason, that had really set us off. We'd laughed so hard some blueberry pancake had shot right out of my nose – which only made things worse. The poor server didn't know what to do.

'I figured out why I was doing that.' Claire giggles now.

'Doing what? Eating enough to feed a small army?'

'Yeah.' She laughs. 'It was a famine thing.'

'A famine thing?'

Claire has come up with some outlandish theories in her day, but even I want to know how she can link her greedy raids in Vegas to the Irish famine of the 1800s when thousands died of hunger and even more emigrated to avoid starvation.

'I reckon we Irish go mad at the all-you-can-eat buffets

feel, deep in our subconscious, that we

ungry again – like we did during the potato

lective-consciousness thing.'

o you stuffing your face in the Luxor Hotel was

r ancestors starved?'

She chuckles, knowing how absurd this sounds.

. . . it could just be because you're a pig.'

We both dissolve into giggles again. God, it feels good to laugh. It feels like I haven't had a good laugh in a million years.

'Speaking of pigs, I'm thinking of getting a real one when I move down here,' she says.

I guffaw again – that's a good one.

'No, seriously. I mean it. I might even get goats.'

'Goats?'

'Yes. For milk. And hens too. I'll probably become self-sufficient.'

'Claire, have you ever actually tasted goat's milk?' I ask. 'It's vile.'

'I'll get used to it,' she answers airily.

'And how will you survive without your espressos – or will you be too busy collecting eggs to miss those?' I snigger.

'I'll be fine,' she says. 'Anyway, I've given up coffee, remember?'

'But you've lived in the city all your life. How are you going to cope when you're miles away from the nearest shop?'

We've already passed through the village of Glacken and, by the look of things, it doesn't even have a proper supermarket, let alone a coffee shop or a wine bar. Who knows where the nearest decent nightclub is?

'Maggie – look at the scenery!' she says gleefully. 'It's heaven on earth down here! I won't care about shops!'

'You think?' I say.

'Yeah, I mean, just look at all this.' Claire gestures to the fields that surround the lane we're currently crawling up. 'You'd never see this in the city.'

'You're right about that,' I agree, eyeing the herd of cows trotting slowly along in front of us. An elderly farmer is ambling behind them, as if we have all the time in the world to get to where we need to go. He tipped his hat at us when we rounded the bend and came face to face with dozens of black and white rear ends, but since then he's simply continued meandering up the road at a snail's pace. Claire's sporty BMW is now travelling at less than 10 k.p.h. per hour.

'Do you think you should bip him?' I ask, a wave of impatience washing over me. It's going to take us all day to get to the cottage at this rate.

'Maggie, you can't bip a farmer because his cows aren't going fast enough for you. This is the country – he has right of way if he needs to move the herd from one field to another.' Suddenly Claire seems to know all the rules and regulations of country life – or, at least, she's pretending to.

'Well, there has to be a quicker way of doing it. I mean, can't he make them go any faster?'

My hand is itching to honk the horn. It's infuriating the way the farmer is just strolling along. It looks like he's going as slow as he possibly can on *purpose*, and he's encouraging his cows to do the same. We're almost stationary now.

'What's your rush? You need to slow down and smell the roses, Mags.' Claire leans her head back against the car seat and rolls down the window. 'Take a nice big breath – doesn't that fresh country air smell wonderful?'

I inhale and then splutter with the shock of the ghastly stench that assaults my nostrils. 'It smells like cow shit, Claire, if that's what you mean,' I gasp, covering my mouth and nose with my sleeve. 'Shut that window, quick.'

'Come on, Maggie,' Claire laughs, 'it's all part of country living!'

'Well, good luck to you. I prefer nice city diesel fumes myself.'

'Even if it's polluting your lungs?'

'I'd choose polluted lungs over that any day,' I say, as a cow pauses directly in front of the car. It lifts its tail and a great whoosh of green slime spatters all over its legs and the road. 'Oh, God, I'm going to be sick,' I mutter, as Claire giggles beside me. My stomach heaves – I may never drink milk again. Up close and personal, cows aren't nearly as cute as they look in those TV ads for cheese. I've never noticed before, but they aren't at all cuddly: their legs are really spindly and their bodies are out of proportion to their heads. Looking at them now, I realize they're positively ugly and the way they poop themselves all the time is really gross. What if some of that poop ends up in the milk? I know the manufacturers pasteurize and everything – but does that even work? I make a silent vow to swear off all dairy products for the foreseeable future, just in case. Of course, that might make it tricky to have my favourite toasted cheese sandwich, but it'll be worth it.

I can't take my eyes off the green slime that now seems to be sliding down the back legs of almost every cow in the herd ahead. Isn't there something they could wear to stop all that stuff dripping everywhere? Some sort of cow nappy maybe? Surely all that gunk can't be good for the environment. Didn't I read somewhere that cow gas is one of the main contributors to the destruction of the ozone layer? These ugly animals are the reason we're all getting fried alive by the hole in the atmosphere. I've a good mind to give that slowcoach farmer a piece of my mind about it.

'How can you not love all this . . . greenery?' Claire breathes. 'I mean, don't you find it so restful?'

There's a look of rapture on her unmade-up features. I'm almost starting to get used to her without makeup now – and somehow she's seeming less naked without the warpaint. Her skin is great – really clear and dewy, almost like she's wearing illuminating concealer, except I know she's not because she's already told me she's decided to go barefaced to allow her skin to detox. I have to admit, it may just be working – her face is aglow. She's an advertisement for the *au naturel* look.

'Restful? Are you kidding me?' I snap. 'If that farmer doesn't get out of our way soon I'm going to have a coronary right here. Or else I'm going to massacre all his cows.'

I imagine jumping into the driver's seat, revving the motor and ploughing through the entire herd – for a split second it makes me feel better.

'Is that a sycamore, do you think?' Claire says idly, pointing to the branches of a tree that are brushing against the car as we inch past.

'I don't know, but it's scratching your paintwork,' I say. 'Honestly, who's in charge of pruning the hedgerow round here? It's completely overgrown – how are people supposed to get by without destroying their cars?'

I wince as more branches scrape against the passenger door – the lane is so narrow it's impossible to avoid them.

'It's the countryside, Maggie.' Claire laughs. 'I believe the hedgerows are *allowed* to grow. It's not like a city garden where you practically have to measure your grass to make sure it doesn't get too high!'

'There's a lot to be said for a bit of order, you know,' I reply, resisting the urge to push Claire aside and step on the accelerator. 'Those hedges are so . . . untidy. And they must be a hazard.'

'To what?' Claire smirks. 'The cows?'

The cows have slowed down even more. A few have now

stopped completely to chew the grass at the side of the road. The farmer is nowhere to be seen – surely he should stay at the back to make them move along? Or he should have a sheepdog at least to keep them on their toes. Or do sheepdogs only work with sheep? I'm not sure, but in these recessionary times they should learn to multitask. They should be back here, forcing these cows to move along. Because these are definitely the dimmest cows in Ireland. Possibly the world.

'Well, I'm going to buy a book about trees so I can recognize all the different species,' Claire says. 'Nature is just fascinating! I want to learn all about conifers, deciduous trees, evergreens. I want to be able to tell them apart.'

'You never cared about trees before,' I say sharply. Maybe a bit too sharply. It's not a crime to want to learn about trees, I suppose, but I'm getting totally fed up with Claire rewriting her entire personal history to make herself sound like a soft and cuddly person when in fact she's nothing of the sort.

'Yes, I did,' she replies.

'No, Claire, you didn't,' I snap. 'In fact, if I recall, you even refused to have a real Christmas tree in your living room last year – you said you couldn't stand the smell. And you hated having to vacuum the needles out of your rug – remember?'

There's silence in the car. I may have gone too far but, honestly, Claire has lost the run of herself. What is the point of learning about trees? What possible use is that ever going to be in daily life?

'You're right,' she says quietly, and even though I feel a little bad, I sigh with relief. Finally, she's seen sense. She realizes this whole charade is a complete waste of time. I had to be brutally honest with her, but if it's made her see the light it's been worth it. And she can't be too cross with me because she's still smiling.

'Can you believe I was that self-centred?'

'Sorry?' I'm confused now.

'Imagine, I was so self-obsessed that I couldn't even appreciate the wonder of nature! My God, I was a monster.' She shakes her head, as if she just cannot grasp the fact that she ever had a plastic, pre-decorated Christmas tree from Homebase in her pristine living room.

'You weren't self-centred, Claire, you were normal.'

'No, I was wasting my life. And now I'm going to devote it to things that are really important.'

'Like learning the difference between tree species?' This is all going horribly wrong. I thought she'd seen how silly this country plan is, but in some strange and warped way, I've actually managed to validate her new lifestyle choices. Which is just my luck.

'You think it's a waste of time,' she says calmly.

I raise my eyebrows in response.

'Well, if I'm going to be living down here full time, I'm going to need to learn the lingo. I can't go round thinking oaks are sycamores, can I? I'd be a laughing stock.'

'But will you really care what the locals think about you? I wouldn't say they're exactly . . . sophisticated.'

As we sped through Glacken I'd spotted one or two people. It was difficult to see what they looked like, but from their casual attire I'm guessing that none of them knows what the big fashion trends of the season are.

'Well, I'll want to fit in,' Claire says. 'After all, when I set up my practice I'll be part of the community.'

'Do you really think you'll have anything in common with the villagers, though?'

'What do you mean?' she asks.

'Well, have you ever heard the expression "kissing cousins"?' I say.

'Yeah, why?'

61

'This place is so remote, I'd say everyone is related. *Very closely* related, if you catch my drift.'

'Maggie, are you trying to tell me I'll be surrounded by inbreds?' Claire throws her head back and roars with laughter.

'You said it, not me.' I shrug my shoulders. 'All I'm saying is country people aren't what we're used to. Don't expect too much from them.'

'From the backward culchies, you mean? You're unbelievable, Maggie!'

'Well, let's face it, it's not exactly café society down here, is it?'

'It's café society I'm trying to get away from.' Claire sighs. Then she grips my arm. 'Oh. My. God!' she whispers. 'I can't believe it!'

'What? What is it?'

I take my eyes off the cow's bottom swaying in front of the windscreen and look to where she's pointing. I can't see anything, except more trees and overgrown bushes.

'It's a baby rabbit!'

I see a small furry ball move in the hedgerow. 'That's not a rabbit,' I say, squinting. 'It looks like a rat.'

'It's not a rat – rats don't have little bunny tails. I want to take a photo.'

She's stopped the car and is scrabbling in her wretched patchwork bag for the state-of-the-art digital camera I gave her for her birthday last year. I suppose I should be grateful she didn't give it away with the rest of the stuff she carted down to the charity shop. Stuff she used to treasure but now thinks clutters her mind. I'm just grateful she didn't chuck out her Chanel too – that's gone into storage. I'm still hoping she'll give it to me eventually.

'Are you mad?' I cry. 'We're never going to get there at this rate!'

'But I've always wanted to see a real baby rabbit!'

'Get down to the pet shop on Earl Street, then,' I say. 'I hear there's plenty of them there – you can even buy one to boil, if you like.'

'Now, now, Maggie.' She pulls out the camera and leans close to the windscreen to get her shot.

'Aren't you at least going to get out of the car?' I ask.

'I don't want to frighten it.' She clicks the shutter. 'Ah, look how gorgeous it is, Mags.'

'I suppose,' I say. The bunny *is* quite cute, the way it's nibbling the grass, its little whiskers quivering in the air. It's oblivious to us, just like the cows. What is it about the animals around here that makes them so confident and self-possessed?

'It probably has myxomatosis, though,' I add, in case she gets any funny ideas – like wanting to coax it inside the car with us. God knows what she's going to suggest next – she's been playing a lot of wild cards recently. Time was she would have wolfed rabbit *au vin* for supper in a snooty restaurant – now it wouldn't surprise me if she wanted to adopt one from the wild.

'OK, I think I've got the shots. I'll keep the camera out, though, just in case I spot anything else. There's probably loads of amazing wildlife here.'

'Hark at you, Dr Dolittle,' I gripe, as she turns the car key in the ignition again.

At least the road before us has almost cleared of cows at last. We finally turn the last bend and there, right in front of us, is the picture-perfect Rose Cottage.

Rule Five: *Keep an open mind*

'Oh. My. God. This place is amazing!' Claire bounds up to the cottage door, panting like a six-week-old puppy. 'Have you ever seen anything so *adorable*?' She stands back to admire the trelliswork that runs across the doorway and points out the weathervane on the roof.

I fix a cynical look to my face before I answer. It's critical that Claire doesn't get her hopes up about this place. For all we know it could be infested with mice the size of hamsters. 'It's OK, I guess,' I say, acting like I'm unimpressed with what I see. Secretly, though, I have to admit the cottage is a lot better than I ever imagined it would be. Instead of the tumbledown shack I'd expected, the place looks in pretty good order. There's a neat garden out front and the roof does look as if it's been replaced pretty recently – the photos Claire had shown me hadn't been touched up. Still, I don't get my hopes up. God only knows what we'll see inside – it's probably a complete horror show in there. At best, it could be a nightmare of seventies chic. At worst, the place could be covered with mildew and dripping damp. There may even be a few resident rodents. I've seen hundreds of homes in my years working in Hanly's and I've come to expect the very worst of all of them, no matter how promising they may look from the outside.

'Ooooh, look at the décor – it's *gorgeous*!'

Claire now has her nose flattened against the traditional sash window pane and is peering inside. 'I just love the colour scheme, don't you? All those pale walls mean you can introduce colour with fabric. Isn't that blue dresser divine? Do you

64

think it's original to the cottage? Maybe it's been used by families for hundreds of years – isn't that an amazing thought? I could be part of history in the making!'

She's practically drooling over a pine dresser that's been painted Tiffany blue. Far from being an original feature, the landlord probably bought it for half nothing at an auction, then slapped some paint on to make it presentable – it's bound to be crawling with woodworm. Claire has a lot to learn about how these people operate. If she goes on appearances alone, she'll have the wool pulled over her eyes good and proper.

'Don't get your hopes up,' I warn. 'Décor can hide a multitude of things.'

'Like what?' She turns to face me, her eyes shining with excitement. I know she's already imagining herself arranging antique crockery on the dresser that she thinks has been used by generations before her.

'Like rot. Or wood lice. Or worse.' I do my best to sound gloomy, even though I somehow inexplicably quite like the cottage. There's something about the place. Still, it won't do to become in any way emotional about it – I have to keep a cool head for negotiations. Looking for possible negatives everywhere ensures I'm able to do just that. It's a trick I've learned from working in Hanly's.

'Well, it's not like I'm buying the place – I'm sure I could get along with a few woodlice!'

Claire dismisses my concerns with a wave. Nothing is going to burst her bubble, not even my cynicism and pessimism. She's genuinely excited at the thought of moving here.

'Still, there's no sign of the landlord.' I glance at my watch. 'He's late.' I look meaningfully at her.

'So what?' she asks, right on cue.

'Well. It's nothing, I suppose.' I pause to make sure she knows that I mean exactly the opposite. 'It's just that good landlords are usually on time. Being late means he's not reliable. Like he may not show up in an emergency.'

'What kind of an emergency?' She frowns.

This is good – I have her worried: I can tell from the way her brow has furrowed that she's thinking about the implications of this.

'Well, you never know what may happen,' I say, as vaguely and as ominously as possible. Luckily, I'm very good at playing this game – as a child, imagining the disasters that could befall me was one of my favourite pastimes. Mind you, Theresa usually beat me: her version of catastrophe was always off the charts.

'Try me.' Her voice sounds sort of edgy. Like maybe she's getting scared – just a little.

I don't want to terrify her, of course not. I just want her to know what she might be getting herself into. I wouldn't be a good friend if I didn't.

'Well...' I rack my brains for some top-notch disasters, the sort that could scare the bejaysus out of her without scarring her for life. 'The water mains could burst and flood the place. Or the gas oven could explode. That sort of thing.'

'The gas oven could explode?' She doesn't look too frightened by that.

'Yes.' I'm sticking to my guns. 'It happens more than you think. These sorts of landlords don't take due care of their property, you see, that's the problem. They just cram as many people as they can through the door and collect the money at the start of the month. That's all it is to them – money. Most of them are money mad.'

'But he's not trying to cram anyone in, Maggie.' Claire is clearly bemused.

'Yes . . . that's what he says *now*,' I reply darkly. 'It could change.'

'What does *that* mean?' She cocks her head.

66

'Well, you never can tell what these sorts have planned. Once he gets you to commit he could try to squeeze in more tenants. Who knows how many?'

'Like in a tenement?'

'Exactly!' I say. I'm delighted she's catching my drift at last. I was beginning to think I'd never get through to her.

'You're worrying about nothing,' she says. 'This is the twenty-first century, Maggie. I'll be signing a lease – that'll protect me surely.'

'It may,' I say airily, 'it may not. Sometimes a lease isn't even worth the paper it's written on. You can't be too careful.'

'Well, I think you're overreacting.' Claire smiles. 'Everything will be fine. Besides, Edward already knows it's just you and me. I told him our plan. I mean, if you agree to it, of course . . .'

'Well . . . he *is* late, that's all I'm saying.'

I don't want to let go of this point – it seems important somehow. Claire is pretty confident that I'll agree to live here while she's in India. The look in her eye tells me so. I need to pare back her expectations – we haven't even stepped inside the door yet. This is the problem with her voyage of self-discovery – she genuinely feels enthusiastic about things instead of hating everything on sight like she did before. Surprisingly, it's turning out to be a very inconvenient trait.

'Not by much. And I'm sure he has a reasonable explanation. Anyway, what's time if you think about it really? Just another constraint inflicted by society. It's so much simpler and less stressful not to focus on these sorts of trivialities too much.'

My jaw drops. Timekeeping used to be such a bugbear of Claire's. I was once fifteen minutes late meeting her for a pizza date and she didn't speak to me for a week afterwards. Even then, I had to endure the my-time-is-valuable lecture *twice*!

'Maybe he does have some sort of explanation,' I say ominously. 'But he could have called us back to tell us. That's what a responsible, law-abiding landlord would have done.'

I turn away from Claire and decide to examine the external window-ledges for peeling paint or anything else sinister. Unfortunately the surface is smooth and glossy – they've been touched up recently, obviously in an effort to make the place look as good as possible. God knows what's lurking underneath. This cowboy could have done a quick paint job to disguise how rotten the place is – I've seen it all before. Behind the perfect exterior there may be crumbling walls or a termite infestation.

'Look – here he is now!' Claire says, undisguised excitement in her voice. 'See? He wasn't *that* late!'

A battered green Land Rover squeals to a stop at the gate. That's a surprise – maybe this guy really doesn't have money, after all. Or maybe it's a ploy – maybe he's driven here purposely in the oldest car he has to make it look like he's penniless – that's a smart move. He probably has a fleet of top-of-the-range Bentleys in his custom-built garage at home. Well, if he thinks that old trick will work on me, he can think again. I steel myself: this guy could be a proper operator. Just because we're in the middle of nowhere doesn't mean the place isn't crawling with con men.

As I watch, a very tall man in a raggy jumper and filthy jeans leaps out and I realize this can't be the landlord after all – he's far too scruffy. He must have sent an employee to talk to us instead. This is probably the caretaker he pays less than the minimum wage to run the place. 'That's not the lord of the manor, Claire,' I say. 'His wife – what's her name? June – obviously couldn't make it so he sent his caretaker with the keys. Imagine! He can't even turn up to meet us – that's pretty shoddy of him.'

'Wow . . . he's *gorgeous*.' Claire whistles low under her breath. 'If he's a caretaker he can take care of me anytime.'

I take a good look at him as he gets closer. He *is* rather handsome – if you're into the whole country just-rolled-out-of-a-haystack look. He's at least six foot two, and even though his face is weather-beaten, there's something undeniably attractive about his craggy features and long, rangy limbs. I can't tell what colour hair he has because he has a waxed cap rammed on his head but even from here I can see that his eyes are an unusually bright blue.

'Hello there!' the man calls, striding up the path towards us. 'I'm so sorry I'm late. Polly fell off her pony and I had to bandage her wrist. And then there was an incident with a bucket . . .'

A small child trots behind him, plaits flying and looking mutinous, her wrist bandaged neatly with white tape.

'Don't be silly.' Claire simpers, smiling sweetly at him. 'It's no problem.'

'I'm Edward,' he says, offering her his hand.

'Oh, so you're *not* the caretaker, then?' Claire flashes a sneaky smile in my direction and shakes his hand with gusto.

If I didn't know better, I'd swear she was batting her eyelashes at him.

'Caretaker? No, there is no caretaker.' He smiles. 'Just me.'

They both laugh gamely at his little joke.

'Well, you'll do nicely!' Claire is giggling like a teenager – she *is* flirting with him. 'I'm Claire and this is my friend Maggie Baxter. I told you about her on the phone – she might take over the lease while I'm away.'

'Of course. Nice to meet you, Maggie.'

He nods politely at me and I nod coldly back at him. If he thinks he can charm me with this nicey-nicey act, he's mistaken. I can see right through it.

69

'And this young lady is Polly.' Edward tugs gently at the child, who's still hiding behind his back. 'Don't you want to come out and say hello?' he asks her.

'No.' Polly sulks and I can't help smiling. This kid isn't going to perform in public for anyone – I can tell by the stubborn look on her plump little face. She's furious for some reason, and no amount of cajoling is going to make her acquiesce to the social graces.

'Hi, Polly!' Claire chirps, seemingly oblivious to the child's bad temper. 'Aren't you cute?'

'Not really.' Polly looks murderous and I have to stifle a laugh by pretending to cough into my hand. This child is not going to be charmed.

'Oh.' Claire is taken aback and a little flustered that Polly is being so obstinately rude.

'Sorry about that,' Edward says, shuffling about, embarrassed. 'She's in a very bad temper. She's usually a lot nicer than this.'

'No, I'm not.' Polly snorts.

'Polly, please behave,' Edward says, his voice strained.

'No! I won't.' Polly stamps her foot. 'You're mean, mean, mean! You're the biggest meanie *ever* in the *world*.'

This is getting more interesting by the minute and it occurs to me that it couldn't be playing out better. Claire has never been a big fan of children – much less children who are as naughty as this one. She's always subscribed to the school of thought that children should be seen and not heard so, hopefully, this scene will plant another seed of doubt in her mind about moving here. After all, Edward and his family live close by – if she lived here, she'd have to engage with them, probably on a daily basis. Dealing with Polly every day would wear anyone out. Edward looks exhausted, that's for sure.

I will Polly to do something really vile to turn Claire off for good. If she vomited right here on the step, or even better when we get into the kitchen, that would be excellent. Claire has never been able to tolerate other people puking – seeing a small child barf up her breakfast would guarantee that she'd run screaming for the hills. Then we could go back to the city where we belong. Claire could give up this ashram idea and get another hedge-fund job. I could even become her assistant – it'd be just like that movie *Working Girl*. I'd be the lovely Melanie Griffith and Claire could be the mean Sigourney Weaver. It'd be great – much better than living here.

'I'm sure she's a lovely little girl,' Claire says soothingly, apparently anxious for Polly to like her.

'No, I'm *not*.' Polly stamps her other foot, her pudgy little face getting redder.

'*Polly*.' Edward's voice is warning.

'One little fall and you make me get off – that is so *stupid*. I'm not a baby – I'm six.'

'Honey, you sprained your wrist – you can't ride with a hurt arm.' He says this with the exhaustion of someone who's been through this reasoned argument a million times already.

'Yes, I *can*.' The child glares at her father. 'You just won't let me. *Mum* would let me.'

'Polly. We'll talk about this later.'

'I don't want to talk to you again.' Polly pouts. '*Ever*.'

'OK, I'm sure that can be arranged.' He grins at his daughter, so she knows he doesn't really mean it. 'Now, why don't I let these ladies in to take a look at the cottage?'

He smiles ruefully at us and Claire smiles back sympathetically, obviously wanting to communicate that she knows how difficult and trying young children can be. I, on the other hand, make sure to look blankly at him in return. If he thinks he's going to charm me with this caring-daddy routine he's wrong. I'm here to let him know that the customer is king – and if

Claire likes this place and decides she's going to rent it, instead of starring in *Working Girl* with me, then I'm going to drive a very tough bargain for her. The recession means it's a renters' market so we have everything going for us. The ball is in our court and I'm going to make sure this Edward knows it, cute obstinate kid or not.

'Right, let's get in, then.' He takes a bunch of assorted keys from his jeans pocket and wriggles one into the lock with difficulty. 'The door is a little sticky, sorry,' he says, as he struggles to get it open.

'Why? Is there damp?' I ask. I glance at Claire. She won't want to move into a place where water's trickling down the walls. She could pick up all sorts of infections – I read in the paper last week that TB is back on the rise again and surely living in a damp environment could heighten her chances of developing it. I make a mental note to mention this to her. Claire has always been very careful about her health – she takes a cocktail of vitamins and minerals that would put an Olympic athlete to shame.

'Damp?' Confusion is written on Edward's face. I have to hand it to him – he's got the perfectly innocent I-can't-imagine-what-you-mean expression off pat.

'Yes – damp,' I repeat, my eyes boring into his. 'You do know what damp is, right?'

'Yes, of course.'

He glances at Claire, who's glaring at me. Maybe I should tone things down, just a little. I don't want to be completely unsupportive: I just don't want to lose her to this place. If she moves here when she gets back from India, I'll barely get to see her and I'd miss her so much. It suddenly strikes me why I don't want Claire to come here. I've already lost Dermot and Dom at Hanly's and I don't want to lose her too. Everything is changing far too fast, so fast I can barely keep up. I want things to stay as they were before the blasted global economy went into meltdown.

'I know you won't mind me asking,' I say, rearranging my face to seem less fierce, 'but as Claire's friend I think it's imperative to be aware of any . . . pitfalls associated with the property. I'm sure you'll agree?'

I choose my words very carefully. I don't want him to know I'm an ex-estate agent necessarily, that's none of his business – besides, Claire has made me swear not to lord it about too much – but I do want to let him know he's not dealing with some dumb *ingénue*. I'm on the ball and ready to take him down if he tries anything sneaky.

'Of course,' he says, looking at me strangely, as if he's wondering what he did to offend me. 'Well, the door is a little stiff but that's because it's rarely used, that's all. It should loosen up once someone moves in.'

'So there's no damp, then?' I raise my eyebrows to show I'm wise to any sly moves he may try to get over us.

'No, definitely no damp.' He smiles at me, but I don't smile back. I want him to know I won't stand for any funny business.

'What about wood rot?' I stare him down.

'No wood rot either.' He smiles again, nervously now.

Good, I've got him on the hop. Right where I want him.

'Oh, this is *gorgeous*!' Claire breathes, as Edward puts his shoulder to the door to nudge it open and she tumbles through. 'It's just *perfect*!'

'Yes, we like it,' Edward says, smiling warmly at her. 'It's been painted recently and all the appliances have been replaced – the fridge, dishwasher, and washing-machine are all new. I have the instructions pinned to the noticeboard in the pantry, just in case you need them.'

'She hasn't said she's taking it yet,' I say, keeping my voice neutral. 'Let's not get carried away!' I can't help thinking that there *is* something lovely about the cottage, though. There's a really peaceful quality about it . . . I push these thoughts from my mind – it's vital I don't let my feelings show.

'You have a *pantry*?' Claire squeals. 'Oh, wow! I've always wanted a pantry!'

'Yes, they're great,' Edward agrees. 'You can keep all your food together, and because the walls are so thick it's always nice and cool in there. You could probably get away without a fridge, to be honest, but obviously I've provided one.'

'Well, you'd have to!' I laugh darkly. 'Otherwise she could get E. coli, couldn't she?'

'E. coli?' Edward says.

'Yes, if her food wasn't refrigerated properly – she couldn't be relying on some old pantry, now, could she? We're not living in the Dark Ages.'

'You're right.' Edward grins. 'Of course, usually E. coli is transmitted to humans through animal faeces or undercooked beef, not food that hasn't been chilled properly.'

'Salmonella, then,' I retort. I'm furious with myself for making that stupid mistake. I should have known he'd be *au fait* with the ins and outs of E. coli. I shouldn't have tried to bluff it.

'Well, it doesn't matter – does it? – because there's a brilliant fridge right here!' Claire interrupts, beaming at Edward. I can sense she's just about to whip her cheque book from her damn patchwork handbag and write him a deposit for the first three months here and now.

'And just look at these floorboards,' she enthuses, batting her eyelashes at Edward once more, 'are they original?'

She's being completely over the top in her fake enthusiasm – if he thinks she likes the place this much he'll try to push up the rent even higher than it already is.

'Yes. They are – we had them sanded and then oiled. It was a long process, but they turned out pretty good in the end.'

'They're *gorgeous*!' Claire claps her hands with glee. 'Are they oak? Oak has such wonderful energy, don't you think?'

'Yes, they are.' He nods. 'I have to say, you have a very good eye.'

They beam happily at each other, like a couple from a home-improvement show on TV who've just been shown the final reveal and can't believe their luck.

'Not very even, though, are they?' I interrupt, kicking at the floor with my boot, determined to burst their happy-clappy bubble. 'I mean, there are so many lumps and bumps. That could be a hazard. What if someone were to trip and hurt themselves?'

'Don't be silly, Maggie,' Claire says lightly. 'That's part of the charm. I don't want to live in a place where the floors are some awful pre-finished laminate. This adds to the character of the cottage. There's such a sense of history here.' She spins to beam at Edward again.

'Won't you miss your polished marble tiles, though, Claire?' I ask. 'She had them specially imported from Italy,' I stage-whisper to Polly.

Polly looks at me blankly. She couldn't care less about any of this. Not that I blame her. Watching three adults tussle about interiors must be mind-numbingly boring.

'Really?' Edward looks very surprised. I get the feeling that importing the most expensive marble available wouldn't be something he'd condone. He's probably some sort of eco-freak. He frowns and I try to hide my grin. This is good – he and Claire were getting far too warm and fuzzy for my liking: driving a wedge between them before they start comparing refurbishing tips is vital.

'No, I won't miss them at all.' Claire glowers, her face hot with embarrassment now I've revealed her as the snob she can be. What's up with her, anyway? She can't really like the oak – she boasted about those marble floors for months after they were installed.

'But you're so used to them, Claire!' I say. 'She loves her luxury,' I add, to Edward, smiling with superiority to let him know that this ramshackle place definitely won't do for Claire – she has far grander tastes.

'Actually, I hate that marble,' Claire says quickly. 'It's so cold. Sustainable woods are far superior. And *this* place is absolutely charming – I love everything about it! Even the paint colours are just perfect – that creamy hue is divine. And I love the way you've introduced a splash of colour with the blue dresser.'

Edward removes his cap and I see his hair is a shock of black. The contrast against his tanned skin is startling.

'It was a bit of a nightmare trying to choose the colours, to be honest – that's why we kept everything pretty neutral on the walls. We did use eco-paints, though – they were very expensive but I thought it was important.'

'Wow – that's impressive!' Claire breathes, stepping forward to inspect the nearest wall – like she actually cares about this stuff! Then she leans in and sniffs deeply. She really is making a total fool of herself. 'They smell wonderful!' She sniffs the wall again.

'Don't they?' Edward agrees, smiling broadly, as if it's the most natural thing in the world to go round sniffing walls. He hasn't batted an eyelid at Claire's insane antics – in fact, he's behaving as if she's being completely *normal*.

'There are no nasty fumes – that's what I really like. Some-times,' he lowers his voice, 'sometimes I'm almost tempted to give them a lick!'

Claire bursts out laughing and Edward joins in. Even pouty Polly is giggling at this, although she's covering her mouth with her hand to hide it. It's clear she doesn't want us to know that she's given up the sulking act.

Right, I have to put a stop to this. It's all going horribly wrong. They're getting on far too well. If I don't break up this giggle-fest Claire will think this is the perfect home for her. She's so into destiny and karmic energy now – I can tell she's falling in love with the place already. She probably thinks this is all meant to be, or some sort of bullshit.

'Was it wise, though?' I ask loudly, to break up the laughter. 'Using such expensive finishes on a property that you want to rent?'

'What do you mean?' Edward asks, sobering. I see Polly looking intently at me as she peeps out again from behind her father's back.

'I mean, if you've spent all this money renovating, then you're going to have to recoup the costs somehow, aren't you?'

He looks evenly at me, but I know he's understood my point. Don't try to fleece Claire with the rent because you've made the mistake of using extortionately expensive eco-paints: we're not going to pay for all this nonsensical extravagance, even if you *can* lick the bloody walls.

'I wanted to retain the character of the place,' he replies. 'There was no point doing something cheap and nasty here. The cottage is four hundred years old – I want to preserve it for the next four hundred.'

'Four hundred years old?' Claire squeaks, as if this is the first she knew of it. 'That's *amazing.*'

I glare at her – she already knew full well how old the cottage is: she's been Googling it for long enough. 'Bit small, though, isn't it?' I say. 'How many square feet is it again?' I direct this at Edward, who's leaning against a creamy wall watching me carefully. Polly is holding on to his leg, still staring at me. I catch her eye and she sticks out her tongue. It takes all my self-control not to giggle. The girl has gumption and I can't help warming to her, even if she is naughty.

'Just under six hundred,' he replies.

'Nice and cosy.' Claire beams.

'A tight squeeze, more like,' I retort. 'Who pays for the utilities?' I fire another question at him. It's important to keep up the pressure in a negotiation like this – let him know who's boss.

'Maggie.' Claire gives me a warning look.

'The utilities are included in the monthly rent,' Edward says, staring at me without blinking.

'Yes, about that,' I start. 'There's no way on earth Claire would even consider paying the rent you've suggested. It's outrageous – the market has moved significantly in the rent-er's favour, you know.'

'Yes, I know.' He sighs, looking completely dejected.

He's probably faking it to make Claire feel sorry for him.

'We would be looking for a significant reduction,' I declare. Now's the time to hit him hard, when he's down.

'Well, like I said in my email, if you were willing to give a hand on the farm now and again we could work something out. I'm not sure if either of you has any experience . . .' His voice trails away and suddenly he seems very unsure about the whole idea, as if he can't believe he ever thought it might work.

'I'd *love* to help!' Claire yelps. 'I really want to get in touch with nature, get back to my roots.'

'Right.' Edward looks doubtful. 'Well, it'd just be working with the ponies, that sort of thing. We operate a full livery service in the stables.'

'No problem,' Claire says confidently, and I turn to gaze at her. Claire can't stand horses – the closest she's ever been to one is sitting in the VIP stand at the New Year's Day races, sipping champagne. Now she's going on like she's some sort of horse whisperer. I'll bet she doesn't even know what a livery service is. I certainly don't.

'I don't want her near my pony!' Polly stamps her foot and folds her arms and I see Claire deflate a little. It's really bothering her that Polly seems to have taken an intense dislike to her – which is strange: she doesn't usually care what other people think of her.

'Are you insured?' I interject.

'Maggie, what are you talking about?' Claire says crossly.

'Insurance is vital, Claire. Farm accidents are very common unfortunately. What if, say, a pony kicked you in the head?'

'Kicked me in the head?' Claire is trying to pretend she's not nervous at this idea, but a flicker of fear crosses her face. She's not an animal person – she was never able to control Charlie the poodle and he was only a miniature. How will she cope with plus size animals?

'Yes, ponies can be fiery – isn't that right, Edward? I mean, just look at Polly here – her own pony threw her this morning. She sounds vicious.'

'She's *not* vicious!' Polly shouts, stamping her foot and glowering at me. 'Tell her, Dad!'

'She's not vicious,' Edward says wearily, 'just a little frisky.'

'Ah, yes, but being frisky can lead to accidents, am I right?'

'I guess so . . .' Edward looks at Claire, who is definitely nervous now. Perfect.

'Yeah, people get paralysed and even killed all the time on farms. Isn't that right?' I say. 'If he doesn't have insurance you'd be in serious trouble. Mind you, even if he does have insurance, it wouldn't help if you had to spend the rest of your days in a wheelchair, would it? No amount of money could recompense for that.'

Edward's face is white. Good. I want to turn Claire off

moving to the country, not encourage her to become a farm-hand. 'We *do* have insurance,' he says coldly.

'We should just take your word for that, I suppose,' I scoff.

'No. You can see the certificate, if you like,' he replies. 'It's in the office. But you're right. If something dreadful happened I'm sure no amount of money could make it right.'

'That won't be necessary,' Claire interrupts. 'I love this cottage and I'd like to take it. Maggie, are you in or out?'

She eyes me brazenly and I gape at her, appalled. The landlord isn't supposed to be privy to our private conversations about the property. We're supposed to have this sort of discussion once he's left or is at least out of earshot. She knows that – what's she playing at? I make eyes at her to stop her talking, but she ignores me. It might be my imagination, but she has a rather rebellious expression. As if she's decided to defy me deliberately.

'Make up your mind, Maggie,' she says mildly now. 'Unless, of course, you want to call your mum and dad? Or Theresa, maybe?'

There's an unmistakable hint of steel in her eyes. She *knows* I don't want to go into the details of my predicament with my family. She's challenging me, there's no two ways about it. Not all of her hedge-fund personality has disappeared under her dog-eaten clothes and dodgy handbag. The options run through my mind: I can stay in the city and have no job and nowhere to live, or I can move here for a while and have Claire pay for everything. There's no alternative, really.

'OK, then,' I sigh, mentally waving goodbye to my *Working Girl* fantasy. I'm never going to be quirky Melanie Griffith in a shoulder-padded power suit, thanks to Claire's bull-headedness. It's such a shame – that look is so on trend right now and I reckon I could carry it off, no problem. Not like those jeggings – they're a total fashion nightmare.

'Great!' Claire joyfully claps her hands together. 'Why don't

I pop up to the main house with you now, Edward, and sign the lease?'

Edward looks doubtful. He eyes me, as if he's trying to decide whether or not he's making a horrible mistake and if I'm going to be more trouble than I'm worth.

'Yes, OK, then . . .' he says at last. But he's not sure: I can tell by the conflicted expression on his face.

'It'd be better if you took a copy of the lease away with you and got your lawyer to cast his eye over it, Claire,' I say hastily. It's my last-ditch attempt to get her to see reason, not to jump into everything so quickly.

'Don't be silly!' Claire tinkles, guiding Edward through the front door, Polly at his heels. 'This will only take a minute.'

Then they all exit, Claire chattering excitedly as they go, and I'm left standing alone by the blue dresser, wondering how it all went so wrong, because somehow it now looks like I'm moving to the country – whether I like it or not.

Rule Six: *Expect the unexpected*

'I can't believe you're moving to the country!' Dom's voice sounds very far away in Melbourne.

I'm on the way to Rose Cottage, talking to him on my head-set as I drive, and the reception keeps dipping in and out of coverage because of the blasted country roads. I don't like them one little bit – I've gone through so many potholes it'll be a miracle if I ever get there in one piece.

'Just temporarily, Dom,' I correct him. 'Until Claire gets back from India.'

'But still! I can't believe it! What on earth possessed you to do that? You *hate* the country!'

'Well, I don't *hate* it as such,' I say.

I'm starting to regret calling Dom, just a little. He thinks this whole country idea is hilarious and it's making me even more nervous and unsure about it than I already am – something I'd thought was impossible.

'Maggie, you once told me that if you ever had to live beyond the motorway you'd go bonkers.'

'I was *exaggerating*, Dom,' I reply.

Trust him to remember. I vaguely recall saying something like that over a few after-work drinks and he's never forgotten it. Not surprising – the man has the memory of an African elephant. He can recall the most mundane of conversations, something his delusional mother likes to think qualifies him for Mensa membership. She even sent him the application form once – she honestly believes he has a gift.

'Anyway, you've moved to Australia,' I say, changing the subject. 'What's the difference?'

'The difference, dear Maggie, is a whole lot of girls in string bikinis. You're going to live in the sticks! I just can't imagine you mucking out ponies or digging up spuds. You'd be useless at that sort of stuff.'

He's convulsing with mirth at the end of the line and I can't help feeling a little aggrieved. It won't be *that* bad. Besides, I have absolutely no intention of dealing with any animals – that's part of Claire's agreement with the landlord, not mine.

'I'm not *that* useless,' I say. 'I could dig potatoes if I wanted to.'

'Yeah, right.' Dom guffaws. 'I don't know anyone less suited to country life than you!'

'I'll be fine,' I protest. 'I can hoe vegetables just as well as anyone else.'

'When was the last time you hoed a vegetable, Maggie?' Dom snorts.

The truth is, of course, that I've never hoed a vegetable in my life. I'm not even sure if hoeing is the correct term for what you do with vegetables. Is hoeing something to do with weeding? I think so. But I'm not sure – not that I'm going to admit that to Dom.

'Actually, my dad had a brilliant vegetable patch when I was a kid,' I say. 'I spent lots of time helping him out. If you need any hoeing done, I'm your woman.'

This part is true. Dad *did* have a vegetable patch when I was young. He loved pottering about in our tiny garden fiddling with his bedding plants and talking to the grass. But I never helped him out. Not once. I was usually inside watching MTV or talking to my friends on the phone. I feel a real pang of regret now that I didn't spend more time with him then – it would have been a lovely way for us to bond. Why didn't I see that?

As it is, I've lied to him and Mum about why I'm leaving the city for a while: I told them I was working on a new property development in the country and they accepted this explanation without question. The guilt is killing me, but I know it's for the best. I don't want them worrying about me any more than they have since the split. They seem to be over the shock of me leaving Robert, but Mum still makes sad references to having 'lost a son', and Dad has been less than subtle about the old spinster jokes. It's why I've told Theresa the same thing – if I have to listen to her lecture me about being left on the shelf one more time I'll find a shelf myself and cheerfully jump off it.

'So, what did you grow?' Dom's voice interrupts my rueful thoughts.

'Sorry?'

'In this wonderful vegetable patch of yours, what did you grow?'

I try to remember what sorts of things Dad grew. There was a lot of lettuce. Not that I ever ate much of that, of course. Unless food came in a can, smothered in tomato sauce, I wasn't interested. God, I must have been a pain in the butt – how did Mum and Dad ever put up with my picky ways?

'Lettuce. I grew lettuce,' I say confidently. He can't fault me for that.

'What else?'

'Peas,' I ad lib. 'And . . . spring onions.'

I'm almost sure I remember Dad growing spring onions in a row near the lettuces – I can still remember their strong smell.

'Right . . .' He doesn't sound too convinced. 'Well, if you change your mind and want to move down here, Maggie, you know I'll welcome you with open arms. You could rub the suntan lotion into my back – or anywhere else that might take your fancy. I've got very sensitive skin, you know . . .'

'I'd only cramp your style, stud,' I joke. 'Besides, I don't like the heat. That Australian sun would kill me.'

'Really?' Dom is shocked. 'God, it's bliss!' he says. 'I plan to spend the next few months soaking up the rays, surfing and drinking beer.'

'And work? Is that in your plan?'

'Work? Do they actually work here?' He laughs. 'I think I'll concentrate on finding myself for a while. And I'll let all the hot women find me too!'

Obviously Dom has fallen on his feet, which doesn't really surprise me. He's a jammy bugger. He always managed to worm his way out of trouble in the office. I lost count of the times that Dermot caught him on the Internet when he was supposed to be working and he always got away with it.

'So you're scoring, then?' Dom hasn't got into the specific details yet, which is unusual for him. 'Had many threesomes, have you?' I ask.

There's a pause on the line.

'Not exactly,' Dom admits.

'What? But I thought your cousin Pierce said that threesomes were ten a penny over there.'

'Yes, well,' Dom's voice is strained, 'myself and Pierce have parted ways.'

'You have? Why?'

'He lied about the threesomes, the bastard. He's never had one in his life.'

'Not even in the Jacuzzi?' I giggle. Isn't that what Pierce had told him?

'He doesn't have a Jacuzzi.'

'No Jacuzzi?'

This is hilarious – maybe Dom isn't having such a fantastic time, after all.

'No.' He sighs. 'Not even a paddling pool.'

'I'm sorry, Dom.'

'That's OK.' He brightens. 'The action is still excellent – I got really badly sunburned the other day and the nurse in the ER was a little ride – I'm meeting her next week.'

'You had to go to the emergency room with sunburn?'

That sounds serious. Dom is very fair-skinned – which is why he's addicted to self-tanners. I even caught him brushing bronzer on his chest once.

'Yeah. That bastard Pierce gave me baby oil – he said it'd give me a real glow. Anyway, I got fried. Still, it was worth it – that nurse who smeared the camomile lotion on me loved my Irish accent. I'm in there!'

'Dom, you're a disgrace,' I tell him. 'I can't believe you picked up an on-duty nurse!'

'The Aussie chicks love my Irish charm, Maggie, what can I tell you?'

'And I bet you're laying that on nice and thick, am I right?'

'As thick as I can to be sure, to be sure!' he says, in his best Oirish accent. 'They can't get enough of it.'

'I suppose you've been using your Gaelic trick, too?'

'Maggie, I can't help it if they like me to whisper sweet nothings to them in my native tongue, can I?'

'Dom, reciting the Our Father in Irish and pretending that what you're saying is something deep and meaningful is very dishonest.'

Dom likes to pull this stunt on foreign girls. He lets on he's a fluent Irish speaker and then proceeds to charm them by reciting a few prayers he learned as a boy at school. When they ask what he's said he claims he's just told them how they're the most beautiful girl on the planet.

'Maggie, Maggie, these women don't care what it is I'm actually saying, they just love the way I say it. That nurse certainly did.'

'You're a tramp,' I say. 'Now I have to go. I've just pulled up outside the cottage.'

'OK, my little country bumpkin. Don't forget to send me some teabags and crisps when you get a chance, will you? That bastard Pierce robbed the last parcel Mum sent me.'

'OK, I will.' Dom loves his mugs of tea and crisps sandwiches.

'Great – thanks. You take care of yourself and keep in touch.'

The phone goes dead and, with a pang, I realize how much I miss him. Even when, or if, I get another job, it'll never be as much fun as it was working with Dom. He's an annoying, sexist, lewd perve, but he's such a good laugh.

Suddenly I feel very alone. Dom is gone and Claire is too. She flew out to India days ago and is now meditating somewhere halfway round the world, surrounded by like-minded spiritual types. I've only spoken to her once since she got there because mobile-phone use is discouraged in the ashram. Apparently having people gabbing on the phone to their friends back in civilization can put the pilgrims off their daily meditations – at least, that's what Claire has been told.

I for one am suspicious. I can't help thinking that the ashram leaders or gurus or whatever they're called might be trying to stop her talking to her friends on the outside for a more sinister reason. What if this place is some sort of cult? What if they're brainwashing her right now? Persuading her to 'donate' her worldly goods and possessions to them? You read about it all the time in the papers – innocent people duped by sophisticated cults. Next thing you know Claire might be calling to say she's become the fourth wife of some long-bearded freak and is never coming back. My only consolation is that I've already Googled this ashram place and from what I can make out it looks above board. There are glowing recommendations on there from pilgrims who've travelled across the world to meet this guru person: they seem to have enjoyed the experience and returned to their regular lives afterwards. None of them looks glassy-eyed or intimidated.

Then again, the website could be a scam too. The cult could have a web designer brainwashed and creating the whole thing from some dungeon underground. All the testimonies could be fake. All the happy photos of pilgrims grinning blissfully in their yoga pants could be Photoshopped – you just never know.

Claire has promised to call as often as she can, just to reassure me that she's safe, but I can't help worrying all the same. The reality that I'm going to be all alone in a strange place with no one to talk to is hitting me hard now. This was one aspect of the situation I hadn't thought through fully when I finally agreed to the idea. I'm used to having constant banter in the office with Dermot and Dom and speaking on the phone to clients, even though that had quietened down in the past few months. But I like to be with people. I like talking. Who am I going to talk to in the country? The cows?

Easing my legs out of the car, I take in the cottage before me. I have to admit it looks even better than I remember, pretty and inviting and cosy, and as I walk up the narrow path to the front door, I start to believe that this may have been a good idea. I need some down-time before I throw myself back into trying to find a job. Some time to just think. And, like Claire says, I'm doing her a favour. Now that she's in India, I can keep an eye on the place for her. *And* she's paying the rent – that's another massive plus because money is tight and it's only going to get tighter.

I rummage under the mat for the key. It's there – just as Edward said it would be.

It's hard to believe that round here they still think it's safe

88

enough to leave a house key under a mat in broad daylight but, then, what do I know about country life? Maybe everyone leaves their door unlocked at night too. I can't imagine doing that – I need at least three locks and a chain to feel safe. I'm going to have to ask Edward to install a few extras first thing, although if I remember rightly, this door is so stiff that no burglar would be able to gain easy access.

I scoop up the key, but before I can prepare myself to do battle with the stiff lock, the door swings open before me, creaking gently as it does.

'Hello?' I call.

Maybe Edward is here. He knows I'm moving in today – maybe he's let himself in to give the place a final airing before I arrive. Unlikely, seeing as he's probably the typical selfish landlord who just wants to make a fast buck with minimum responsibility, but it is possible.

There's no answer so I try again. 'Hello?'

'Who are *you*?'

A teenage girl stalks into the room, tugging her T-shirt down over her navel. Her face is flushed and her blonde hair tousled, like she's just been wrestling someone.

'I might ask you the same question.' I eye her up and down.

She doesn't look like your average burglar but, then, I have no idea what an average burglar looks like. Do they wear balaclavas these days? Probably not. Still, she looks far too young and far too flustered to be breaking and entering. She can only be about fifteen at most.

'My name is Matilda Kirwan and I own this cottage,' she says, with the confidence of someone twice her age. She pushes her hair back behind her ears and smoothes her T-shirt with the other hand. 'You're trespassing. You'd better leave right now, or I'll have to call Security.'

'You *own* this cottage?' I try not to laugh, but the conceited look on her face is so funny it's hard not to. She's lying through her teeth — although I have to hand it to her, she's pulling it off quite well. If I didn't know for a fact that her father owns this cottage I'd almost believe her. She is quite obviously Edward's elder daughter: she's a larger carbon copy of the obstinate Polly.

'Yes, I do,' she pouts, eyeing me viciously, 'and you are trespassing on private property. Leave immediately before I have to — take action.'

She pulls a mobile phone from her jeans pocket and flips it open, glaring at me defiantly.

'You're pretty young to own a cottage, aren't you?' I smile.

'Technically my father owns it,' she sniffs snootily, narrowing her eyes at me, 'but it'll be mine soon enough. So, you'd better get out or I'll have you . . . arrested.'

'I see. Well, Matilda,' I keep my voice as neutral as I can, 'I think there's been some sort of misunderstanding. I'm here to rent the place. My name is Maggie — your father was expecting me.'

'Rent? Here?' The girl's face falls and suddenly she looks far younger. 'What do you mean?'

This news has evidently come as a surprise to her. I wonder why her father hasn't told her what he's doing. 'I'm going to live here for a while, until my friend Claire gets back from the ashram anyway, and then she'll live here . . .' It all sounds a bit ridiculous and convoluted when I say it out loud like that.

'There must be some sort of mistake,' the girl snaps, but a flicker of confusion in her eyes tells me she's suddenly doubting herself. 'This cottage is not for rent.'

I pass a hand across my brow — my head is starting to throb and a wave of exhaustion washes over me. The drive here is beginning to take its toll — all those potholes were hell. 'Listen,

Matilda, I'm sorry if this comes as some sort of . . . shock to you, but I *am* moving in. Your father has rented this property. Didn't he mention it?'

'There's been some sort of misunderstanding.' Matilda's eyes are cold now. 'Like I said, the cottage is not for rent. Not now. Not ever. My father wouldn't agree to something like that unless he discussed it with me first.'

I hear a thud from the bedroom. Someone else is in there – Matilda isn't alone – which may account for her mussed-up hair and flushed face. Hearing the noise she blinks rapidly, but says nothing.

'OK. If you don't believe me,' I say, 'I have the contract right here.'

I rummage in my handbag and pull out the lease that Claire signed. Shaking it smooth, I hand it to her.

Matilda scans the document and, seeing her father's signature at the bottom, gasps aloud.

I shift uncomfortably from foot to foot. This isn't exactly how I imagined I might settle in here. Obviously darling Matilda and her father have some issues they need to resolve. She apparently had no clue that Rose Cottage was being rented and she certainly isn't overjoyed about it.

'Right.' She flings the lease back at me. 'Daniel!' she calls, over her shoulder. 'Come out, we're leaving.'

A teenage boy appears from behind the bedroom door, his pockmarked face red with embarrassment. Just as I suspected, Matilda hasn't been alone. From the look of things she and this boy have been using the cottage as their love nest. It's sort of sweet, really – puppy love can be very powerful. I wasn't much older than this girl when I met Robert and I was sure then that he was the one for me. He wasn't, of course, but it took me years to figure that out. A fresh pang of remorse hits me as I think about poor Robert. I wonder how he's doing

– whether he's forgiven me for leaving and ruining his life, like he said I had.

'Let's go,' Matilda snaps at the boy. 'I'm sick of being here – it smells.'

She glares at me again, then marches out through the open front door, the boy shuffling behind her, and I'm left standing in the room, unsure of what to do. It looks like I interrupted a snogging session between Matilda and this skinny boy. I wonder if her mother and father know about her boyfriend? Probably not. Teenagers are very good at hiding things – Edward and his wife probably have no idea what their elder daughter is getting up to, or with whom. Now all I can do is keep out of her way and hope she does the same. It's not the best start to my stay here but more trouble is the last thing I need.

Sighing, I go back outside to try to haul my bags from the boot. They're so heavy I'm probably going to have to drag them up the garden path. It's as I'm trying to decide which way to manoeuvre the first one that I notice the scratches on the side of the car. They aren't from any tree branches on a country lane, though – they are long and even and very, very deep.

With a shock, I suddenly realize that this was no accident: these scratches have been made deliberately. Someone has just viciously keyed the passenger door, and I think I can guess exactly who it was. It looks like I've made my first enemy here and I've only just arrived – it may be some sort of world record.

Rule Seven: *Honesty is the best policy*

I wake up sweating, trying to free myself from the bedding that's tangled around my legs. I feel like I'm bandaged in it, it's wound so tightly round me – I must have been thrashing around pretty hard.

I know what's woken me. I was having that dream again – the one where I'm falling, and no matter how hard I try to grasp on to something to stop myself crashing to certain gory death, I can't. I've been having it for a while now but it still manages to scare the daylights out of me every time. I know what it means, of course, because in the time-honoured tradition of my love affair with Google I looked it up on-line. Having a nightmare about falling without ever hitting the ground means I feel out of control in my life – not very surprising, really, considering how wonderfully things are going for me at the moment.

Usually Robert features somewhere in the dream too: he stands in the background, watches me fall, then sadly turns the other way. Even my subconscious feels guilty that I left him. Theresa would have a field day with that one. Dream psychology is another of her passions: she analyses every single dream she can remember. Of course, taking the little blue pills causes weird ones sometimes, but she documents these, too, because keeping in touch with your psyche is vital, she says, even if you are just a little too fond of prescription drugs and your dreams are more hallucinations.

I rub my face and lie catching my breath, telling myself it was only a nightmare, that I'm fine, really. It takes a minute for my eyes to adjust to my unfamiliar surroundings. I'd been expecting to see the cool blue tones of my own bedroom walls and instead a warm yellow glow infuses the room. But unless someone has been busy painting in the middle of the night when I was out cold, I'm not in my flat in the city – the one that Dermot lets me rent for peanuts. I'm somewhere else entirely.

And there's something else as well – that *noise*. What is it? It sounds like . . . like a hundred birds sitting on my head singing their tiny little lungs out. In my half-awake, half-asleep state I can't figure out what it could be. Is it the TV? A mobile phone's ringtone? What the hell is that racket?

And then it hits me. Of *course*. I'm not at home. I'm in Rose Cottage and that noise isn't the TV or some weird ringtone: it's birds squawking for real. Knowing my luck, word has got round that a real live city slicker has come to stay and every blasted mangy bird for miles around has converged on the window-ledge especially to aggravate me. The din is *horrendous*. How do people stand it? It's noise pollution, that's what it is. It's deafening – worse than any city traffic I've ever heard. I'd take wailing city sirens over that – that *chirruping* any day.

Rolling across the bed, I reach for my watch to see what time it is: eight forty-five a.m. I've slept almost twelve hours straight. I can't believe it. Obviously the drive down really knocked me for six. I can barely remember what I did after I'd dragged my suitcases inside. From the grimy feel of my skin, I definitely didn't take off my makeup – which I'm now regretting because I can almost hear my pores cheerily clogging up as I lie here. Maybe Claire has the right idea – if I stopped wearing makeup altogether I wouldn't have to spend so much time every night taking it all off. It's tempting. No one knows me down here – I could get away with it. Then again, the thought of leaving the house without a few layers of slap terrifies me. It's something I've grappled with on and off for years – in my drunker moments I've even considered getting permanent makeup tattooed on. The only thing that stops me is my fear of needles – unless I'm out cold there's no way anyone can touch me with one.

Pushing myself out of bed, I make my way into the kitchen to look for coffee. I need a really strong cup to kick-start my day – otherwise it takes me for ever to get going. Not that's there's any major rush, I suppose – it's not like I have a job to go to. That thought depresses me even further. How many mornings have I woken up, longing for a day off just to do nothing? Now that day has come and it's the worst feeling in the world. I'd do anything to be back home, getting ready to troop into Hanly's and spend the day filing. I'd gladly listen to Dom's sexist banter all day long if it meant I could have my job back. I wouldn't complain once – not even if Solid Mahogany rang a million times. Poor old Dermot's bound to be struggling with her calls – he never could handle her and her high-maintenance ways.

I rummage around the tiny kitchen for a while, looking for a percolator. The original oak floors that Claire admired so much are nicely warmed by the sunlight that's peeking through the sash windows. Even though I scoffed at those boards when we viewed the house, I have to admit they make a pleasant change – usually I'm shivering on the porcelain tiles in the flat. Still, they're probably a terrible dirt trap.

I nose in every cupboard, but I still can't spot a percolator so I flick on the kettle – instant will have to do for now. It never gives me the same boost – I may need two cups.

I'm leaning against the counter, waiting for the kettle to boil, when I hear a thump at the door that makes me jump. Who can that be? I'm not expecting anyone – I don't know a soul here. Unless . . . unless it's stroppy Matilda. Maybe she had a think about what to say to make me go back to the city. She was absolutely furious when she left me – maybe she's come back to challenge me again, demand that I go. I wouldn't put it past her – she's a cheeky kid, that's for sure.

There's another knock, more insistent this time. If it *is* Matilda, she's not going away and suddenly I'm very annoyed. That girl has no right to arrive on my doorstep, practically at the crack of dawn. I'm going to give her a piece of my mind – keying my car like that was outrageous, a criminal act. In fact, I'd be perfectly within my rights to report it to the police. Who knows what the consequences could be? Probation, maybe – even community service.

I wrench the door open, prepared to do battle, but Edward and little Polly – looking as mutinous as ever in a navy blue school uniform – are standing there. There's no sign of Matilda.

'Hi!' Edward smiles at me.

'Um, hi,' I say. This is awkward. Last time I saw this guy I was dissing this cottage – the one I'm now living in. I feel just a little foolish, but I try not to let it show.

'We just wanted to check that you were settling in well,' Edward says. 'I hope you have everything you need – I left some basic provisions in the pantry for you.'

Is he a little nervous? It seems he is. He looks as if he doesn't know how I'll react to him turning up on the doorstep. Like I might bite his head off. Which I suppose, to be fair, I sort of did last time we met. 'Yes, everything's fine, thanks,' I say.

I tug my T-shirt down round me. Maybe I should have pulled on my jeans before I opened the door. I slept in the top I drove here in because I was too tired to look for my pyjamas. Suddenly I feel a little self-conscious that I'm not dressed – this T-shirt is barely covering my bottom. Still, that's not my fault – it's not as if I'd been expecting anyone to drop by so ludicrously early, especially not my temporary landlord and his child.

'Good, that's good. Um, I'm sorry I dropped by so early,' he says now, as though he's reading my mind. 'We're just on our way to school so I thought I'd check everything was all right. I should have realized you'd be relaxing on your first morning here – that was stupid of me.'

'No, it's fine.' I force myself to smile. There's no point making mortal enemies with the landlord – that's what I've always told my clients. Maintaining a civil relationship is best and Edward looks friendly enough – he's obviously decided not to hold my criticism of him or his precious Rose Cottage against me.

'What's that on your face?' Polly pipes up. 'It looks really weird!'

I glance in the mirror by the door. Black streaks of mascara are round my eyes. I look a fright. 'That's makeup I didn't take off last night,' I reply. There's no point trying to hide from this one – she's as sharp as a tack.

She nods, her little face scrunched up with concentration, obviously trying to think what I remind her of. 'You look like a . . . panda,' she decides eventually.

'Polly!' her father admonishes.

'That's OK.' I sigh. 'She's probably right. I was just so tired from the drive down here, I guess I fell asleep before I had a chance to clean up properly. Plus, this mascara is the long-lasting type.'

'What does that mean?' Polly asks.

'It means that if you put enough on, it lasts all day,' I answer.

'But doesn't that mean it's hard to get off?' Polly says.

'Well, yes, it does,' I admit.

'Why do you use it, then?'

'I don't really know,' I reply. She has a point. This stuff is a nightmare to remove. 'I guess I'm a sucker for advertising.'

'Did you sleep in *that*?' she goes on, pointing at my chest.

'Yes, I did.'

Out of the corner of my eye, I see Edward wince.

'Don't you have pyjamas?' she asks curiously.

'Yes, I do. I just haven't unpacked yet.'

This kid is a question a second. I can barely keep up.

'My Pooh Bear ones are my favourites,' she announces. 'You can borrow them if you like. Matilda says they're only for babies but she doesn't know anything.'

'She doesn't?' I say, trying not to laugh out loud. She *is* pretty cute, even if she's very forthright in her opinions.

'No, she's naff.'

'Naff?'

'Yeah, naff. Naff is my favourite word.'

'Is it?'

How am I having a conversation with a six-year-old child about her favourite words? I need a coffee, fast.

'Yeah, I try to use it ten times every day. That's what Mrs Ryan told us to do with our favourite words.'

'Mrs Ryan?'

'Mrs Ryan is Polly's teacher,' Edward explains. 'Her very long-suffering teacher.' His cheeks are red. He's mortified by Polly's ramblings.

'What does "long-suffering" mean?' Polly says.

'It means that she puts up with quite a lot,' Edward replies.

'Do you mean what I said about her chin?'

'What did you say about it?' I ask. This sounds interesting.

'I told her she had a hairy chin.'

Edward physically cringes.

'You did?' I giggle. I can imagine Polly speaking her mind, just like that.

'Yes, I did.' She puffs out her chest. 'She has a chin just like a Billy Goat Gruff.'

'It gets better.' Edward rolls his eyes.

'Why? What happened then?' I ask Polly.

'She came in the next day and the hair was gone, but her chin was really red. So I told her she looked like the troll. You know, the one who lived under the bridge.'

'She'd waxed her chin?' I look at Edward.

'It took a long time to live down,' he says.

'I've told her about *you* already,' Polly says to me.

'You have?' God, what has she said?

'Yes, I told her I thought you were naff when I first met you, but Daddy said I had to give you a second chance because we need the money.'

'Polly!' Edward gasps. 'I'm sorry about this,' he says. 'I probably should have brought Polly to school before I stopped by . . .'

'I can see your pants, you know,' Polly interrupts. 'They're pretty naff too.'

I'm wearing my oldest pair, of course I am. Are they really on show? I can't bear to look. Edward is cringing again. Is it because of his daughter and her never-ending questions or the state of my pants? I can't be sure.

'Do you always sleep this late?' Polly goes on.

She's on a roll and I can tell she's using her opportunity to extract as much information as possible from me. Are Theresa's twins going to be like this in years to come? How will she cope? They can't even talk properly yet and they have her run ragged. I can only imagine what it's going to be like when they can have a conversation. It makes my head spin just to think about it.

'Polly!' Edward says. 'That's enough questions. I'm sorry,' he says to me.

'That's OK. She's right – it is late.'

They obviously think I'm inexcusably lazy. Usually, of

course, I'd be at my desk at this hour. Not knowing why, I decide to lie, to save face. It's one thing to admit to not removing makeup, but I don't want them to think I have nothing better to do than laze in bed all morning when everyone else is up saving the world. Edward definitely thinks I'm a layabout. While Polly has been rabbiting on, he's barely said a word.

'Well, we'd better get going,' he says briskly. 'I think Polly has embarrassed me quite enough for one day – and I still have the school gate to get through.'

I laugh at this – even I know that school gates can be dangerous places.

'Actually,' I blurt, as they turn to leave, 'I don't usually sleep this late. Normally I'm up at the crack of dawn, you know . . . to work out . . .'

This is a grade-A fabrication. I never work out. The truth is, I never roll out of bed until I really have to. Still, Edward will never know I'm not a fitness fanatic. Well, not unless he catches sight of the flabby thighs I'm trying to hide with this blasted T-shirt. Why didn't I grab something else before I answered the door? I shuffle back inside a little so he can't see.

'Really?' Edward sounds interested. 'What do you do?'

'Sorry?' I say, wishing I hadn't opened my mouth. What on earth made me decide to fib like that? I don't have to impress this person. What's it to him if I lie in bed till teatime?

'To keep fit?' He goes on. 'What sort of workout do you do?'

'Um, I run,' I say brightly. 'I run a lot – it's great, you know, for the mind. And the body, of course. It's very . . . therapeutic.'

God, that sounds weak. He'll never fall for it – even Polly is sceptical. From the way she's looking at me she knows I couldn't run for a bus. Anyone who got a close-up of my rear could testify to that fact. Still, that's the sort of thing that people who do exercise say, isn't it? That it's all very worthy and good for the mind, body and spirit?

'Daddy runs every morning!' Polly pipes up again. 'And then you come back and make me breakfast – don't you, Daddy?'

'That's right, Polly. Poached eggs on toast – your favourite.'

Edward smooths Polly's hair. There's a tangled knotty bit at the back that her mum must have missed brushing.

'Do *you* like eggs?' Polly directs another question at me.

'Sure, yes.'

'Which way?'

'Which way?' I repeat.

'Yes, which way – poached, fried or scrambled?'

'Or fertilized?' I laugh.

Then I see Polly's face. Shit. That was a grown-up joke. I shouldn't have said it. 'Um, scrambled, I think,' I mumble. I can't admit that I haven't touched an egg since that time I got thrashed in an end-of-term egg fight in college – I was washing scrambled eggs out of my hair for days afterwards.

'Urgh. I hate scrambled.' Polly makes a face. 'They make my insides go wobbly.'

'They do? Oh, no.' I make to go back inside. It's time to end the chit-chat. I need my coffee and I need to put a halt to this awkward conversation.

'So – how many do you do?'

Edward's not letting me go yet.

'How many do I do?' I look at him blankly. What does he mean? How many eggs do I eat at a time?

'How many K do you do? On your runs?'

His face is eager, like he actually expects me to answer him.

'K?'

'Kilometres,' Polly says. 'Don't you know that?'

Does he mean how far do I run every morning on my fictitious outings? His face says he does – that's exactly what he means. I try to think. What should I say? Twenty? That sounds like a lot, but maybe it's not really. I decide to try it. 'Twenty?' I chance.

'You run twenty K every day?' Edward is incredulous. Even Polly looks stunned, as if she knows something I don't. I'm obviously very far off the mark.

'Well, not every day,' I backtrack. 'Just sometimes. Once a week, maybe twice.'

'Wow, that's impressive.' He whistles. 'You must be very fit.'

I back in behind the door so he can't take a closer look at me – if he does he'll know there's no way I could run anywhere without collapsing into a breathless heap after about two minutes. How on earth did I get myself into this? 'Not really. To be honest, I've been letting things slide recently.'

I pull the door towards me so he gets the hint and takes off, taking his cute, outspoken daughter with him. This charade has gone on long enough.

'You should go running with Daddy!' Polly says. 'Shouldn't she, Dad?'

'Um, yes, of course . . .' Edward seems unsure. 'If you like. There are some excellent tow-paths round the village – I could show you.'

Oh, no. I can't go jogging with him – he'd suss me out in five minutes flat. 'Um, I'm not sure,' I mutter. This is a nightmare.

'Of course not. I'm sorry,' he says quickly, his expression changing when he sees the reluctance in my face.

'No, it's not that . . .' I start. Now I feel bad. I didn't mean to insult him – I just need to get out of this mortifying situation.

Polly is looking from him to me, bemused. What's going on here? her face says. Are all grown-ups as mad as these two?

'Honestly, forget it.' He's brisk now, taking Polly by the hand and turning towards the gate. 'I'll see you after lunch – you can start with the ponies then.'

Eh? Start with the ponies? I'd almost forgotten that part.

Claire was getting a reduction in her rent because she'd agreed to work for free. I don't want to hold up that side of the bargain. I'm not a horsy person. I'm not an animal person full stop. As far as I can see, they're all smelly, slobbery inconveniences. I wouldn't be any good at grooming or whatever it is Claire agreed to do. Her poodle Charlie almost took my fingers off once when I tried to pet him – that had been right before he'd pooped in her Balenciaga handbag. I might even have scared the poor mutt into doing it. He seemed terrified by me. Then again, he did have some serious issues – he used to chase his tail far more than could ever be considered normal.

'About that . . .' I call after him.

'I'll meet you at the stables at two,' Edward shouts from the gate. Suddenly this guy is desperate to leave. He's dragging Polly up the path as fast as her little legs can carry her.

'The stables?' I echo.

'Yes, they're behind the main house – just follow your nose.'

What does he mean, follow my nose? Can he mean that the gross horsy odour will be so repulsively pungent that all I'll have to do is sniff the air to find him? Just like some sort of warped version of the old Bisto ad? He said he operates a livery service – which I found out means he stables horses for other people – but what does that involve exactly? I have no idea.

But I can't ask any more: Edward has already strapped Polly into the back seat and jumped into the battered Land Rover. As I watch, he roars away up the lane, Polly's chubby little hand waving out of the open window as they go.

Rule Eight: *Never work with children or animals*

'So, you see, I'm probably not the best person to work with the ponies,' I explain, 'but once Claire gets back she can help you out.'

I've just finished telling Edward why I can't help him in the stables and I'm very happy with how my little speech has gone – he's let me rabbit on without interrupting so obviously he agrees that me doing anything remotely farmhand-related with his animals is out of the question. The relief I feel is enormous.

'I see.' Edward smiles as I pause to catch my breath.

He's being very understanding, which is pretty decent of him. Maybe he's not as bad as I thought.

'Sorry about that,' I add, trying to look a lot sorrier than I actually feel. 'I hope it's not too much of an inconvenience.'

'It's OK,' he goes on. 'I know what the issue is.'

'Issue? What issue?' I frown at him.

'You're nervous of animals. Some people are cautious around ponies – it's nothing to be ashamed of, honestly.'

'I'm not nervous.' I bristle. 'It's just that they don't like me. They don't react well to me. It's like I said . . .'

'They can sense your anxiety, that's all,' Edward says, his blue eyes crinkling at the edges. 'They *know* you're afraid – they pick up on it.'

'It's not that I'm *afraid* exactly,' I say. Well, maybe I am, just a little, but I'm not telling him that.

'Animals are very clever – far cleverer than we give them credit for. You need to feel in control when you're handling them. You can fake it for a while, until the confidence comes more naturally. There's nothing to worry about. I'll show you what to do.'

I've heard this theory before, from my dad, but I'm not convinced. After all, I tried to be in control with Claire's maniac poodle and that didn't get me very far – I'd been lucky not to lose a finger. 'How can they tell if I'm . . . you know . . . nervous?' I ask. There's no harm in asking. I'm not admitting anything as such.

'It's the physiology of the animal kingdom,' Edward says. 'Your pupils dilate when you're afraid, your heart rate increases – animals can sense these things.'

'That's like when you're attracted to someone, isn't it?' I blurt out, remembering something I read once. 'You know – your pupils dilate if you fancy someone?'

'Exactly,' he replies, smiling again. 'Our bodies never lie – all you have to do is look for the signs.'

'Right.' I can feel a blush creeping up round my neck. I can't believe I said something so stupid about fancying people to a complete stranger. He must think I'm a total idiot. 'So, all I have to do is show the ponies who's boss?' I ask, clearing my throat and trying to regain some composure.

'Well, yes, you can be gentle and firm at the same time,' he replies. 'Tell you what, we'll start with one of the quieter ponies, OK? Let's take Saffy here – she's Polly's.' He gestures to a stable where a grey pony stands watching us over the half-door, a bored expression on her face.

'You should probably change into your boots before we begin,' he says.

'Which boots would they be?' I ask. I'm wearing my trainers – it was a toss-up between those and my camel Uggs. I'm glad I went for the trainers, though – they co-ordinate really well with the blue velvet Juicy Couture tracksuit I have on. I've nailed the country look, for sure.

'Your wellingtons?' he says.

'Wellingtons?'

'You didn't bring any?'

He looks at my trainers, as if he's not sure they're going to suit.

'No.' I shake my head. 'Why?'

'Well, those designer trainers you're wearing are going to get ruined,' he says. 'Maybe I could go back to the house – see if I can find something else for you . . .'

Damn! Why didn't I bring my fabulous wellies from Avoca with me? The ones with the diamanté on the side. This would have been the perfect opportunity to wear them. I've only ever worn them once before – to a weekend music festival – and loads of people admired them then. They would have worked so well here – I'd have looked so cute pottering about in them, just like something from a country catalogue. Mind you, the stable yard isn't even that mucky – the ground is dusty but otherwise it's fine. My trainers are hardly going to be ruined by standing here. It's not like the festival – that was a mudbath. Anyway, those wellies wouldn't have matched my Juicy tracksuit half as well as my trainers.

'It looks pretty safe to me,' I say, trying to sound confident. 'I'll be fine.'

For some reason, I suddenly want to prove to Edward that I'm not the nervous city girl he seems to think I am. I *am* scared, but he doesn't need to know that. Besides, I don't have much choice but to try. If I outright refuse to help out, I might put Claire's lease in jeopardy. He could ask me to leave so he can get cheap help somewhere else. I don't want Claire to return from India and find she's got nowhere to live – I have a responsibility at least to *try* to uphold the terms of the agreement. If I try, then he can't evict me, right? Maybe once he sees that the horses don't like me he'll let me off the hook scot-free. After all, ponies are valuable commodities and most of these don't even belong to him – he takes care of them for other people. They're part of his livelihood. He won't want me messing with them – maybe spooking them or doing them some sort of injury.

'OK, if you say so.' Edward looks doubtful. 'I'll lead Saffy out for you so you can get started.' He steps inside the stable, slips what he tells me is a halter over the pony's neck then leads her out into the yard. So far, so easy. Maybe this is going to be straightforward after all.

'Hi, Saffy,' he says cheerfully, tying her to the wall and rubbing her nose, 'you look gorgeous today.'

I laugh at this – he's talking to the pony as if she really understands him.

'Saffy likes to be complimented,' he explains. 'She's a pretty girl, aren't you, Saffy?'

The pony throws her head and bats her eyes at Edward, as if she's flirting with him. 'What's wrong with her leg?' I ask.

'Ah, that. Yeah, Drya kicked her out in the meadow and poor Saffy got a nasty cut – she's just finishing her antibiotics now.'

Why would one pony kick another so fiercely that they need bandaging all the way up the leg? That doesn't sound safe. Are they all as vicious? What if one of them kicks me, just like I warned Claire? I'd been exaggerating the farm-injury story to make Claire think twice about moving here and now it turns out that it's true. Maybe I should take a look at Edward's insurance policy, after all – I could fax it to a city lawyer, get him to give it the once-over. Not that it will help if I'm killed, of course.

'Don't worry, we won't let you near Drya,' Edward says solemnly, seeing my expression. 'She's a difficult horse – no one is to touch her but me.'

I gulp. I don't like the sound of this Drya – she must be a monster.

'Now, Saffy,' he turns back to the grey pony, 'this is Maggie. Maggie is new so I want you to be nice.'

The pony shakes her head and rolls her eyes. She doesn't look too impressed with me. Is it my imagination or is she smirking at my trainers?

'Now, now, she's not that bad, Saffy.' Edward laughs as if the pony has just told him she thinks I'm a hopeless case. 'So behave.'

I laugh nervously. That pony is definitely making faces at me. Can she tell I'm a disaster around animals? Christ, how did I get myself into this?

'So, Maggie,' Edward turns back to me, 'here's the pitchfork – and you can dump everything in here.' He points to a rusty wheelbarrow lying against the stone wall.

'What's that for? Are we cutting her mane or something?'

'Cutting her mane?' Edward repeats, evidently confused.

'Yes, while we groom her. Are you going to put all the hair we cut from her mane in the wheelbarrow? You probably use it to make things, right?' I'm sure I heard somewhere that horse hair is used to stuff things – cushions, maybe? They obviously collect it in the wheelbarrow and then bring it some-where to be used again. It's quite commendable, really. Eco-friendly and all that. Still, horse-hair cushions must be pretty uncomfortable – not to talk of smelly.

Edward stifles a laugh. 'You think we're grooming Saffy?'

'Well, yes.' What the hell is so funny?

Saffy harrumphs, like she's laughing at me too.

'Maggie, I'm sorry if you misunderstood,' he says, mouth still twitching. 'But you're not trimming Saffy's mane – you're mucking out her stable.'

'Mucking out her stable?' I echo.

'Yes.' I follow Edward's gaze to the interior of the stable. I can see large lumps of horse poo all over the straw. And damp patches. There are definite damp patches.

My stomach lurches. He wants me to pick up that pongy mess. He wants me to use the pitchfork to pick it up and then put it in the wheelbarrow. Oh, God.

I can feel his eyes on me and I try not to blanch at the thought. I can't deal with this stinky mess – he can't expect me to.

'I'm afraid the antibiotics have unsettled her stomach a little . . .'

That's the understatement of the millennium – there's poo everywhere and the stench is unbearable. I close my eyes briefly and will myself not to hurl. 'So I see,' I say.

'Do you think you can manage?'

I have to try. For Claire's sake. One little stable won't hurt me. If I can just get through this, it'll all be OK. 'Yes,' I squeak.

'Great.' Edward seems pleased. 'The manure pile is round the back.'

'And that is . . .?'

'Where you dump everything.'

'Right, of course.' Like I should be expected to know that.

'So, I think that's it. I'll lead them all out while you get started. Once you're finished with Saffy, you can do Pedlar next door and work your way around the block. Stop when you get to Drya. Like I said, she's a little . . . highly strung. I'll handle her. And that's how the routine will go every day.'

'Every day?' I look at him blankly.

'Yes.'

'You mean,' I splutter, the truth dawning on me, 'you mean you have to do this *every* day?'

'Well, of course! We muck out every morning.'

109

'But isn't that a little unnecessary?' I ask. 'Surely a good clean-out every couple of days would be OK?'

'Maggie, for a horse to be healthy and happy it must be kept clean and dry. That means mucking out every day. No exceptions.'

'No exceptions?'

'No. An unclean stable can lead to infections. We don't want that, do we?'

'Of course not.'

'That's why a daily clean is essential – and then, once a week, we strip the stall completely.'

'What does that mean?' I feel dizzy. That can't be good.

'It means you fill the wheelbarrow until the stall floor is bare. Then you use a shovel to scrape up any remnants of bedding and the broom to sweep it clean. After that, you put down stable disinfectant and let the floor dry before re-bedding.'

With that, Edward smiles at me and walks away.

'Right,' I say, to thin air. I'm aghast. He expects me to clean *all* these stables every day? And then do a complete strip every week? I run my eyes around the block and count six different stalls, excluding that of the dreaded Drya. I'm going to have to muck out every one of these? The idea is mind-boggling. I grip the pitchfork just to stay upright. How has this happened? How have I ended up here, about to do something I wouldn't even ask my worst enemy to do? It's impossible.

But it doesn't seem I have much choice. If I refuse, what might happen? Claire might lose the lease on the cottage, that's what. And it would be my fault.

'You're not going to muck out wearing those things, are you?' A hard voice interrupts my thoughts and I swing round to see a tall, grey-haired woman staring at my feet, contempt on her lined features.

Why is everyone so hung up on footwear round here? What is the big issue? 'Oh, hi,' I say, deciding to ignore the trainers comment. 'I don't believe we've met. I'm Maggie.'

It's nice to see another female face, even if this woman isn't exactly glowing with welcoming warmth. She doesn't look thrilled to meet me, that's for sure. 'I'm June,' she replies curtly.

June? This is Edward's wife? Wow – but she's so *wrinkly*. She looks old enough to be his mother. She must be a real-life cougar – isn't that what they're called? Older women who marry younger men? I'm a little stunned by this development. I can't imagine Edward and this woman together – they seem so different. Still, there's no accounting for taste, or attraction, I suppose.

'You're Edward's wife, of course!' I smile to cover my surprise that Edward is apparently married to a granny. 'Well, I'm very happy to meet you.'

The expression on June's face turns even sourer. '*What* did you just say?' she barks.

I blink. Have I insulted her in some way? Maybe they're not actually married and she hates being called his wife. Why is she looking at me like she wants to kill me? Talk about over-reacting. 'Sorry, do you prefer to be called his life partner?' I stutter.

'His *life partner*?' June hisses. 'I'm hardly his life partner. Are you blind? I'm far too old to be married to someone Edward's age. I'm his mother-in-law.'

Oh. Shit. I'm mortified.

'I'm sorry,' I say. 'So you have the same name as your daughter?'

'I *had*.' June looks at me coldly.

'Had?'

Now I'm really confused – what is she talking about? This

place is full of lunatics. They *are* all too closely related – I knew it.

'Yes. I *had*. That's what I said. You're hardly deaf as well as blind, I take it? My daughter June, Edward's wife, was killed three years ago in a riding accident in Glacken Woods.'

I see tears prick at her eyes as she says it, although I can tell she's desperately trying to swallow them back. She doesn't want me to see her getting upset – that much is clear. 'Oh, I'm sorry – I didn't know,' I manage to say. 'That's really terrible.' I've quite obviously brought all the pain flooding back for the poor woman – the reality of the situation is hitting her afresh, all because of my stupidity. How could I have made such a ridiculous mistake? I'd just assumed that when Edward kept referring to June he meant his wife. No one ever said anything about anyone being tragically killed. Now I've gone and upset this June no end – the anguish is etched on her face.

'Yes. It was.' June turns on her heel and walks off abruptly, angrily wiping away a tear.

I feel absolutely awful. No wonder Edward was so touchy about the insurance thing when I first questioned him about it. When he said something like no amount of money could bring back a loved one, this was what he'd meant. He'd been talking about his dead wife. I can't believe I put my foot in it so badly – now, as well as Matilda, I've made a second enemy in June. I'll be in *Guinness World Records* yet.

Stepping into Saffy's stall, I decide to do a really good job for Edward – it's the least I can do to make up for what I said. My left foot squelches into something and I look down to see my best trainer embedded in a fresh batch of dung. There are splatters of smelly gunk dripping all over the hems of my precious Juicy tracksuit. Maybe this wasn't the thing to wear after all – how on earth am I ever going to get that mess out of the blue velvet?

'Thanks for that.' I sigh and, outside, Saffy farts loudly in reply. Her meaning is clear – she certainly doesn't think I'm going to last long here and I have a doomed feeling she's probably right.

Rule Nine: *Remember that he who angers you conquers you*

'They all look great, thanks, Maggie,' Edward says. 'You're getting really good – I think you're a natural at this.' He closes the last stable door and smiles at me, but I don't think I could smile back even if I wanted to.

It's week two of my stay, and I'm so exhausted I can't feel my arms. I don't think that's a good sign. Either I've had some sort of mini-stroke, or spending hours mucking out all those ponies every day has damaged the nerve endings in my upper body. By my calculations, I've spent almost three hours today shifting wet and soiled bedding, although I'm not sure if that can be right – it's as if time stood still while I was desperately trying to breathe without gagging. It's been like that every morning – I try to work while holding my breath so I don't retch. I'm never going to get used to the awful stink. Not if I do this a million times, which I quite possibly will before Claire gets back.

'Saffy looks a little better, don't you think?' Edward leans over the pony's stable door and gently strokes her nose. She nuzzles happily into his hand.

'I think so,' I say, leaning on my pitchfork for support. I feel like I might keel over any second. I had no idea when I started here that, as well as being a disgustingly smelly job, mucking out is so physically demanding it can make me weak. I've been sweating in places I never knew I could – it's positively vile. My beloved Juicy tracksuit is now a shadow of its former self and I've given up trying to protect it. I've packed away my best city clothes and am now rotating my oldest jeans and my destroyed tracksuit bottoms every day – all sense of style and fashion has gone out the window.

'Still, I might get the vet back to check on her again.' Edward fondles Saffy's ears. 'We don't want her to get any worse. Were the rest OK today?'

'Yes, fine,' I wheeze. I never thought it would happen, but even though I find the work exhausting, I've actually become less nervous in just a few days here. Edward was right: the trick is to act confident with the ponies. If I concentrate on doing that it seems to go smoothly enough. I haven't been kicked or bitten yet in any case: all of them are well behaved and let me lead them out and tie them to the wall without trampling me to death, if I pretend I'm not quaking inside. Thankfully, I still haven't needed to go near Drya – I hear her stamping and harrumphing in her stall every morning and I'm terrified even by that.

'Great. So, what are you going to do with the rest of your day?'

Lie down and die? The words are on the tip of my tongue, but I don't say them. That would sound really pathetic. 'I'm not sure yet,' I say, pushing my hair from my eyes.

It feels like I have dirt in every single crevice. It'll take ages to get it all off, just like it does every day – I've already worked my way through two very expensive Jo Malone shower gels trying to scrub the smell from my skin. Once that's done, I have no idea what I'll do with my time. There's no TV or even Internet access in the cottage – it's like being stuck in some kind of time warp. Most days I've just flicked through the collection of *Vogue* magazines I brought with me from the city. It's almost painful to do that, of course – not because seeing all the high-fashion shots reminds me of how far from the real world I am, but because my hands are now a puzzle of calluses, broken nails and split skin. No matter how much intensive moisturizer I apply, nothing can improve them – not even the special cotton gloves I wear at night to help the salve sink in. I'm beginning to have farmhand fingers – it's very depressing.

'Isn't the light amazing today?' Edward says softly, gazing at the sky.

I look to where he's pointing and see the dappled pinks and oranges that linger among the clouds. He's right – the light *is* amazing today. I hadn't noticed.

A vision of sitting in front of my easel, paintbrush in hand, suddenly pops into my mind. That sky would be such a treat to capture on paper – even the idea of it sends a delicious shiver of anticipation up my spine. Ever since Claire reminded me of how much I used to love it, the idea of trying to paint again has been swirling about in my head.

'So, how's Claire getting on in India?' Edward asks, and I snap back to the stable yard.

'Fine, I think,' I reply. I've been wondering the same thing myself. If only I could call her – it's so strange not to be able to talk to her when I want to. Claire always used to pride herself on being available 24/7 when she worked with the hedge fund – her BlackBerry used to be welded to her hand. How is she getting on without constant access to the rest of the world? She must be going through serious cold turkey, even if she did wean herself off texting before she left, along with caffeine and cigarettes. It has to be weird to be so far away from civilization. Then again, I haven't exactly been keeping up to date with current events either – it's almost as if I'm inhabiting a parallel universe. I have no idea what's been happening in the world since I got here.

'She told me she's hoping to set up a holistic therapy practice when she gets back,' Edward goes on.

'Yes, that's true.' I nod. 'Do you think the villagers will like that sort of thing?' I can't imagine they will. After all, these country bumpkins probably don't believe in all that mumbo-jumbo – they'll run a mile. Maybe I should tell Claire that. Drop a gentle hint that her grand plan is probably a waste of time and that the villagers will never take to it. Perhaps then she'll go back to the city and we can do the *Working Girl* thing. The more I think about this idea, the more appealing it is.

'I think they will, actually,' Edward says unexpectedly. 'There's a *reiki* healer in the next village – he's very popular. There's a three-week waiting list for an appointment.'

'A *reiki* healer?' I'm gobsmacked. 'In the middle of the country?'

'Yes.' Edward laughs. 'Are you surprised, Maggie?'

'Well, I am a little,' I confess.

'Why? Do you think we're a bunch of inbred ignoramuses?'

His tone is teasing but he's hit the nail on the head and I think he knows it. 'Of course not,' I say, lowering my chin so he can't see the guilty expression on my face.

'So, what do *you* do for a living, then? Claire told me all about her plans, but she never said why you're here.'

He sounds curious – damn. I've been waiting for this question – in fact, if I was him I would have insisted on finding out my occupation far earlier. For all he knows I could be some sort of drug-dealer – I could be planning to turn Rose Cottage into a crack den. He never even asked to see references – nothing. He just accepted me on face value. That was incredibly trusting of him. And incredibly naïve.

'Um . . .' I search for something to say. I don't want to say I'm an unemployed estate agent – that doesn't sound very impressive. Not that I need to impress him, of course.

'Dad!'

Edward swivels from me to the sound of this shrill cry and I exhale. Saved by the bell.

Matilda, his teenage tearaway, prances into the yard, a smaller, mousy-looking girl in tow. It's the first time I've seen her since our encounter in the cottage.

'Matilda, come and say hello,' Edward calls. 'This is Maggie – you two haven't met yet, have you? Maggie is renting Rose Cottage and helping out in the yard while she's here – I told you, remember?'

There's no edge to Edward's voice, which is a big surprise. Surely they had a huge argument about me. After all, Matilda was so angry when she stormed out, I was positive she'd have marched straight to her father to demand an explanation. I haven't broached it with him – his family affairs are his business – but by the calm tone of his introduction now, it seems that Matilda didn't confront him at all.

She glares at me, her eyes hard. Now it clicks into place. She didn't tell her father about our argument because that would have meant confessing to being alone in the cottage with her boyfriend. Clearly, this isn't something she wants Edward to know. She obviously thought twice about saying anything.

By the expression on her face now, she's weighing up her options again. Should she admit that she's met me before? Or should she pretend this is the first time she's clapped eyes on me? 'Tell my dad,' her eyes flash for an instant, 'tell him that you found me in the cottage with a boy – let's see what he'll say.'

I'm being challenged, I'm sure of it. I can inform Edward that I've already met his charming daughter making out with her spotty boyfriend in the cottage – or I can pretend I've never seen her before. It doesn't take me long to make up my mind: it's really none of my business. Matilda isn't my daughter and the way she behaves isn't my concern. 'Hello, Matilda.' I smile sweetly. 'Nice to meet you.'

Matilda clamps her lips together and says nothing. It's almost as if she's disappointed. As if she'd been sure I was going to out her.

'*Matilda!*' Edward says, his voice a little strained. 'Please say hello.'

'Hello,' she mutters, then turns her back to me. The message is loud and clear – just because I didn't snitch doesn't mean she's going to be any nicer to me.

'Dad, Chloë and I want to hack out. I'm taking Drya.'

'Matilda,' Edward's tone is stern now, 'I've told you before. No one rides Drya.'

'There's nothing wrong with her – you can't keep her locked up all the time, it's not fair.' Matilda pouts, her face suddenly very much like her younger sister's. 'I'm not a child.'

'Drya is a very disturbed animal. She's not safe to ride – you know that.'

'I can handle her.'

'No. You can't.'

'You think I can't. Just because –'

'*Matilda,*' Edward's voice shakes with anger, 'I said no, and that's final.'

This is embarrassing and I suddenly want the ground to open up and swallow me whole – unlike the mousy Chloë, who seems to be thoroughly enjoying every second of the argument: she's drinking in every detail with relish.

The air between Edward and his daughter crackles with tension for what seems like for ever and then Matilda turns. 'Funny, isn't it?' she spits. 'You won't let your own daughter ride her favourite horse, but you'll let a complete stranger work in the stables. An *amateur*.' She glares at me.

'That's enough, Matilda!' Edward is furious. 'Why must you act like this?'

I hang my head. Matilda doesn't think I'm good enough

even to muck out. She's probably right – what do I know about horses? Nothing.

'Saddle up Pedlar and Romeo,' Edward says, 'and make sure you rub them down when you get back – I don't want either of them getting a chill.'

'Whatever,' Matilda grunts, and her friend giggles nervously as they disappear into the tack room.

'That was *major*!' I hear Chloë hiss with excitement to Matilda as they leave. 'Your family is so dramatic – it's better than watching *EastEnders*!'

'Sorry about that.' Edward rubs his hand across his brow in agitation. 'Drya was her mother's horse. Matilda has been . . . Anyway, you don't need to know our family history.' He smiles ruefully. 'Go and enjoy the rest of the afternoon.'

He was about to talk about his dead wife, I'm sure of it. Should I mention that I know all about it? That I've already met his mother-in-law? That I mortally offended her? Maybe not. This probably isn't the right time and I don't want the day to turn into an episode of a TV soap for real – there's been enough drama already.

'OK,' I say. 'I am a bit tired.'

'Yes, mucking out is hard work. Still, you're so fit – that must be really standing to you.'

'Fit?' I laugh cynically. 'Hardly!' Where did he get that idea?

Edward looks momentarily confused. 'But what about the running?'

Crap. Of course – I told him I run a stupid number of kilometres every week. Whatever possessed me to do that? 'Ah, yes,' I say, racking my brain for some sort of plausible theory. 'But you use different muscle groups when you're mucking out, of course. It takes some getting used to.'

'Right.' He doesn't look too convinced, probably because he's a real runner himself. He knows I'm bullshitting.

'But I *am* aerobically fit,' I bluff, 'so that helps.' I hope he can't see the sweat dripping down my neck – it'd be a dead giveaway that I'm actually totally knackered.

'Excuse me,' he says, glancing at his phone and moving away as it begins to ring in his hand. 'It's the vet and I have to talk to her about Saffy.'

Once he's out of sight I collapse on the stone steps, exhausted. It's funny, but even though I'm totally shattered, there is a perverse pleasure in knowing that all the ponies are clean and content. Manual labour can be quite satisfying in a strange sort of way.

'Tired, are you?' Matilda trots by on Pedlar, a large yellow pony, her friend Chloë in her wake on Romeo.

'I guess I am,' I reply, squinting up at her. The sun is high in the sky, blinding me.

'Serves you right,' she sneers, adjusting her hard hat. 'You have no business being here. Anyone could tell that you haven't a clue what you're doing.'

'Your dad doesn't seem to think I've done too badly,' I say. God, what a piece of work Matilda is.

'He's lying,' she snipes. 'He thinks you're hopeless as well.'

'Actually, he told me I'd done quite a good job.' I look her in the eye. I'm not going to let her get away with talking to me like that.

'You didn't really –' She throws her head back and laughs. 'You didn't really *believe* him, did you? Chloë, listen to this! Maggie here thinks she's doing a good job! Isn't that hilarious?'

Chloë giggles, hiding her freckled face behind her hand.

'The truth is,' Matilda goes on, 'Dad doesn't think anything of the sort. He told me you were hopeless, but he has to put up with you because he's no other choice. He needs cheap labour to do the yard work and you're his only option. He said a monkey could do it too, if it was trained properly.'

I feel the colour rise to my cheeks. Edward said he was really happy with my work. That I was a natural. 'That's not true,' I reply.

'You think not?' Matilda sneers. 'You think he would really tolerate you here unless you were paying rent and working for nothing? Walk on, Pedlar,' she commands, and her horse obediently sashays out of the yard, just before Edward re-appears.

'I'm going into the village later,' he says to me, snapping his phone shut. 'Would you like me to pick up some supplies for you?'

'No, thank you,' I reply frostily. If he's been talking about me behind my back, I'm not going to bother trying to be friendly any more. I'll do my bit working in the stables to keep the cottage safe for Claire but that's it. No more chit-chat.

'Are you sure?' He smiles at me, a look of confusion on his face. He has no idea why I'm suddenly so chilly towards him and I'm certainly not going to fill him in. If he's devious enough to be nice to my face and laugh at me behind my back he doesn't deserve to know. Let him try to figure it out for himself. Or let his darling daughter tell him.

'I *do* need some provisions,' I sniff in response, 'but I'll go into the village and get them for myself.'

I haul myself off the step and try to stalk away with dignity. It's difficult because every muscle in my body is screaming in vicious agony, but I manage it. That'll show him – this is a professional agreement, nothing more. There'll be no more friendly conversation. Not one word.

Rule Ten: *When in Rome, do as the Romans do*

'A pint of milk, please.'

'Right you are.' The shopkeeper reaches under the counter and hands me the milk from some invisible fridge, smiling all the while.

From the look of this tiny shop, I'm not convinced it's exactly safe to buy anything here – there's a hodgepodge of biscuits, mixed with dusty tins of peas and boxes of crisps on the shelves, next to what look like cartons of nails. And thread. And what might be a hammer. Although it could be some sort of ornament.

But I don't have much choice: I've already wandered up and down the street a few times, just to make sure I haven't missed anything, but apart from a butcher, a pub and a petrol station with sacks of coal heaped outside, there doesn't seem to be much else to the village.

There's certainly no supermarket so this little shop, with the old-fashioned sign that says 'Village Store', will have to do.

'Thank you.' I smile back at him.

With his striped apron and bushy handlebar moustache, the shopkeeper looks as if he's been transported straight from the 1920s and plonked into the twenty-first century.

'Like Rose Cottage, do you?'

'Excuse me?' I ask, pausing from counting the money from my purse on to the counter for him. I don't want to check whether the milk is still in date until I leave the shop. Even I know that would be rude.

'The cottage? Like it, do you?'

He must know who I am — word obviously travels fast in this part of the country.

'Yes, it's fine, thanks,' I answer politely.

There's no point in telling him that mucking out ponies isn't my idea of a good time. Or that I seem to be making enemies everywhere I go. Country life certainly isn't the bed of roses Claire believed it would be.

'Edward is a nice fella,' the man continues. 'Of course it's been hard for him — you know . . . since his wife passed on.' He shakes his head sorrowfully. 'Awful, that was.'

'Yes, I suppose so,' I say. I just want to pay for the milk and go. I don't want to talk about Edward or his life. It's really nothing to do with me. I'm here to do a job, that's all. Besides, I don't need reminding of how badly I put my foot in it with June.

'I'm sure you've met his girls by now — that little Polly's a right 'un, isn't she?'

'Yes . . .'

Why all the conversation? You don't get this in the city. There you can just hand over the money, get your goods and go. You don't even have to meet the eye of the person who serves you if you don't want to and no one thinks anything of it. It's a far simpler system — all this small-talk is exhausting.

'I remember,' he leans back and crosses his arms, as if he's going to recount a long story, 'I remember one day she came in here looking for ice cream. But she didn't just want one — oh, no, she wanted two.'

'Really?'

I flick my eyes across the shelves to see if there's any wine in here — I'm starting to feel the need for a serious drink. I can't spot any. Maybe they have it out the back. There's a shabby red curtain on the wall — it could be behind there.

'It was the funniest thing — guess who she wanted the other one for!'

'I have no idea,' I reply.

Or maybe he keeps it under the counter – in the invisible fridge with the milk? I doubt if he has anything good but I don't really care – I'll drink any old plonk right now. Maybe he has some *poitín* somewhere. I've heard these country villages are awash with that stuff – maybe there's some sort of code I need to know before he'll sell it to me. I wonder what it could be.

'Ah, go on. Take a guess. Guess who she wanted it for!'

Is this guy for real? I don't have time to be playing these sorts of silly games with him – I just want to pay for my milk and go. And maybe get some wine. Or *poitín*. Or anything alcohol-related. Mouthwash?

'Go on, guess!' he insists.

If I don't make some sort of effort I'm never going to escape. 'Her sister?' I try. Would Polly buy an ice cream for Matilda? I doubt it – but then again, who knows how that crazy family works?

'Matilda? Poor child – she's had it tough and no mistake. But it's not her, no. Guess again.'

This man seems to like Matilda – maybe there's more to Her Sulkiness than meets the eye. I suppose it's pretty hard to be a teenager and it must be even harder to be a teenager when you have no mother to look out for you. That said, the girl does need a serious attitude adjustment. Maybe even a spell in a teenage boot camp – that might sort her out. I try to imagine Matilda being told to drop and do fifty press-ups – she'd probably tell the drill sergeant where to get off.

'Her father?' I try.

'No.' He beams at me, enjoying the game.

'Her grandmother?'

'*Her?* No, that one wouldn't need an ice cream – she's already the Ice Queen of the Village!'

He cackles madly at his own joke and I suddenly warm to him – obviously Edward's mother-in-law isn't Mrs Popularity. That's a relief – so it's not just me.

'Go on, take another guess.'

'I really don't know,' I reply, feeling defeated. 'I don't know anyone else here.'

'OK, I'll tell you then. The second ice cream was for . . . her pony! Isn't that gas? The child was getting an ice cream for her pony!'

He cackles madly again, and I can't help but grin back at him. 'She *is* pony mad,' I say. 'She's crazy about Saffy.'

'Yes,' he wipes tears of mirth from his eyes with the edge of his apron, 'she's exactly like her mother, God rest her. Fiery and headstrong, just the same. Everyone knew that Drya was a danger, but June couldn't be told. It was a tragedy waiting to happen . . .' He shakes his head.

Drya? Edward's wife was killed when she fell off Drya? Now I understand fully. No wonder he doesn't want anyone to touch that horse.

'Yes, well.' I suddenly feel uncomfortable. 'I'd better get going, thanks.' I push the money towards him and scoop up my milk carton.

But before I can run, the shopkeeper is off again. 'So, what do you do, then?' he asks, planting his elbows on the counter and leaning in closer to me.

'What do you mean?' I spy a tin of corned beef behind his head – I didn't know that stuff was still available. I haven't seen it since I was a child. Mind you, the tin looks as if it could have been here since then.

'For a living – what do you do for a living? No one in the village has been able to find out – you're a proper little mystery!'

'Oh.' I pause. I don't particularly want to tell him that I'm an estate agent. In my experience, this never makes people feel at ease. Especially now times have changed – everyone seems to think that estate agents made so much money in the good years that now they deserve to die slow, painful deaths. In any case, calling myself an estate agent isn't true any more – not now that I'm unemployed. My stomach does a little flip when I think about that. I've been managing to push the unemployment spectre out of my mind quite successfully so far, but the truth of the situation is that I'm living in a strange village, where almost everyone I've met dislikes me, shovelling horse crap every day. It's utterly depressing.

'I'm a . . . I'm an artist,' I say quickly, plucking the occupation from thin air. Where did that come from? True, I've been thinking about painting a lot, but I can't call myself an artist. It really is appalling how many lies I've told recently – I lied to Edward about running and now I'm lying to this perfectly nice man about my occupation. Of course, Edward lied to me too: he said I was good with the horses and then slated me to Matilda. But, still, that's no excuse. What's happening to me? Is the country air scrambling my brain? Maybe I'm having some sort of nervous breakdown. I'll have to call Theresa later and list my symptoms, get her diagnosis. Theresa loves nothing more than a threatened breakdown. She can spot one a mile off. One of her favourite pastimes is sitting in Starbucks, earmarking which of the frazzled mothers will crack next. She's almost always right.

'An *artist*?' The shop owner is impressed. 'Hear that, Peg?'

A small wiry woman with tightly curled hair suddenly pops her head up from underneath the counter and I jump with fright. Where has she been hiding? In the invisible fridge with the milk?

'What's that, Ted?'

Ted and Peg? Are they having me on? This is like something out of a badly written TV sitcom.

'This is the girl who's renting Rose Cottage from Edward – Maggie Baxter. She's an *artist*!'

Wow. He knows my full name too. That's pretty impressive.

'Maggie!' Peg calls, as if I'm some sort of long-lost relative. 'Let me have a look at you.' She eyes me from head to toe, taking me in. 'Well, they were right, Ted – she's a looker!'

'She is that!' Ted is now happily munching a Mars Bar.

'Ted,' Peg scolds him, 'where are your manners?'

'Sorry, Maggie,' he says, chocolate seeping from the corners of his mouth. 'Will you have a Mars Bar?'

'No, I'm fine, thanks,' I say.

'Not everyone wants to eat Mars Bars, Ted,' Peg says. 'He's not supposed to have them, Maggie. Addicted to them, he is. Eats half a dozen a day and him a martyr to his cholesterol.'

'My cholesterol is fine!' Ted protests.

'Dr Martin doesn't think so!' Peg argues hotly.

'Ah, what does he know? A harmless little Mars Bar won't kill me.'

'Maybe one wouldn't, Ted. But half a dozen? He just won't listen to me, Maggie.' Peg sighs. 'Any excuse and he's munching – is it any wonder that his cholesterol is through the roof? Dr Martin says it's a medical mystery he's survived this long.'

'Now, Peg,' Ted says, 'Maggie here doesn't want to be hearing about my insides.'

'You're right.' Peg pauses mid-rant. 'I'm sorry, Maggie. We're being very rude. Now, an artist, are you? Isn't that very exotic! No one thought that, did they, Ted?'

'No, they didn't,' Ted agrees. 'Betty in the butcher's was sure you were on the run.'

'On the run?' I gulp.

'Yes – you know, from some sort of tragedy. A broken relationship, maybe.' Peg's eyes light up at the thought and then she composes herself again. 'But don't mind Betty, she's a nosy article – she'll know your business before you know it yourself. Hear the grass grow, that one would!'

'She won't like that we've found out before she has – will she, Peg?' Ted says.

'No, she won't!' Peg rubs her hands together with glee. 'She'll be green with envy! Serves her right, too – she's been lording it over us ever since she was the first to find out about the supermarket.' Her face suddenly darkens and the shop goes deathly quiet. I have no idea why.

'So, Maggie,' Ted says, breaking the tense silence, 'what do you use?'

'How do you mean?' I sidle closer to the door, eager to make my escape. I don't want to be rude – they seem nice, but I don't want to make any more chit-chat. Making chit-chat is dangerous: it leads to lies, lies and more lies. Am I becoming a compulsive liar, perhaps? It isn't beyond the realms of possibility.

'To paint – what medium do you use, oils or watercolours, like?' Ted isn't letting me go.

I try to think what would sound legitimate. 'Um, a bit of both,' I say.

'A bit of both!' Peg is delighted with this news. 'That's mighty altogether. And have you had many?'

'Many?' I struggle to decide what she means by that. Why is it that everything she says seems to be some sort of riddle? Is that normal practice round here?

'Many exhibitions? Of your work?'

'Oh, right. Yes, a few,' I say, finally understanding what she means. 'You know how it is.' God, I'm being so dishonest – what's happening to me?

'That's fantastic!' Ted says, beaming, and I blush.

It's terrible to lie like this, but I don't want to hurt their feelings now – they're so enthusiastic.

'Do you think you'll have an exhibition here? Oh, my God,

Ted! What will I wear?' Peg's face falls. 'I'll never fit into that dress I got for Billy Nolan's wedding. And *you*! That's it!' She grabs the Mars Bar from his hand. 'You have to give up those things. You can't make a show of poor Maggie here – she'll expect us to look the part when all her city friends come for the exhibition. Won't you, Maggie?'

'Um, I . . .' I'm stuck for words.

'Everyone will be delighted when we tell them,' Ted says, eyeing the Mars Bar in Peg's grip. He's definitely trying to figure out how to get it back.

'They will. They'll be delighted!' Peg echoes.

'Everyone?'

'The villagers, of course! We've all been wondering about you – it's a real privilege to have an artist here.'

'Edward wouldn't tell us a thing about you,' Ted says sorrowfully. 'He's a lovely fellow, but he's useless for news.'

'Not a thing!' Peg agrees. 'Not what age you were, what you did – nothing! Wait till I tell them all!' She's almost dancing with excitement.

'Ah, don't go telling anyone,' I say. It'll be too awful if people think I'm a real artist. Why couldn't I have said I was something else – something less interesting?

Peg's face falls. 'Not tell them? But sure that'll be no fun, no fun at all. What's the point in knowing you're a real live artist if I can't tell anyone?'

'Not tell anyone? Why not?' Ted asks.

This pair is a proper double-act – one stops and the other starts. 'Well, you know . . .' I try to dodge the question. This has gone too far – I can't have the whole village believing I'm something I'm not.

'*I* know why she doesn't want anyone to find out!' Ted suddenly bangs his fist on the countertop and I flinch, the milk carton jumping in my hand.

'You do?' Peg looks bewildered.

'It's obvious!' Ted roars, his fleshy cheeks wobbling with mirth and his handlebar moustache quivering with his unbridled excitement.

'Ah, Ted, stop leading me on!' Peg begs. 'Tell me why.'

'She's obviously working on something top secret!' He whispers the last bit – like he's some sort of CIA agent. I get the feeling Ted probably likes to watch *CSI*.

'Are you?' Peg breathes, her face changing visibly as she gazes at me. She looks almost . . . almost awestruck.

I blink rapidly, trying to decide what to do. If I confess that I'm not an artist working on a secret assignment, I'll look very foolish and they'll be disappointed. They want a little drama to brighten up their lives. Plus, I don't want them to think I'm a barefaced liar – even if they are complete strangers. Maybe I'll just go along with it, let them believe this untruth. What harm can it do, really? It's not like I'm some sort of con woman or anything.

'You caught me!' I smile at them both. 'I'm working on a top-secret commission and I'm hiding out in the cottage to get some peace and quiet.'

'I *knew* it!' Ted bangs the countertop again and I grip my milk carton tightly this time. 'I just *knew* it!'

'You have a psychic streak, Ted.' Peg slaps him on the back, thrilled. 'You definitely do. I always said it, didn't I?'

'You did, girl.' Ted beams at her.

I get the distinct feeling they want to embrace – they look like they could hop on each other with the pure thrill of it all.

'He foresaw poor Blackie Dempsey's death,' Peg informs me, her delighted little face suddenly solemn once more. 'Isn't that right, Ted?'

'It is. More's the pity,' Ted says, solemn too. 'Poor old Blackie.'

'He had a dream that Blackie was going to die, didn't you?' Peg pats Ted's hand and Ted nods. 'He met a terrible end,' Peg says to me. 'Really gruesome it was.'

'What happened?' I ask, almost afraid to enquire.

'Jean Dolan reversed over him. Decapitated he was, Lord have mercy on his soul.'

Peg and Ted drop their heads in respect to poor Blackie.

'Decapitated?' I'm appalled. 'That's awful!'

'It was, Maggie, it was,' Peg says. 'His little head rolled down Pender's Hill and Johnny Ryan found it in the gutter, didn't he, Ted? He was only eight, the poor cratur.'

'He was that,' Ted agrees. 'The poor child was never right after it.'

I grip the counter, feeling faint. An eight-year-old child found a man's head rolling down the street? This is horrific – why didn't I ever hear any of this on the news? 'A man's head?' I stutter. 'A man's head rolled down Pender's Hill?'

Peg and Ted look at each other, then roar with laughter. 'Where did you get that cracked idea from?' Ted guffaws.

'Well, you said . . .' I look from one to the other in confusion. Are they completely insane? 'You just said that Jean Dolan reversed over Blackie Dempsey and decapitated him and then his head rolled down Pender's Hill.'

'Oh, oh . . .' Peg and Ted are convulsing with laughter. They're gripping each other and rocking back and forth with glee.

'Blackie wasn't a man, Maggie,' Ted gasps. 'He was a tom cat!'

They fall against each other again, shaking with mirth.

'Aye, a randy old tom at that – every cat in the parish celebrated when he went to his Maker!' Peg roars. 'You're priceless, Maggie – you really are a howl a minute!'

A tom cat. Right. How the hell was I supposed to know

that? They called him by a first and last name. Who gives a cat a last name? It's ridiculous!

'I can't believe –' Peg pants '– I can't believe you thought Blackie was a – a man!'

They both collapse into more fits of giggles. 'That's the best one I've ever heard!'

'Well, 'bye, then,' I blurt, feeling like a prize idiot for the millionth time in just a few days. How could I have been so stupid? I have to get out of this twilight zone, quick. Yanking the shop door open, I rush outside gripping my milk, the sound of Peg and Ted roaring with laughter ringing in my ears as the door swings behind me.

Rule Eleven: *Appearances can be deceptive*

'Well, *excuse* me!'

I gasp as my carton of hard-won milk bounces off a pair of pointy bosoms encased in a pale pink cashmere twinset and hits the path with a splat. 'I'm very sorry.' I stoop to pick it up. 'I didn't see you there.' Luckily, the carton is still in one piece because I don't fancy going back in and starting all over again with Peg and Ted. Even the thought terrifies me. Who knows what other insane stories they'll tell me?

Miss Twinset smooths herself down and adjusts the strand of pearls at her neck. I can tell they're real – they're exactly like some I saw once in a swanky city-centre jeweller's: gorgeous. In fact, with one glance, I see that this woman has completely nailed that whole prim-and-proper look – that *Mad Men* vibe is very in right now but I can't believe Glacken society has embraced such a high-fashion concept. Maybe I should pull out some of my best outfits and stop slobbing about in smelly things that are smeared with horse manure. After all, I wouldn't be seen dead looking like this in the city – I'd rather die. I should have showered and changed before I came into the village – why did I just assume that everyone would be grubby and old-fashioned and no one would notice? How have I let my standards slip so badly? The truth of the matter is I hadn't expected to meet anyone like this, not in a million years. It serves me right for making that presumption, I suppose.

'That's quite all right,' Miss Twinset says. 'No real harm done.'

She smiles coldly at me, her gaze penetrating. I know instantly that she doesn't believe there's no harm done – she looks like she'd happily skin me alive for so much as touching her. She's certainly not sweet and innocent, like her image suggests.

I go to make my way past her, not wanting to engage in any more conversation, but she subtly blocks my path. 'You must be the new tenant in Edward's cottage. Maggie, isn't it?'

'That's right,' I mutter. Wow! Word really does travel fast in this neck of the woods. Everyone seems to know who I am.

'I thought so. My name is Odette Ffrench. Two *f*s. I'm the vet here in Glacken.' She announces this with an air of supreme authority – as if by being a country vet she should be regarded as some sort of royalty.

I take her proffered hand – she has a bone-crushing grip and I wince as she clasps my fingers briefly, yet agonizingly in her palm. How can she look so ladylike and be so freakishly strong? What does she do – work out with some sort of handheld device to build up her muscle strength?

'So, how do you like Glacken so far?'

Her eyes drift from my scraped-back hair to my filthy clothes. I can tell she thinks I'm some sort of riff-raff by my grubby attire and I cringe under her gaze – I must look a proper state and I probably smell even worse. I'm almost sure I see her nose wrinkle in distaste. 'It's very nice,' I reply carefully.

'And Edward? I'm sure he's helping you to settle in.'

'Yes,' I say. If calling me useless behind my back counts as helping – but I keep that thought to myself.

'I'm a very good friend of Edward's – you may have heard that.'

There's a certain tone in her voice – she's not threatening me exactly, but she's definitely trying to convey a particular message. I just haven't figured out what it might be. 'Um, no, I don't think I have.'

No one mentioned an Odette, did they? Perhaps someone did and I've forgotten – I've been so tired from the physical activity it's all one big blur.

I glance to my left and see the unmistakable heads of Peg and Ted peering out from the shop window. They're watching this little encounter.

'Well, I am.' She lowers her voice, as if she's afraid she may be overheard. 'If I'm frank, we're more than friends, really.'

'What do you mean?' I watch as she fiddles with the pearl necklace draped round her neck. I'm starting to think she's not doing high fashion, after all. Maybe her attire isn't an ironic nod to the 1950s. Maybe she just dresses like an eighty-year-old woman.

'We're in a relationship but we're trying to be discreet about it, if you know what I mean,' she continues.

'Why's that?' Odette is making me feel very uncomfortable – there's something creepy about her eyes. She looks almost wolf-like. As if she might gobble me up in a second.

'Well, out of respect for his deceased wife, of course. Edward doesn't want all the villagers . . .' she whips her head around to make sure no one is watching and I catch Peg and Ted ducking out of view '. . . to know about us. Not just yet. It wouldn't be . . . proper.'

'I see.' Why is she telling me all this? What does it have to do with me?

'Yes. So now you know.'

'Sorry?' I'm completely lost. I'm also sweaty and tired, and I'm dying for a cup of tea.

'I think it's important to tell you about Edward and me,' she says, 'in case there's any . . . confusion.' She stares directly at me.

'Excuse me?' I've no idea what Odette is talking about. Why

136

would I care who Edward has a relationship with? I have to say, though, that I'm very surprised he's going out with this woman – she strikes me as a nasty piece of work and I already dislike her intensely from her super-sleek bobbed hair to the tip of her pointy stilettos. I could never imagine him with her – she's far too glacial for him, surely. Then again, even if Edward seems nice enough, he may not be. After all, his daughter claims he's been less than complimentary about me. I have to remember that.

Odette frowns, as if she can't understand why I'm so stupid. Then suddenly the penny drops. I realize she's staking her claim on Edward. She thinks I'm interested in him!

'Well, Edward has been quite vulnerable since his wife passed away,' she says. 'Certain types might want to take . . . advantage of that.' She picks a minuscule speck of fluff from her arm and flicks it away with her sharp nails.

'What exactly are you suggesting?' I glare at her. I feel a bubble of anger rise inside me – how dare she imply that I'm some sort of predator, stalking Edward?

'I'm not suggesting anything,' she says coolly, rearranging her twinset so that it sits just so on the waist of her tweed skirt. 'I'm just disseminating the information so we're clear.'

Then she gazes steadily at me again. She definitely gets Botox – her forehead hasn't moved once during this conversation. In fact, her entire face is almost frozen. Whoever did it hasn't done much of a job – good Botox can make you look years younger and fresher. Claire used to swear by it before she turned all happy-clappy, but her face never looked anything like this – like a freaky life-size plastic doll's. Then again, Claire used to attend the most expensive dermatologist in the city for regular top-ups. Miss Twinset here could be injecting herself with something from her veterinary bag to cut corners.

What can Edward see in her? And what about the children

– what must they make of her? If they even know about her, that is. Maybe Edward hasn't broken it to his children that he's dating Odette – she did say they're trying to keep their relationship quiet. I wonder what Matilda will do when she finds out – I can't imagine her throwing her arms round Odette and welcoming her into the family. And Polly will definitely have something to say: she's not one to hold back her opinion, even if she is only six.

'Listen, Odette, I have a boyfriend back home, OK?' I say coldly. 'I'm spoken for, so you don't need to worry.' This lie trips off my tongue and I don't feel an iota of guilt about it.

'You do?' Odette's eyes light up.

'Yes.' Another lie, but she's not to know, is she?

A vision of Robert crying openly as I left him pops into my head and I say a silent prayer that he's doing better now. He really didn't take the break-up well – watching him dissolve into tears like that had made it so difficult to see through my decision. If I hadn't known deep inside that I was making the right choice for both of us I might have faltered right then and there.

'Well, that's a different matter.' Odette smoothes out her twin-set again and then straightens her pearl necklace once more so that it lies neatly against her *décolletage*. 'I'm glad we got that sorted out. Will he be paying you a visit, this boyfriend of yours?'

'I don't know,' I reply frostily. 'Now, if you don't mind, I really need to get on.'

I inch my way round her – if I don't have that tea soon my throat will close up completely.

'Of course. I'll leave you to it.'

She smiles benignly at me as she walks away and I grit my teeth at her in return. This place is full of crackpots. Either they *are* all related or there's something in the water. I'll have to boil the kettle more than once before I make my tea.

I watch warily as she crosses the road, then lowers herself

into a pretty swanky red sports car and takes off at high speed, leaving a trail of dust behind her. It's certainly not conventional transport for a country vet. Then again, Odette is not what I ever pictured a country vet would look like. I'll bet she makes a point of being glamorous at all times – she probably looks just as good when she's helping a cow to calve. I can't imagine her ever breaking into an unseemly sweat or letting a mere animal muss her perfection.

She's certainly made it abundantly clear how the village hierarchy works: the country vet is obviously a powerful member of the community and she's made damn sure I understand this. She's also made it very clear that Edward is off limits – she couldn't have been any plainer if she'd pulled plans for the big house's remodel from her handbag. She's intent on becoming Mrs Edward Kirwan, Lady of the Manor, and nothing will stop her. Not the villagers, Edward's daughters, or his mother-in-law. She'd have them all for breakfast and not think twice.

I'm in my car, instinctively indicating to pull out, even though there isn't another vehicle to be seen on the street other than a parked Massey Ferguson tractor with a missing wheel, when Peg and Ted come rushing from the shop.

'Maggie! Maggie!' they shout in unison, bounding up the path.

I think about taking off and pretending I don't hear them, but it's too late.

'We're sorry to bother you,' Peg pants at my window.

'But we wanted to apologize,' Ted continues.

'Apologize?'

'Yes,' Peg says, looking ashamed. 'We shouldn't have laughed at you in the shop.'

'No, we shouldn't, it was rude,' Ted agrees, nodding earnestly. 'It was very improper. Very funny, mind, but still very improper.'

'You weren't to know that Blackie was a tom cat,' Peg goes on.

'No, you weren't.' Ted's mouth twitches at the corners. 'Although it was hilarious.' He breaks into chuckles.

'Now, Ted, don't set me off,' Peg says, struggling to stay serious. 'You know you've a very infectious laugh – you'll start me going again and Maggie here will think we're terrible.'

'You're right.' Ted composes himself. 'Anyway, Maggie, we wanted to say we're sorry.'

'Yes, we're sorry,' Peg chimes in, as if they've practised it beforehand.

'That's OK,' I say. I can't hold it against them – thinking back, it was pretty funny, even if they are certifiable. 'Let's forget it, shall we?'

Now that I've accepted their apology they can go back to their shop feeling happy and I can get on with making that cup of tea.

'Well, there is one other thing,' Ted says.

'There is?' Why doesn't this surprise me?

'Yes. You see, we've had a brainwave,' Peg continues. 'It's about the supermarket.'

'The supermarket?' I look at the leaflet that Peg has shoved into my hands. 'Save Glacken Village!' it screams, in large red lettering.

'Xanta is trying to build one of its cut-price supermarkets just outside the village,' she says, her voice wavering.

'And that would be a bad thing?' Surely a Xanta store would do brilliant business round here – value supermarkets have been popping up all over the country since the recession hit. The papers say they're the only businesses benefiting from the downturn – people want value for money in their trolley now more than ever.

'Of course it would be a bad thing, Maggie.' Peg looks at

me as if I'm the crazy one. 'We don't want one of those awful places here – it would change the village for ever.'

I can't help thinking that Glacken could do with a bit of a change. Maybe this supermarket could force it to step out of the musty past and into the present. But I don't say this because Peg and Ted look positively distraught at the idea.

'So, we've started a campaign,' Peg goes on.

'A campaign to stop the supermarket destroying the community,' Ted adds. 'Because if it's built no one will bother coming into the village any more – there'll be no passing traffic.'

'And if there's no passing traffic then . . .' Tears well in Peg's eyes and she's unable to go on.

Ted reaches out to grip her hand. 'It'll be OK, girl,' he says firmly. 'If I have to lie down in front of a bulldozer to stop this thing I will!'

'Ah, Ted, you're an ole dote.' Peg smiles unsteadily at him. 'We think you could help, Maggie. We need someone like you.' Her eyes are pleading. 'There's a meeting tonight for both sides to air their views. Will you come?'

'Both sides?'

'Yes, *some* people, naming no names, think this supermarket is a good idea.' Peg's face darkens.

'She means that Odette,' Ted explains.

'*She* thinks it's a great idea!' Peg cries bitterly. 'What would she know about it?'

'Now, now, Peg, take it easy,' Ted counsels. 'So, Maggie, will you come?' He turns back to me.

'Um, I'm not sure what I could do,' I say uneasily. 'I don't know anything about supermarkets.' And I don't want to be dragged into village politics – all this is nothing to do with me.

'But you have an artistic brain – we could do with one of those,' Ted says.

'Artists look at the world differently,' Peg adds confidently. 'You'll probably be able to come up with some brilliant ideas.'

'And you'll be able to paint some posters,' Ted suggests. 'You know – for the campaign, like.'

'Ted! That's a brilliant idea!' Peg says, beaming up at him. 'You're a genius so you are!'

'Ah, no, I'm not,' Ted says bashfully.

'You are. You're far too modest – isn't he, Maggie?' She gazes adoringly at him. 'We're married for thirty-two years, did you know that?'

'No, I didn't,' I reply. How could I possibly know that? I only met them for the first time today. These two are complete crackpots.

'Yes, thirty-two years of wedded bliss and he still manages to surprise me every day,' Peg says in wonder.

Ted clutches her hand and they stare lovingly at each other.

I don't know what to say. And, anyway, I don't have to say much because they're far too busy cooing over each other to notice me any more.

'Thanks for the leaflet anyway.' I go to drive away, hoping they're so wrapped up in each other that they've forgotten about me and I can escape.

'Wait!' Peg springs away from Ted and grabs my arm. 'Please come tonight, Maggie – we need you.'

'Yes,' Ted says. 'Please come.'

'There'll be cake,' Peg adds, like that might be enough to persuade me.

'And you can meet everyone,' Ted goes on. 'They're going to love you. Although you've already met Odette.'

Peg's face twists again at the mention of her name. 'Don't let her put you off,' she leans in close to me and whispers. 'The rest of us are nothing like her.'

'Nothing *at all* like her,' Ted agrees passionately.

'But there's no point getting into all that now.' Peg nudges Ted. 'Maggie will find out soon enough.'

'You're right!' Ted agrees cheerfully. 'So, we'll see you tonight, then, in the parish hall at seven p.m. There'll be tea and sandwiches, as well as cake, so don't be late.'

'Oh, that reminds me, Ted, I forgot to boil the eggs.' Peg is in an immediate flap at the mention of sandwiches.

'Quick so, we'd better go – there'll be murder if you don't bring your egg sandwiches.' Ted swats her bottom and Peg giggles girlishly.

'Go on out of that, you cheeky pup! But you're right, I'd better get moving – that Betty in the butcher's would only love it if I didn't make any. She's been trying to outdo me with her sausage rolls for years, hasn't she, Ted?'

'She has that, my love, but who wants a limp sausage roll?'

'Ah, Ted, they're not that bad.' Peg looks thrilled with this verdict.

'They are so – everyone avoids them like the plague. Not like your sandwiches, Peg – no one can resist them. They have a special ingredient,' he says to me.

'Do they?' This is surreal.

'Oh, yes, indeed they do. But I can't tell you what that is – if I did, I'd have to kill you! Now, the hall is just across the road – we'll see you there.'

I twist my head to see a squat grey building, but before I can make an excuse about why I can't attend the meeting, Peg and Ted have bounded away again. I'm left sitting speechless in my car, the milk carton, which has decided to spring a leak after its altercation with Odette's pointy bosoms, dripping slowly into my lap.

Rule Twelve: *Proceed with due caution*

'Order!' Peg roars, her cheeks pink.

I'm impressed that she can project her voice so successfully across such a crowded room – for a small woman she can really pack a punch.

'Order!' she bellows again, and everyone stops chattering.

'Now settle down, people,' she says sternly. 'Let's not frighten the new girl!'

I squirm with mortification in my seat. When I first got here, Ted himself guided me to a place in the front row, then handed me a cup of tea and one of Peg's famous egg sandwiches. I have to admit, they *are* delicious – I've half a mind to ask her for the secret recipe. I've sat here, trying to look inconspicuous, ever since, but I'm keenly aware that people are staring at me curiously and I'm feeling incredibly self-conscious.

'Now,' Peg says, 'this is Maggie. Maggie is an internationally recognized artist so we're very lucky to have her here in the village. The great news is, she's agreed to give us some input about the proposed supermarket development. Isn't that marvellous?'

Internationally recognized artist? I never said that! I never even hinted that. I just said I was a painter – how has she made that leap?

I look at Peg's happy expression and I know she's inflating my importance to impress the audience, half of whom are now craning their necks to see me.

'Now, Maggie, if you'd like to say a few words.'

Say a few words? I look wildly at Ted, who's smiling broadly at me and gesturing with his hands that I'm expected to stand up and say something. There's polite, if muted, clapping as I rise from my seat.

What on earth do they expect me to say? How did I ever agree to come? I wouldn't be here at all if Peg and Ted hadn't arrived at my door at six forty-five p.m., declared they were there to give me a lift to the meeting and bundled me into their little white van. I suddenly long to be curled up in front of a flat-screen TV, back in the city, where I feel safe and I'm not dragged to mad places I don't want to go to.

'Hello, everybody.' I look around the room and three dozen pairs of beady eyes stare back at me. They don't look all that friendly. Some seem downright surly.

'Um, my name is Maggie and I'd be delighted to help in any way I can,' I stutter.

I see an overweight man in a blue wool jumper fold his arms and roll his eyes, like he doesn't believe a word I'm saying. He's right not to, of course – I don't really want to help at all and I have no intention of sticking round here for long enough to find out what happens with the supermarket. By then I'll be gone. Long, long gone.

'Maggie said she'd do a few posters for us!' Ted beams proudly. 'Isn't that great altogether?'

The crowd don't look all that enthusiastic. I distinctly hear someone mutter, 'Big swing.' It might have been the man in the blue jumper – I can't be sure.

'What approach do you think we should take, Maggie?' Peg asks earnestly, just before I lower myself back into my seat. My muscles are screaming in agony from the stable work – I feel tired and stiff all over.

'Approach?'

'To the proposed supermarket development. Should we be peaceful or more "active", if you know what I mean?'

There's an excited murmur when she says that – clearly a few of the locals are in favour of some sort of civil disobedience to liven things up.

'We could form a human chain round the site!' a middle-aged woman in a floral dress calls.

'That's a stupid idea.' The overweight man in the blue jumper snorts. 'And it's illegal.' He looks certain of this.

'It's not stupid,' another woman, in a dark jacket, interrupts.

'It is. And, anyway, even if it's not illegal, there aren't enough of us to form a chain round a development site,' Blue Jumper retorts.

'We could do a nude calendar to raise awareness!' someone shouts from the back of the hall.

'Yeah, I'll pose naked behind my pitchfork – how about that?' someone else bellows.

There's a wave of laughter at this suggestion.

'Order!' Peg yells. 'Come on now, lads, stop wasting time!'

'The supermarket is a great idea. We should be welcoming it with open arms, not trying to stop it.' A man in a tweed hat has stood to address the room.

'I agree!' a voice calls. 'We need jobs! We don't all want to die farming, you know!'

The hall erupts. It looks like people are fairly divided about the supermarket development: some passionately oppose it and others welcome it. How on earth will they come to some agreement? This is complete chaos.

'Good evening, everyone,' a sharp voice blasts, cutting right through the noise with ease.

I turn to see Odette Ffrench, two *f*s, walking purposefully towards the front of the room.

'What's she doing here?' Ted mutters to Peg. 'I thought she wasn't coming tonight.'

'She wasn't supposed to,' Peg replies, out of the corner

of her mouth. 'The sly dog – she can't bear to miss a thing.'

'Apologies for my tardiness,' Odette says crisply. 'I was delayed at an important meeting elsewhere. Let me just quickly set up and then we can continue.'

She doesn't elaborate about where she's been – it's as if she wants people to speculate about what the important meeting might have been about.

I hover over my seat, unsure what to do next. Should I sit down? Everyone has fallen completely silent now that Odette has made an appearance – she's obviously organizing this entire thing because they all seem to be looking to her for leadership. All except Peg and Ted, who are glowering openly in her direction.

'Maggie here was just about to make some new suggestions,' Ted offers. 'I think she should continue.'

'I second that!' Peg says quickly, backing him up.

'Maggie, how nice to see you again.' Odette bares her sparkling teeth at me. 'And what a surprise.' She's more than just displeased: she's livid that I'm here.

'We invited her,' Peg says stoutly.

'Of course you did. Well, she's very welcome, even if she is somewhat of an . . . outsider.' Odette lingers carefully over the word, so everyone knows what she means – outsiders are not to be trusted.

'Why don't you continue, Maggie?' Peg says. 'You were just about to say something.'

I crouch over my chair, half standing, half squatting. Should I say another word or just slide back into my seat in silence? The way Odette is staring at me is scary.

'You timetabled her contribution, did you?' she interrupts, before I can reply.

Ted and Peg glance at each other.

'We thought we'd just let her speak,' Peg says, looking furtive.

'Off the cuff, do you mean?' Odette replies, her lips pursing slightly. 'Right. And that would be lovely. But, as you know, if we don't stick to the agenda things have a habit of getting out of control. If Maggie's little talk isn't timetabled then she really should speak at the end – when we address any other business.'

'I think we could make an exception, just this once.' Ted pouts.

'Yes, of course we could, Ted,' Odette agrees brightly, 'and we *can*, if you like. But if we do that then everyone will expect there to be exceptions every time we meet. Unless you're happy for that to happen?'

Her voice is sickly sweet, but there's no escaping what she means. I start to sweat. Have I somehow become a pawn in this game of cat and mouse? It feels like it.

'No.' A look of defeated resignation crosses Ted's face and he slumps back into his chair.

'Right, then.' Odette is smug in victory. 'Well, why don't I get the ball rolling? You can distribute the agenda I took the liberty of printing up and we'll start with Item One.'

Three hours later, I'm wedged between Peg and Ted in the snug of the local pub, wondering how I came to be there.

I'm completely up to speed on the proposals for the new supermarket. There are two distinct camps: Odette leads the pro contingent, Ted and Peg lead the dissenters and everyone else seems to be rowing in behind. There still has been no real agreement about what to do, despite Odette's best efforts to convince everyone that the supermarket could herald a new dawn for the village and Peg and Ted's attempts to explain that it would sound the death knell for country life.

'I think I'd better go home,' I say quietly, anxious to leave before someone plants a drink in front of me and I can't escape. 'I'm really very tired – I probably should get some sleep.'

This is no lie: I'm exhausted after another very long day and all I want to do is crawl into bed.

'Sleep?' Ted says cheerfully. 'Can't you sleep when you're dead? Sure the night is young!'

'Yes, and sure why would you want to go back to the cottage all alone?' Peg clucks, linking her arm through mine.

'Have a drink!' Ted insists.

'Yes. You could have a Cosmopolitan,' Peg suggests. 'Matty makes a lovely Cosmo, doesn't he, Ted? They're never too bitter, not like some you can get.'

'Who's Matty?' I ask, taken aback. Cosmopolitans? In the middle of nowhere? Surely all these muckers only ever drink pints of stout – maybe whiskey chasers if they're feeling wild.

'Matty is the publican, of course,' Ted answers. 'His Cosmos are legendary round here. But I prefer the White Russians myself – they have a great kick.'

'Or Slippery Nipples.' Peg licks her lips. 'I love a nice Slippery Nipple.'

'Um, I'm not sure I could manage a cocktail, actually,' I murmur. 'Maybe a glass of wine . . .'

It's useless to resist. If I have just one drink I can leave straight afterwards and no one will be offended.

'Well, he has a wonderful wine list,' Peg enthuses. 'It's very extensive, isn't it, Ted?'

'It sure is.' Ted smiles. 'That Château de la Guiche is something special.'

'Oh, yes, that's lovely! You could have a glass of that, Maggie.'

'OK,' I agree, slightly stunned. Château de la Guiche? Isn't that the rare red I read about in the wine pages of the *Irish Times*? The one that's won awards? How come a small country pub stocks it?

Within minutes, I'm sipping the most delicious glass of wine I've had in a long time.

I have to admit, this is a revelation. I never would have imagined that the village had a place like this. It's an old-fashioned pub, that's true, but the décor is cosy, not twee, and the wine list is the best I've seen in ages. Could it be possible that I misjudged this place?

'So, Maggie. What made you want to move to Rose Cottage?' A woman with a shiny face leans across the table between the empty glasses that have already piled up. These people can drink – and how.

'Em, I just wanted to get away from the city, I suppose,' I murmur. I don't really want to get into the real reason I'm here. It's far too complicated.

'Right. So, no other reason, then?' the woman probes.

I can see Peg glaring at her, as if she wants to lean across and slap her hard. Why does she look so furious?

'She's working on a special commission, Betty,' she announces suddenly, as if unable to stop herself.

Betty? Betty from the butcher's? No wonder Peg's so cross – isn't she the limp-sausage-roll woman? The one who competes with Peg's egg sandwiches? There's obviously a fierce rivalry there – I saw both of them circling the buffet earlier, keeping an eye on which food was most popular with the locals in the hall, sandwiches or sausage rolls. I might have imagined it, but I'm almost sure Peg was jotting a tally on the back of her hand.

Now Peg's face is dangerously flushed. She has two empty Cosmopolitan glasses in front of her and the drinks have quite obviously gone straight to her head.

'Is that right?' Betty says tightly. 'Isn't that marvellous?'

'Yes, it is.' Peg smirks, as if she's thrilled she met and befriended me before Betty had a chance to.

'Who's it for, this commission?' Odette interrupts, shaking her impeccably groomed hair and looking me in the eye. She's kept quiet until now, but she doesn't believe a word of my story, I can tell.

I take a sip of my wine and try to decide how to answer that. Odette has it in for me, I know. Luckily Peg jumps to my rescue. 'It's top secret!' she says defiantly. 'She can't divulge a thing about it. Isn't that right, Maggie?'

'I didn't know artists' work was so cloak-and-dagger.' Odette stirs her gin and tonic with her swizzle stick and smiles sweetly.

'Well, my client is a very private person,' I say, egged on by her smug expression. 'I have to respect his wishes.' I don't feel bad about lying – I don't think I've ever disliked anyone more.

'I see.' Odette doesn't look convinced. 'Where did you say you've exhibited again?'

'Oh, lots of places,' I answer airily, taking another gulp of wine for courage. 'All over, really.' Telling lies is quite easy. And it's getting easier with each sip of this delicious wine.

'She's very highly regarded,' I hear Peg confide loftily to Betty from the butcher's. 'We're lucky to have her – very lucky.'

'I see.' Odette regards me carefully. 'I must Google you, take a look at your work.'

Crap. If she does that she'll find out that this is all a lie. 'Well, I don't paint under my own name, of course,' I say.

'You don't?' Odette raises an expertly plucked eyebrow. 'Why ever not?'

It feels like the entire table swivels towards me to hear my reply.

I clear my throat and try to think of some reasonable excuse to make this sound plausible.

'Edward!' Odette looks past me to the door of the pub, her face suddenly alight. 'Come and sit here!'

I breathe a sigh of relief and relax my shoulders. Now that her boyfriend is here, hopefully she'll lose interest in interrogating me.

'Hi there!' Edward says, as everybody calls hello. They all look delighted to see him – he's obviously popular. 'Sorry I missed the meeting.'

For a split second Odette's face reveals her devastation – she must have thought he'd been there to witness her little victory earlier in the hall. She wants very badly to impress him: that much is clear.

I can sense that Edward is standing directly behind me, but I don't turn to greet him. I'm still very annoyed that he called me useless behind my back when I've been trying my hardest to muck out properly.

'Edward, sit here.' Odette pats a space beside her on the bench. 'There's plenty of room.'

That's for sure – everyone avoided sitting beside Odette when we came in, even those on the pro-supermarket side of the community.

'Thanks, Odette,' Edward says easily. 'Let me just get everyone a drink first.'

People call out what they want and then I hear his voice in my ear. 'And you, Maggie, what would you like?'

'I'm fine, thank you,' I say, concentrating very hard on staring straight ahead. 'I still have this.' I indicate the wine glass in front of me, which still has a drain of red liquid in the bottom. It was absolutely divine and I'd love another, but I'm not going to let Edward buy it for me. No way. Not after what he said about me to Matilda.

'But it looks like you may need another in a minute.' I can hear the smile in his voice. 'Why don't you tell me what that is?'

'It's Château de la Guiche, Edward,' Peg volunteers cheerfully. 'And you *should* get her another, we need to celebrate – Maggie here is our new arts representative!'

'Is that right?' Edward whistles. 'That's great news altogether! I did hear you were a famous artist.'

'You did?' I snap my head round to look at him. Who told him that? Peg probably.

'Yes. A little bird told me.' He smiles again. 'You're a dark horse, Maggie. I'd love to see some of your work.'

'Maybe some time,' I mutter into my glass. God, this is mortifying – this charade has gone way too far. Now everyone thinks I'm something I'm not. What if they find out the truth? It will be so embarrassing.

'So, what do you think we should do about the supermarket? I'm intrigued.' Edward's staring intently at me and I shift nervously under his scrutiny. I really wish he'd stop talking to me – it's making me feel very uncomfortable. Why is he pretending to be interested in my opinion? He thinks I'm a dumb city girl – Matilda told me so and I believe her. For one thing, every time he talks to me he has this strange little smirk playing round his lips – like he's mocking me.

'I don't know,' I reply curtly. Go away and play with your prissy girlfriend, I add silently in my head.

'Oh, come on,' he persists. 'A smart city girl like you – you must have a very interesting perspective on the issue.'

There it is again – he's making fun of me! 'Well, it's complicated.' I stare at him, remembering my vow to try to maintain a civil and professional relationship, for Claire's sake. 'There are no black or white answers, I would say.'

'You're right.' He smiles at me. 'That's what I think too. Now let me get you that wine.' He walks away to order the drinks before I can protest.

He's just back and setting the round on the table when Peg pipes up: 'Let's have a toast!' she calls.

Is it my imagination, or is she slurring slightly?

'Yes, shush everyone!' Ted knocks his glass on the table to quieten the crowd. 'Behave now!'

Peg clears her throat and everyone leans in to listen to what she has to say. She's obviously going to speak about the supermarket development, maybe say that she hopes it will all work out in the end. It'll be a mini miracle if it does. 'We'd like to officially welcome Maggie to Glacken,' she says, swaying a little in her seat.

Eh? Why is she talking about me? I snap my head up and find that she's gazing at me, a wide smile on her face.

'We're honoured to have her here with us,' she goes on, 'and even though we don't know her all that well yet, we love her already. Here's to Maggie!' Peg raises her glass, the liquid slopping gently over the edge as she sways, and everyone else follows suit.

'Here's to Maggie!' they cry. 'We love her already!'

Oh, God. I grip the glass that Edward has handed me and try not to die on the spot. I can't believe she's done that.

'Speech, speech!' Ted calls. 'Go on, Maggie!' he urges, when he sees my stricken face. 'It's tradition.'

'I'm not very good at speeches,' I demur. And I definitely don't want to draw any more attention to myself than I have already.

'Come on, Maggie,' Edward says, 'we're waiting!'

Why is he smiling at me like that? Like he's a nice person? I know he's not – not after what he said about me. Still, he does have such lovely twinkling eyes. Maybe he's not all bad. Maybe Matilda made a mistake.

'OK,' I stutter. 'Well . . . it's lovely to meet you all,' I begin. 'I've never been anywhere quite like Glacken before . . .'

'And you never will again!' someone calls.

'. . . but it's nice to be here. So . . . may the road rise before you and may the wind always be at your back!'

154

Everyone looks a bit confused by that – maybe it was the wrong thing to say – but it's the only Irish blessing I can remember.

'And so say all of us!' Edward calls, and I grin at him in relief.

'And so say all of us!' everyone else cries. I slump back into my seat and almost drain my wine in one gulp.

It has an amazing kick when you knock it back fast like that. As it heats my insides and goes straight to my head, I look around and smile happily. The villagers really are very nice – I'm actually enjoying being here sharing a drink with them, in spite of my reservations about the inbreeding and the insanity. Maybe I was too hasty, jumping to unfair conclusions about country life. This might be the best night out I've had in yonks – everyone's so relaxed and chilled, not like in a city-centre wine bar where they're far too busy posing to enjoy themselves.

I'm basking in this contented glow of camaraderie when I catch Odette's eye. She doesn't look friendly like all the others: instead she's glaring at me with undisguised hatred, patently furious that Edward has been speaking to me, including me in village life. She wants to leap across and stab me with her swizzle stick – it's written all over her face. In fact, from her expression alone, I know for sure I've just made enemy number three.

Rule Thirteen: *Try something new every day*

'You're late.'

Matilda, Edward's fiery teenage daughter, is standing on the front step, dressed in cream jodhpurs, a fitted hacking jacket and riding boots. Her surly face is caked with too-dark foundation, her eyes are lined with thick black kohl and her hair has been viciously blow-dried poker straight. It's obviously a special occasion.

'Late? What are you talking about?' I ask, rubbing the sleep from my eyes and squinting against the bright sun streaming through the door. God, my head hurts.

'The *gymkhana*?' Matilda says, her voice dripping with contempt. 'You were supposed to be at the stables an hour ago to help get everything ready.'

She eyes me from head to toe, taking in my crumpled T-shirt and bleary eyes. A haughty sneer plays round her lips. She thinks I'm very old and very past it, I can tell. She may be right.

'I have no idea what you're talking about,' I say. 'Besides, it's my day off.'

I suddenly realize that my head is throbbing quite a bit. How many glasses of that rare red did I have last night? I lost count after the first three. And then there were the Slippery Nipples Peg insisted I try. Oh, God.

'You get a day off, then, do you?' she snipes. 'I didn't know that was in the help's contract.'

I don't have to answer to this upstart, and I don't have to tolerate her rude behaviour either, troubled past or not. It's not my fault she's so angry about life. I go to close the door, but in a flash she jams her riding-boot-clad foot in the way so I can't.

'Dad said you offered to help. Believe me, I wouldn't be here otherwise.' She flicks her silky sheet of hair. It's not just a straight-up blow-dry – she must have been up since dawn pulling a GHD through it again and again. I recognize a ceramic-hair-straightener addiction when I see one.

'Well, your dad was mistaken.' I push the door firmly against her foot. 'I've never heard of this gymkhana. And I certainly didn't volunteer to help out. Now, if you'll excuse me, I'm going back to bed.'

Matilda shrugs, then takes her foot away. 'Fine with me,' she says. 'I said you'd be a liability anyway.'

'What's that supposed to mean?' I pull the door open a crack. How dare she call me a liability?

'You don't know the first thing about horses, remember?' she calls over her shoulder, as she struts back up the garden path. 'You'd probably jinx the entire event. Dad already told me that renting Rose Cottage to a no-hoper like you was a very bad idea – he knew you'd let him down today.'

Furious, I slam the door. How dare that little whippersnapper speak to me like that? She needs a good talking-to and next time I see her precious father I'm going to tell him so. And while I'm at it, I'm going to tell him exactly what I think of him too – the nerve of him calling me a no-hoper!

I'm just snuggling back under the covers, pounding my feather pillow to make it more comfortable, when I hear the knocking again. It's louder than ever. Matilda is back.

Seeing red, I jump from the bed and race to open it. This is ridiculous. It's bad enough that I have to help in the stables during the week, but I'm certainly not going to at the weekends as well. I'm going to give this brat Matilda a piece of my mind. If she thinks she can intimidate me, she's wrong.

'Maggie, what are you doing? We're all waiting for you.'

Edward is standing on the doorstep, his rangy limbs filling the frame.

'Excuse me?' I blink at him.

Who does he think he is, barging in here unannounced at the crack of dawn on a Saturday morning? This is outrageous! It's my day off – which means I can lie in bed all day and do absolutely nothing. Does no one around here understand that simple concept?

'You were supposed to be at the stables over an hour ago. What happened?'

'I'm not working today!' I snap, my temper fraying. 'But I've been disturbed so often already this morning my day off is already ruined.'

'Don't you remember?' Edward's voice is suddenly softer.

'Remember what?'

'Last night. In the pub. You said you wanted to help at the gymkhana today.'

'I did not.' I'm 100 per cent sure about this. I didn't volunteer to do anything of the sort. I had a few drinks and chatted to the locals, that's all. There was no mention of any gymkhana.

'I told you that Polly and Matilda were going to a gymkhana and you volunteered to help,' Edward explains patiently.

'No, I didn't.' What's he on about?

'Yes. You did. You said you'd grown really fond of Saffy and you wanted to come today. You were really enthusiastic about it.'

Cold fear creeps up my spine. That sounds just a teeny bit familiar.

'It was just after the sing-song,' he prompts.

'Sing-song?' I croak.

'Yes,' his eyes dance, 'you have a great voice, I have to say. All the villagers thought so – you really got everyone going.'

Oh my God. I must have been very drunk. I don't sing unless I'm legless and from what Edward is saying it's as if I started some sort of session. Would I have done that? Why can't I remember? Then again, there's a lot about the night that's pretty fuzzy. Like how I got home, for example.

'You weren't . . . you weren't *drunk*, were you?' Edward says now, breaking into a broad grin. 'You do *remember* our conversation?'

I quickly decide that I can't admit I have no proper recollection of the conversation whatsoever. That would be too humiliating. I'll have to lie. Luckily, I'm getting good at telling fibs – it's almost becoming second nature now.

'Of course I remember,' I say stoutly. 'I just overslept, that's all. Sorry.'

'I see. Well, do you still want to come?'

'Um . . .' I pause. My head's throbbing full-on now. All I want to do is go back to bed.

'Of course if you're hung-over, I totally understand.' Edward smirks.

'I'm not hung-over! I just need to get ready.'

I can't let him believe I'm a useless fool – he apparently already thinks that and I'm damned if I'm going to confirm it for him.

'How long will that take?' He peers at my crumpled T-shirt.

I remember that this is not the first time he's seen me with very little on, and I blush. 'Let me just grab a few things and I'll be right there,' I say, shoving the door closed. There's no way he's going to smirk at me in that condescending way and imply I'm a lush when I'm not. Lushes don't drink rare wines that are featured in the *Irish Times*. They don't have scintillating conversations about being an artist either. Crap. A horrible flashback assaults me – was I really talking to people about my fake art career? Did I tell them I paint under an assumed name? I vaguely remember getting carried away and describing where I get my inspiration from and how long it generally takes me to complete a painting from beginning to end. Sweet Jesus. Did I tell the fat man in the blue wool jumper that I'd done a few nudes? A wave of nausea washes over me – I obviously drank far too much. I can't remember getting home or into bed. I must have been hammered. All I can hope is that everyone else was too so they mightn't have noticed as much.

People were definitely singing Irish rebel songs at some point – they only sing those when they're stocious, right? I feel a little better when I realize that if everyone was as drunk as I was, they won't remember the stupid things I said or the lies I told. What possessed me to go on like I was a real artist? From what I can remember, Peg and Ted egged me on, and once I started I just couldn't stop. I distinctly recall the way Odette observed me as I waffled – her face said she didn't believe a word of what I was saying.

And the way she looked at me when Edward offered me a lift home . . . Oh God. Now I remember. Edward drove me back here – he even helped open the sticky door when I had a fit of giggles.

Did I really harp on about the pony phase I went through when I was nine? The one I quickly shook off when I discovered boys? Did I tell him I used to read pony books and even dreamed of having a pony of my own?

I did. I definitely did. It's all true. CRAP.

Not only did I do just that, but then I begged – yes, begged – to go to the gymkhana today. I've made a complete and utter tit of myself. Again.

A few hours later, I'm leaning against a fence, watching a chestnut horse trot slowly around the arena, its rider sitting stiffly immobile on its back. Dressage is so incredibly boring. So far, all the competitors have done more or less the same thing – which has amounted to little more than walking slowly round the ring looking deadly serious, as far as I can see.

'Is this it?' I say to Edward, trying to stifle another yawn. He has a look of intense concentration on his face – he's fascinated by this stuff.

'This guy's a champion,' he whispers back. 'The command he has of his mount is outstanding.'

I strain to see what he's talking about. Am I missing something? No, the chestnut is still trotting round the arena, just like before. *Boooo*ring. 'Don't they do a few tricks?' I whisper. I know that talking in a normal voice is a no-no – I've already been shushed twice by people further down.

'Tricks?' Edward shakes his head, his eyes never moving from the chestnut mare. 'No, it's all about control. Control and mutual respect.'

'I could do that, for goodness' sake.' I sigh as the horse starts to zigzag slowly across the arena, taking small precise steps. Wouldn't it be more exciting if they livened things up a bit? Maybe did a few circus moves? If someone balanced on the horse's back and juggled plates I might sit up and take notice – otherwise I'm struggling to stay awake.

'No offence, Maggie, but it takes years of training to achieve that flawless gait. He's been riding since he was Polly's age. Probably training every single day of his life.' Edward smiles. 'Dressage is a very complicated event. The skill is in making it look easy.'

'Well, it's a complete waste of time,' I mutter. 'Why on earth would anyone want to do that?' Who would want to waste half their life training for a sport that could send spectators to sleep? It's ridiculous. I know I sound incredibly grumpy, but I just can't help it. I have a shocking hangover. I spent the entire journey to the showground trying to hold it together – but it wasn't easy, especially because a very highly strung Polly chattered endlessly during the trip. She could give anyone a headache at the best of times. Matilda, on the other hand, barely uttered a word and hared away the second Edward eased the Land Rover and horsebox into a parking space. We haven't seen her since and I get the impression that Edward is worried sick about her and what she might be getting up to.

'It's my turn soon!' Polly bounces about, her plaits flying. Today is Polly's first proper event and she's beyond excited: she can't wait to show the judges what she and Saffy can do.

'Ssh . . . you've got to be a little quieter, Polly.' Edward tousles her hair. 'We can't distract the rider.'

'Do you think I'll win, Maggie?' Polly tries hard to whisper. She isn't very good at it – she seems to think that shouting is much more fun.

'I'm sure you have a very good chance, Polly,' I smile at her. Not that I know anything about this sort of stuff, of course, but if enthusiasm counts for anything then Polly will win by a mile. She's very cute – but, God, she's loud. She's been rabbiting on at high volume for hours about her chances of winning a rosette and it made the drive hellish. I had to concentrate very hard on not vomiting: I knew the smug Matilda, in the back seat, was willing me to be sick, and I was determined not to give her the satisfaction. Besides, throwing up all over my landlord wouldn't have been very classy. Edward has already seen me so drunk that he had to prop me up on the way home, and that's quite enough disgrace for one week. A vision of me swaying drunkenly against his shoulder is just one of the excruciating flashbacks I've experienced this morning. I now suspect that he may have had to physically hold me upright while he tried to open the door to Rose Cottage. The thought makes me burn with shame. He hasn't mentioned it, but I know, I just know, by the smirk that's been playing around his mouth all morning that he finds the whole situation highly entertaining.

'Daddy, will I win? Do you think I'll win?' Polly hops at Edward's feet.

She really, really wants to win – she kept her fingers crossed the whole way in the jeep, just in case, which caused an almighty row when Matilda told her that was only a silly superstition and meant nothing. Polly retaliated by telling her older sister that she looked really naff with her face all weird and her hair so stupid. There'd been murder.

'It's not about the winning, Polly, it's about taking part,' Edward says. 'That's what's important.'

Polly rolls her eyes. 'Dad, you are so naff!' she says. 'I don't care about taking part – I want to *win*.'

'Now, let's keep cool, OK?' Edward plants a kiss on top of her head. 'We don't want to get overexcited.'

'OK, Dad, I'll keep cool,' she says solemnly, before squirming out of her father's arms again.

'I'm glad to hear it, Polly. A cool head goes a long way,' a female voice says directly behind us and we all turn.

It's June. The Ice Queen of Glacken. This is all I need. What's she doing here?

'Granny!' Polly launches herself at her grandmother's thighs and hugs them tightly. 'You said you couldn't come!'

'I couldn't miss my granddaughter's first dressage event, could I? That wouldn't do. Hello, Edward.' June nods at her son-in-law but completely ignores me, as if I'm the hired help and she doesn't have to acknowledge my existence. You don't have to engage with the staff and, from the expression on June's face, that's exactly what she thinks I am.

I cringe inside as she turns away, her face a mask of ice. It's obvious I haven't been forgiven for the stupid mistake I made. June is holding on to her grudge with a vengeance.

'It's my turn soon, Granny,' Polly chatters. 'Do you think I'll win?'

'Did you cross your fingers?' June asks.

It seems she takes Polly's superstitious streak seriously, even when other people don't.

'Yes,' Polly replies solemnly.

'Well, so did I.' June squats to whisper in her granddaughter's ear. 'I think your chances are very high indeed.'

'I *knew* it!' Polly squeals, hardly able to contain herself with excitement. 'I'm going to win! I'm going to win!'

'Let's go, Polly,' Edward says, taking Polly by the hand. 'I don't want to lose you in the crowd. We have to get your event number.'

My heart plummets. I'm going to be left alone with the charming June. What will I say to her? Should I pretend to have narcolepsy and just fall asleep so we don't have to converse?

'Wish me luck! Wish me luck!' Polly shouts, as she scrambles away.

'I'm keeping everything crossed,' June calls, winking at the little girl.

Polly winks back and gives her a thumbs-up.

'She's so like her mother at that age,' June says, under her breath, as if forgetting where she is for a moment.

This is so awkward. If I could just break the ice, we might be able to start again. I never meant to upset the old woman – it was a genuine mistake, thinking she was Edward's wife. Surely she can see that.

'Do you like dressage?' I say, when Edward and Polly disappear out of sight.

June flinches and raises her chin an inch, as if she's not going to dignify me with an answer.

'Edward explained that it's all about control,' I go on. Maybe if I try just a little harder it might work. June can't stand here in total silence – she'll have to respond sooner or later.

'He's right, control is key,' she says coolly.

I'm stupidly pleased – it's actually worked! We started off on the wrong foot, yes, but hope isn't lost – maybe we can be friends. A wave of loneliness washes over me suddenly. If only I had Claire to chat to. But Claire is too busy finding herself in India: I haven't spoken to her in ages. And I don't want to call Mum and Dad or Theresa, just in case I give the game away about my situation. I've been keeping in touch with them through cheerful, but vague, texts.

'And if you could control your *mouth* and stop chattering,' June goes on, 'I would like to watch the event. In silence.' She stares coldly at me.

'Sorry?' I can't have heard her properly.

'I said, be quiet. Who do you think you are? Just because you're renting Rose Cottage doesn't give you the right to tag along on family outings. You have no place here with Edward and Polly, looking so cosy. No place whatsoever. Polly's own *mother* is going to miss her first equestrian event. If she's not here to see it, then you certainly shouldn't be. I have no intention of allowing you to elbow your way into our family, so why don't you pack your bags and go back to the city, where you belong?'

June turns back to watch the event, her face cold and hard.

'Oh.' I'm speechless with shock. What can I say to that? She's never going to like me, no matter what I say or do. She's already decided that I'm a pointless waste of space and now she seems to think I'm somehow muscling in on her family too. The irony is, I wouldn't even be at this stupid gymkhana except I wanted to prove a point to Edward.

I stumble away, tears pricking my eyes. June really dislikes me. And she's not the only one. Matilda hates me too, and so does Odette. Even Edward only tolerates me because of the work I do. After all, he said a monkey could be trained to do the same.

Suddenly I know that coming to the country has been a terrible mistake. I don't fit in here – it's never going to work. I'll have to tell Claire, then go back to the city and take my chances looking for another job. Maybe I *could* stay with Dermot and Yvonne for a while – it mightn't be that bad living with my ex-boss and his gold-digger wife.

Just as I'm contemplating spending every evening listening to Yvonne talking about her colour-coded shoe collection, my phone buzzes in my pocket.

'Hi, Maggie!'

It's Claire. I can hardly believe it.

'I'd just finished *ashtanga* when I got a funny feeling,' she jabbers. 'I felt my inner voice telling me to contact you so I asked for special privilege to call home. How's country living? Is it *amazing?*'

I debate telling Claire the truth – that I'm lonely and miserable and hated – but something stops me. Maybe my own inner voice, which seems to be screaming, 'Keep quiet!'

'It's fine,' I say. 'Are you having a fantastic time?'

'Oh, yes!'

I sidestep a pat of horse dung and grip the phone tighter to my ear so I can hear properly. The line is pretty bad. 'That's great.' My voice sounds hollow, even to me.

'Maggie, thank you so much for staying in Rose Cottage until I get back,' she gushes now. 'I'm really grateful. I know you had some reservations about it – you're such a good friend.'

'Yes . . . About that, Claire.' I clear my throat. This is it – my chance to back out of the agreement.

'What is it? Is something wrong?' Claire is instantly anxious.

'No, there's nothing wrong as such. It's just that life at Rose Cottage isn't exactly how I thought it would be . . .' I try to pick my words carefully. It's vital not to spring the news on Claire all in one go. After all, she's thousands of miles away – I don't want to upset her.

'What do you mean?'

'Well, it's quite a lot of work,' I answer. That'll do for starters – I'll build up to the bit about everyone hating me.

'Physical work, do you mean?' Claire asks. 'I can't wait for that! After years of sitting at my PC, working up a proper sweat will be fantastic! Are the horses just *amazing*?'

'Um, they're certainly interesting,' I reply. 'But the thing is, Claire, I'm not sure it's for me.'

'*All under-eight riders to the arena in the next five minutes, please!*' the speakers blare.

'Where are you, Maggie?' Claire asks. 'What's that noise?'

'I'm at a gymkhana!' I shout, the noise of another announcement on the intercom almost deafening me.

'A what?' Claire bellows.

'A gymkhana!' I yell.

'Wow! Talk about getting into the spirit of things!' Claire shouts back. 'I'm so proud of you, Maggie. Thank you so much for doing this for me – you're the best friend ever. Now I've got to go – the fruit platter's here. If I don't get to it first I'll be stuck with all the bloody bananas again.'

There's a loud click in my ear. Claire's gone and I haven't managed to tell her how I really feel. I shove the phone back into my pocket and try to decide what to do next. I need a coffee, and fast, to help me focus. Luckily, there are lots of refreshment tents dotted round the field – hopefully they do a decent brew, not the instant stuff I've been forced to drink in the cottage.

Picking the small, shabby tent closest to me, I pull the flap aside and duck into the gloomy interior. As my eyes adjust to the blackness, I realize I've made a mistake. This isn't a coffee tent, it's some sort of storage facility. Just my bloody luck – I can't even get a coffee properly. Can this day get any worse?

As I fumble for the flap to make my way back out again, I hear the unmistakable sound of muffled crying. Straining my eyes, I can just about make out the shape of a girl huddled in a corner, her knees pulled close to her chest and her face buried in her hands. 'Hey, are you OK?' I call.

The girl is sobbing really hard – it sounds like she's inconsolable. 'I'm fine,' she croaks hoarsely. 'Just leave me alone.'

'You don't sound fine,' I say softly. The poor girl's heartbroken.

'Well, I am, so just leave me *alone*!'

With that, she jumps up and shoves her way past me. As she does, I catch sight of her mascara-streaked face in the darkness and I gasp. This is no stranger – it's Matilda.

Rule Fourteen: *Keep cool under fire*

'If we get stuck will we have to sleep in the Land Rover, Dad?'
Polly asks.

'It won't come to that, Polly.' Edward's face is grim. 'We'll
find a petrol station soon.'

'Yes, but if we *do* get stuck, will we sleep in our seats or the
horsebox?'

I swallow nervously. Neither option sounds very appealing.

'I can't believe I forgot to fill up with diesel before we set
off this morning,' Edward mutters. 'That was so stupid of me
– I'm really sorry about this, Maggie.'

'That's OK,' I say, feeling sick but trying not to let it show.

If I have to sleep in this Land Rover I'll have hysterics but I
don't want to say that out loud because it might frighten Polly.

'There's bound to be a petrol station round the next bend,'
I say instead, with little conviction, as the red warning light
flashes angrily on the dashboard. It's been doing that for the
last forty minutes at least – which means this vehicle is now
being powered by thin air as far as I can see. If we were on
the motorway we'd be fine – there'd be service stations every
few miles – but this is a country road. God only knows where
the next garage might be.

'I can't believe I won first prize, can you, Maggie?' Polly
chirps from the back, forgetting about the diesel drama. 'I
knew crossing my fingers for luck would work!'

'It's fantastic, Polly,' I tell her. 'You did really well.'

'Thanks! Wasn't Saffy brilliant, Dad? This is the best day of
my life *ever*!'

'Yes, she was,' Edward grins, 'and you were too. Well done, darling.'

I see Polly beaming at her father in the rear-view mirror and my heart warms – it's clear she idolizes him and laps up his praise.

'You did really well too, Matilda,' Edward says warmly, to his elder daughter. 'Congratulations.'

'Third place is hardly doing well.' Matilda stares out of the window, her expression unreadable.

'Third place is excellent – there was some very stiff competition,' Edward cajoles.

'Or maybe I was just crap.'

'I didn't say that.' Edward is suddenly wary. 'You did brilliantly – why can't you just believe me when I tell you?'

'I dunno, Dad,' she replies, her voice edgy now. 'Maybe it's because you don't always tell me the truth.'

'What does *that* mean?' Edward asks.

'I thought you were great, Matilda,' I offer, in an effort to break the tension. The last thing we need is another argument – especially if we're going to be stuck on the side of the road for the night. Besides, I've been feeling awful since I caught Matilda crying her eyes out. I don't know what's wrong, but I've decided to make an extra effort with her for the rest of my stay here – however long that is. Even if she acts far older, she's only a child, and from the look on her tear-stained face when she dashed from that tent, something seriously upset her today.

'Thanks, that means so much,' she sneers sarcastically. 'Especially because you're such an *expert*.'

'Matilda!' Edward gasps. 'That's uncalled for – why are you being so rude?'

'It's OK,' I say quietly. 'She's right. I know nothing about horses.'

'Well, Saffy likes you!' Polly sticks up for me. 'She told me!'

'How can a pony tell you something like that, you twit?' Matilda snorts. 'What are you – telepathic?'

'What's "tel-er-patethic", Daddy?' Polly's little face is creased with anxiety. 'Will I die from it?'

'No, honey, of course you won't. Matilda, why can't you be nicer to your little sister?' Edward sounds weary. 'Can't you try to get on – just for the trip home?'

If we ever make it home, I think. We're already running on empty. Who knows when this thing will give up the ghost and simply grind to a halt? 'I like Saffy too, Polly,' I say to reassure her. 'And you do a great job with her.' It's true – I *do* like Saffy. I suddenly remember confiding drunkenly to Edward that I'd come to love all the ponies, even though I'd been so nervous to begin with. Did I tell him I was sure they could talk to me in their own way? Oh, God. I did. I told him that Saffy smiled at me the other day and that Pedlar frowned to remind me to lock the stable door properly. He must think I'm a complete mentaller.

Polly beams at me, content, completely oblivious that I'm cringing inside at my drunken stupidity. 'I'm going to be a vet when I grow up,' she says.

'That'll be handy.' Edward grins. 'Odette's fees cripple me – I hope you'll give me a discount.'

'I don't like Odette,' Polly announces. 'She's mean.'

'Polly . . .' Edward's voice is warning.

'It's true!' Polly protests. 'She pretends to be nice when you're around, but she's a big faker. Just like Mary Devlin.'

'Who's Mary Devlin?' I ask.

'Polly's friend in school,' Edward replies.

'She's *not* my friend!' Polly protests.

'Isn't she?' Edward asks, glancing at Polly in the rear-view mirror.

'No way!' Polly yells. 'She always pretends to be nice just

before lunch, in case anyone has any sweets in their lunchbox, but she's mean the rest of the time. That's just like Odette, Maggie – she's nice when Daddy's there, but she's mean when he's not. *And* Saffy doesn't like her either. Not like you, Maggie – Saffy *loves* you!'

I can't help but giggle – when Polly doesn't like someone or something she isn't shy about expressing it. I quickly turn the giggle into a cough – after all, Edward and Odette are going out: I don't want to diss his girlfriend, even if she is a cashmere-wearing battleaxe. Obviously, Polly and Matilda know nothing of their relationship – and it's clear Edward isn't about to declare his intentions.

'What do *you* want to be when you grow up, Maggie?' Polly says now, turning her attention fully to me.

I laugh – that's a very good question. If only I knew the answer.

'Maggie is an artist, Polly,' Edward says, and I shift uncomfortably.

Everyone has latched on to the ridiculous idea that I'm some sort of world-renowned artist. Maybe because, in fairness, I haven't exactly set the record straight about my so-called career.

'You mean like a painter?' Polly asks.

'Yes – isn't that exciting?' Edward replies.

'I *love* painting!' Polly wriggles excitedly in her seat.

'I'm so happy for you.' Matilda rolls her eyes.

'What do you like about it, Polly?' I ask her, trying to ignore the dislike in Matilda's voice. It's impossible to develop any sort of rapport with the girl, no matter how hard I try. Obviously something's bothering her, but does she have to be so abrasive? So dismissive? Was I like that as a teenager? So angry with everyone?

'Everything! And guess what? I got my face painted once – like a fairy. Will you do that for me?'

'Sure I will.' I smile at her. I've never painted anyone's face before – but it can't be that difficult, right?

'Brilliant! Did you hear that, Matilda? Maggie's going to paint my face for me!'

'Whoop-de-doo.' Matilda sighs. 'Let's throw a party.'

'Well, *I* think it's brilliant!' Polly punches the air. 'Saffy will love it.'

'Saffy is a *pony*, Polly,' Matilda says. 'She won't know if you have your face painted or not.'

'Yes, she will,' Polly insists. 'She's very smart. She'll know.'

'Whatever.' Matilda rolls her eyes again, then catches mine in the rear-view mirror. Her expression is defiant, as if she's deciding whether she'll talk to me or not. 'So, Maggie,' she says, her voice hard to read, 'do you like Rose Cottage?'

I'm so taken aback that she's actually speaking directly to me that I swallow before I answer. Edward flinches in the driving seat. He doesn't know where this is headed either. 'Yes, I do,' I answer truthfully. The cottage is lovely – it's just my life that's screwed up.

'What do you like about it most?' Polly joins in, hoping for a game.

'Um, let me think . . . The roses round the door are really pretty,' I say finally.

'My mother planted them,' Matilda says, her voice icy. 'Didn't she, Dad?'

'Yes,' Edward says, hesitating for a beat, 'she did.'

'In fact, my mother did most of the work on the cottage garden, wouldn't you say?'

'That's true,' he says. 'She loved gardening.'

Matilda narrows her eyes at me in the mirror.

'It's beautifully done,' I say, trying to ignore the fact that she's looking at me with such accusation and loathing.

173

'So, Maggie,' Matilda's eyes burn into my forehead, 'you have a boyfriend, do you?'

'Matilda! That's none of our business!' Edward's voice is stern.

'Sorry, I was only asking.' I see her smirk.

'Do you, Maggie – have a boyfriend?' Polly says.

'Um, sort of,' I reply, feeling my cheeks redden again.

A flat no is the correct answer to that question. After all, Robert and I are ancient history, but I've already told Odette that I'm in a relationship, so I don't want to contradict myself now. God, this is getting complicated.

'What does that mean?' Polly asks, her little face creasing.

'It means that you don't get to ask Maggie anything else, madam,' Edward interjects. 'What must she think of us, prying into her affairs like this? I'm sorry, Maggie.' He turns his head a fraction and flicks his eyes away from the road for a second to smile at me.

'That's OK,' I murmur.

Trust Matilda to press that particular button – as if she knew it was my weak spot. If she ever finds out about my fake art career, she'll have a field day, I know that for sure.

'I'm never going to have a boyfriend,' Polly announces with determination. 'Boys are *gross*!'

'You won't think that in a few years.' Edward laughs and I join in, relieved that the heat of the conversation is off me at least.

'I will! They're yuk!' Polly exclaims, wrinkling her nose. 'Do you want to know what Freddy Doyle did the other day?'

'Freddy Doyle is Polly's favourite boy in school,' Edward explains to me, out of the corner of his mouth.

'He is *not*!' Polly yells passionately. 'I hate him!'

'There's a fine line between love and hate, Polly.' Edward's eyes twinkle. 'Tell us what he did.'

'He picked his nose and rubbed the snot into his jumper!'

'That's disgusting!' Matilda curls her lip.

'I *know*,' Polly says, agreeing with her older sister for once, 'and another day he picked his nose and *ate* it! With his *mouth*!'

'As opposed to his ear?' Edward laughs.

'That's vile!' Matilda says.

'Boys get a bit nicer when they grow up, Polly,' I tell her. 'Trust me.'

'Well, I'm still never going to have a boyfriend.' She shakes her head at the very idea. 'Not like Matilda.'

'Shut *up*, you little weed!' Matilda snarls. 'I do *not* have a boyfriend!'

'Yes, you do! Matilda and Daniel sitting in a tree, K-I-S-S-I-N-G,' Polly sings, then sticks out her tongue and makes puking gestures. 'Yuk!'

Daniel – that's the name of the spotty adolescent I met on the first day at Rose Cottage.

'Shut up, Polly. I'm warning you.' Matilda sounds menacing.

I glance at Edward, who seems oblivious to this part of the conversation. His eyes are darting anxiously between the diesel gauge and the road. I know from his expression that if we don't find a petrol station soon we're scuppered.

'There it is – at last!' he exclaims.

I see lights ahead and I exhale. The idea of being stuck in this vehicle with Edward and his two daughters overnight isn't appealing – especially because World War Three is just about to break out in the back seat.

'That's a relief – I was getting a little worried there,' Edward admits, pulling off the road and manoeuvring up to the diesel pump. 'I'll only be a few minutes.'

'It can't have been easy coming here on your own,' Matilda says innocently, as soon as her father climbs out.

'It's been OK.'

I look out of the window and will Edward to hurry. I get a horrible feeling that there's more to Matilda's comment than meets the eye – I'm at her mercy now he isn't here.

'You must miss the city, though – all those fantastic shops . . .'

'There are some great shops,' I admit, a fierce longing hitting me to see the shoe department of Brown Thomas. It used to be one of my favourite pastimes, just wandering about in there, fondling Louboutins and dreaming. Most of my decent shoes are crammed into suitcases at the moment – I'm officially living in my stinky trainers, which are caked with all sorts.

'And then there's your friends . . . or your boyfriend . . . or whoever . . .'

I suddenly wonder if Robert is dating. It's not beyond the realms of possibility that he is – after all, it's been months since we split up. It would be good if he found someone else to share his life with – he is a nice guy, after all. Just not the guy for me.

'I mean, when you're so used to city life, being all alone in that cottage must be lonely.' Matilda's voice interrupts my thoughts again.

'It's not so bad,' I say, watching as Edward struggles with the pump. It looks as if it's jammed. I pray for it to loosen before Matilda can ask any more of her searching questions.

'Really? Aren't you spooked, though?' she goes on.

'Spooked? Why would I be spooked?'

Edward finally wrestles the pump free and starts to fill the tank – thank God for that.

'Well, you're all alone in that cottage at night in the dark. Doesn't it . . . freak you out?'

I hear Polly snore softly – she's fallen asleep. That's probably a good thing. 'Not really,' I reply. I hadn't actually thought about that – but I *am* all alone in the cottage at night. What if something happened? What would I do? It's not like I have neighbours downstairs to keep an ear out for me, like I had in the city. Even if I barely knew their names, they would have helped in an emergency. Wouldn't they?

'Wow – you're brave. I don't think I could bear being on my own in there.' She shudders. 'Especially, you know, after last year.'

'Last year? What happened last year?'

'Oh.' She looks surprised. 'Didn't Dad tell you? There were loads of burglaries in Glacken.'

'No, he didn't mention it.' I try to keep my voice calm, as if I'm not screaming inside, which of course I am. Burglaries? Oh, God, I'd die if I was ever broken into. Why didn't Edward tell me about that? He wasn't obliged to, of course, but still, he might have let me know – I'm probably the ideal target for gangsters. Single woman, living all alone, no vicious dog on site and no previous experience of any sort of self-defence. I must fit the victim profile perfectly.

'Yeah, it was really creepy. No one knew who it was – some people thought it was a local. You know, someone with a grudge.'

A local with a grudge? Who could that be? All the locals I've met so far have been nice – eccentric, maybe, but not the type who'd do any breaking and entering in their spare time. Then again, what do I know, really? Appearances can be deceptive. That fat man in the blue jumper at the meeting could be a criminal for all I know. Come to think of it, he did have shifty eyes. And he was quite aggressive. I make a mental note to watch him from now on.

'Yeah, there's *lots* of bad feeling between people here,' Matilda goes on ominously. 'It can get pretty nasty.'

'You mean like feuds?' I've heard of these country feuds – they can be passed on from generation to generation.

Families can be mortal enemies for donkey's years, often about the simplest of things, like right of way across a field. 'Isn't that sort of thing usually about land?' I ask, suddenly feeling very uneasy.

What if someone's granny used to live in Rose Cottage and they don't take kindly to a blow-in moving in? What if I become a target? An innocent victim of gangland warfare? It wouldn't be called gangland warfare down here, of course, maybe culchie warfare – but it would amount to the same thing: me, dead.

'It can be land, yes,' Matilda confirms. 'Of course, it being a local was just *one* of the theories. It might have been the Mad Man of the Woods.'

Matilda turns her face away from me and looks out of the window. I follow her gaze, feeling a little shaky. There's no one at the diesel pump any more – Edward has disappeared inside to pay.

'What Mad Man of the Woods?'

'I shouldn't get into it – I don't want to scare you.'

'Tell me.' My voice is shaking.

'Honestly, it's probably nothing to worry about.'

'Tell me.' I want to know who this man is now.

'OK, if you insist.' Matilda shrugs her shoulders. 'There's a man who camps out in the woods sometimes – he's been doing it for years. People say he's crazy.'

'What do you mean, crazy?'

'Oh, the usual stuff. He talks to himself, that sort of thing.'

'Talking to yourself isn't illegal,' I say. Matilda's just trying to frighten me, that's all. This guy is probably harmless.

'You're right,' she muses. 'But the story goes that he has some sort of criminal record. He might be on the run.'

'That's a little far-fetched, don't you think?' She's making all this up, it's so obvious.

178

'Yeah, you're right, it *does* sound far-fetched,' she agrees. 'I'm sure it's all nonsense. But there were the knives, of course.'

'Knives?'

'Yeah, a local farmer found a stash of knives in the woods – it was really odd. And then all the burglaries started . . .'

'Did they catch him?' I say, genuinely nervous now. Maybe there's more truth in this story than I'd thought.

'That's the really weird part. He disappeared, and then the burglaries stopped.'

'So, if it *was* him, he's moved on.' I sigh with relief. Thank God for that.

'You'd think so – but there's a rumour going round that he was seen in the woods again recently.'

'Do you mean Glacken Woods?' My heart quickens as I put two and two together. Don't they back on to the cottage?

'Yeah, apparently the same farmer who found the knives swears he saw the man a few weeks ago. He reckons he might have been hiding out all along. The woods are pretty deep – God knows what goes on in there.'

'What do you mean?' My heart flutters with fear. None of this sounds good, even if she is just trying to scare me. Those woods are far too close to the cottage.

'Well, you know. Wooded areas can be a magnet for all sorts of . . . deviants.' She lingers on the word, a sinister edge to her voice.

Deviants? Knife stashes? I feel sick: this place is far more dangerous than the city!

'But I wouldn't worry about it,' she continues, her tone more casual now. 'You know how people can be. They love to spread silly stories about nothing.'

'Everything all right?'

A gust of wind engulfs the interior of the Land Rover as

179

Edward opens the door and jumps back into the driver's seat, oblivious to the conversation we've just had.

'Fine, Dad!' Matilda smiles.

'Good. Well, we should be home in an hour or so. I could just about *murder* a cup of tea, couldn't you?'

Matilda raises an eyebrow at me and I wince. If what she says is true, then that's not all that could be murdered round here.

I close my eyes and try to block out everything she's just told me. She was just winding me up: there probably *is* no Mad Man of the Woods – we're not living in the Middle Ages after all. This man is just a myth, a figment of a lonely farmer's fertile imagination. Of course, there is the small matter of the knives. But, then, these stories always get blown out of all proportion. That farmer probably found one small knife and then the rumour mill started. There's nothing to worry about. Nothing at all.

Rule Fifteen: *Find your fun where you can*

'Maggie, you know how you're a painter?' Polly asks, as she rubs Saffy's nose.

'Yes,' I say reticently. Technically, I'm not lying to her – I'm not a professional of course, as half the village seems to think, but I did paint her face as she asked me to. She was so delighted with the tiny stars and flowers I drew on her cheeks one morning last week that she now seems to think I'm some sort of Van Gogh. Luckily, she hasn't asked to see any of my artwork yet – because there is none.

'Will you teach *me* how to paint?' she says. 'I want to learn how to draw properly. Mary Devlin says I'm crap at art.'

'Does she now?' I say. Her father wouldn't be happy if he heard her using that word, but I can't very well correct her – I'm not her parent, after all. 'Well, Mary Devlin doesn't know very much, does she?'

'She brought a dead hedgehog into school the other day. All the other kids thought it was really cool.' Polly's face is glum.

'And you didn't?'

'No,' she pouts. 'Who wants to see a squashed hedgehog in a cornflakes box?'

'Not very many people, I imagine,' I say. I've seen any number of dead animals on the road since I came here and it takes some getting used to, even if the locals are completely blasé about it. Peg told me that Betty from the butcher's sometimes makes stew with road kill, although I can't be sure she wasn't exaggerating slightly. There was an unspoken suggestion that Peg wasn't quite certain what ended up in Betty's sausage rolls, although I tried to ignore that. I secretly tried Betty's sausage rolls last week when she pressed some on me in the street and they weren't half bad. Not that I can ever admit that to Peg – she and Betty are sworn enemies and I get the very strong impression that Peg doesn't like me even passing the time of day with her.

'So will you teach me?'

'Sure I will, Polly.' I smile back. She really is very cute. 'But I bet you can paint perfectly well without me.'

'I'd like you to help.'

'OK, then, I will some day.' I heave a large pile of straw bedding to the door of the stable, then attempt to sweep the floor – it's strip day so everything has to be cleared and then washed out. It's a dirty job but I'm getting much quicker at it. It still leaves me a little breathless, though, even after a few weeks' practice.

'Which day?'

'Sorry?'

'Which day will you teach me how to paint?'

'I'm not sure,' I fudge. 'Some day soon.'

'I know what *that* means.' Polly sighs dramatically and rolls her eyes like a pro.

She must have been watching her older sister for inspiration. Matilda is the Queen of the Rolling Eyes. 'You should be careful, Polly,' I say. 'If the wind changes your eyes will stay like that.'

'That's only an old wives' tale,' she tuts knowledgeably. 'Everyone knows that.'

'They do?' I always used to be really scared to roll my eyes as a child in case they got stuck – but Polly is a lot smarter than I ever was.

'Yeah. Anyway, I know what you mean when you say "some day soon",' she says now.

'Eh?'

'When grown-ups say "some day soon", they mean "never".'

'That's not true.' Except it is. This kid is sharp. It's like she can see straight through my bullshit.

Maybe Theresa's right: maybe children *can* see into your soul. Theresa says both her twins have a 'second eye' – they seem to know what she's thinking or even if she has a sneaky ciggie when they nap. She can tell they know from the accusing way they look at her sometimes. As far as Theresa's concerned, smoking the occasional Marlboro Light is no big deal – she reckons it's a miracle she's not on anything stronger than nicotine, she has so much to deal with. She told me a few days ago that there's talk at her mothers' group that a wilder mum – one who doesn't even *believe* in the naughty step, a scandal in itself – can actually score cocaine. Theresa says the only thing stopping her giving in to temptation is the worry of what might happen if she did: she doesn't want to turn into some sort of crack whore – and it's not as if she can rely on Malcolm to look after the twins properly if she's carted off to rehab. He'd have no clue how to grill potato waffles the way the twins like them – he can't even find the toaster.

'Yes, it is.' Polly's voice snaps me back to the present. 'Daddy says it all the time. I keep asking him when we can go hacking in Glacken Woods and all he says is "Some day soon." I know what *that* means. It means "never".'

'I see.'

I daren't say any more. Glacken Woods? That's where Polly's mum had her accident. It's also a haven for deviants, according to Matilda. No wonder Edward doesn't want Polly to go there.

'Mummy used to paint with me,' Polly announces out of nowhere.

'Did she?' I'm not sure what to say to that. Should I say I'm sorry her mother is dead? Are you supposed to acknowledge death to children?

'Mummy's dead.' Polly looks at me with clear hazel eyes. She doesn't sound upset – more matter-of-fact.

'I heard that.'

'Yes. She fell off her horse and then she died.'

'That's very sad.' I'm just following her lead, stating the obvious and not being overly emotional.

'Yes, it was.' Polly sighs. 'Daddy was sad for a long time.'

'I'm sure he was.'

'He's cheered up a bit now.' Polly smiles. 'I think it's because of you!'

'Me?' What do I have to do with it?

'He likes you.'

'No, he doesn't.' He likes me mucking out the stables, and that's about it.

'Yes, he does. He like-likes you. I can tell.'

'What does that mean?'

'He wants to fall in love with you.'

'Don't be silly!' I laugh. Where did she get that idea from? Edward only tolerates me because Claire is renting Rose Cottage and I provide cheap labour. He wouldn't choose to have me around, not unless he really had to. And he certainly doesn't want to fall in love with me. For one thing he's already in love with the vet from hell.

'I'm *not* silly,' Polly insists. 'I saw it on TV. The man and the woman in the movie *pretended* they didn't want to fall in love but they did, really. All they needed was a little help. And someone to get rid of the wicked witch.'

'The wicked witch?'

'Yes – that's Odette.' She looks around as if she's afraid Odette might pop up from behind a bale of straw. 'In the movie, the dragon ate the witch in the end, but I don't know what we'll do to kill off Odette. I've never seen a dragon in real life, have you?'

'No, I haven't. It sounds like an interesting movie, though – what was it called?'

Polly scrunches up her face with the effort of trying to recall. 'I can't remember,' she says at last, 'but there was lots of kissing. That part was gross. I hate kissing. Do you?'

How do I answer that? 'I haven't been kissed in a long time,' I say eventually, trying to brush over the subject.

'*Really?*' Polly's eyes widen. 'Doesn't your boyfriend kiss you? That's what all grown-ups do.'

My boyfriend – that's right. I told them all I had a boyfriend in the city. Nice one.

'You don't have a boyfriend, do you?' Polly smiles knowingly. 'You told a lie.'

'It's complicated, Polly.'

'I know what *that* means. It means you're lying! Show me your tongue!'

'I will not.'

'You have to! Show it to me – if there's a black spot on it then you're lying!'

If that was true my entire tongue would be black – I've told so many lies since I got here that I can barely keep track of them all. 'Let's move on, shall we?' I say briskly, to change the subject.

Changing the subject is another one of Theresa's fail-safe ploys with the twins. She can talk about fifteen different subjects in less than three minutes – she timed herself once. 'Tell me, Polly,' I ask, keeping my voice neutral, 'what's your favourite colour?' Favourite colours – that's a safe topic. Probably the number-one safe topic actually.

'I don't know.' She frowns, thankfully forgetting about the lying thing. 'Mummy loved blue. Do you like blue?'

'Yes,' I agree.

Hmm . . . maybe not so safe.

'Is it your favourite colour?'

I think about this. I don't want to hurt her feelings by saying that blue isn't my favourite, but then again she'll know immediately if I don't tell the truth. 'Blue does have a lot to recommend it,' I muse, 'but I've always preferred yellow, to be honest.'

'I like yellow too.' She smiles at me and I smile back. The gap in her teeth is adorable.

'How about next week?' I say, unable to stop myself. This child is so sweet – what harm can it do to paint with her for a bit?

'For painting?' Polly claps her hands with excitement.

'Yes – for painting.'

'Oh, thank you, Maggie,' she squeals, and throws herself at me, wrapping her plump little arms round my waist. 'Thank you, thank you, thank you!'

I hug her back, my heart unexpectedly full. Who knew such a small thing could make her so happy?

'What's all the excitement about?' I look up to see Edward standing at the stable door, wiping his hands on his overalls.

'Daddy!' Polly launches herself at him like a rocket, careering across the floor and skidding to a stop millimetres away from him.

'Hello there!' He scoops her up and hugs her tightly to him.

'Dad! Put me down!' she yelps. 'I'm not a baby any more, you know!'

'Sorry, Poll,' Edward says, setting her down. 'I keep forgetting.'

'Well, try to remember! I'm six now – you can't be lifting me up all the time.'

'You're practically a teenager, I know.' Edward winks at me

over Polly's head and I smile back – I can't help it. They're so cute together.

'I have something to tell you,' Polly announces. 'Guess what it is!'

'You're leaving home?'

'Dad!'

'Sorry. Um, let me think . . . you have a new boyfriend?'

'*Dad!*' Polly pulls a disgusted face.

'Well, I don't know then, I give up.'

'Maggie's going to teach me how to paint!' she yells, her chubby cheeks pink with pleasure.

'Is she now? Aren't you lucky?'

'I hope you don't mind,' I say. Maybe it was inappropriate to agree to it without consulting him first. Suddenly I feel a little uncomfortable – Edward may not want to agree to this plan. Maybe I shouldn't have opened my big mouth.

'Of course not. And Polly is obviously thrilled.'

He smiles at me, his eyes warm and liquid, and something strange stirs inside me. Maybe I'm hungry – mucking out is hard work.

'Dad, guess what Maggie's favourite colour is?' Polly is hopping from one foot to the other.

'Um . . . purple?'

'Purple? Urgh, no, Dad! It's yellow. The same as me!'

'How cool!' He grins at me now.

What is it about the way he's looking at me? I just can't put my finger on it.

'Yeah. Mum's favourite colour was blue, but Maggie says yellow is better and I think she's right.'

'I didn't actually say yellow was better than blue!' I start. God, I hope he doesn't think I was badmouthing his dead wife. 'I just prefer yellow, that's all.'

It sounds totally lame.

'I like yellow too,' Edward says. 'It's so . . . cheerful.'

Phew – he's not insulted after all.

'Do you, Dad? Do you hear that, Maggie? You and Daddy like the exact same colour! That's just like in the movies!' She winks knowingly at me and I make a face at her to be quiet. The last thing I need is for her to ask her father if he 'like-likes' me. Things are awkward enough.

'Edward!' A shrill voice sears through the yard. 'Oh – there you are!'

It's Odette – and she doesn't look too happy.

'Oh, hi, Odette,' Edward says, turning to greet her.

'What are you doing here?' Polly says, glaring at Odette, unable to contain her intense dislike, and I try to stifle a laugh. From what Polly just told me, Odette is her version of the wicked witch.

'Oh, Polly, hello,' Odette says, as if the little girl is an annoying fly she's just found in her soup. 'I was just passing and thought I'd pop in and take another look at Saffy's leg. Make sure she's OK.' She turns her high-voltage smile on Edward.

'That's very kind of you, Odette,' Edward replies, looking a tad flummoxed by her sudden appearance from nowhere. From his expression, he's not overly thrilled to see her either. Interesting. Very interesting.

'Saffy's OK now,' Polly huffs. 'She doesn't need to see you.'

'Well, better safe than sorry, isn't that right?' Odette tinkles. 'Why don't you lead her out and I can see how she looks?'

'Honestly, Odette, she's fine,' Edward says. 'Right as rain.'

'Still, I'd just like to check her again. I couldn't live with myself if anything happened to her . . .'

'What do you mean?' Polly is immediately alarmed. If anything ever happened to her precious Saffy she'd be bereft.

'Well, infections can *look* like they've cleared,' Odette says, 'but sometimes they linger . . .'

'And?' Polly's little face is white with fear and I resist the urge to lean across and slap Odette hard. It's like she's deliberately trying to scare her. She knows how Polly feels about her pony – there's nothing on earth more precious to that child.

'Well, then,' Odette looks deadly serious, 'the infection can travel through the bloodstream and head to the heart. It can be fatal.'

'You mean Saffy could die?' Polly whimpers.

'That's not going to happen, darling,' Edward consoles his daughter. 'Odette, I don't think that's what you meant, is it?' He is clearly very annoyed that she has put such a notion into Polly's head. She's an idiot – doesn't she realize that six-year-olds are very impressionable?

'No, of course it isn't,' Odette backtracks, visibly alarmed by Edward's tone. 'There's probably no need to check her. I was only trying to help. Maybe I should go.'

'No! Don't go!' Polly screams, terrified. 'Dad, let's get Saffy, quick! I want her to be safe!'

'OK, it can't hurt, I suppose.' Edward looks oddly at Odette, then follows Polly as she bounds away to Saffy's stable.

'So, Maggie.' Odette places her veterinary bag on the ground. 'I must say you look quite at home – it's amazing that you've settled in so quickly.'

'Well, I don't know . . .' I wipe my grimy hands on my tracksuit. I've given up all hope of it ever recovering from this experience – even the Juicy logo on the bum is barely legible any more. My jeans are the same – no matter how much I wash them, they still look filthy.

'Oh, no,' Odette says. 'I think you're fitting in very well for such a city girl. It's all so . . . cosy.'

'I wouldn't say that.' There's nothing cosy about mucking out. But then I get the feeling that's not exactly what Odette is referring to. I really don't want to talk to this woman: she makes me feel very uncomfortable – and more so because she's dressed immaculately, as always, even though she's on call, while I'm soaked in sweat and probably looking a complete fright.

'I just don't know how you do it all, Maggie,' she goes on, steadfastly ignoring what I've just said. 'I mean, you're here to paint – that's what I understand anyway – and yet you're finding time to do so much else as well. It's so . . . commendable.'

I can tell from her tone that 'commendable' is not the word she wants to use. 'What do you mean, Odette?'

'Well, here you are, working so hard in the stables . . .'

'That's part of the lease agreement.' It's not as if I want to work here, even if I have grown very fond of the ponies. They all have such different personalities – the thought of not seeing them every morning when I go home makes me feel a little sad. The city seems almost like a foreign country now. With a shock, I suddenly realize I haven't really thought about it in days.

'It's part of the lease agreement?' Odette's eyes widen. It looks like this revelation is news to her.

'Well, yes – didn't Edward tell you?' How strange that he hadn't said anything – surely if they're in a relationship they should be discussing this sort of thing.

'Of course, that's right. I forgot,' Odette says quickly. 'But it's not just here, in the stables. You're getting so involved in village life as well.'

'I suppose you're talking about the supermarket?' I sigh.

'Well, yes. How *are* you finding the time to develop an interest in it as well as everything else you do? Are you Superwoman?' She makes an attempt to laugh girlishly, but it sounds more like a strangled sob.

I put my broom against the wall – there's no point in trying to work when Odette is buzzing in my ear. 'Peg and Ted asked me to. I couldn't really refuse.'

'That's very worthy of you. But what have Peg and Ted ever done for you exactly?' She smiles tightly at me and her white teeth gleam.

She's had veneers, I'm almost sure of it – her teeth are way beyond what could be considered naturally perfect. 'I'm not sure what you mean,' I say.

'Well, you're certainly going out of your way to help them out, but why? That's what's puzzling.'

'I like them. They asked me for my opinion.'

'Yes, it seems straightforward enough,' she muses, tucking a stray strand of her glossy hair behind her impossibly petite ears. Has she had them pinned back? For a second I thought I spotted a tiny scar behind one lobe. 'And yet . . . something doesn't quite add up. I mean, they *are* complete strangers, after all.'

'That doesn't mean I can't like them,' I retort.

'No, of course not. It's just that it makes so little sense. You swoop in, set up house, then throw yourself into village concerns so vigorously. It does seem . . . unusual . . . don't you think?'

'Are you saying I'm not allowed to be involved in the community, Odette? Is that it?'

'Of course not.' She smiles again, but there's an unmistakably threatening air about her. 'I'm just a little confused, that's all. And then, of course, there's Edward.'

'What does Edward have to do with it?'

'You're spending so much time together. You even went to the gymkhana with him.' Her eyes are boring into mine.

'I was helping out.'

'Helping out. I see. That's what you're calling it.'

'I *was* helping out!' I protest.

'So you didn't beg him to go, then?'

I feel a red heat inch up my neck. Did Edward tell her that? That I'd drunkenly pleaded with him to take me along? He wouldn't have – would he? Unless . . . unless he's been talking about me behind my back to Odette as well as to Matilda. The thought makes me squirm with embarrassment: he's obviously been having a real laugh at me when I'm not around.

'I have things to do, Odette.' I grab the brush and go to make my way past her, but she doesn't budge.

'Would you like to share what you were discussing?'

'Excuse me?' I can't believe this.

'What you two discussed. You were together for hours on the journey there and back. Maybe you'd like to share with me what you spoke about.'

Somewhere inside me a little spark ignites. This woman has gone too far. And maybe, just maybe, this is an opportunity to teach Edward a lesson too. If I stir things up a bit between them, he'll have to deal with the consequences. Odette is not a woman to be crossed – I can only imagine what it must be like to be in a relationship with someone like her. And Edward deserves some hassle. It might teach him to stop talking about me when I'm not around.

'I can't reveal that, I'm afraid, Odette,' I say slowly, arching an eyebrow suggestively at her.

'What?' she barks, then tries to compose herself. 'I mean, why not?'

'Well, because the conversation that Edward and I had was private. I couldn't possibly tell you what we discussed. It would be . . . betraying a confidence.'

I pause meaningfully to allow her to digest the implication. She's absolutely furious – her face is turning a deep purple colour that clashes unbecomingly with her baby blue jacket. It's very, very satisfying.

'Are you telling me that you won't divulge what you spoke about?'

A small vein in her neck is bulging and I stifle a giggle. This is brilliantly funny but I don't want to burst into laughter and give the game away. 'It's not that I won't . . .' I say, trying to control the urge to dissolve into hysterics. 'It's that I can't. I'd love to be able to tell you, Odette, but when someone asks you to keep a secret, you can't very well tell people, can you?'

'A secret? What secret?'

Her eyes are bugging from her head now and I can see she's struggling to regain her composure. Good. She'll probably kill Edward for this – it serves him right for making fun of me. 'That's not for me to say.' I lower my eyes. 'If Edward wants everyone to know, I'm sure he'll tell.'

'I'm not exactly everyone,' she spits.

'Of course, I know that,' I concur. 'And you and Edward are close so I'm sure he'll confide in you very soon. After all, you said yourself that you two have a very special relationship.'

I watch as she battles to control the rage that threatens to explode on her face.

'I know!' I say, as if the thought has just occurred to me. 'Why don't you ask him about it? Here he comes now.'

Edward and Polly are walking towards us, leading Saffy. The little pony doesn't look too pleased to be dragged from her stall to meet the vet. She hates being poked and prodded. I can't help wishing she'd kick Odette, just to mark her card. That would be priceless.

'I – I –' Odette splutters.

'I'll leave you to it, shall I?' I say sweetly. 'I have so much artwork to catch up on – the commissions are coming thick and fast. I just can't keep up!' With that, I turn on my heel and leave, a big fat grin on my face. It may have been a bit mean to goad Odette like that, but it serves her right for being so hateful. Besides, it was the best fun I've had in ages.

Rule Sixteen: *Beware wolves in sheep's clothing*

'I like your gold hot pants,' I say to Odette.

She does have good legs, to be fair, although I'm not sure if her pearls and twinset go all that well with the overall look. A belly top might have been better.

'Thanks,' she replies. *'I bought them on eBay. Now, give me that mic. It's my turn on the karaoke machine.'*

'What are you going to sing?' I ask curiously.

'"Secret Lovers", of course! For Edward!' She wiggles her hips, then leaps on to the stage, and the crowd in Matty's pub goes wild.

I wake suddenly. What a funny dream. It's such a shame I won't get to see what happens next. Still grinning, I reach to turn on the bedside lamp and illuminate the inky blackness. I have no idea what woke me or what time it is. It's so dark here – there isn't even a chink of light peeking through the curtains, not like the city where there's always a street lamp to depend on. My fingers are just grappling with the switch when I hear it. A rustle outside the window. Someone's there. Someone's trying to break in! I know immediately who it is – it's the Mad Man of the Woods Matilda told me about! He's back. He's heard that a single city girl is living alone in Rose Cottage and he's come to ransack the place and do God knows what to me. He must have been hiding out in Glacken Woods all this time. He could have been spying on me since I got here – he could have been watching my every move, waiting for this opportunity to pounce.

I lie frozen with fear, my heart thumping. What on earth should I do? Turn on the light to scare him away, scream for help, try to phone the police?

Before I can decide, I hear a muffled grunting. He's trying to get in through the window – if I don't do something I'll be murdered in my bed. Forcing myself to move, I leap up, grab my mobile phone and bolt from the room, my mind racing. I need to get out of here before he gets in. Not stopping to think any more, I wrench open the cottage door, run up the path and on to the road towards Edward's – he'll know what to do. Heart pounding, I race along, my knees almost buckling with fear. At last I see the manor house and, with one final gigantic effort, I sprint to the front door and hammer on it until Edward appears, his sleepy face startled.

I've obviously woken him up because he's wearing rumpled pyjamas – not that I would care if he was standing there in his long johns. I just want him to help me.

'The Mad Man's trying to kill me!' I gasp, my breath ragged from the exertion of sprinting all the way.

'What?'

'In the cottage! The Mad Man of the Woods!' I feel a trickle of sweat roll down my neck and into my cleavage. I probably haven't run that fast since I won the egg-and-spoon race back in primary school.

'A mad man?'

'Yes,' I pant. God, is he dense? Which part of this does he not understand? 'He was trying to break into the cottage – I heard him trying to climb through the window,' I manage to wheeze. Then I promptly burst into tears. This is all too much.

'Right.' His face is grim now. 'I'll get the keys.'

The keys? How about a rifle? He must have a rifle surely. For hunting? We are in the country, right?

'What on earth is going on?'

June appears behind Edward and frowns at me. She's wearing a long white nightdress and has old-fashioned rag curlers in her hair. Evidently she's been woken from a deep sleep too and she's very displeased.

'Maggie thinks there may be someone trying to break into the cottage, June,' Edward says. 'I'm just going to have a look.'

'A burglar? That's ridiculous!'

'I heard noises!' I snuffle through my tears. 'Someone was rattling the window.'

'Nonsense!' she tuts. 'It was probably the wind in the trees. Honestly, what a lot of fuss over nothing – you've woken the entire house!'

'It *wasn't* the wind!' I protest, rubbing my dripping nose on my arm. I'm suddenly very conscious that I'm barely dressed and Edward and June are watching me shiver in a teeny T-shirt. This must be the third time Edward has seen me like this. But what can I do? It's not like I had time to pull on my dressing-gown before I ran screaming from the scene of the crime that was about to be committed.

'Well, let's check it out, shall we? I'll be back as soon as I can, June.'

Edward shrugs on a fleece, then takes me by the elbow and steers me outside towards his Land Rover. I can see June scowling at me as we leave, her bushy grey eyebrows pulled low over her cold eyes.

'Don't worry, Maggie, it's probably nothing,' he says, opening the passenger door for me and looking away as I try to hoist myself up without exposing my bottom to him. Of course I'm wearing my greyest knickers. And my legs are probably the hairiest they've ever been. The city-centre waxing appointments are long gone and I haven't bothered to shave for weeks now – my legs look like the Black Forest. Edward must be repulsed, not that I care what he thinks, of course.

'Would you like a hand or . . .?' he offers, as I struggle to get in, tugging my T-shirt down around me as best I can.

The dismay on his face tells me he doesn't know where to look.

'I'm fine,' I snap, annoyed that he and his horrible witch of a mother-in-law are dismissing my fears. I've almost been murdered and they're reacting as if it's nothing serious. Is this the way people conduct themselves here? Are they so used to rampant violence that they don't bat an eyelid when something like this happens? Maybe they're all suffering from violence fatigue. Or maybe some local tipped off the Mad Man that I'd moved in. For all I know, half the village is in cahoots with gangs of professional thugs who roam the countryside just waiting to attack vulnerable women. They're probably all in on it.

'Like I say, it was probably nothing,' he says, as the engine jumps into life.

'It was *not* nothing.' I glare at him. 'I heard someone trying to get in. He was – he was . . . grunting. God knows what he was up to.' I shiver at the thought of what I may have escaped from – it doesn't bear thinking about.

'OK,' he says. 'Well, if someone was trying to get in, I'll deal with him.'

Deal with him? What does that mean? Maybe he has got a gun, after all. 'Do you mean shoot him?' I tuck my legs beneath me to try to keep warm. I can't stop shivering, which is obviously the shock of what's happened.

'Shoot him?' He turns to look at me. 'Why would I shoot him?'

'Well, isn't that what you do down here?'

'What? You mean like vigilantes?'

'Well, yes. That's what I heard anyway.' I distinctly remember reading that country folk dealt with crime in their own way – which I took to mean an odd bullet or two in the kneecap for anyone who broke the law.

'Maggie, this is Glacken village, not the Wild West.' Edward chuckles to himself. 'We don't go round shooting people, even if they *are* breaking and entering. If . . .' he pauses and looks sideways at me '. . . that's what happened.'

'I'm telling you,' I say very loudly and clearly, so there can be no mistake, 'someone was trying to climb into my bedroom window. I'm not making it up – I know what I heard.'

'OK, OK,' he says. 'I'm not saying I don't believe you – it's just that it would be pretty unusual for something like this to happen round here. It's usually pretty quiet.'

'Except for last year, I suppose?' I snap. I can't believe he's still not acknowledging all those burglaries that Matilda told me about. 'Or have you conveniently forgotten about that?'

'Last year?' he says, sounding confused.

'Yes, last year – when there were all those break-ins?'

'Break-ins?'

It's hard to read his expression because the interior of the Land Rover is so dark, but he's certainly managing to sound surprised. Why the cover-up? 'Yes,' I bark impatiently. 'And the Mad Man who's been camping out in the woods? The one with the criminal record?'

Why is he keeping up this pretence of not knowing anything about it? Maybe he's worried that I'll leave the cottage and he'll have no help in the stables until Claire gets back. After all, this piece of information could be grounds for discounting the lease agreement. He's probably covering up the truth because he doesn't want to be left in the lurch. But isn't that dishonest? The more I think about it, the more convinced I am. Maybe Edward didn't exactly have a legal obligation to tell me about the break-ins, but didn't he have some sort of moral responsibility?

Wait till I tell Claire about this – she'll die. Being attacked in the middle of the night wasn't part of the bargain when I agreed to move here and take her place.

'You think that there's a mad man camping out in the woods,' he repeats.

'Yes, Edward, Matilda told me. He had a stash of knives – I know all about it. And I also know that he was spotted again recently, so you can stop pretending.'

'Right.' He clears his throat. 'Well, let's not jump to any conclusions. Maybe we should just wait and see, OK? Here, let me turn on the heater – your teeth are chattering. You've had a shock.'

A blast of hot air hits me and I rub my arms to warm myself. He's right – I *have* had a shock. A very major one. I *knew* coming here was a bad idea – I just didn't realize how bad. I should have stayed in the city – where it's safe.

Less than a minute later, Edward pulls up outside the cottage and my stomach churns. God knows where the weirdo is now or what he's doing. Maybe he's inside going through my underwear. He could be a predator. A pervert. It doesn't bear thinking about.

'Well, it seems quiet,' Edward says calmly.

'You don't expect him to advertise that he's here, do you?' I snap. 'He's hardly going to have the lights on and a welcome mat at the door! He's a dangerous *criminal*.' I can feel tears pricking the backs of my eyes again. Edward isn't taking this situation seriously. It's obvious he doesn't believe me. He thinks I'm some overreacting female, petrified of my own shadow.

'Aren't you going to call the police?' I demand now.

'Yes.' Edward thinks about this. 'I'm sure Jimmy would come if I called him, but I don't want to wake him up at this time of night – he goes to bed by eleven. Let's just take a look first.'

'Jimmy? Who's Jimmy?'

'The local guard.'

'The local guard goes to bed by eleven?'

'He likes to, yes. He's an early riser, you see. He walks his greyhounds at six every morning – he's like clockwork. Didn't you meet him that evening in the village hall?'

'I don't remember being introduced to a guard. Then again, I met quite a few people. It was pretty crowded.'

'He was definitely there. He can seem a bit gruff sometimes, but he's a nice fella underneath. He rescued those dogs from a shelter – they were about to be put down.'

'Hang on a second.' I start to put two and two together. 'Are you telling me that everyone round here knows that this Jimmy goes to bed at eleven every night?'

Edward considers this. 'I suppose they do, yes. He doesn't make a secret of it.'

'So, if you were a criminal, all you'd have to do is wait until after eleven to commit a crime and you'd get away with it?'

'Well, now, like I said, there wouldn't be much of that round here. Most folk are tucked up in bed pretty early.'

'But this Jimmy – he's the only guard in the village?'

'Yes, the one and only,' Edward agrees.

'And you don't like to disturb him in the middle of the night?' I've never heard anything so ludicrous. Isn't that why we pay our taxes, for goodness' sake?

'Well, I'd call him if there was some sort of emergency. But not unless it was absolutely necessary. It wouldn't be fair. Like I said, he's an early riser.'

'And you don't think that me almost being killed by an intruder is an absolute emergency?' I can't believe this – I'm starting to fume.

'I think that may be a slight exaggeration, Maggie,' Edward says, pulling on his waxed hat, 'don't you?'

'Not really, no.' I'm at boiling point. 'If it wasn't for my very quick response in getting out of the cottage, you could have been looking at a homicide. Jimmy would have been dealing with a murder inquiry – would he have got out of bed for that, do you think?'

'Now, that would have been a first for Glacken,' Edward says. 'The locals would definitely be talking about you then, even more than they are now.'

'The locals are talking about me?'

'Of course.' He opens his door. 'The beautiful stranger in Rose Cottage is all anyone is talking about.'

Beautiful stranger? His face is in the shadows, but I can tell by his voice that he's teasing me again.

'Well, you go ahead and have a look, if you want,' I say, as he gets out, 'but don't expect me to come with you.'

'You'd better lock the door behind me, then,' he says. 'You know – to be on the safe side.'

I'm out in a nanosecond. If that thug knows I'm on my own he's bound to come and get me. For all I know, he could be watching us right now, from the safety of the cottage. God only knows what could happen if I was left alone.

'So, you're coming, then?' Edward says, switching on a torch he's pulled from his pocket.

'Yes,' I mutter. 'I'm coming.'

'Here, take this so.' He shrugs off his fleece and hands it to me. 'It's pretty cold and that T-shirt of yours is pretty short. Maybe you should think about borrowing Polly's Pooh Bear pyjamas.'

I can hear the smile in his voice, even if it's so dark I can't fully see his face. Either way I'm offended. The cheek of him! I have a good mind to throw his grubby old fleece back in his face. Then, again, he's right – it is freezing and now I've cooled down after my sprint to the big house I'm shivering with the cold and the shock. Refusing it would be biting off my nose to spite my face. I slip my arms into the sleeves and zip it up.

It's still warm from his body and almost immediately I feel better, I'm not sure why. Maybe it's the lovely musky smell – but the feeling of it wrapped snugly round me is actually quite nice . . .

'Now we're ready to face these terrorists,' he says.

'Are you trying to be funny?' I shake myself out of my reverie. 'There *was* someone there – I heard them.'

'I'm sure there was,' he says again, and I'm not sure if he's being patronizing or reassuring – it's so hard to see anything in the pitch blackness. 'Now, stay behind me – OK?'

I grip Edward's fleece tightly round me, my hands trembling with nerves. Who knows what might be going on inside the cottage?

Holding his finger to his lips, a sign that I should keep quiet, he creeps forward and I stick close behind him. We tiptoe together through the open front door, left swinging after I sprinted from the place. Before my eyes adjust to the interior gloom of the cottage I can hear a rustling sound and I'm terrified. He's still here – I can't see him but I can hear him. I stumble forward and grab Edward's back to balance myself. What will we do if he really *is* violent? Suddenly I wish I'd done those martial-arts classes I always threatened to take up. I try to remember what you're supposed to do if you're attacked – go for the eyes, I think, or is it the groin? Maybe both, although that could be tricky to do at the same time.

My head is spinning with the possibilities when I hear the switch click and I blink to adjust my eyes to the bright light. What's Edward doing? Now we're going to come face to face with the intruder! Surely it would be better to get out of here and call Jimmy – this is a legitimate emergency and we won't stand a chance against a hardened criminal, not unless Edward has a black belt he hasn't told me about. He doesn't look the type to be able to throw a mean karate chop, but you never can tell. People have hidden depths – like, who could have thought that Claire would up and go to India? If she doesn't get brainwashed and decide to stay, I'll kill her when she gets back for forcing me to come here – it's been the worst mistake of my life. All the years I've lived in the city, I've never been broken into. Not even when I was next door to that crack den during college – the dealers were quite decent once you looked past the criminal activity. They even loaned me sugar once when I ran out.

Blinking in the bright light, I look wildly round the room, trying to figure out where the burglar might be. I can still hear the rustling, but I can't see anyone. He must have heard us coming – he's probably hiding somewhere clever, ready to jump out and murder us. This isn't the way I want to die, draped in a smelly fleece in the middle of nowhere. I'm too young to meet my Maker – there's so much I still want to do. I want a Chanel 2.55 clutch, I want a pair of limited-edition Jimmy Choos. But most of all . . . I want to paint. I can't believe it's taken me until now to realize this. But it's too late – I'm going to die tonight before I have a chance to pursue my real passion. I really *am* a tragic heroine.

'I think I know who did this,' Edward says gravely, as my life flashes before my eyes.

'You do?'

I have a death grip on his back and I'm not letting go. Funnily enough, even though I'm scared witless, I can't help noticing that his back is very lean, yet muscly too. A nice combination.

'Yes.' He stalks over to the bedroom door, me shuffling behind, and flings it open. The rustling gets even louder. 'Mabel – is that you?'

Mabel? Who's Mabel? That's not a name a hardened criminal would use. What's going on?

'Come here and look at this,' Edward says, his face solemn.

I peep over his shoulder, still uncertain whether it's safe, and there, in the middle of the room, stands what looks like a sheep, munching happily on my best La Perla bra and knickers. She turns to gaze at us, an expression of mild surprise on her black face. As she does, I catch a glimpse of my prized turquoise lace and silk G-string disappearing down her gullet. An underwear-eating sheep called Mabel is my burglar.

Rule Seventeen: *Keep calm and carry on*

'I'm really sorry, Maggie,' Edward says, as Mabel trots past us and back outside, a look of smug satisfaction on her face. 'Mabel is infamous for doing things like that. She broke into the linen cupboard in the big house once and ate my mother-in-law's best tablecloth – the girls thought it was hilarious, but June was furious.'

A picture of the charming June flashes into my mind. I can imagine her flipping her lid if a sheep chewed her best linen – that woman would take no prisoners. It's a wonder Mabel lived to tell the tale and didn't end up on the Sunday dinner table.

'It must have been Mabel you heard rustling outside your bedroom window in the bushes. She obviously came through the front door when you ran out.' He's trying his best not to laugh – he thinks this is hilarious.

'What wonderful detective work.' I scowl, furious that a dumb animal has made me look like a prize idiot.

Even though I'm relieved that a lunatic isn't stalking me, I also feel stupid that it wasn't a real intruder after all the fuss I made. I'm sure June will have a good old laugh when she hears what really happened. She'll probably tell everyone in the village what a fool I am – my cheeks burn at the idea that everyone will be talking about the city girl who thought a harmless sheep was a burglar.

'She's more of a pet than anything else,' Edward goes on. 'The children weaned her from when she was a lamb. She thinks she's human, really – that's why she's always trying to get indoors.'

'That sheep thinks she's human?' The sarcasm drips from

my voice, but Edward seems to miss it. Or else he's deliberately ignoring it, I can't be sure.

'Yes. Her mother rejected her, you see, so we hand-fed her. She loved her bottles of warm milk. See – almost human.'

'Well, I can understand why her mother rejected her,' I say now, surveying the chaos before me. Mabel has rampaged through the cottage, knocking over almost everything in her path. It's going to take for ever to clear up the mess.

'What do you mean?' Edward says.

'She's so badly behaved. No wonder her mother didn't want to know her – she's out of control.'

'She's not exactly out of control.' He smiles.

'You think?' I raise an eyebrow. Is he blind? The stupid sheep has made mincemeat of my underwear drawer. 'How would you describe her behaviour then?'

'Well,' he says, smiling again, 'she's . . . feisty. Let's put it like that.'

'You can put it any way you want,' I sniff, annoyed. 'As far as I'm concerned she should be for sale on a supermarket shelf somewhere. Beside a jar of mint sauce preferably.'

'Oh, no, we couldn't do that! She's almost like one of the family. Besides . . . I like feisty.'

I pick up some remnants of underwear from the floor and glare at him. It looks like Mabel had a proper feast – most of it is ruined.

'It could have been worse,' he suggests.

'How's that?'

'Well, I know Mabel has done a lot of damage, but at least it wasn't the Mad Man of the Woods like you thought, right?'

Something in his face registers with me and suddenly it all clicks into place. 'There never *was* a Mad Man of the Woods, was there?' I say.

'Not that I've heard of, no . . .'

'So . . . your lovely daughter made up that story to scare me. She told me that a dangerous criminal was on the loose, just to make me feel frightened.'

'It might have been her idea of a joke,' he offers.

'It wasn't very funny,' I say. 'I was absolutely terrified. I thought I was going to be killed.'

'I'm really sorry, Maggie.' Edward is serious now. 'She shouldn't have done that. I'll be grounding her as punishment.'

'I certainly hope so,' I fume. 'Do you have any idea how much good underwear costs? Do you realize how much damage that sheep has actually done?'

He looks momentarily embarrassed, but I'm too annoyed to care. It's his daughter's fault that at least a few hundred euros' worth of my best lingerie is now fit for the bin.

'I wouldn't . . . I don't have any idea,' he mumbles, his cheeks flushing.

'One set alone can cost a couple of hundred euro,' I announce. 'That kind of money doesn't grow on trees, you know. Or maybe it does for you – but it certainly doesn't for me.' A wave of self-pity washes over me. I'm unemployed and practically homeless. I'll probably never be able to afford nice undies again. I'll be wearing grey baggy knickers for years to come, possibly for the rest of my life.

'I really *am* sorry, Maggie.' He bows his head. 'It won't happen again.'

'Humph,' I grunt. He does look sorry, to be fair. And I suppose this isn't his fault. Not that I'll tell him so.

'Let me help you to clear up,' he says, stooping to pick up some of my precious collection of magazines that fell to the floor when Mabel barged through the living room. I guess I should be grateful she didn't chew her way through those too.

'You like fashion, I see,' he comments, as he rearranges my *Vogue* back issues into a neat pile.

'I used to,' I sigh, 'when I had a life.'

My city wardrobe seems like a million years ago now that I'm living in my oldest, tattiest gear and my stinky trainers. I've even abandoned full makeup. Making that sort of effort seems a bit pointless when everything just gets covered in yard dirt all the time. And it's not like there's anywhere exciting to go, even at night.

'I guess Glacken isn't very cool, is it?' he says. 'It's probably a very big change for you, compared to all the glamour of the city.'

'You could say that.' I nudge the coffee-table back into place.

'Still, it's good for your art.'

'I suppose so,' I mumble. I don't want to talk about my fake art career – not now.

'Where do you keep it?'

'What's that?' I pretend not to hear him properly.

'Your artwork. Where do you keep it all?'

He looks curiously round the room. There's not a single piece of my so-called art anywhere to be seen, of course.

I frantically try to think of something to say. Should I just come clean? Tell him that this has been a stupid misunderstanding? I never meant everyone to believe I was an artist – this whole thing has just developed a life of its own. Then again, it mightn't be the right time to reveal my double identity – after all, I've already dragged him from his bed because of a sheep burglar. Breaking the news that I've been lying all this time would only make this mess even worse.

'It's in the boot of the car,' I say.

'The boot of the car? Really?'

'Yes,' I bluff. 'Once I've completed a work I need to remove it from the house – to let the creative juices continue to flow.' God, that is such bullshit. How do I come up with this stuff?

'I see.' He nods, as if this makes perfect sense. 'So what are you working on next?'

'I'm not sure,' I reply. 'The muse hasn't struck yet.' Muse? This is terrible.

'Will you let me see some one day? If I promise to keep Mabel under lock and key?'

I roll my eyes at him. I guess it is a little funny, even if I want to make kebabs of that Mabel.

'Maybe you can do my portrait?' a gruff voice says.

I spin to see a fat man in a blue jumper in the doorway. It's that man from the meeting – the aggressive one with the shifty eyes. What's he doing here? And why does he have a notebook in his hand?

'Jimmy, why are you here?' Edward's face falls.

Jimmy? The fat man in the blue jumper is the local guard? The one who doesn't like to be disturbed after eleven?

'I'm here because I got a call to say that there'd been some sort of emergency,' Jimmy says. He doesn't look too happy. 'Do you want to tell me what's going on?'

I look wildly at Edward. How can we ever explain this mess?

'Well,' Edward clears his throat, 'it was all a misunderstanding, Jimmy. Maggie here thought someone was breaking in . . .'

Jimmy starts to write. '"Someone was breaking in,"' he repeats, word by word. 'Go on.'

'Well, no, that's not exactly what happened,' I interrupt, and he lifts his head.

'You're changing your story, are you?' he says, narrowing his eyes at me suspiciously, as if he doesn't like the look of me one little bit.

'Well, no, I'm not changing my story. I did *think* someone was breaking in.'

'You're not retracting your previous statement?' He pauses, holding the pencil away from his notebook.

'No, I *did* think that originally,' I say.

'So you're sticking to the original version of events, then? Because if you're changing it, I have to start again.' He waves the notebook impatiently at me. 'Time-wasting is a criminal offence, you know.'

'Jimmy,' Edward weighs in, 'Maggie *did* think there was a burglar trying to get into the cottage, but it turns out there wasn't.'

Jimmy writes all this down, painfully slowly. 'So,' he says, once he's finished, 'can you explain why you thought a robbery was being committed? That's a serious allegation to make.'

I shift uneasily, tugging Edward's fleece down round me. Why is he making me feel like I've done something wrong? I'm the victim here. Well, I would have been the victim if the burglar had been human. But that's not the point.

'There was rustling in the bushes,' I say. 'There were noises.'

'Noises.' He writes this down. 'But you're sure now it wasn't a burglar.'

'No,' Edward confesses. 'It was Mabel. The sheep.'

'The sheep.' Jimmy pauses. 'So if all this was a fuss about nothing – can you tell me why I'm standing here now so instead of tucked up in my bed? I have greyhounds to walk in the morning, you know. They like to be out at six a.m., no later. How can I be expected to do that now? It's gone three.'

'Sorry about that,' Edward says, winking at me as Jimmy stuffs his notebook into his pocket. 'June never should have called you. I didn't ask her to.'

'June? June didn't call me.' He snorts, glowering at me. 'The woman knows better than that. She knows about dogs. She knows about routine.'

'Well, if it wasn't June, who was it?' I ask.

'You know right well who it was, miss,' he says. 'It was *you* – *you* called me.' He waggles his finger at me. 'And I've a good mind to caution you. This is pure messing. I don't like messing.'

'I *didn't* call you!' I protest. 'I wanted to – but Edward said he'd deal with it.'

'That's right – she didn't call you, Jimmy,' Edward agrees with me. 'I was with her the whole time.'

I smile gratefully at him – at least he's sticking up for me. That's nice of him. And he gave me his fleece when I was cold. That was nice too. Maybe he's not so bad.

He smiles back at me and I suddenly notice the way his eyes dance when he does. If I wasn't so furious about Mabel, I might even think he was cute. Really cute . . . Why didn't I notice that before?

'Well, *someone* who said they were you called me and begged me to come out here. If it wasn't you, then I don't know who it was. Mabel the sheep, maybe?' Jimmy stalks back out of the door, huffing about wasting police time and resources.

I look at Edward again, all thoughts of his dancing eyes gone as the implication of what Jimmy just said hits me hard. I can tell by Edward's face that he's realized who did this, just as I have: it was Matilda, I'm sure of it. She wasn't just playing a silly prank when she spun that tale about the Mad Man of the Woods. She was really trying to frighten me. And now this. She must have heard all the commotion at the manor earlier and then called Jimmy to make things worse. She wants me out of here and I have a funny feeling she's not going to give up trying to get rid of me any time soon.

Rule Eighteen: *Be a good neighbour*

'The very woman!' Ted exclaims, as I walk into the Village Store.

'Maggie!' Peg beams. 'We're delighted to see you!'

I cringe – it's obvious that Peg and Ted have just been talking about me and I can guess exactly why: word has already spread about Mabel the sheep. 'Hi, Peg, Ted.'

I'm regretting coming into Glacken, but it's not like I had a choice – not unless I wanted to make the thirty-mile round trip to the nearest supermarket. Mind you, I'm beginning to think that's exactly what I should have done – at least then I wouldn't have had to face the villagers. One or two definitely smirked at me as I parked my car on the main street – now I know why.

'Now, don't worry, pet, people aren't laughing at you,' Ted says. 'Well, not much, anyway.'

He's trying to keep a straight face. I know what this means: it means that the entire village is talking about Mabel breaking into the cottage. I should have known that it would be impossible to keep a secret round here – I'll never live it down.

I wonder who told them. It must have been Edward. He's probably told everyone and had a really good laugh at my expense. So much for him and his stupid dancing eyes.

'I thought I was being broken into,' I try to explain, feeling the red heat of embarrassment creep up my neck towards my cheeks. They must think I'm a clueless city girl. It all sounds a little silly now, in the cold light of day.

'Of course you did, and why wouldn't you?' Peg is

understanding. 'That Mabel is a holy terror for frightening people. That's the problem with feeding the runts. They start to think they're human.'

'That's what Edward said!' I gasp.

So he wasn't teasing me then – maybe that part was true.

'And he's right.' Peg nods. 'Rescued lambs can grow up thinking their place is indoors beside the fire, not out in the pasture. That Mabel especially – she's a cheeky thing, no mistake.'

'When I heard her at the window, I was convinced someone was trying to get in,' I explain.

'And, of course, it's so dark here at night – terrifying if you're not used to it,' Ted adds.

A weight's been lifted off my shoulders. They know exactly how I feel.

'That's it!' I whoop. 'It's so black – noises can seem . . . magnified.'

'Well, of course they can – the long nights would put the fear of God in you unless you were used to it. I sometimes get a little spooked myself and I'm born and bred in Glacken,' Peg confides.

I suspect Peg made up that bit so that I won't feel any more embarrassed than I already do, but because they're both being so understanding and not at all judgemental, everything seems somehow much better. I had been feeling pretty foolish about the whole incident, but they're so kind. Maybe it wasn't such a stupid mistake to make, after all.

'I didn't think I was afraid of the dark, but I've never seen darkness like I have here. It's really scary,' I confess.

'Ah, sure, it's nothing to be ashamed of. Lots of people have irrational fears,' Peg says. 'I'll let you into a little secret, will I? I used to be afraid of flying until I was cured. Wasn't I, Ted?'

'You were that,' Ted agrees, looking fondly at her.

'Yes, terrified I was. And then I was hypnotized and sure it doesn't bother me now at all. You should try it.'

'What – hypnosis?' I'm not sure about this idea. Not at all sure.

'Yes, it's absolutely brilliant. I couldn't even look at a plane before I had it done and now I've no problem at all. Do I, Ted?'

'No, she can fly whenever she wants to. She's a little trouper so she is!' He puffs out his chest proudly.

'So do you travel a lot more,' I ask, 'now that you're not afraid to fly?'

'Oh, no, I hate travelling.' Peg beams at me. 'I prefer to stay at home. Sure why would I want to leave the village? Everything I need is here. Isn't that right, Ted?'

'That's right,' Ted agrees, pulling the wrapper off a new Mars Bar and diving into it.

I can't help but think he looks a little sad, as if he wouldn't mind packing his suitcases and taking off on an adventure, with Peg as his sidekick travelling companion.

Peg seems oblivious to this, though.

'But I thought you said you could fly now, since you've had the hypnosis?' Isn't that what she said? Did I misunderstand her?

'Ah, yes, I could if I *wanted* to,' Peg nods, 'but I've never flown anywhere.'

'You've never been on a plane, even though you're no longer afraid to fly?'

This is so weird.

'No. Never. But if I *wanted* to, then I could.' She's looking at me as if I'm the one who is a sandwich short of a picnic.

'Because of the hypnosis,' I say.

'That's right. Now, the other thing you could try is exposure therapy.'

'Exposure therapy?'

'Yes. It's when you surround yourself by the thing you fear so you learn not to fear it any more. It's supposed to be very effective – if you don't want to go the hypnosis route, like. It really worked for a friend of mine who was terrified of mice.'

'Nelly Reilly,' Ted interjects, as if I should know who Nelly Reilly is.

'That's right, Ted,' Peg agrees. 'Ted has a wonderful way with names, don't you, Ted? He never forgets a name.'

'That's the Mars Bars, Maggie,' Ted says. 'Chocolate is full of antioxidants – good for the old grey matter.' He taps the chocolate wrapper on the side of his head.

'Not so good for the cholesterol, though,' Peg frowns.

'You can't have it every way, girl,' Ted says mildly, taking another massive bite of Mars Bar and chewing slowly.

'So, Nelly Reilly?' I prompt Peg – if I don't we could be here all day.

'Ah, yes . . . Nelly Reilly.' Peg gathers her thoughts. 'She had exposure therapy to cure her of her mouse phobia, and she can pick up a mouse now – no problem.'

'Why would she ever need to pick up a mouse?' I ask. Why would anyone ever want to touch a rodent? That's abnormal, surely. Catch one in a trap, yes, but touch one? No way.

'Because she works in a pet shop, of course!' Peg looks as me curiously, as if I should know this. 'Why else?'

'Do you know, I read the other day about this woman who found a dead mouse in a jar of spaghetti sauce?' Ted interrupts. 'They reckon it fell in just before the jar was sealed in the factory. You wouldn't credit that now, would you?'

He chews slowly on another chunk of Mars Bar as he contemplates this scenario.

I blanch. Oh, God, I'll never buy another jar of spaghetti sauce ever again.

'Oh, sorry, Maggie, that was very insensitive of me,' Ted says. 'I don't know what I'm thinking this morning. You don't want to be hearing those kinds of stories. Would you like a Mars Bar, maybe? They're very good for shock – it's the sugar, you see.'

'No thanks,' I say.

'Anyway, we're glad you're OK after your awful fright with Mabel,' Peg says.

'We heard Edward took very good care of you anyway,' Ted says.

'He's such a lovely man,' Peg adds. 'And so lonely since his poor wife died. I don't know why someone doesn't snap him right up. Not that *some* people haven't tried hard enough, mind you.'

Peg raises her eyes to Ted and he nods back, but says nothing. They must be talking about Odette – maybe that secret relationship isn't as secret as she'd like to think.

'He told you all about it, I suppose?' I ask.

'Edward?' they gasp in unison.

'God, no,' Peg says. 'Edward never told us a thing. He's useless for news – we told you that.'

'Yes,' Ted agrees sadly. 'He's far too discreet – especially about people he likes.'

People he likes? Do they mean me?

'He'd never say a bad word about you, Maggie – protective of you, he is.'

'He is?'

'Oh, yes. Guards your privacy so he does.'

So he hasn't been talking about me. Right. That's a bit of a turn-up for the books. I thought he'd been laughing about me with half the village. I even tried to teach him a lesson by stirring things with Odette . . . Maybe that wasn't such a good idea.

'Now, enough of all that. We're glad you're here, because we wanted to talk to you. Didn't we, Ted?'

'We did. The thing is, we feel bad.'

'Why?' I'm confused.

'Because we haven't brought you out – shown you the high life, like!' Ted grins.

'The high life?' What kind of high life can there be around here?

'Yes,' Peg goes on. 'I said to Ted the other night, "Really, Maggie must think we're the worst sort of neighbours." Didn't I, Ted?'

'You did.'

'I don't think that,' I say.

'Well, the worst sort of muckers, then. We haven't brought you anywhere nice since you came to Glacken.'

'You brought me to the pub,' I remind them.

'That's true,' Ted says. 'We took you to Matty's.'

'Ah, yes, but that was work-related,' Peg crows. 'We haven't brought you anywhere just for laughs, to experience the social scene.'

'The social scene?'

'Yes, we have to take you out somewhere exciting! Somewhere fun!'

'So, this is the plan. We're going to a ball.' Ted rubs his hands together with glee.

'A ball?'

'Yes, a hunt ball. It'll be great *craic*! We haven't been for a few years, but what better excuse now that you're here? It'll be a blast!'

I don't know what to make of this. On the one hand, the thought of a decent night out is tempting. On the other, could a hunt ball count as a decent night out? It's hardly very cool – it's probably like an old-fashioned dinner dance.

'Well, I'm not sure I can make it, actually,' I stall. I need time to think. I can't just accept straight away without knowing what I'm letting myself in for. I have to do some research – Google this type of thing, at least.

'Of course you can!' Ted laughs. 'And I'm driving so you needn't worry about a thing.'

'Right.'

How am I going to get out of this?

'Now, if you need anything to wear, Maggie, don't hesitate to ask.' Peg's sincere face is worried. 'These things are very fancy affairs . . .' She looks at my grubby outfit doubtfully.

'Yes, Peg has some lovely dresses, if you need to borrow anything,' Ted chimes in.

Of course – Peg and Ted haven't seen me in anything other than jeans or tracksuits. They've no idea that I have a glamorous city wardrobe just itching to be worn. No wonder Peg looks so worried – she probably thinks I have absolutely nothing to wear to a hunt ball. She may think I'll turn up smelling of horse dung, with straw in my hair. She has no clue that I used to have a whole other life – a life where I dressed for success, wore proper makeup and styled my hair every day. That life seems so far away.

'I have a lovely blue dress that would suit you perfectly,' Peg goes on.

'That's OK, thanks, Peg. I have a few bits and pieces I can pull together,' I say.

I could give my D&G dress an outing. The thought jumps into my head and makes me tingle. I love that black dress – it's the perfect mix of sexy and classic: not too slutty, not too prissy, but an ideal blend of both. Last time I wore it, to a work dinner with Dermot and Dom, Dom told me if he didn't know me better he'd have given me ten out of ten. A back-handed compliment, yes, but I was chuffed all the same.

Thinking about it now, I can't remember the last time I went out properly. Dom nagged me for ages to go clubbing with him after Robert and I broke up, but I never succumbed, no matter how much he begged.

Maybe an outing would be fun. OK, so I've never been to a hunt ball before and I have no idea what's involved, but how bad could it be? As long as they don't actually expect me to go hunting, it'll be bearable, surely.

'Wonderful! So you're on?' Peg squeaks.

'OK, then,' I agree. 'Why not?'

'Great!' She and Ted high-five each other.

'Now, before I forget, I made this for you – I was going to drop it up to the cottage, but now that you're here I don't have to!' Peg hands me a casserole dish, its top covered with tinfoil.

'What is it?'

'Oh, just a little dinner. I thought you might like it if you were feeling shaky – you know, after . . . Mabel.'

'You made me dinner?'

'It's nothing really,' she says. 'Now, it needs to be reheated in a hot oven for about twenty minutes. Add a little salt and pepper, if you like.'

'Thanks, Peg, that's really kind of you.' I smile gratefully at her.

'No problem.' She grins. 'Sure isn't that what friends are for?'

I'm taken aback by what she's said. I can tell from her expression that she genuinely counts me as a friend, even though we've known each other for such a short time. That's why she's cooked this for me. It would never occur to me to cook for anyone, not even my closest friends in the city, yet it's such a simple and lovely thing to do.

'Well, thanks again,' I say. 'It was really thoughtful of you.'

'Don't mention it,' she beams. 'It's nothing special.'

'It's her shepherd's pie.' Ted winks at me. 'Delicious, it is!'

'Now, Ted, don't be boasting.' Peg swats at him with her hands.

'That recipe won an award at the farmer's market last year,' Ted adds. 'Beat Betty's it did.'

'Well, she came second,' Peg says graciously. 'That wasn't so bad.'

'Shepherd's pie's my absolute favourite!' I sniff the dish appreciatively, suddenly transported back to my childhood. I haven't had it for years – I used to love it with ketchup and mushy peas on the side.

As if she's reading my mind, Peg rummages behind the counter and brings forth a tin from its depths. 'Mushy peas,' she says, winking. 'You can't beat them.'

'Peg!' I say, astounded. 'I love mushy peas!'

'Well, of course you do,' she replies, as if it's the most normal thing in the world to be able to read my mind like that. 'Doesn't everyone?'

I can't remember the last time anyone besides Mum made a homemade meal especially for me. Any dinner parties I've been to in the last few years weren't exactly home-cooked affairs – usually whoever hosted bought everything in ready-made. Sometimes, at the posher dos, there was a caterer, even waiting staff. In retrospect it all seems so opulent and over the top. Peg is acting like this is nothing unusual, but I would never think about making something to eat for any of my neighbours. In fact, I barely knew any of my neighbours back in the city, except to nod to. Ted and Peg have made a real effort to include me since I've been here. I guess that's why they call it a community – people look out for each other.

'Thank you again, Peg,' I say, feeling a little overwhelmed. They've been so kind to me.

'You're very welcome. So, we'll see you on Thursday for our big night out. We'll pick you up at seven.'

'OK.' I smile. 'I'm looking forward to it.'

'Great! You don't mind sharing the back seat with Edward and Matilda, do you?'

Edward and Matilda? 'They're coming too?'

'Oh, yes! Didn't I mention that?' Peg asks. 'I'm such a feather-head, honestly.'

'We thought they could do with a good night out as well,' Ted explains. 'Blow off the cobwebs a bit, let the old hair down. There'll be lots of teenagers there too, so Matilda should have a great time.'

'Sure, I know what you mean,' I lie.

The warm, fuzzy feeling I'd been enjoying disappears in a puff of smoke as I realize I've agreed to go to this ball with my landlord and his teenage daughter – the one who hates my guts. Great. That's just great.

'So, get your glad rags out!' Ted cheers. 'It's going to be a brilliant night – I can feel it in me waters.'

My heart sinks as he unwraps another Mars Bar and takes a celebratory bite. Ted's wrong. This isn't going to be a brilliant night, it's going to be one big disaster – I can feel it *my* waters, or I would if I knew where they were exactly.

Rule Nineteen: *Dance like no one's watching*

'I'm not sure about this beef.' Peg pokes the meat on her plate with her fork. 'I think it's off.'

'Really?'

I cut a tiny corner from my steak and chew it slowly. It tastes delicious but I'm afraid to say so. What if Betty from the butcher's supplied the meat? If I compliment anything to do with her Peg will be royally offended, and I certainly don't want that, not when she and Ted have been so nice to me.

'It's a little chewy,' I concede, and she smiles knowingly at me.

'You're right,' she agrees. 'It hasn't been hung properly, that's the problem.'

'Do you think so?'

'Oh, yes. If beef isn't hung properly it can taste like card-board.'

'The vegetables are nice enough, though.' I'm hoping this is the right thing to say – I get the feeling I shouldn't praise anything too much.

'Yes,' she agrees half-heartedly. 'Of course, they would have been far nicer if they were steamed.'

'True,' I say, and she smiles at me, happy I concur.

'So, Maggie, what do you think of the hunt ball so far?' Edward leans across the table to talk to me.

He's wearing a black tux and he looks sensational – nothing like a trussed-up waiter, unlike poor Ted who keeps pulling at his bow-tie, as if it's slowly strangling him.

I've spent most of the night so far trying to avoid talking

to Edward mostly because although Odette isn't sitting with us, she's floating round the room somewhere. However, there is another reason I'm reluctant to engage in conversation and that's because every time I look at him I experience a strange fluttering in my chest. A fluttering that's making me feel very uneasy indeed. 'I like it,' I answer politely, carefully cutting up some more beef into tiny little pieces. Concentrating on doing that minimizes the sizzling embarrassment I feel every time he looks at me.

'Not too boring for you?'

'No,' I reply, dicing my carrots and pushing them round my plate. Why am I so hot and bothered?

'It's too boring for *me*!' Matilda groans. 'Why can't I go and talk to my friends?' She looks longingly across the room to where a gang of teenagers are sitting together, tossing napkins back and forth across the table at each other. She spent the entire journey here in Peg and Ted's little white van in stony silence and she's barely uttered a word to anyone all night. I'd no idea why she'd even agreed to come until I spotted Daniel with the group on the other side of the room. Obviously he's the motivation behind her get-up. Her strapless, backless, barely there black dress is incredibly short and she's plastered fake tan on every visible inch of skin. It's a look that any city teenage girl would be proud of, and apparently it's just as popular here in the middle of nowhere. When she took off the modest wrap she had draped around her shoulders to reveal what was underneath I saw Edward pale. Despite many discreet hints from him, she has since refused to put it back on.

'You can talk to them when we've finished our meal, Matilda,' Edward says mildly, trying to defuse the tension.

'I *have* finished.' Matilda pushes her plate away. 'It was disgusting.'

'Didn't you like *any* of it, Matilda?' Ted asks, his face creased with worry as if he's somehow personally responsible for this.

'I'm a vegetarian,' Matilda replies. 'Meat offends me.'

'A vegetarian, you say?' Ted is interested. 'Why is that? Is it for health reasons?'

'Not exactly,' Matilda says coolly. 'I just decided I don't want to eat anything with a face, that's all.'

'Anything with a face, eh?' Ted repeats. 'Did you hear that, Peg?'

'What's that?' Peg isn't paying any attention to the conversation, she's far too busy carefully observing someone else. I follow her gaze to another table – where Betty from the butcher's, in a purple satin sleeveless gown, is tucking into the beef with relish. As I watch she takes the gravy boat and drenches her plate with another generous helping.

'Matilda here says she won't eat anything with a face.'

'That's nice,' Peg says distractedly, her eyes glued to Betty's fleshy shoulders.

'Since when, Matilda?' Edward scoffs lightly. 'You had a beefburger last week, if I remember rightly.'

'A lot has changed since then,' she says loftily. 'Not that you would ever notice.'

'Ah, yes, a week is a long time in the life of a teenager,' Ted says, dabbing at his mouth with his napkin. 'Even I know that.'

Matilda stares at him, eyes narrowed, as if she can't quite believe he was ever a teenager.

'Did I ever tell you that I saw the Beatles perform live once?' he says to her, out of the blue.

'No way!' Matilda forgets to be cool for a second and her jaw drops in genuine admiration.

'Yes, I did. They weren't that good, though.'

'The Beatles weren't that good?' Matilda is astounded.

'No. I never did like Paul McCartney – far too saccharine.

Now the Stones – they were class. Jagger knew how to play a crowd. Of course, I can barely remember that gig – I'd smoked so much hash beforehand, I was really out of it.'

'You smoked *hash*?' Matilda can't believe her ears.

'Of course,' Ted replies. 'Ah, the music's starting – great!'

'Oh, God, not this crowd,' Matilda mutters, suddenly remembering to be stroppy again.

A group of five is setting up on the stage, all dressed in identical blue suits and blue suede shoes, their hair slicked back into greasy quiffs. 'Who are they?' I ask.

'The oldest swingers in town.' Matilda groans. 'They're *brutal*.'

'They're not that bad,' Edward remonstrates.

'You're right, they're worse. I'm outta here, Dad, see you later.'

Before Edward can protest, Matilda stalks away from the table. She's heading straight for Daniel. He doesn't even lift his head to say hello as she sashays towards him, wobbling a little on her heels. He's completely ignoring her – I'd forgotten how charming teenage boys can be.

'Maggie, will you give me the honour of this first dance?' Ted bows formally in front of me as the band swings into life.

'I'm not much of a waltzer, Ted,' I warn him.

'And neither am I, so we'll be perfectly matched.'

'Go on, Maggie.' Peg is no longer watching Betty. 'It'll give me the chance to quiz Edward here about his love life!'

Edward shifts in his seat and a pink colour creeps into his cheeks.

'You're a terrible woman, Peg,' Ted guffaws. 'You're making the poor man blush.' He swings me away from the table and on to the dance-floor, which is already packed with people. Apparently the city phobia about being the first to move doesn't apply here – everyone is happy to get out and start to

226

enjoy themselves immediately. It's quite refreshing, even though Ted is stamping all over my precious Prada sling-backs. He wasn't lying – he's no dancer.

'So, Maggie, how are you enjoying country life?' he asks me now, as we sway around the floor.

'I like it,' I reply. 'It's certainly not dull, that's for sure.'

'Did you think it was going to be?'

I bite my lip. Damn. I don't want to offend him, not when he and Peg have invited me here tonight.

'Don't worry, you're not insulting me. I was terrified when I moved to Glacken first.'

'You're not from here?' I had simply assumed he was. He certainly *sounds* as if he is.

'Oh, no.' He shakes his head. 'I'm a blow-in, like you.'

'Where are you from, then?'

'I'm from Lyross.'

'Where's that?'

'About ten miles away.'

Is he serious? He thinks he's a blow-in because he moved to Glacken from a village ten miles away? 'That's not very far,' I say.

'Geographically, no. But psychologically it may as well be a million light years away.'

'Really?'

'Oh, yes. It took people a long time to accept me into the community. I'm still known as Ted from Lyross among the villagers, even though I've been here for thirty-odd years.'

'Wow,' I say. 'That's mad.'

'Yes, even my children would have been considered blow-ins. It takes generations for the villagers to really accept an outsider. The children didn't happen for us, of course.'

A flicker of grief passes across his face as he says this but I pretend not to see it. I don't want to embarrass him.

'Still, I'm glad to be here,' he goes on. 'I did my travelling in my youth.'

'You did? Where to?'

'All over, really – Australia, America, South Africa . . .'

'You travelled all over the world?' I'm gobsmacked. I never would have guessed that.

'I did, yes.' He smiles a little wistfully. 'I worked on the ships before I settled down. It was a wonderful life. But that was before I met Peg, of course – she put a halt to my gallop.'

'Do you ever miss it?' I ask, curious.

Ted glances across to where Peg is chatting to Edward. 'Between you and me, I do,' he admits. 'Sometimes I think I'd love to go exploring – you know, take off with no great plan and just see what happens. But Peg . . .'

'She's more of a home bird?'

'Yes, she is,' he says. 'We *were* planning to travel – when we found out that children weren't going to happen for us. But the years just seemed to pass us by. Peg was nervous about flying, too, of course . . .'

'She's over that now, though.'

'Yes, she is. But she still doesn't really want to go, and now there's this supermarket thing. I don't want to push her . . .'

'What are you two talking about?' Peg is at Ted's shoulder. I'd never even noticed her coming.

'Nothing, sweetheart!' Ted fixes a smile to his face.

'I see. Nothing, was it?' Peg smiles back. 'Well, Maggie, I hope you don't mind if I interrupt you? I'd like to take my husband for a whirl.'

'Of course.' I kiss Ted's whiskery cheek. 'That was lovely, Ted, thank you,' I whisper. He squeezes my hand and I squeeze his back in return – the message is clear: this conversation stays between us.

I turn to go back to the table as Ted takes Peg's hand and

bump straight into Edward's torso. Where did he come from? It's as if he appeared out of thin air at my side.

'Would you like to dance?' he asks quietly, his eyes locked on mine.

I gaze at him, my heart suddenly pounding in my ears. Odette is here somewhere – what will she do to me if she sees us dancing together? She'll have a canary, that's what. A vision of her launching herself across the floor to rip the hair from my head flashes into my mind. Then again, such a public display wouldn't be exactly her style. She'd probably do something far sneakier – like slip a cyanide pill into my drink. I get the feeling Odette would like to watch me die a slow and very painful death.

Then Edward smiles hesitantly at me and instantly I make up my mind. I don't care what Odette thinks or what she does: all I know is that I want to dance with him. It's almost as if I'm longing, yes, longing, to feel his body close to mine. Which can't be right, can it?

I nod yes to him and he slips his arm around me. It's nothing like dancing with Ted. Edward moves smoothly, his hand resting lightly on the small of my back, guiding me. For once I actually feel like I'm waltzing properly and not just being frogmarched about. If I could only stop my knees knocking together with nerves it would be even better.

'You look beautiful tonight, Maggie,' he says in my ear, as we move together across the floor.

'Thanks, so do you,' I reply. 'Not beautiful, of course. You look well. That's what I mean. Very well. Clean too. You look really clean.' I sound like an idiot. Why can't I think before I speak – what is *wrong* with me?

'Thank you,' he says solemnly. 'It took me quite a while to scrub up.'

'Me too!' I exclaim, then bite my lip again. Why did I have

to go and say that? What a stupid thing to admit, even if it's true. It's been so long since I've been anywhere remotely fancy that it took for ever to do my hair and makeup. I couldn't even check how I looked because there's no full-length mirror in the cottage but I think my D&G dress is OK – it slipped on and zipped up easier than usual. I may have lost a few pounds from all the mucking out, which is an up-side to all the sweating and scrubbing that I hadn't thought of.

An awkward silence descends between us and I desperately try to think of something intelligent to say. My mind is completely blank. For some reason not a single thing, intelligent or otherwise, comes to mind. Could it be because he's so close? His hand is still resting on the small of my back and all I can think about is the heat of his fingers on my skin. But thinking like that is insane. The only reason he asked me to dance is because he's being polite. Anything else is in my head.

'Thanks for offering to teach Polly how to paint,' he says at last, and I exhale with relief that the ice has been broken. Now I know for sure that I've lost weight – the last time I wore this dress I had to hold my breath all night I was so nervous the seams would pop.

'That's no problem. She's a lovely kid. I probably should have asked you first, though, before I said it to her,' I babble.

'It was probably less you offering and more her suggesting – am I right?' He chuckles.

'I don't mind, honestly,' I say. 'It'll be fun.'

'Well, she can't wait – it's all she can talk about.'

'I hope it lives up to her expectations.'

'A private lesson with an award-winning artist?' He whistles. 'I'm sure she'll love every minute.'

I cringe as he says this. Why, oh, why did I ever pretend to be something I'm not? I feel like such a fraud – probably because that's exactly what I am.

Should I confess here and now? I do want to tell him the truth, but something is stopping me. It's so lovely moving slowly together to the music that I can't bear to spoil the moment. And baring my soul, revealing all, would definitely do that because something tells me that Edward wouldn't be impressed with my story.

'Was Polly sad she couldn't come tonight?' I ask, to change the subject.

'Not really. She thinks balls are naff,' he laughs. 'Besides, June has promised to make her hot chocolate as a treat.'

'They're very close, aren't they?' I ask, bumping against him as the floor becomes more crowded. If we get any closer together we'll need special equipment to prise us apart – it's not such an unappealing idea, not when, under my fingers, I can feel Edward's taut, lean back. The same back that I clung to when we were investigating the burglary at Rose Cottage. Who knew a back could be such a thing of beauty?

'Yes, they are. June is great with her. It's just that she can be a little . . .' Edward searches for the right word to describe his mother-in-law '. . . colder with everyone else.'

Ain't that the truth! June is a pussycat with her younger granddaughter – but she's a vicious tiger with everyone else. Should I tell him what she said to me at the gymkhana? That I should pack my bags and go back to the city? It's tempting, but what good would it do? June hates me, and snitching on her won't change that. I decide to keep quiet.

'By the way, I've spoken to Matilda about what she did,' he goes on. 'After tonight she's grounded for two weeks.'

'Ouch.' I wince. 'I'm guessing that didn't go down too well.' Two weeks is a long time in the life of a teenage girl – no wonder she was so quiet on the journey here.

'No, it didn't,' he admits, looking pained. 'But she knows

what she did was wrong. Making up that story about a mad man was way out of order. And then to call Jimmy as well . . .'

'She doesn't like me very much.' I state the obvious.

'It's not you, as such,' he says. 'I think she's just struggled since her mum died. It's been especially hard on her.'

'I can imagine,' I say. 'Losing your mother at such a difficult age must be terrible.' Suddenly I feel really guilty that Matilda will be grounded because of what she did.

I look to where she and Daniel are now slow-dancing nearby. Matilda looks like she's in seventh heaven, although her spotty boyfriend seems supremely bored. Should I tell Edward that I caught them together in the cottage? If I tell him will he forbid them to see each other? That might make it worse.

'I think it's been easier on Polly,' he says. 'She remembers her mum, but she was so young when she died, it didn't have quite the same impact.'

'She's such a character,' I say, thinking about Polly. 'She's fearless, isn't she?'

'Yes, I wish she wasn't, to be honest. Then she mightn't get into so much trouble. Or get *me* into so much trouble, I should say.'

'Nah, I think she's great just the way she is.' I giggle. 'Things never get boring with her around!'

Edward grins – I can see he's very proud of his little girl. 'She never stops talking, that's for sure,' he says.

'You got that right!'

'Matilda used to be just like her.' He sighs. 'She's clammed up completely since her mum died.'

'Teenage girls can be a mystery at the best of times,' I agree.

'What about you, Maggie? You're pretty mysterious yourself.'

'No, I'm not.' I blush.

'Yes, you are,' he teases. 'Tell me something, was coming here your idea?'

'Well, I did want to escape city life,' I murmur. 'I wanted a break.' And I had no job and nowhere to live, my inner voice adds.

'But it was Claire who persuaded you that coming here was the right choice to make?'

'More or less,' I admit.

'I thought as much. You hated it at first, didn't you?' he probes.

'Hate is a very strong word,' I say. 'It was just all so different from what I was used to, I suppose.'

'And how do you feel about it now?' he says. 'Are you just biding your time until you can leave?'

Something in his tone makes me look up. He's gazing at me, his eyes searching my face.

'No, I like it here,' I reply, my voice suddenly hoarse. It's true. I do like it. I like it an awful lot.

'Good,' he whispers, his grip tightening around my waist. 'Because I'm finding it hard to remember what it was like before you came.'

We stare at each other, and I swallow. What does that mean? Am I imagining it or is an electric current fizzing between us?

'OK, everyone, now we're going to speed things up a bit!' the lead singer bellows into his mic, and the spell between us is broken as the band begins to rock out to a much faster song. Instantly I feel like an awkward teenager when the slow set ends at the youth-club disco. I have no idea what to do or say. If I could rush outside and smoke an illicit ciggie with a pack of my giggly girlfriends I probably would.

'Would you like a drink?' Edward's hand drops from my waist and he steps back from me.

'Sure,' I reply, my head spinning. I'm not a silly teenager, I'm an adult, and I have to try to remember to act like one. 'I'll just go and powder my nose.'

'Powder my nose'? Where did that come from? Where do I think I am – in some sort of Victorian drama? I stumble away from him, embarrassed to have said something so stupid and trying to think straight. Did I dream the way he looked at me or misinterpret the meaning in his words? I must have. It was only a friendly dance, nothing more. There can't have been electricity between us. Maybe the beef *was* bad, like Peg said. That must be why my tummy is now filled with jiving butterflies.

'Enjoy that little rendezvous, did you?' Odette is at my side before I reach the Ladies.

'It was only a dance, Odette,' I say, tempted to turn and run. 'Completely innocent.'

'I hope so, Maggie,' she says icily. 'It's taken Edward a long time to get over his wife and move on. But now he has – and he's moving on with me. Understand?'

'Yes, I understand perfectly.' I look into Odette's eyes and they gleam back at me, the message crystal clear.

'Good. Then we all know where we stand.' She marches away, her chiffon dress swishing behind her. It seems to whisper menacingly as she moves: 'Keep away, keep away.'

Rule Twenty: *Fake it till you make it*

'Have you seen this?' Peg shoves a newspaper at me.

I lean across the shop counter to get a better look. 'Super-market Chain Promises Twenty New Jobs!' screams the headline.

'Can you believe it?' Ted says, his face creased with indigna-tion. 'They'll stop at nothing to get what they want.'

I quickly scan the article to get the general gist of the thing. It looks like the new supermarket is on a serious PR campaign to garner support in the village. Someone has leaked the news that the development will bring at least twenty jobs to the area – possibly more. And the supermarket says it won't employ any outsiders, not even in the management positions. They want locals to fill the jobs. The paper says the top brass wants the store to be 'part of the community' and having locals working on the shop floor is their 'top priority'. It's a smart move, and obviously intended to get the villagers on-side.

'I suppose it *would* provide new jobs for the village,' I say doubtfully, not knowing how they're going to take this opin-ion. Anytime anyone has suggested that the locality could do with the jobs, Peg and Ted have pooh-poohed the idea.

'Bah!' Peg huffs. 'No one here would take a job with those – those monsters. We'd rather die.'

'That's right!' Ted agrees.

'Ted said he'd lie down in front of a bulldozer first, didn't you, Ted?' Peg looks very determined. 'He has a rebel heart, even if his cholesterol is sky high. Glacken could be put on the map for it – just like Tiananmen Square!'

Ted looks a little nervous at this – I'm guessing that Peg might expect him to follow through on his promise if push came to shove.

'They're hardly monsters, though, are they?' I suggest carefully. 'I mean, business is business and all that. And it does say here that they want to be part of the community – that could be a genuine sentiment.'

'How can you say that, Maggie?' Peg looks mortally offended. 'I thought you knew where we were coming from, what we *stood* for. If that supermarket moves to the village it will destroy everything! It's not about cheap tomatoes that have been imported from Spain – this is about a way of life. I thought you understood that. You of all people. We can't back down at the first hurdle. That would mean we had no moral compass.'

Peg makes to take the newspaper from me, tears glittering in her eyes. This has all gone wrong. I never meant to upset her or Ted, just point out that some people in the village may welcome new job opportunities, which are pretty few and far between, these days – I should know. I don't want to offend either of them – I'm actually really fond of them both, something I've recently come to realize.

'I'm sorry, Peg,' I backtrack. 'Of course I know what this means to you all. I was just trying to be objective.'

'We don't want people to go without jobs, Maggie,' Ted says, looking wounded. 'We're not that insensitive.'

Then he reaches for another Mars Bar and tears off the wrapper. That won't do anything for his cholesterol problem: if he has a heart-attack here and now it'll be my fault. I desperately try to remember any of the first aid I learned in Girl Guides as I watch him munch, but my mind is a complete and utter blank. If Ted collapses and goes into cardiac arrest right in front of me I won't be able to do a thing to stop it – and I can't help feeling it'll serve me right for being so thoughtless.

Peg looks at Ted, then back at me, as if I have totally betrayed her trust and, to make matters worse, I have hounded her beloved husband to his certain artery-clogged death-by-chocolate.

'I really didn't mean to upset you, Peg,' I try. 'I said the wrong thing, I'm sorry.'

She shoots me another injured look. God, she's really good at this. I feel awful, like a traitor.

'Tell you what, why don't we convene another meeting?' I blurt. The words are out of my mouth before I know it. I have no idea why I just suggested that – especially because getting myself more embroiled in village politics is the last thing I want to do. But seeing Peg tearful and distressed has really got to me and I have to do something to make her feel better. I can't take the accusatory looks any more.

'Why would you do that?' She eyes me suspiciously.

Simply expressing my doubts about the supermarket has made her wary of me. Still, this is progress. At least she's talking again. 'Because I want to help. Honestly I do. If we have another meeting we can talk it through and try to come up with something to combat this – this . . .' I search for the right words to express myself '. . . PR exercise.'

'What do you know about PR?' she says cautiously. But there's a definite glint of interest.

'Loads,' I gush, eager to impress them both. 'I used to manage all the PR campaigns in the office.'

This is true. We never hired a PR agency at Hanly's. It was up to Dom and me to come up with campaigns to help sell the properties we had on the books and we were pretty good at it. We started off sending pens to journalists and progressed to organizing champagne lunches to schmooze the media whenever a new development came on to the market. Dermot was never too comfortable with those lunches – he always thought that developments should speak for themselves. I wonder how he is and whether Yvonne, his gold-digging wife, has upped and left him now that she knows the truth. If she knows the truth. From the way Dermot was talking before I left, he was going to hide the dire financial situation from her for as long as possible.

'What office?' Peg stares at me blankly and I suddenly remember that she thinks I'm a full-time artist, not an unemployed estate agent. I can't confess now. If I do, then she'll never trust me again.

'I mean the office in the gallery,' I say quickly, thinking on my feet. 'When I had my exhibitions we had to invite press, whip up a bit of media interest, that sort of thing.'

'Oh, right.' Peg's eyes light up. 'What sort of things did you do?'

'Well, we sent them gifts.' I grab at straws.

'Gifts?' Ted echoes.

'Yes – you know, to butter them up. Make sure we got a mention in the press.'

'You gave them stuff to get in the paper?'

'Sometimes. Everyone does it. It's common practice – journalists expect to get goodie-bags, it's part of the PR thing. Like a perk of the job.'

I'm anxious she understands that I wasn't doing anything wrong – that would make things even worse.

'Goodie-bags?' Peg says. 'Like actors get at the Oscars? I've read about that in *Hello!*. They get all sorts in them, don't they? Like diamonds. Celebs love their diamonds.'

'Well, yes. We didn't do anything as fancy as the Oscars obviously – we couldn't afford to give out diamonds, that's for sure!'

I laugh to break the tension, but Peg doesn't join in. She's busy, lost in thought.

'I get you.' Ted is intrigued. 'You give them stuff, they give you good press.'

'Something like that – you scratch their back, they scratch yours. I'm not saying we have to do that in this case, of course.'

'Say no more. We understand *exactly* what you're getting at,' Peg says, 'don't we, Ted?'

'I think we do, my love, I think we do. Leave it with us, Maggie – we'll round up the troops. I'll text you with the details, OK?' Ted is delighted.

'OK,' I say.

'In fact, I'll send a group text to everyone, let them know what's happening. I can do it on-line.'

'You can?' How does he know how to do that?

'Yes, of course.'

'You should tweet about it too, Ted,' Peg says.

'You're right, my love, I'll update my Twitter account with the details – good idea. Do you use it yourself, Maggie?'

'What? The Internet?'

'No, Twitter.' He looks at me eagerly.

'Twitter? No, I don't.'

'Ah, you should!' Peg chimes in. 'It's a great yoke for keeping in touch. Isn't it, Ted?'

'It is. You can let everyone know what you're up to.'

'Of course, some people, naming no names, use it for their own self-promotion purposes.' Peg's mouth tightens.

'Betty from the butcher's,' Ted explains. 'She updates her account far too much.'

'She does!' Peg confirms. 'I mean, do we all need to know about some stupid sausage-roll competition she won? No, we do not.'

'Twitter shouldn't be used to blow your own trumpet,' Ted says.

'You're right, Ted. It's not that sort of medium. Now

Facebook – that's what she should be using, much more up her street. Jimmy likes his Facebook, too, doesn't he, Ted?'

'He does. Jimmy loves Facebook,' Ted agrees.

'Jimmy? The guard?'

'Yes. That's how he found those dogs of his – the ones he rescued. One of his Facebook friends tipped him off.'

'Right.'

'Nice fella, Jimmy.'

'He is,' Peg agrees. 'Sound as a pound.'

There's a pause. An undeniably pregnant pause.

'Of course, you have to be very careful what you say to him, like.'

'You do?' Crap. What did I say to him that night in Rose Cottage?

'Ah, yeah, you do.'

'Jimmy likes to take notes – keep records. It's the promotion thing, you see.'

'The promotion?'

'Yes, the inspector likes the note-taking, and Jimmy reckons if he does it enough he'll be promoted.' Ted nods.

'It's why he walks those greyhounds at the crack of dawn too. He likes to see what people are up to early in the morning,' Peg explains.

'You mean he spies on people?'

'Well, it's not spying exactly,' Peg says.

Really? That's what it sounds like to me. No wonder he was so eager to write down everything I said that night.

'No, not spying,' Ted agrees. 'More keeping an eye on things.'

'That's how Betty was caught, isn't it, Ted?' Peg's face lights up at the memory.

'It is! Getting dodgy meat deliveries she was – she wasn't meeting health regulations. Jimmy had the whole thing written down. The health inspectors were very interested in his notes. *Very* interested.'

'She's lucky she's still in business.' Peg smirks.

'She is,' Ted agrees.

This is surreal. Absolutely surreal.

'No wonder we couldn't find you on-line so, Maggie,' Ted says. 'You're a bit of a technological dinosaur.'

'Um, yes, I guess I am,' I say. They were looking for me on-line? Oh, no. I never thought about that.

'Yes, there was only one other Maggie Baxter on there – some estate agent in the city,' Ted says. 'Isn't that funny? Your namesake is an estate agent, imagine that!'

'But of course you use a pseudonym to paint, don't you, Maggie?' Peg says. 'That's why we couldn't find you.'

'Um, yes, I do,' I say. I'm holding my breath.

This is it: the game is up. It's all over. Any second now, they're going to ask me what that pseudonym is. I brace myself, but the question never comes. They're too distracted by the idea of another meeting, which they're now discussing passionately. 'I'd better get on,' I say eventually.

'Yes, of course. Why don't you leave your list here and we'll drop the groceries up to the cottage for you?' Peg smiles.

'You do home delivery?'

'Of course!' She giggles. 'This is the twenty-first century, Maggie – we don't live in prehistoric times. You can email us your list next time, if you like. Lots of people do.'

'I don't have Internet access,' I say, gobsmacked. A tiny village shop, with dusty tins of Spam on its shelves, accepts email orders?

'No Internet access?' Ted is aghast. 'How can you live without email? That's very unreasonable – you'll have to speak to Edward about it.'

'You will,' Peg says solemnly. 'He can't expect you to live

241

without the web – sure how would you watch the new *Desperate Housewives* otherwise?'

'You'd be forever waiting to see it on the telly,' Ted agrees. 'It's so much easier to stream it on-line, isn't it?'

I stagger back into the street, as if I'm emerging from some sort of time-travelling vortex, my head spinning. Facebook? Twitter? Web streaming? What's going on? I would have confidently bet my life that Peg and Ted had never even *heard* of the Internet, let alone be so *au fait* with it. They defy my expectations on so many levels, it's mind-boggling.

I'm wandering back towards my car when I spot Odette approaching in the distance, her pastel twinset rippling under the midday sun. She's the last person on earth I want to meet. Well, maybe not the last person – I wouldn't exactly like to run into Robert either. But running into my ex is hardly likely here.

Looking wildly to right and left, I search desperately for somewhere to hide. My car is too far away – I'll never make it there in time. Should I do a *Starsky and Hutch* roll under the abandoned Massey Ferguson with the missing wheel? Or go back into the Village Store? Doing the roll is the more attractive option: I may get killed but at least I won't have to explain myself to Peg and Ted.

I'm just getting ready to launch myself under the tractor when I spot the gate to the churchyard. Of course! I'll hide in there – there'll be no chance of Odette seeing me then. Ducking through the shabby little gate, I walk quickly down a gravel path and find myself in a small graveyard. I'm just about to hide behind a headstone when I see Edward sitting by a grave, deep in thought, his head bowed. I stop stock still at the unexpected sight of him. Of course: this must be where June is buried. He's paying his respects to his dead wife and I've just walked in on a very private moment.

242

I try to figure out what to do. Should I call out, let him know I've seen him? Or should I get the hell out of here before he spots me?

I'm frozen by indecision when he turns his head a fraction and I see his face. God, he looks absolutely devastated – he's ghostly white and raw grief is etched on his features. There's no way I want him to know I've seen him. I have to get out of here, fast.

Holding my breath, I start to tiptoe backwards, praying he doesn't see me inching my way out. This is obviously an intensely painful moment for him and I don't want him to think I'm spying, or being disrespectful. Crunching backwards across the gravel, I anxiously keep my eyes fixed on his face, willing him not to hear me. But I needn't worry – he doesn't notice a thing: he's so preoccupied he may as well be on another planet. As I watch, he lays a bouquet of red roses on the grave. Then he says something – I can't be sure what, but it sounds like a muffled 'I love you.'

Far from being over her, like Odette said, Edward is clearly still very much in love with his dead wife. Of course he is – it makes sense. People don't just forget their wives, especially when they were as wonderful as everyone says June was. Edward is obviously still pining for her. It's only natural he still loves and misses her – you can't forget someone you've shared your life with. Someone you've had two children with. He will probably love and miss her for the rest of his life. No one will ever really fill the void she left when she died – not for him, or Matilda and Polly. Not Odette, not anyone.

I shake my head to clear it – why am I even thinking about this? It's not like it has anything to do with me. But seeing Edward looking so lost and vulnerable has brought home to me the enormity of the situation. He's still a grieving widower and there won't be another woman in his life for a long time.

Not properly. This realization hits me like a tidal wave and I feel physically winded. What's wrong with me? Why do I feel so rattled? Why has seeing Edward like that unsettled me so much? And what is this strange feeling I can't seem to shake?

Stumbling from the graveyard, my mind reeling, I try to make sense of it all. Why am I so affected by a man I couldn't care less about?

Rule Twenty-one: *Two heads are better than one*

'Can I have an espresso, please?'

I've slipped into Matty's pub to catch my breath. Seeing Edward in the graveyard has flustered me, although I'm still not sure why.

Matty has a really good coffee menu – it's a pity I didn't stick to it the night I polished off all the rare red wine and the cocktails and made a total drunken fool of myself. He even has my favourite brand of espresso – the one that's so difficult to find in town.

'No problem, Maggie.' Matty smiles at me. 'Why don't you take a seat and I'll drop it over to you? The one by the window is nice and sunny.'

I murmur my thanks, pleasantly surprised that Matty remembers my name – it's really nice to have someone know who you are. In the city everyone is so anonymous. I've been getting my espresso in the same Coast Coffee for two years now and the staff still don't recognize me or remember what I like to order. I've always wanted to swan into a place and say, 'I'll have my usual, please!' You'd get laughed at for saying something like that in the city, but here you can get away with it. If I lived here permanently, this would be my local. I don't have a local in town, just a series of bars and nightclubs full of strangers.

This pub is different: it's so full of character. The worn old pine floorboards are a mellowed ochre colour and the light streaming through the stained-glass windows dapples beautifully on the pale cream walls. There are delightful watercolours dotted around in groups of two or three, adding some interest to the simple scheme. They look like originals of local scenes – I recognize the village church, the pretty bridge and even Peg and Ted's shop front.

I settle into my seat and lean back, closing my eyes almost involuntarily, enjoying the warmth of the sun on my face. Matty was right – this is a lovely, sunny spot. It really is very restful in here.

'It looks like you need this,' a man's voice says, just as I'm drifting off, and I jolt upright. It's Edward, holding a coffee cup.

For a second I think I must be asleep. It can't be him – he isn't really standing in front of me. I'm just dreaming. Then I come to and realize it's not a hallucination – Edward is right here. 'Oh,' I redden, 'I wasn't asleep, I was just . . .'

'Resting your eyes?'

'Exactly.' I smooth my hair behind my ears and try to stop blushing. What's he doing here? And why is my heart suddenly hammering in my chest?

'Matty asked me to give you your espresso.'

I take the cup from him and gulp the hot liquid, scalding the back of my throat. I can't believe I was almost asleep in a pub in the middle of the day. Edward must think I'm a complete idiot. And, God, his eyes are so blue – and the way they twinkle when he smiles . . . I take another gulp of my coffee. Why am I thinking like this? What's wrong with me today?

'It's nice in here,' I mumble, for something to say.

'Yes, it's a good spot to get away from the madding crowd,' Edward replies, shoving his hands into his pockets.

We both glance out of the window, where a solitary person wanders up the street.

'Hardly the madding crowd.' I raise an eyebrow at him.

'Well, the *maddening* crowd, then.' He laughs. 'I was going to have a coffee myself. Would you mind if I join you or would you prefer to be alone?'

I hesitate. For some reason, I feel stupidly pleased that he's suggested joining me but I can't pinpoint why. It's definitely a bad idea: Odette wouldn't like us to be having a drink together – she made it perfectly clear she doesn't want me spending any time at all with Edward. Then again, it's not like we're doing anything wrong: a landlord and his tenant having a coffee is a completely innocent scenario.

Besides, even if Edward wasn't seeing Odette, which he is, he still has the ghost of his dead wife in his life – very much in his life if his display in the graveyard was anything to go by. There's absolutely nothing between us. Not that I want there to be.

All these thoughts race through my mind as Edward stands before me, waiting to hear my verdict. Why am I making such a big deal of it? If I don't answer him soon, he'll think I'm a proper weirdo. It's not like he's just asked me to marry him! God, what made me make that comparison? *What* is *wrong* with me today?

'Sure.' I shrug, trying to sound casual. I need to hang on to some shred of self-respect – he did find me practically snoring in broad daylight after all.

'Great,' he says. 'I could do with a caffeine shot – Matty does the best coffee, don't you think?'

I nod: it's wonderful – miles better than anything I've ever had in Coast Coffee, that's for sure.

Pulling up a stool to the table, he calls across to Matty for another espresso. 'So, I hear there's going to be another meeting about the supermarket.'

'Bloody hell, word travels fast here!' I gasp. 'How did you know that?'

'Ted texted me. He and Peg are pretty excited about your PR campaign.'

'What PR campaign is that?' I ask, my hammering heart now sinking to my toes. This doesn't sound good.

'Apparently they're going to start a PR campaign to get the press onside. Peg's already planning the goodie-bags. She's pretty sure her prize-winning organic tomatoes will impress the journalists.'

I feel faint. 'Goodie-bags?'

'Yes, you know, "like at the Oscars",' he says seriously, repeating what Peg said earlier, word for word.

'I didn't say anything about goodie-bags,' I protest. 'Well, I may have mentioned them, but only as an example of the things PRs do sometimes. I didn't mean we need to do the same . . .'

He must think I'm on drugs – making up press goodie-bags with organic tomatoes is an insane idea.

'That's funny.' He looks puzzled. 'Ted definitely said something about goodie-bags. He was talking about putting cabbages in there too.'

'Cabbages?' He can't be serious.

'Yes. And turnips. Although I tried to put him off those – turnips aren't everyone's cup of tea.' His eyes dance and suddenly I know he's teasing me again.

'You're joking.'

'Well, I am about the cabbages and turnips, yes, but Peg *is* very keen about the organic tomatoes.'

Oh, crap. Peg really thinks that giving journalists soggy tomatoes will make a difference to the supermarket outcome. And that's my fault. I never should have mentioned those damn goodie-bags in the first place.

'Peg has a heart of gold,' Edward says, evidently seeing the horror on my face, 'but she can get a little carried away sometimes. We'll talk her out of it, don't worry.'

'What do you mean?'

'Well,' he stirs the coffee that Matty has carefully placed in front of him, 'she feels very strongly about the supermarket so it stands to reason she's fairly emotional about it. She's grasping at straws.'

'The goodie-bags?'

'Exactly. She wants to stop the development, but to her, it's more than just about corporate greed or the loss of village life. It's about family.'

'Family?'

'Yes. The shop that she and Ted run has been in Peg's family for generations. She feels a huge responsibility to keep it going.'

'But businesses fold all the time,' I say. 'It won't be her fault if she can't stop the supermarket. The Xanta Group is very powerful – they have hundreds of stores all over Europe already.'

'You're right,' he agrees. 'It won't be her fault. But Peg won't see it that way. She'll blame herself for destroying her father's legacy. That's the way she views it. Her whole world is tied up in that little shop, and if she has to close it, she feels she'll lose part of her own identity. And because she and Ted have no children, this means everything to her. Do you see what I mean?'

I'm beginning to understand Peg's passion for stopping the supermarket. It's not just about money or keeping her little village shop profitable, it's about her past.

'That's why she resisted the estate agents for so long too,' Edward adds. 'She wouldn't sell out, no matter what they offered her.' The tone of his voice has changed and his twinkling eyes are now like flint.

'Estate agents?' I repeat. Why does he look so irate suddenly?

'Yes, they came sniffing round the village, saying they had

a cash buyer for the shop. Xanta was behind it, of course. Peg and Ted weren't the only ones approached.'

'The supermarket group wanted to buy up property in the village?' This is a common enough ploy – corporations often try to buy out dissenters in order to push a planning application through.

'Yeah, but it didn't work.' Edward's face twists. 'Peg and Ted wouldn't play ball. That's been the one good thing about the property crash. Finally those good-for-nothing crooks are getting their comeuppance.'

'What do you mean?' I squeak, suddenly very nervous. Why does he sound so bitter?

'All those low-life scumbags are the same – selfish, greedy criminals, only out for their own good.' His voice is shaking with anger.

'You're not a fan of estate agents, I take it?' I ask, my hand suddenly trembling. I put down my coffee cup so he won't notice.

'I hope they all rot in hell.'

'What's wrong with them?' I ask numbly. Why do I feel so sick? So what if he hates estate agents? Why should I take it personally or even care? It's nothing to do with me.

'I'm sorry, Maggie, you must think I'm insane,' he says now, his expression wretched.

'No, not at all,' I reply, my insides churning.

He looks at his hands, as if trying to decide whether to continue. 'The morning that my wife was killed, we had an argument about the manor house,' he says quietly. 'She'd had an estate agent over to value the place and he'd given her the hard sell – said we'd make millions if we put it on the market, that sort of thing.'

'I see.' That sounds familiar. 'But you didn't want to sell?'

'No, I didn't. And neither did her mother. We both thought

it was important to try to hold on to the house if we could. It's the children's heritage – it's up to us to safeguard it for them.'

'But your wife didn't feel the same?'

'No,' Edward says, his voice bleak. 'Even though she grew up here, she always wanted to escape. She wanted a different kind of life – one where she didn't have to work so hard all the time. Maybe she was right. I could be passing on a mill-stone for the kids.'

'Country living certainly isn't easy,' I say. I've never worked so hard in my life, that's for sure.

'You're right. Matilda will probably leave Glacken the minute she turns eighteen. She already hates it here. Sometimes I think she blames me for what happened.'

'How could she?' I ask, shocked. 'It was an accident.'

'You haven't heard the whole story yet,' he says, his face pale. 'After the estate agent's visit, we had a dreadful argument. June felt we should take the money and run. I disagreed and she took off into Glacken Woods on Drya and . . . well, I'm sure you heard what happened then.'

'Sort of,' I mumble.

'We never should have argued, of course, I blame myself for that, but if the estate agent hadn't come, then . . .'

The rest hangs in the air, but the meaning is clear: he blames a greedy estate agent for the death of his wife.

'Anyway,' Edward shakes his head as if to clear it, 'enough about that. Let's change the subject. How do you think the supermarket thing is going to pan out?'

I take another sip of coffee to try to steady myself. Edward hates estate agents. What would he say if he knew I'd been one? 'Well,' I start, 'if I'm brutally honest, I think that Peg and Ted don't have a rat's chance of stopping a huge conglomerate like Xanta. The supermarket will be pushed through. It's just a question of when.' There – I've admitted it. It might be the first truthful thing I've said since I came here.

'You're probably right,' Edward says, nodding. 'But if the development is going to happen anyway, there must be a way to use it to our advantage – don't you think so?'

'How's that?'

'Well, maybe we can make it work for us in some way.'

'Go on.'

I crunch into one of the oatmeal cookies that Matty placed on the saucer. It's delicious. I make a mental note to ask him which brand they are. It's the perfect blend of crunchy and chewy, not too sweet, not too salty.

'OK, let's think this through rationally.' Edward leans forward, placing both elbows on the table as he does so. The scent of horse wafts across to me. For once it doesn't smell that bad, in fact it smells almost . . . inviting. That can't be right.

'If this cheap supermarket opens on the outskirts of the village, people will travel to it,' he says.

'Definitely.' I'm trying to concentrate on what he's saying, not the way his lips move when he speaks. 'Those supermarkets are really popular. People want value, especially now.'

'But even if people *do* travel to the supermarket, that doesn't mean they'll come into the village itself,' he goes on.

'Agreed.'

'So, the village won't necessarily benefit from the development.'

'Exactly,' I say. 'In fact, it could make things even worse – just like Peg thinks it will. There would be no passing trade any more.'

'Right.'

'So, what do you propose?' I'm really curious now.

'I think we need a regeneration plan for the village, one that can improve our profile and encourage people to visit. We need a unique selling point.'

'A USP.'

'A USP. Right.' He smiles at me.

'And what do you think this USP is?' I smile back. It's impossible not to – his enthusiasm is infectious. And his eyes – a person could melt into them.

'I think we should try to market the village as an area of cultural significance. That's our USP. What do you think?'

Cultural significance? This place? Is he joking? 'Well, Glacken isn't exactly a cultural hotspot,' I say.

'Not now – but we could develop it. Make it a destination of choice for artists round the country, maybe even the world. We'll need buy-in from Xanta, of course, get them to fund some sort of cultural-development plan on the back of the supermarket. They won't refuse if we agree not to oppose the build.'

'They scratch our back, we scratch theirs?'

'Something like that, yes.'

It's a very interesting idea – he's right. If we could tie Xanta into providing funding, the village could benefit from a new lease of life. There are snags, though. Has he thought it all through? 'But why do you think artists would be interested in coming here?' I ask.

'You tell me.'

'Eh?' I look at him blankly.

'You're an artist, right? Why did you come here?'

'Well,' I bluster, 'that's different. I'm only here till Claire gets back.'

'Yes, but you like it so far?'

'It's not too bad, I suppose.' I lower my eyes. The way he's looking at me is making me feel very strange.

'And you've been inspired to work since you've been here?'

'Work?'

'Yes. On your commissions?'

I raise my head to see he's looking straight at me. Crap. 'Um, yes.'

'You've found the village inspiring?'

'I guess so.'

'So, it stands to reason that if you do, others would too. If Xanta agrees to provide the funding we could have an artists' retreat – Glacken could become a real craft village destination.'

'A craft village destination?'

'Yes!' His face is alight with enthusiasm. 'There could be a gallery, maybe even workshops for craftspeople of all persuasions. All we need is some investment – and Xanta can provide that. It's the cash cow.'

'But, Edward, I think there's something you're forgetting.'

'What's that?' His blue eyes stare at me in puzzlement.

'Peg and Ted. They'll never agree to it. They want to stop the supermarket at all costs. This plan would devastate them.'

'You're right.' His face falls in disappointment. 'They'll probably hate the idea.'

'Maybe I'm wrong,' I backtrack. 'They might change their minds. You could bring it up at the meeting – see what they think.'

He looks so devastated that I'm suddenly desperate to find a way to make the plan work.

'Me?' He laughs, his tone hollow.

'The idea is really good,' I protest.

'Maggie, I'm a farmer. I know about horses and land, not the arts.'

'Anyone can have an opinion about the arts, surely.'

'That may be true,' he smiles ruefully, 'but who am I to plan a cultural regeneration? What would I know about culture?

Here I am, covered with horse hair, trying to convert people to art. It's a bit of a joke. I'm sorry for wasting your time.'

He drains his coffee cup and gets up to go, but something in his face makes me speak. 'Hang on, Edward, don't be so hard on yourself,' I say.

'What do you mean?' He stuffs his hands into his pockets like before. Like an embarrassed teenage boy.

'Trying to promote art and culture isn't pointless. It's a very worthwhile idea.' What would you know about it? a little voice inside me hisses, but I try to ignore it.

He looks down. Now that the heat of the moment has passed, when he somehow felt he could express his thoughts freely, he seems really unsure of himself. 'You would say that,' he says, almost shyly. 'It *is* your bread and butter – you *are* an artist, after all.'

If only he knew how far off the mark he was. I currently make no bread and butter at all, let alone by anything to do with art. 'Well, let's think about it some more,' I suggest, sounding uncannily as if I know what I'm talking about. 'Don't discount it yet. Maybe there's a way we can sell it to Peg and Ted so that it doesn't seem like a personal attack.'

I think I see a flicker of hope cross his face.

'Maybe you're right,' he smiles slowly, 'maybe there could be some way . . .'

'So we'll think about it?' I ask.

'Yes, let's do that.'

He offers me his hand to help me up and I take it, hoping he's strong enough to pull me from my seat. The one and only time Robert ever tried to lift me – when I fell and twisted my ankle in Crete – he did in his back. He had to have a painkiller shot and I felt like a prize heifer for months afterwards. It would be utterly mortifying if the same thing happened with Edward. But, mercifully, he lifts me upwards as if I were as light as a feather and I grin at him, suddenly feeling I could float on air.

Our eyes lock and then it hits me. *Now* I know why I felt so weird when I saw him in the graveyard. It all clicks into place. Inappropriate and twisted as it is, I was jealous. Jealous of his dead wife. Jealous when I saw how much he misses her. How much he must have loved her. Because the truth is, Polly is right: I 'like-like' this man. A man who has a dead wife I can never live up to, a girlfriend who will kill me if she knows how I feel, a mother-in-law who thinks I'm the hired help and a daughter who hates me.

I can barely believe it, but there's no denying it any more – I'm drawn to Edward in a way I've never been drawn to anyone before. But it couldn't work. I mean, besides all the complications in his life, he's just told me he hates estate agents. He thinks I'm an artist – he has no idea that I've been spinning a web of deceit since I got here. And if he ever found out . . . Well, who knows what would happen?

'So . . . see you at the stables,' I mutter, before I let go his hand and bolt for the door.

I have to escape. I have to get out of here. I can't look him in the eye any more because if I do I have a horrible feeling he'll know the truth – that everything I've ever told him has been a lie.

Rule Twenty-two: *There's nothing to fear but fear itself*

'Like this?'

Polly squeezes some paint on to the tray in front of her, watching with glee as a worm of yellow spurts out.

'That's perfect,' I say. 'Not too much, not too little, just the right amount.'

She beams at me and my heart lifts – she's such a funny little thing.

'I'm not going to use any pink,' she announces grimly. 'Pink is *naff*!'

'OK.'

Polly rarely does what you'd expect of a six-year-old girl. She's what Theresa would call 'unusual in her tastes'. One of her twins is exactly the same – Max refuses to watch *Bob the Builder* like his brother. Instead, he insists on watching *Come Dine With Me* while he has his bottle every night before bedtime. He gets very excited if *fruits de mer* is included on the menu, even though the closest he's ever come to tasting seafood has been mashed-up sardines.

Theresa was quite worried about it at first: would he be picked on by other kids? Would he ever find a soul-mate who understood his TV tastes? Would he be marginalized by society at large? But she says she's made her peace with it now. In fact, she's decided to be actively optimistic about the situation. Being actively optimistic is one of Theresa's new life rules. She says it's a very handy approach to take to things because it can be used in almost every type of daily situation. Say, for example, the toast burns in the morning: this just means that she will eat fewer carbs that day. If one of the twins throws up on her head, as they often do, her hair may soak up vital nutrients from the carrot purée they had for lunch and be extra shiny. Every scenario has an up-side.

She's decided to believe that Max's unusual love for bad telly at such an early age means he'll turn into a celebrity chef with his own TV series, and when that happens, she intends to be 100 per cent supportive. She may also be an executive producer, because that's where the big bucks are.

Of course, Malcolm isn't at all pleased. He wants both boys to be accountants and studiously ignore all their creative impulses, like he did. They've already had some serious arguments about it – Theresa says that trying to stifle Max's tastes by playing *Bob the Builder* on a loop is an assault on his civil rights.

There's no way anyone could stifle Polly. She has campaigned very hard to get me here, and now that I am, it looks like she's determined to thoroughly enjoy herself, pink or no pink. We're in the kitchen of the main house, a selection of paints on the table before us and our easels ready. Edward said this might be the perfect place to have our painting session: the floors are tiled and it really won't matter if we make a mess, which is pretty much guaranteed. Polly is wearing a washable polyester apron, just in case. I was really nervous in case I met June again – but I didn't mention that little detail to Edward when he suggested this venue: it seemed childish to do so. Thankfully, there's been no sign of her – it was the charming Matilda who let me in earlier, with a sulky scowl and a bare hello, but I haven't seen either of them since. I know June must be around somewhere, though – I suspect she'd never let me be alone with Polly if she had her way.

'What will I paint, Maggie?' A look of concern crosses Polly's face, making her round cheeks sag a fraction and her smooth forehead crease.

'What do you feel like painting?'

Her brow furrows in concentration. 'I'd like to paint Saffy eating a carrot,' she says finally.

'That's a great idea.' Saffy is never far from Polly's mind. 'Then just go ahead and do that.'

'Are you sure?' She still looks worried. 'What if I get it wrong?'

'You can't get it wrong, Polly,' I say. 'There's no such thing.'

'Really?' Her face brightens immediately.

'Yes, really. All art is subjective.'

'What does "subjective" mean?'

'It means that beauty is in the eye of the beholder and if *you* like it then that's all that matters.'

Happy with this explanation, she dips her brush into her paint and gets to work, splashing the colours on to the page with generous strokes. Within seconds the paper is sodden, a wonderful mess of rainbow hues, and she is singing happily.

'Aren't *you* going to paint?' she stops suddenly to ask me, cocking her head to one side.

'Yes, of course,' I bluff. 'I'm just waiting for inspiration.'

'What does that mean?'

'It means that, unlike you, who have so many great ideas,' I explain, 'it takes me longer to come up with anything worthwhile.'

Thank God Edward is out on the farm somewhere – I'd die if I had to do this in front of him. Ever since I realized how I feel about him I've been keeping out of his way – it seems the safest option somehow.

'You should paint those flowers.' Polly points to a jug of gladioli on the scrubbed-pine table.

She's right – the colours are wonderful and the chipped old vase has great character. The composition could make a wonderful picture. 'Do you think so?' I ask.

'Yeah. It'd be cool!'

She dips her brush into her paint again and attacks her paper with passion and I stifle a giggle. I don't want her to think I'm laughing at her but her enthusiasm is so joyful. It's infectious.

Taking a deep breath, I try to relax and clear my mind of the inner voice that's telling me I can't possibly do this. Instead I try to remember the bolt of inspiration that hit me when I thought a burglar was about to kill me. As my life flashed before my eyes, my one big regret was not painting. I have to learn something from that. All I have to do is give myself permission to let go – that's what Claire, and probably Theresa, would say.

Taking a deep breath, I look at the flowers, drinking in their shape and form, and then I slowly begin to paint. The feel of the brush on the paper is wonderful and, within minutes, I'm lost in the act of simply sliding it back and forth across the page. The rhythm is so calming that soon it's silenced all my inner critics. I'd forgotten how much I love this feeling of complete absorption in the moment. Why ever did I stop painting? It's so soothing, so relaxing. It's taken me so long to get back to this place, this place where the world stands still and it's just you and the paint – it feels amazing.

'Wow!' Someone whistles. 'That's great!'

I whirl to see Edward standing behind me, staring intently at my picture, his arms crossed. Oh, no. I never meant anyone to see this – especially not him. Why's he here anyway? He's supposed to be out doing farm stuff – whatever that might be. Instead he's no more than two feet away from me. And he looks so . . . gorgeous. Mud-spattered and smelly as always, but still . . . gorgeous. God, I really am in trouble.

'Please don't look,' I mutter, staring at the ground to hide my embarrassment. 'It's not very good.'

'It's great!' Edward enthuses. 'You've captured the scene

perfectly – the way the sunlight reflects off the petals. It's fantastic!'

'No, it was only a scribble, really,' I protest. 'Please don't even look at it. It's nothing.'

'But, Maggie,' he says, eyes wide, 'it's *really* good. You're very talented. To make such a wonderful picture from such a simple scene – that's amazing.'

'Well . . . thanks,' I say shyly, torn between being utterly mortified and feeling a little proud. I still don't think it's much good – but he seems to, which is very gratifying.

'Is *mine* good, Daddy?' Polly is hopping excitedly before him, her face aglow.

'Let me take a look,' he says seriously, pretending he'll have to consider her work properly. 'I'll have to see. Hmm . . .'

Polly watches anxiously as her father studies her wild *mélange* of colours at length, waiting impatiently for his verdict.

'I have to say . . .'

'Yes? Yes?' She can barely contain her excitement.

'I have to say . . .'

'Hurry up, Dad!'

'I have to say . . . it's the most brilliant picture I've ever seen.'

'Really?' She dances delightedly before him.

'Yes, really. What do you think, Maggie?' he asks solemnly.

I think you're possibly the nicest father on the planet, I want to say, but I don't. 'I have to agree with you, Edward.' I nod. 'Polly is very advanced for her age.'

'Quite clearly.'

'What does that mean?' Polly asks.

'It means you're extremely talented, Polly,' I tell her. 'You should be very proud of yourself.'

'Now, where will we hang this masterpiece?' Edward says.

'How about the fridge?' Polly squeals.

'Oh, no, somewhere much better than that. Just a second,

I've got an idea.' He bounds out of the door on some secret mission.

'What's going on here?' a clipped voice says, as he disappears from view.

It's June – and, from her icy expression, she's not exactly overjoyed to see me.

'We're painting, Granny!' Polly giggles, bouncing towards her grandmother and wrapping her plump little arms round her waist. 'Come and see what I've done!'

I place the paintbrush back in the jug of water before me. I can feel June's eyes boring a hole through my head, and when I glance round I'm proved right – she's glaring at me with unconcealed hatred.

'That's very nice, Polly.' She smiles tightly as Polly whirls in front of her creation, describing it in a breathless monologue.

'. . . and Maggie said I could paint whatever I wanted to, so I said I really wanted to paint Saffy with a carrot, and she said I should go right ahead and that there's no right or wrong way to paint . . .' Her sweet little voice babbles on and on, explaining in minute detail how she came to paint this particular scene. Meanwhile, I'm busy trying to ignore the way June is looking at me.

'Polly,' June squats to her granddaughter's eye level, interrupting her mid-flow, 'will you run out to the yard and see if you can find Henry? I haven't seen him all morning.'

'He's such a naughty cat, isn't he, Granny?' Polly sighs melodramatically, wiping her paint-spattered hands on her apron. 'I'll have to have stern words with him.'

'Yes, you will,' June says, smiling at her. 'He'll listen to you.'

'That's right.' She skips happily out of the door. 'He will!'

June and I are now alone in the kitchen and the air suddenly feels icier than before. 'So, what are *you* painting?' June asks, slowly making her way across the room to look at my picture.

'Oh, I was just messing around,' I murmur. 'It's nothing really.'

'But Edward tells me you're a talented artist,' she says. 'Surely talented artists don't just mess around.'

'I'm not that talented.' I pull my easel towards me, not wanting her to see my picture. She'll know for sure that I'm not a real artist if she sees my efforts.

'You're not shy, are you, Maggie?' She cocks an eyebrow at me.

'I never let anyone see a work in progress,' I reply, bluffing. 'It's bad luck.'

'Is that what Edward is to you too?' June's face contorts.

'Excuse me?' What's she insinuating now?

'Is he your next work in progress? Are you going to work on him until he's just right?'

'I don't know what you mean,' I respond, flustered by her tone and the cold look in her eyes. Can she tell I like Edward? Does she somehow know that I'm drawn to him?

'I think you do, Maggie,' she says, her eyes dark. 'I think you know exactly what I mean. Volunteering to help Polly with her painting was clever, but you and I both know why you really suggested this one-to-one lesson.'

'We do?'

June is so close I can almost feel her breath on my face.

'Of course we do,' she spits. 'You think Edward is a fine catch. You wouldn't be the first to think that. But you can stop playing these silly games and trying to get to him through his children because it just won't work.'

'I'm not trying to do that!' I gasp. I'm not, am I? Is that why I volunteered to help Polly? No, it can't be. I like Polly – I really, truly like her, regardless of how I feel about her father. I would never use a child in that way. Besides, Edward is spoken for, in more ways than one.

'Yes, you are.' Her expression is glacial. 'But there's only one problem – he's still in love with my daughter and he always will be. Your plan will never work. Never.'

Well, that's true – I've seen it for myself. Edward does still love his wife, even if she's passed away.

Before I can say anything else, Polly bounds back into the kitchen, a tabby cat in her arms. 'Granny,' she squeals with excitement, 'I found Henry! You'll never guess where he was.' The cat mews loudly and struggles to escape from Polly's arms.

'Where was he, darling?' June's voice loses its bitter edge and becomes instantly warm and sunny.

'He was hiding under the gorse bush.' Polly's eyes shine. 'He'd just caught a mouse – look!'

With that, Polly drops the cat, digs her hand into her pocket and pulls out a mangled mouse. She holds it aloft by its scaly tail – its little head is dangling by a sinew from its neck. At first I think she's joking – that can't possibly be a proper mouse she has in her hand: it must be one of those plastic joke things you can buy. I had one myself as a child. It's amazing how lifelike they make them now – this looks so real.

'Polly!' June gasps. 'Drop that at once. I've told you a million times you can't bring dead rodents into the house under any circumstances.'

'But, Granny,' Polly protests, 'it's a really big one!'

With a jolt, I realize the creature in Polly's hand is not a fake. There's a dead, head-almost-severed-from-its-tiny-body mouse in the kitchen. An arm's length away from me. A few weeks ago it would have made me sick. Now I'm able to be in the same room and not run screaming. Maybe it's all the road kill I've seen since I came here, but I'm not scared, not a bit.

'Polly,' June says, 'I'm sure you're frightening, Maggie. She's from the city – she's not used to seeing dead rodents like this. Are you OK, Maggie? You look a little white – do you need to sit down, maybe? Put your head between your legs?'

The note of sarcasm in her voice is unmistakable. She's almost willing me to faint so that Polly will think I'm some weak city slicker. 'I'm fine, thank you, June,' I reply calmly. 'But I do think you should put that away, Polly, don't you? It's time to get back to work.'

'OK, Maggie, if you say so.' Polly skips back to the door, and swings the mouse outside by its tail.

I glance at June and I could be mistaken but I think I see respect in her formidable features.

'Ladies!' Edward calls, striding back into the kitchen. 'I found what I was looking for. Polly, give me your painting. I have something here that will finish it off just perfectly.'

'What is it?' Polly shouts. 'What is it?'

'It's a frame, of course – a very special frame for a very special painting.'

'You're going to frame it?' Polly holds her picture aloft.

'Yes, I am!' Edward grins. 'That way I can look at it every day. Don't you think it's a good idea?'

'What do you think, Maggie?' Polly asks me.

She's unsure if the idea has merit, or if it's completely naff. 'I think it's a brilliant idea, Polly,' I assure her. 'All the best art is framed – it means this picture is very special indeed.'

'Thanks, Dad!' Polly is thrilled, her pudgy little face beaming with joy.

Edward has managed to make this moment really special for her – something she'll always remember. As Polly flings herself into her father's arms and he stoops to hug her, I glance across the room to see June surveying the scene. She's watching with a very peculiar look on her face, tears glittering in her eyes. She stares straight at me momentarily, her expression much softer than before, then slips silently out of the door, letting it creak gently behind her.

'Did you get the text?' Edward asks, seemingly oblivious to June's disappearing act.

'What text?' I ask.

'From Ted – there's another meeting about the supermarket on Thursday.'

'Oh, right.' I lower my eyes from his, suddenly too embarrassed even to look at him properly. I'm like some kind of soppy teenager – it's ridiculous.

'This could be our chance,' he goes on.

'Our chance?' What does he mean by that? I whip my head back up. Does he mean us? Does he feel the same as I do?

'Our chance to sell the arts development project idea to everyone, of course,' he says. 'What did you think?'

'Of course!' I bluster. God, if he only knew what I was really thinking.

'So, are you ready? Will we take on the village?'

'I'm not sure . . . I'm an outsider, after all. The villagers mightn't take too kindly to me getting involved.'

'You're not an outsider, Maggie, you're one of us now. Isn't she, Polly?'

'Yeah, Maggie, you are.' Polly grins.

Then Edward smiles at me and my heart melts. How can I refuse him? If he asked me to muck out a hundred stables right this second I might just do it. 'OK,' I say. 'Why not? We don't have anything to lose, do we?'

'Great!' he says, ruffling Polly's hair. 'Let's hope they don't eat us alive!'

Rule Twenty-three: *Rules are made to be broken*

'I'm so glad you agree, Edward,' Odette croons smugly, from the stage. 'This supermarket will be a wonderful opportunity for the village – one we *must* exploit if we're not to lag further behind than we already are.' She stares meaningfully at Peg and Ted, who are sitting in the front row of the packed hall, their arms folded across their chests, looking mutinous.

'Well, I don't exactly agree with *everything* you propose, Odette,' Edward says coolly.

'You don't?' Odette's eyes widen, as if she can't imagine why anyone would ever disagree with anything she had to say. She really is a player. A player in pearls and a cashmere twin-set, which I've discovered can be the most dangerous kind.

'Let me elaborate,' he says. 'I think that the supermarket *could* help Glacken, yes. It could bring us some much-needed employment for a start.'

Odette nods energetically and there's a murmur of approval in the hall.

'But,' Edward continues, 'on the other hand, we don't want to destroy the unique quality that the village has. It's that quality that makes Glacken special. And I think we can agree that this village is very special to all of us.'

There's an outburst of applause at this, led by Peg and Ted clapping and cheering enthusiastically. Ted is dying to give Edward a standing ovation already, I can see that.

'What are you getting at, Edward?' Odette asks crossly, momentarily forgetting to be sweetness and light to her beloved.

Seeing Edward's surprise at her impatient tone, she remembers to smile at him again. This woman is like Jekyll and Hyde – what does he see in her? I just can't understand it.

'Well,' Edward glances at me, 'Maggie and I were chatting about it and we think we've come up with a plan that we believe could work.'

My face warms. It must be because everyone is staring at me – it can't be because Edward's cornflower blue eyes are locked on mine. Can it?

Half of the crowd has swivelled to see where I am. I try not to give in to the urge to sink down in my seat and hide. Instead I force myself to smile gamely, as if I'm the type of person who could have a plan about things. And I desperately try to forget the way Edward just looked at me. He's looking at me like that because I'm here to support his arts idea, nothing more. After all, he and Odette are together. This fantasy that there's some sort of connection between us is in my mind.

'You and *Maggie*?' Odette's voice cracks and she shuffles the papers before her to compose herself and buy some time. I can tell she's rattled because she's got a death grip on her precious documents; her pearly pink manicured talons are almost ripping through them with rage.

'Yes. Maggie,' Edward confirms, smiling at me. 'As you all know, Maggie is a celebrated artist here to complete an important commission.'

I wince as Edward says this. Whatever made me lie so stupidly like that? If only I'd told him the truth – that I'm an out-of-work estate agent . . . Maybe he wouldn't have cared. Then again, from the way he reacted when we spoke about estate agents, he hates them all. Anyway, it's too late to confess now that everyone here thinks I'm an artist. A massive wave of guilt washes over me. I feel terrible for letting them all believe I'm something I'm not. I try to push that thought away, though, because if I focus on it, I'll never be able to speak or say anything remotely useful and I know that Edward is depending on me to contribute. Watching him talk with such conviction about the place he loves is moving. I'm rooting for people to support his idea and I want to be involved, even though I know I should probably just walk away before I land myself in even more trouble. Something is making me stay, though, and I know that something is Edward. The little voice in my head can't be denied: I'm here because I genuinely don't want to leave. I want to stay because of Edward and the way I feel about him.

'. . . and Maggie feels that Glacken has something special to offer too.' Edward is still speaking. 'So, we've put our heads together,' Odette shivers visibly, 'and we both think that Glacken could be promoted as an artists' retreat.'

'An artists' retreat?' Odette's voice is withering. 'That's your big plan?'

'Yes,' Edward says. 'We could invite painters from all over the world to come here to work. We could establish a gallery – we could even have a festival.'

A festival? That wasn't something we'd spoken about – obviously Edward has put even more thought into this proposal. A festival is a brilliant idea. Nothing too grungy or like Glastonbury of course, something civilized. There could be showings, demonstrations, that sort of thing. The locals could rent out rooms to guests, Matty would make a fortune in the pub, and Peg and Ted would be set up. The more I think about it, the better it sounds.

'But, Edward,' Ted interrupts him, 'how would that help us?'

'I don't like those festivals, Edward.' Peg is unconvinced. 'It's all sex and drugs.'

'Yeah,' someone shouts, 'we don't want that sort of thing going on here.'

'Yes, we do!' someone else calls, and there's a ripple of laughter in the hall.

'There could be naked mud-wrestling or orgies. I saw that on the TV!' Betty from the butcher's bounces excitedly beside me, a basket of steaming sausage rolls at her feet. She's already tried to entice me with one, but I had to resist. I can't let Peg see me fraternizing with her. I may sneak one later, though, when she's otherwise occupied.

'Keep dreaming, Betty,' Jimmy the guard, in his blue wool jumper, says.

A heated debate breaks out about the possibility of an orgy happening in a muddy field.

'No, no, listen,' Edward shouts. 'I don't mean anything like Glastonbury – of course that wouldn't work here. I'm talking about something much more cultured. You know, like that literary festival they have at Hay-on-Wye.'

'I've heard of that,' Ted says. 'They had Dan Brown there one year.'

'Did they?' Peg perks up. 'Do you think Dan Brown will come here too?' she asks, her eyes widening.

'Don't be ridiculous,' Betty from the butcher's says. 'Dan Brown will never come to Glacken.'

'Well, why wouldn't he?' Peg pouts. 'What's wrong with Glacken? We're just as good as that Hay-on-Wye place.'

'I'd say we're better,' Ted agrees. 'Far better. Dan Brown would be a fool not to come here.'

'But he's not an artist, Ted.' Betty sniffs. 'He's a *writer*.'

'Well, we could have that girl, then,' Peg says. 'You know, the one who puts all her filthy rubbish on her bed.'

'Tracey Emin?' Jimmy the guard pales.

'Yes, that's her. She could come. Or that man.'

'Let me guess, the one who floats dead cows in formaldehyde?' Jimmy puts his head in his hands.

'Yes!' Peg looks jubilant. 'Now, he wouldn't be my cup of tea, but it would get the village great publicity. He's always in the papers.'

'Listen! LISTEN!' Edward bellows. Everyone falls silent again. 'If, and I say if, this project got off the ground and was in any way successful, it could attract tourists. The *right* sort of tourists.' He smiles. 'It could generate business for us all.'

Peg and Ted begin to look a little hopeful. 'So you think our shop could be saved, Edward?' Peg asks.

'No one can say for sure,' Edward answers honestly, 'but it's worth a shot.'

There's a loud hum in the room as everyone leans in to their neighbour to chat about the plan.

'Order.' Odette raps her little hammer on the table in front of her. 'Order!'

Everyone falls silent again.

'Edward.' She fake-smiles at him. 'This is a nice idea. But there's one problem.'

'What's that?' I pipe up. It seems unfair to let Edward do all the talking. I need to help him out.

'I was speaking to Edward,' Odette snipes at me. 'Not you.'

'That's OK, Odette,' Edward interrupts. 'Maggie should have some input. She's the expert, after all.'

I blush as he says this – God, I feel terrible for lying to him. Why on earth did I ever do that?

'OK,' Odette doesn't look too happy, 'if you insist.' She settles her eyes on me. 'So. Maggie. Celebrated artist.' She raises an eyebrow when she says this. 'Who's going to pay for this scheme? Unless you're going to fund the exercise yourself perhaps. Then again, from what I hear, artists don't make much money . . . not until they're dead, that is.'

Peg gasps. She knows exactly what Odette is implying – that she could kill me here and now with her bare hands, given half the chance.

'That's a good question, Odette,' I reply, getting to my feet, 'and one I'm happy to answer.' Lie. I'm not happy to answer this. I'm terrified. Absolutely terrified.

'Great.' Odette leans back in her chair and smiles. 'Please – go ahead.'

'Well . . .' I take a deep breath and try to remain composed '. . .we could look for funding. There are grants we could apply for. The government –'

'The government isn't giving any money to anyone, Maggie,' Odette interrupts, 'or hadn't you noticed that all public funding has completely dried up?'

I clear my throat. She's not going to make this easy for me. 'We could get a private investor,' I go on.

'A private investor?' Odette laughs. 'Please. There *are* no private investors any more.'

'There are still people out there who want to invest in the arts,' I argue, 'especially if there's something in it for them too.' I'm building up to mentioning Xanta. I can't just wade in and drop the bombshell: it would be too much of a shock for everyone. I have to choose my moment carefully.

'We're wasting time.' Odette dismisses me with a wave of her hand. 'It's never going to work.'

'Hang on, Odette,' Edward says, his voice steely. 'Let's just listen to what Maggie is saying.'

'Edward, we need to form a consensus about how best to

proceed. Time is of the essence, and we can't afford to waste any more of it.'

'Some of us *have* formed a consensus,' Ted says. 'Some of us have a very clear consensus.'

'Yeah, who died and made you Queen of the World?' Peg mutters, just loudly enough for those sitting in close proximity to hear.

Odette continues as if she hasn't seen them – it's as if they're a muddy spot on her otherwise perfect landscape, best ignored completely. I know if she could somehow get rid of them both she'd do it in a heartbeat.

'I thought, at this juncture, it would be useful if we had some outside input. To help us focus . . .' Odette pauses meaningfully and an excited murmur runs through the hall as people wonder who she's going to wheel in '. . . so that's why I've invited the chairman of Xanta Ireland here tonight to discuss the development with us.'

'What?' Ted roars, his face pink.

Chaos erupts in the hall and there's a deafening buzz as people process this information.

'Calm down, Ted,' Odette shouts over the din. 'You know full well that Laurence wasn't given a fair hearing last time around. It's only right we listen to what he has to say.'

'The chairman has been here before?' I ask Betty from the butcher's.

'Yes, he came to talk to us a few months ago. It got pretty ugly.'

'It did?'

'Laurence had his own security with him and they tried to throw Ted out of the hall.'

Betty doesn't look too upset by the memory – probably because she and Peg are mortal enemies, even if that has never been openly acknowledged.

Wow. I can't imagine Ted having to be escorted off the premises – he's such a gentle soul. Then again, he can get pretty fiery when it comes to this topic.

'I can't believe you did this behind our backs, Odette,' Peg fumes. 'You've ambushed us!'

'Peg, be reasonable.' Odette shuffles her papers and avoids Peg's eye. 'If I'd told you that Laurence was coming here tonight, you would have refused to attend. This was the only way to get everyone together – it makes perfect sense.'

'Yeah! I want to hear what he has to say,' someone calls from behind me.

'So do I,' someone else agrees.

'He's not a monster, Peg,' a third says, 'and we need the jobs.'

'You see?' Odette smirks smugly.

Peg slouches in her seat – she's very unhappy about this development, very unhappy indeed.

Suddenly there's a flurry of activity at the rear of the hall and a portly man in a pinstripe suit, leather briefcase tucked under his arm, makes his way to the stage.

'Laurence,' Odette coos, kissing him on both cheeks, 'how lovely to see you again.'

'Odette.' He kisses her back. 'You're looking gorgeous as always.'

'Oh, thank you,' she giggles, blushing. 'I'm so glad you could come.'

'My pleasure, my dear, my absolute pleasure. Halloooooo, everyone!' Laurence turns to face the room, his voice booming. 'Thank you for coming here tonight.'

He's so Big Top cheery, I almost expect him to do a little tap dance or pull a rabbit from his briefcase to try to impress us all.

'We wouldn't have come, if we'd known you'd be here,' Ted says loudly, his face stony. 'We were tricked into it.'

'Peg, Ted, it's lovely to see you again.' Laurence beams at them both, ignoring the fact that he's just been insulted.

'I wish I could say the same,' Peg replies. 'But I can't.'

'Ah, now, Peg, don't give me a hard time. I'm not here to ruffle your feathers. I'm here to talk – have a conversation. There's nothing wrong with that, is there?'

'Can snakes have conversations, then?' Peg says.

'Bring your thugs with you again, did you?' Ted adds. 'Or are they waiting for me outside?'

'Ho, ho, you two are a tonic, you really are!'

Laurence's tone is bright, but there's a brittle edge to it. It seems that Peg and Ted are thorns in his side, no matter how he tries to disarm them with the charm offensive that obviously works so well on Odette.

'I told you before, all that was a simple misunderstanding,' he goes on. 'The boys weren't going to harm you, Ted, you know that.'

'I know nothing of the sort!' Ted snaps, his face thunderous. 'They – they manhandled me!'

'They could have killed him!' Peg shouts. 'He has high cholesterol, you know – he could be one Mars Bar away from a heart-attack.'

The crowd erupts into animated conversation again and Laurence shifts nervously from foot to foot, unsure how to proceed. 'Now, now, all that is behind us,' he says. 'It's time to move forward, look to the future.'

'We could have sued the pants off you!' Peg shakes her fist at him. 'We might still!'

'Peg, let's give Laurence a chance to speak. It's only fair,' Odette wades in, patently eager to break the tension.

'Fair doesn't come into it!' someone shouts.

'Hear, hear!' Peg yells.

'Laurence, can you tell us about any recent developments

with regard to the supermarket?' Odette ploughs on, ignoring the interruptions.

'Yes, I can, Odette, certainly.' Laurence clears his throat, and rearranges his jovial features so he instantly looks more serious and businesslike. 'Well, as you are probably all aware, the supermarket has received the preliminary green light from the council.'

'Bah!' Peg huffs. 'That was very convenient.'

'So, bar any objections,' Laurence glances nervously at Peg and Ted, 'we aim to proceed within the next six weeks. We estimate it will take approximately twelve weeks to build the structure and a further twelve before it's fitted out and ready to operate. It'll be state-of-the-art when it's finished. State-of-the-art!'

'How exciting!' Odette breathes.

'I'm happy you think so.' Laurence eyes her.

Is it my imagination or is he looking straight at her breasts?

'So, it will be just over six months before the doors are opened to the general public?' She simpers.

'Yes, six months before it'll be all systems go!' Laurence gives the thumbs-up, trying to play to the crowd.

I realize, with a jolt, that this is just like a beauty pageant: Odette is the smarmy commentator and Laurence is the hopeful contestant trying to impress the audience – not that he could win any prizes with the waistband of his shiny suit straining round his gut like that.

'Six months before the village is ruined, you mean!' someone shouts. Peg and Ted clap furiously.

'Six months. That's right, Odette, that's right.' Laurence tries valiantly to ignore the protests. 'All going well, of course.' He shoots another anxious glance at the front row.

'And I read that you're keen to give locals jobs, Laurence?'

It sounds to me as if Odette and Laurence have prepared

this patter beforehand – it's all too smooth, like it's straight from a press release.

'That's very true, Odette.' Laurence beams. 'Integration into the community is of the utmost importance to Xanta. We value Glacken very much and we'll do our absolute best to employ people from the vicinity.'

'But you won't guarantee it?' a familiar voice asks. It's Edward. He's leaning against a wall, looking intense, as he poses the question. God, he's hot when he's being serious. But I try not to think about that: it's highly inappropriate – especially as his girlfriend is only a few feet away from us both. Odette would strangle me if she had any inkling of my feelings for her boyfriend. Still, I can't help but wonder again what Edward sees in her – they're so different. They even hold opposing views about the supermarket development. Edward is realistic: he knows the supermarket will probably happen but he wants to ensure that the area at least benefits from the development. He genuinely wants what's best for the village. Odette doesn't seem to care about any negative impact and she certainly isn't considering ways to help the community make the most of the situation. I see her narrow her eyes in annoyance at Edward's query – she's not taking kindly to him questioning Laurence publicly like this.

'We'll do our very best,' Laurence repeats jovially. 'But there are no guarantees in life, of course not. We could all be dead tomorrow, I always say that!'

'I wish you were, that's for sure,' Peg says, over the drone of conversation in the room – people aren't happy about this disclosure.

'Edward, there's no point in splitting hairs.' Odette's voice is sweet, but with a warning edge. 'The *majority* of the supermarket's workforce will be made up of locals. Isn't that right, Laurence?'

'That's the plan, Odette!' Laurence booms, smiling happily at the audience. 'That's the plan!'

This guy is a smooth operator underneath all the geniality. He knows exactly what he's doing. He's dishing out vague promises without setting anything in stone – it's a clever ploy.

I catch Edward's eye and he gives a tiny shake of his head. I get the message: tonight is not the time to reveal any more about our arts development idea, not now that Laurence is here – tension is running too high.

I nod back at him to let him know I understand, and he smiles. What is it about that smile that makes me go weak at the knees?

'And do you think the supermarket will attract many customers, Laurence?' Odette is still talking. It's like she's reading from a cheat sheet she prepared in advance – all this *must* have been rehearsed.

'We do indeed, Odette,' Laurence replies. 'In fact, I have projected figures here – let me just get them on to the screen so everyone can see.'

A burly man wheels a projector screen on to the stage and I see Ted pale – this must be one of Laurence's security team, one of the minders who ejected Ted from the hall last time.

Within seconds, the lights are flicked off and the projector is whirring.

'This looks very promising, very promising indeed!' Odette murmurs, as everyone scans the pie chart and graph that have sprung up behind her. There's a jumble of figures running along the bottom – it's all highly complicated, which I suspect is exactly as Laurence wants it. He wants to dazzle the villagers with facts and figures – blind them with science – so they won't put up a fight.

'Who says any of these so-called customers will come into the village, though?' Ted asks. 'The exact opposite could happen! They'll come to the supermarket to do their shopping and then bugger off home again. Glacken will be a ghost town.'

'Well, now,' Laurence pulls an understanding face, 'I take your worries on board, of course I do. But there have been studies done to prove the exact opposite. Here, let me show you.' He rummages in the half-light and pulls another sheet of paper from his briefcase. Odette slides it under the projector. 'See here?' He points to a summary of findings. 'We opened a supermarket in a small village on the west coast two years ago. Like Glacken, the village was close to the development and, like here, certain villagers had their concerns. Which we took seriously, of course. However, if you read the findings you can see that the village benefited directly from the development. Passing trade increased by thirty per cent and so did profits. It's a win-win situation – this study proves it.'

'How fascinating!' Odette croons. 'Isn't it, everyone?'

'Was that an independent study, by any chance?' I hear Edward ask.

I see Odette frown in the projector light. 'Edward, a study is a study,' she says quickly. 'The results speak for themselves.'

'Not exactly, Odette.' Edward's voice is sharp. 'A study can be tweaked to draw almost any conclusion. That's well known.'

'What an extraordinary thing to say!' Laurence barks, his jovial expression hardening a little.

'Edward, please!' Odette gasps. 'This is hardly conducive to good relations.'

'OK, let's assume the study *was* legitimate,' Edward says. The entire room has swivelled to watch him. 'Can you tell me where your supermarket was in relation to the village?'

'I don't know what you mean!' Laurence blusters.

'Don't you?' Edward goes on. 'I bet the store site was such that customers had to drive right *through* this village to get to the supermarket – am I right? If they did then it stands to reason that a certain percentage would stop, thus the increase in trade.'

'I – I . . .' Laurence is looking at the projector as if willing it to give him some answers.

'It's hardly comparable to Glacken, is it?' Edward says. 'No customers will drive through *here* to get to your supermarket, will they, Laurence? The site is far enough away to ensure that.'

There's a murmur in the hall as everyone processes this news. He's right, of course. The two situations are completely different.

'Now, Laurence, I believe you have more news for us.' Odette is desperate to move the conversation forward, away from this topic. It's almost as if she wants the supermarket to be pushed through, no matter what. Why is that?

'Yes, I do.' Laurence rearranges his face into a smile and beams at the darkened hall again. 'I know that some of you were slightly concerned that the supermarket was out of keeping with the landscape.'

'An ugly blot on the countryside, more like!' Peg shouts.

'Yes, well,' Laurence continues, 'in a gesture of goodwill, we've decided to redesign portions of the complex to make it more . . . aesthetically pleasing. Easier on the eye, like.'

'Why's that, Laurence?' Odette asks, right on cue.

'Well, Odette, we feel that the structure must reflect what the community is about – we want it to sit comfortably among you.'

'That was very thoughtful, I must say,' Odette replies.

'Thank you,' Laurence says graciously, as if he thinks he's some sort of hero. 'So, to that end, we have gone to enormous expense to redesign the clothing hall section of the building.'

'You've redesigned just one portion of the overall scheme?' Ted retorts. 'That's big of you.'

'I think you'll agree it makes a huge difference,' Laurence says. 'In fact, just reconfiguring this one section has softened the impact of the whole building. It took a lot of hard work and money to achieve.'

'I'd say it did!' Odette says, her face earnest.

'Yes, but we wanted to get it right,' Laurence says. 'We have a top-class team working on this project – our architect is a genius.'

'Did it take him long to adjust the plans, Laurence?' Odette asks.

'Well, Odette, you can ask him yourself because he's here tonight to answer any of your questions.'

I almost expect him to say, 'Come on down, the price is right!' This is all completely staged, I'm certain of it now.

Everyone cranes their neck to see where this architect is hiding.

'Come on, Robert, step forward – don't be shy!'

Robert? An architect called Robert? That's a creepy coincidence. Then again, there are probably hundreds of architects called Robert – it's not such an unusual name, is it?

It's so hard to see in the darkness, but a shadowy figure is making his way from the rear of the hall. It's bizarre – if I didn't know better it *could* almost be him: the similarity, even in the darkness, is uncanny. But it couldn't be. There's absolutely no way. It's just my mind playing tricks on me, that's all.

'Hmm . . . not bad.' Betty whistles beside me. 'I wouldn't throw him out of the bed for eating crisps, know what I mean?'

It can't be. It can't be. There's no way on earth . . .

As he draws closer I can see his features more clearly and my stomach flips. I can't believe it. It *is* him. It's Robert. My Robert. My ex, Robert. He's Laurence's architect – and he's here in Glacken.

Rule Twenty-four: *Just breathe*

'Hello, everybody, my name is Robert Kilbride and, as Laurence said, I'm the principal architect on the latest Xanta development here in Glacken.'

Robert is standing on the stage beside Laurence. The older man has one arm draped round his shoulders and he's beaming with pride.

How can he be right here, feet away from me? What horrible act of Fate has brought him to the one village in the entire country where I am?

Unless . . . Does he somehow know I'm here? Who could have told him? Claire? Dom? They wouldn't have . . . would they? No, Claire is still on her mission to find herself in India and Dom is busy trying to bed as many Aussie women as possible. They wouldn't have had time to organize this. Mum and Dad wouldn't do it: even if they did think of Robert as the son they never had, they know we'll never get back together.

What about Theresa? She thought I'd made a huge mistake when I broke up with him – she spent long enough telling me so. Would she have sent him here in some sort of deluded plot to get us back together? No, she couldn't have. Even if she thinks I was a fool to leave Robert, she wouldn't go this far, surely. Not unless the kids have finally sent her over the edge, of course. That is quite possible.

I close my eyes briefly, trying to figure it out. It's so surreal. Could I be imagining the entire thing? Maybe this is a nightmare and when I open my eyes it will be over. I ease my eyes open again and my heart sinks. It's not a nightmare. There he is, standing on the stage, smiling at the audience. He's simply dropped into my new life, like an alien from outer space.

Suddenly the greater implications of it hit me. If Robert sees me I'm done for – all my lies will be uncovered and everyone will know the truth about me. *Edward* will know the truth about me. That I'm not who I said I am. That I've been pretending all this time. Worse, that everything I've told him is a lie. What am I going to do? My mind is racing with possibilities as I watch my ex-boyfriend stand smiling, almost within touching distance. Thank God the hall is in darkness – if it wasn't he'd spot me almost immediately.

'What a *ride*,' Betty from the butcher's breathes in my ear. 'He's even better close up!'

The light from the projector is illuminating Robert's unmistakable features. He looks good, even I can see that. Tanned and healthier than I've seen him in years.

I try to concentrate on breathing and not passing out. Betty doesn't seem to have noticed anything amiss so obviously, even though I'm silently hyperventilating, she can't tell that my head is about to explode.

'Robert, how lovely to meet you.' Odette shakes his hand warmly. 'And thank you for travelling all the way down here to speak to us this evening – I know you're a very busy man.'

'It's no problem at all, my pleasure.' Robert smiles indulgently. 'Always happy to help.'

'Robert is a *genius*,' Laurence announces to the floor, and I hear Peg snort loudly, as if she doesn't believe a word of it.

'I wouldn't say that, Laurence.' Robert bashfully ducks the compliment.

'Aw, now, credit where credit is due, Robert. You've done me proud on this, you sure have.' He squeezes Robert's shoulders. 'He's like family to me,' he says to Odette.

'Thank you, Laurence,' Robert says, 'and, more importantly, thank you, everyone, for giving me this opportunity to come here and talk to you tonight.'

'If I'd known beforehand, I would have made sure to sit in the front row.' Betty giggles and nudges me again.

'I'm aware that some of you may have concerns about the supermarket . . .' Robert starts.

'That's putting it mildly,' someone yells from the floor.

'. . . but hopefully, I'll be able to dispel any fears you have about the development. That's why I'm here tonight – I'm here to help.' Robert spreads his hands wide and looks out at the audience, his eyes searching among the seats.

He sounds sincere – but then again, he's good at this sort of thing so it's hard to tell. Even I can't say for sure if he genuinely means it or not and I know practically everything about him – what side of the bed he prefers to sleep on, how he likes his eggs, which football team he supports. How much he loves yellow jelly-babies . . .

I push the last bit from my mind. There's no point in revisiting all that. The thing is, I'm familiar with almost every detail of his life – but I can't tell for sure why he's really here.

'He can help me any day of the week.' Betty digs me violently in the ribs and I gasp loudly. I see Robert frown and scan the audience to see where the noise came from and I drop my chin to my chest to make sure he doesn't recognize me. Not that he would quite possibly – I'm not wearing a scrap of makeup, my hair is pulled back unflatteringly from my face and the sweater I have on is probably fit for the bin.

'I haven't seen a fine thing like that in a long time.' Betty is almost salivating with unconcealed lust. 'Well, except for Edward Kirwan – I'd give him a go too, if I had half a chance!' She nudges me again but this time I bite my lip so I don't make a sound. 'I can't see a ring, can you?' she hisses.

'No.' I shake my head mutely.

'He's fair game so.' She rubs her hands with glee. 'It's about time we had some fresh meat here – do you think he'll come for a drink afterwards?'

'I don't know,' I murmur. My head is spinning. I really need to get out of here.

'So, Robert,' Odette simpers on-stage, 'can you tell us about the new clothing hall?'

'I'd be happy to.' Robert smiles at her and I slide down in my seat.

How can I escape without drawing attention to myself? Robert can't see me now, because the lights are off, but when they're switched on he'll spot me for sure.

'So, we were cognizant of the fact that the building had to sit comfortably in the landscape and we really feel we've achieved just that with this new design,' Robert says.

An image of the reconfigured supermarket appears on the screen.

'See here,' Robert points to the drawing, 'we've significantly reduced the size of this area, to rebalance the entire development.'

'It looks great,' Odette says.

'It looks awful!' someone calls. 'Just as bad as it did before.'

I see Robert's face twist faintly at this criticism of his work.

'It's not that bad,' someone else yells.

'What would you know?' another retorts.

'Order, everyone, please!' Odette bangs her gavel on the table. 'Are there any questions from the floor? Any *practical* questions?'

'Has the construction contract been awarded yet?' I hear Edward ask, and I shrink even further into my seat. Great! The man I love is speaking to the ex I abandoned. As the thought pops into my mind, I realize it's true. I don't just fancy

Edward, I love him. Properly love him. I start to sweat as the truth hits me.

'Not yet,' Robert replies smoothly. 'It will be put out to tender soon.'

'Will any local contractors be considered?'

'Like I say, it will be put out to tender,' Robert says. 'Then we'll whittle down the applications and take it from there. We expect it to be a highly competitive process.'

Laurence winks happily at Odette as Robert says this – I get the feeling that he'll take great satisfaction from getting the most value for his money.

'I wish I could think of something to ask him,' Betty hisses. 'He's such a hottie!'

'What about traffic congestion?' Odette asks, her head cocked to one side, as if she's spent endless nights worrying about this detail.

'That's a very good question, Odette,' Robert replies. 'Under- and over-ground parking will be provided.'

'Plenty of room for everyone, then?' She giggles.

'Oh, yes,' Robert agrees. 'And parking will be free, of course.'

'All those extra cars in the area will do nothing but pollute our beautiful countryside!' Peg is on her feet at the top of the hall. 'You lot are trying to swindle us!'

Robert shoots a concerned glance at Laurence. He's not quite sure how to handle Peg now that she's left her seat – he thinks she's a loose cannon, I can tell.

'We're not trying to swindle anyone, Peg,' Laurence says quickly, in a soothing tone. 'We're trying to improve amenities for the village. Wouldn't you like to be able to get some fresh coriander if you wanted it?'

'I hate coriander.' Peg snorts.

'I love it!' someone calls.

'Me too!' another voice shouts.

'See? You can't stop progress, Peg,' Laurence says, his eyes like flint, 'no matter what.'

'Is that a threat?' Ted is on his feet now. 'Are you threatening my wife?'

'Of course not,' Laurence replies smoothly. 'But she's getting pretty heated. Maybe you should bring her home and give her a cup of tea. Calm her down a bit.'

'You condescending –' In the blink of an eye, Ted is scrambling to get on the stage. 'I'll have you for that!' he roars.

'Jesus, Mary and Joseph!' Laurence sprints to hide behind Odette. 'Lads! Lads! Get this lunatic out of here.'

Two burly men leap from the side of the stage and lunge towards Ted, who is now shadow-boxing at a quaking Laurence. Odette is flapping Ted away, like she might swat at an irritating fly, and Robert is looking on with an expression of sheer bafflement.

'Let go of him, you animals!' Peg screeches, launching herself at one of the thugs, who now has Ted by the collar and is attempting to haul him away.

Everyone is on their feet now and there's pandemonium as the villagers swarm over the stage and join in the mêlée: fists are flying and punches are being thrown left, right and centre. It's suddenly become a free-for-all.

I know this is my chance. If I act now, I'll be gone before the lights come back on and Robert will never know I was here. I move quickly, pushing past Betty who's yelling, 'Get him, get him!'

I'm not sure which side she's on, and I'm not waiting to see. I'm at the door, ready to dive into the night, when I hear Peg cry above the din. 'Help! Somebody help!' she sobs, looking helplessly around her. I glance over my shoulder and see Ted crumpled by the stage, deathly pale. Laurence seems to have been bundled from the hall.

Oh, no. Something has happened to Ted and people are too busy squaring up to each other to notice. If I go back now I'm done for – Robert will see me and the truth will be out. But Ted needs help and Peg is terrified. I've no choice. Pushing all thoughts of what will happen from my mind, I turn and shove my way through the crowd and back towards the stage.

'Maggie!' Peg sobs, when she sees me. 'Maggie, help him, he's having a heart-attack!'

'I'm not having a heart-attack, Peg, don't fuss,' Ted says weakly.

'Are you OK?' I stoop to look at him.

'I don't feel so good, Maggie girl.' He smiles wanly at me. 'It's nothing – I'll be OK in a minute.'

'Don't worry, Ted, you'll be fine,' I say. 'We'll get you out of here.'

Inside, I'm panicking. For once, it seems that Peg isn't exaggerating: Ted doesn't look good. He needs a doctor – fast.

'Sit with him, Peg,' I say, my voice far calmer than I feel. 'I'll call an ambulance.'

'An ambulance?' Her voice shakes.

'Just as a precaution.' I hug her briefly. 'I'm sure he'll be OK, but we don't want to take any chances, do we?'

'No, no,' she cries. 'Oh, Maggie, if anything happens to him, I'll die. He's the love of my life.'

'I know he is, Peg.' I squeeze her tight. 'Now sit and hold his hand – this'll only take a second.'

I make for a quiet corner – there's still bedlam in the hall and I need to make sure the emergency services can hear what I'm saying.

'Maggie?' Edward is at my side as I flip open my phone.

'It's Ted,' I say, quickly dialling 999. 'I think he's having a heart-attack. Stay with them, will you? Peg's in a state.'

'Of course. Don't worry, it'll be OK.' He briefly squeezes my arm, then disappears back into the crowd.

I've given the emergency services the details and am shoving my phone back in my bag when I hear the voice behind me. 'Maggie?'

I don't even have to turn – I know immediately who it is. The game is up.

'Hi, Robert.'

'What . . . what are you doing here?'

Confusion is written all over his face. He didn't know I was in Glacken, that much is obvious. No one told him where I was and he hasn't been stalking me. This is just one big cosmic coincidence – if God exists, she has a very strange sense of humour.

'It's a long story.' I sigh. 'I'm living here now.'

'You've moved? *Here?*' His voice is incredulous as he drinks in my appearance.

'Yes, I have.'

I know why he's so surprised. Notwithstanding that he never imagined bumping into me here, the last time he saw me I was groomed and polished. Now I'm standing in the middle of a remote village hall, dressed in an outfit I would never have left the house in just a few short months ago. I look like . . . like Claire did when she started her journey to her inner self. And Robert looks just like I did when I met her wearing her dog-eaten hoody: shell-shocked. I almost have to stifle a laugh at his expression. This would be comical if it wasn't so tragic.

'But you hate the country!' he says, astonished.

'I don't *hate* it,' I say.

'You *do* – you once said that –'

'If I ever had to live beyond the motorway I'd go bonkers?'

That's what Dom said when I told him I was moving to Glacken. I must have told Robert the same thing.

'Exactly!' He shakes his head, as if he can't quite believe his eyes.

'Well, I guess I was wrong.' I smile sheepishly. 'I like it here. In fact, I love it.'

As I say it, I know it's true. I *do* love Glacken. It's started to feel like home. These people have started to feel like a second family. There are a few mad relations in the pot, of course – Peg and Ted aren't entirely sane – but I love them regardless.

'But what are you doing for work?' Robert asks. 'Is there even an estate agency down here?'

'Not exactly . . .' I fudge. 'I'm keeping busy, you know, with other stuff.'

'Robert!' Odette's voice cuts through our conversation as she rushes to Robert's side. 'Thank God I got Laurence out of here safely. I'm so sorry about this calamity. It's these villagers – some of them are barbaric. The sooner I get out of here myself the better! Oh, Maggie!' She stops chattering when she notices me.

'Hi, Odette,' I say.

'You two know each other?' Robert asks.

'Everyone knows everyone in a small village, Robert,' I reply.

Odette looks from me to Robert, her eyes narrowed, as if she can't quite figure out what's going on. 'Do you . . . do *you* two know each other?'

'Yes, we do,' I reply. There's no point in denying it.

'Maggie and I were together . . .' Robert says, not elaborating any further. But it's clear what he means.

'What? You mean *Robert* is your secret boyfriend?' Odette's eyes widen.

'You have a secret boyfriend?' Robert asks, getting hold of the wrong end of the stick. 'Wow – you *have* been busy, Maggie. Leaving the estate agent's, moving here, getting a secret boyfriend . . . What else have you been up to?'

'Estate agent's?' Odette's mouth is hanging open. She has definitely had veneers – I'm sure of it now. Funny what you notice in a crisis.

'Well, yes,' Robert says, looking even more confused.

'You're not an artist, are you?' Odette says accusingly. 'You never were! You don't paint under a pseudonym at all! That was all a lie! I *knew* it!'

'What's she talking about, Maggie?' Robert asks.

I'm desperately trying to think of something to say. The only possible way out of this mess is an alien abduction. What are the odds of that happening? Slim to none, I should imagine, more's the pity, because being snatched by evil alien life forms intent on using my brain for sinister experiments is far preferable to having to tell the truth.

'Maggie told everyone in the village that she was an award-winning artist!' Odette crows.

Now that she's over the shock of the revelation, it's clear that she's thrilled by the news.

'Well, I didn't exactly say award-winning . . .' I begin.

That's true at least: technically it was Peg and Ted who spread that rumour, not me. I did go along with it, of course. I'm the one to blame for this mess.

'An artist?' Robert guffaws, slapping my back a little too heartily. 'That's hilarious!'

'Why is it hilarious exactly?' I feel the hairs on the back of my neck prickle. OK, so I may have lied, but why does he think the idea of me painting is so outlandish?

'Well, you're not exactly Van Gogh, are you, Mags?' Robert chuckles.

'That's not what she told everyone,' Odette says. 'She led us all up the garden path about her career when she was really living a lie! She even told us she painted under another name – all so she wouldn't be found out!'

'Odette, this was a misunderstanding that got out of control,' I say. 'I never meant to deceive anyone.'

'And we're supposed to believe that, are we?' she sneers. 'When you told everyone you were an artist and all along you were an *estate agent*! You're a joke!'

It's as if the room has become suddenly still and deathly silent as Odette's voice rings out.

I see past her to where Edward is standing, a look of horror on his face. I'm not sure about everyone else, but he has definitely heard every word – he knows the truth about me, that I am what he said he despises most.

I watch as Robert and Odette follow my gaze. There's an undeniable flicker of recognition on their faces: they've seen how I feel about Edward; they know the full truth now.

It's happened – just like I knew it would eventually. My pyramid of lies and deceit has finally come crashing down around my ears.

Rule Twenty-five: *Your health is your wealth*

Three hours later I'm sitting by Ted's hospital bed, gripping Peg's hand tightly as the doctor breaks the news.

'Indigestion?' Peg gasps. 'Are you sure?'

'Yes,' the doctor confirms. 'We've run all the tests. Your husband wasn't having a heart-attack. He ate something that disagreed with him – it's not uncommon. You can go.'

'Oh, thank God, thank God,' Peg cries. She throws her arms around me and hugs me tightly, then flings herself at Ted, who has closed his eyes with relief.

'And what about his cholesterol, Doctor?' she asks, through her tears.

'Well, that *is* far too high. He needs to drastically overhaul his diet.' He passes a healthy-eating diet sheet to Peg, who grabs it with both hands, like it's the last lifejacket on a sinking ship.

'I told you, Ted!' she admonishes. 'No more chocolate!'

'Chocolate?' The doctor is clearly appalled.

'I have an addiction.' Ted hangs his head in shame.

'You'll have to get over that pretty quickly.' The doctor is unsympathetic.

'He's been told to cut down,' Peg says. 'He never pays any attention.'

'Well, if he doesn't start paying attention soon, he'll definitely be on medication for the rest of his life.' The doctor's eyes are steely.

'I will?' Ted pales.

'Yes, you will. Think of this little warning as your last chance to change your ways.' He strides away, a nurse at his heels. There's no time for any more idle conversation, not when he has patients who really *are* at death's door to deal with.

'It looks like you had a lucky escape.' I smile at Ted as Peg sits stroking his hand.

'Aye, it does that.' Ted nods. 'I thought I was a goner then, I really did.'

'What could you have eaten that disagreed with you so much?' Peg asks him, puzzled.

'I had a few Mars Bars?' he offers half-heartedly.

'Yes, but you have half a dozen Mars Bars every day. Why would they suddenly cause this? What else did you eat today? Was there anything different? Anything at all?' Peg can't work it out.

'I can't remember.' Ted seems anxious not to delve into it too much. 'Now, let's get out of here, Peg. The doctor said I could go.'

'The nurse has to come back with the discharge papers yet,' Peg says. 'We've plenty of time to try to figure this out. You heard the doctor – this could be a warning. We have to take it seriously.'

'Maybe I should go,' I suggest. There's something about Ted's guilty expression that I don't like – I don't want to be here when he confesses to Peg what led to his 'heart-attack'.

'No, Maggie, stay.' Peg has a death grip on my arm. 'Let's think. This is important. I thought you were dying, Ted. We can't let this happen again.'

'OK.' Ted looks extremely guilty now.

'So. You had scrambled eggs for breakfast, like always.'

'That's right,' he agrees. 'Then I had two Mars Bars at eleven.'

'You had soup for lunch.'

'Lentil. That's right. And then a Mars Bar for dessert.'

'You had chicken pasta for tea.'

'And two Mars Bars after.'

'So, just like every other day. Was there nothing else? Think, Ted, think!'

'Peg, there was something else . . .'

'There was?' Peg is all ears. 'You didn't have a Moro Bar, did you? You know I can't abide those Moros.'

'No, I didn't have a Moro.' Ted's nose wrinkles in distaste. 'I wouldn't touch one of those – nasty things they are.'

'So, what was it then? A Lion Bar? A Toffee Crisp?'

'No. It was . . .' Ted gulps. 'It was a sausage roll.'

There's silence in the room as we all absorb this information.

'A what?' Peg's voice is barely audible.

'A sausage roll.'

'Where did you get a sausage roll?' Peg asks, her voice icy.

I want to be anywhere but here because I know exactly what's coming next.

'I'm sorry, Peg, I'm so sorry.' Ted breaks down. 'I forgot to bring my emergency Mars Bar to the meeting and then Betty passed by with her basket and I just couldn't resist . . .' He looks at me imploringly, as if he wants me to intervene on his behalf. I look at the floor. He would have been better having a fatal heart-attack and be done with it.

'You – you ate one of Betty's sausage rolls?' Peg's face is disbelieving.

'Yes,' Ted admits, his handlebar moustache quivering with remorse.

'You – you traitor!' Peg hisses, her face a fury. 'How *could* you?'

'I'm weak, Peg,' Ted moans. 'A weak man. Forgive me, you have to forgive me.' He looks properly ill now. Worse than he did in the hall.

I shrink back against the wall, hoping Peg will forget I'm

here. What if she asks me if I ever tasted one? I won't be able to lie. I'll have to tell her. What will she do to me?

'I'll never forgive you for this, Ted. *Never!*' Peg cries, dabbing at her eyes. 'There's nothing worse you could do to me, you know that! That Betty will be laughing up her sleeve now, all right. My own husband – betraying me. I just can't believe it!'

'I didn't mean to do it!' Ted pleads.

'What? Are you trying to tell me you didn't enjoy it, Ted, is that it?' Peg's face is red with rage.

'It meant nothing to me – nothing!'

'I find that hard to believe,' she spits. 'You've probably been lusting after those sausage rolls all along, haven't you?'

'No, I haven't, I swear!'

'Were you thinking about them when you were eating my egg sandwiches, Ted – were you?'

'Never!' Ted is aghast. 'I swear it!'

'Then why don't I believe you? I'm going.' Peg quickly gathers up her things.

'Please don't,' Ted begs.

'Find your own way home,' she calls over her shoulder, as she sweeps from the room. 'Better still, knock on that hussy's door – she might take you in. I hope you both choke on your sausage rolls.'

'Ah, Ted,' I say, when she's gone. 'What possessed you?'

'I was *starving*, Maggie,' he says, his eyes full of tears. 'That Betty's been trying to tempt me for years, waving her sausage rolls under my nose, and I just cracked. I don't know what came over me. Will you go after her? Talk to her for me? Please?'

'Why don't we give her an hour or two, and then I'll try, eh?' I know Peg will need time to calm down. There'll be no point in trying to talk to her now.

'You're probably right.' He sighs. 'Hopefully she'll come round. What a mess.'

'Yes,' I agree.

If he only knew the half of it. Mess doesn't come close to describing my life. There's a long silence as we contemplate our fates.

'I can't believe I went for Laurence like that,' Ted says eventually. 'I just saw red when he insulted Peg.'

'You were pretty nimble on your feet, all right.' I giggle, somehow seeing the funny side.

'Did you see him hide behind his henchmen?' Ted smirks. 'What a coward.'

'If you hadn't had a heart-attack you could have floored him for sure.'

'Wasn't Odette terrible for springing him on us like that, though? Him and his fancy architect.'

'Yes.' I stop laughing. It doesn't seem funny any more.

'What is it, Maggie?' Ted asks. 'Did I say something wrong?'

Suddenly I know I have to tell him the truth. He'll find out soon enough – it's only fair that he hears it from me first. He and Peg have been so good to me and he deserves to know.

'Ted, I have something to tell you,' I start. 'I'm not who you think I am. I'm not an artist.'

'You're not?'

'No.'

'You're not from the Inland Revenue, are you?' he whispers fearfully. 'I was going to sort all that out – I swear.'

'No. I'm not a tax inspector. I'm an estate agent.'

'An *estate agent*?'

'Yes. I don't know why I lied about it. I told one fib and then it all seemed to snowball.'

'Yes,' he says sadly. 'That's what can happen. One lie leads to another.'

'So, now you know.' I wait for Ted to say he never wants to

see or talk to me again. An image of Edward flashes into my mind. What must he think of me now?

'Well, everyone has their secrets, Maggie,' he says. 'I won't judge you, that's for sure. Peg won't either, I know that.'

'You think?'

'No, of course not. Not now you've come clean. Everyone deserves a second chance. I just hope she gives me one too. Besides, you're a good friend – look how you helped us tonight. Peg really wanted you in her hour of need – and so did I.'

'Thanks, Ted.' I lean in to hug him tight. As I do, there's the beep of a text in my pocket.

Flipping open my phone, I see it's from Edward and my heart soars. Maybe he wants to meet me – maybe all isn't lost. I click and read it eagerly, my heart pounding. But it's not the message I hope for.

It's Drya. The wild horse is missing. And so is Matilda.

Rule Twenty-six: *Seize the day*

'Thanks for helping, Robert,' I say. 'You didn't have to.'

'Are you kidding?' Robert says. 'This is an adventure! And it's a great opportunity to try out the four-wheel-drive mode!' He pats the steering-wheel of his jeep and grins at me.

I'd forgotten how much Robert loves his jeep. He even named it after his favourite football player. That was another thing that used to get on my nerves – his long-standing obsession with Fernando Torres. In fairness, though, I can't very well tell him off about it, not when he's driving me round the countryside in the middle of the night, searching for a stroppy teenager he's never even met.

The minute he heard what had happened – that Matilda had gone missing, presumably after galloping off somewhere alone on that mad horse – he volunteered to help. It's made me see him in a different light. Not that I've changed my mind about us, but he's stepped up to the plate tonight when he didn't have to and I really admire that.

'Well, it's still very good of you,' I say. 'It's not like you know Matilda or Edward.'

'Ah, yes, the brooding Edward,' Robert says. 'Is he the hero of the story?'

'What do you mean?' I shift a little uncomfortably in my seat. I know Robert clocked how I looked at Edward earlier – he must have worked out how I secretly feel.

'Well, you're the heroine, obviously, and I'm the villain of the piece. So that makes Edward the hero, right?'

'You're not the villain,' I say quietly. 'If there is a villain it's probably me.'

'Why's that?'

'I haven't exactly told everyone the truth about myself.' That's the understatement of the century.

'So I gathered . . . What's all this about being an artist?' Robert turns his head to glance at me, his expression soft. He's not making fun of me, which is kind of him.

'It's a long story,' I say, 'but everyone here thinks I'm an artist. An award-winning artist.' I wince as I say the words – how stupid am I? Award-winning stupid, that's how.

'Aha.' Robert nods. 'So that explains Odette's reaction.'

'Yes, Odette doesn't particularly like me.' I sigh.

'I picked up on that.' He smiles. 'Not very subtle, is she? What's her role in this little drama? Wicked witch?'

'Some people think so,' I reply, remembering what Polly said.

It seems so long ago now. I feel a pang when I think of the little girl with the big attitude. How will I explain to her that I have to leave? Because that's what I must do. I've no choice: I can't stay here – not now that everyone knows the truth about me. Or they will once the village hotline jumps into action. Everyone will be talking about me, come morning. Once they've polished off the Ted-Peg-Betty triangle, of course – that will take precedence. There probably hasn't been this much scandal in Glacken for years.

'She's certainly dangerous, that's for sure.'

There's a warning in Robert's voice that I can't ignore. 'What do you mean?'

'Well, she's not promoting Laurence's development for the good of her health, let's put it like that . . .'

'You mean he's *paying* her?' I can't believe it.

'Or promising her a new veterinary clinic next door to the supermarket at cut-price rent . . .'

'Wow.' So Odette *has* a vested interest: no wonder she was so keen for the project to be pushed through, regardless of local opposition.

'You really like it here, don't you?' Robert asks.

'Yes, I do. Crazy, I know.' I peer out of the window, straining to see any sign of Matilda or Drya. It's past midnight and it's getting cold – if we don't find her soon, who knows what could happen? She may be in real danger.

'It's not that crazy. People change – I know I have.'

'You have?'

'Yes.' He laughs. 'A girl broke my heart – that was pretty life-changing for a start.'

'I'm sorry, Robert,' I say. A tidal wave of guilt washes over me. Robert is such a nice guy – he never deserved heartache.

'That's OK. You were right – it was for the best. I've learned lots of things about myself since then that I never knew before.'

'Like what?'

'Well, it turns out I'm more adventurous than I ever thought.'

'Really?' I'm doubtful of this. Robert's favourite pastime is charting the financial decline of the country from the comfort of his sofa. He thinks adventurous is ordering extra pepperoni on his pizza.

'I know you'll find it hard to believe, but I've put a stop to the doom-and-gloom watching. I even joined an orienteering club a few months ago.'

'Orienteering? Wow!' I whistle sarcastically, and he laughs.

'I know, I know, orienteering mightn't have much sex appeal but, believe me, it's thrilling enough for me.'

'I'm only kidding.' I smile warmly at him. 'I'm glad for you.'

'Thanks.' He smiles back. 'I love it – it's where I met Maria.'

Aha. There's a new woman – no wonder he has such a spark in his eye. Am I jealous? I search around inside to try to decide.

Nope, nothing. *Nada*. Not even a sniff of the green-eyed monster. 'Who's Maria?' I ask. He's dying to tell me. I have to put him out of his misery.

'My new girlfriend,' he says proudly. 'She's Australian.'

'Australian, eh?' A picture of Dom pops into my mind. I wonder if he's had that threesome yet? Doubtful – he would definitely have called me to boast if he had. Maybe even texted a few photos, if I know Dom.

'Yes, she's from Sydney. She's very sporty. She's taking me bungee-jumping next week.'

I try to erase the image of Dom in bed with two buxom babes and concentrate on Robert. Did he just say bungee-jumping? That can't be right. Robert hates physical challenges. He refused to get into the hotel pool the last time we went away together. Now he's going bungee-jumping? That doesn't make any sense at all.

'I know!' He laughs again, seeing my confused face. 'Isn't it mad? But Maria just brings out the wild side in me. Do you want to know what her motto is?'

I don't really – it's bound to be something corny – but I don't want to hurt his feelings. 'Sure,' I say.

'It's "Seize the day" – isn't that amazing?'

I can see from the misty-eyed look on his face that he genuinely believes Maria has come up with this life-affirming nugget all on her own. 'Amazing,' I agree.

'Yes, she's taught me a lot. Like, what's the point of worrying about the financial crisis and the recession? We're all just passing through – we have to live life to the fullest and follow our dreams, grab our happiness where we can.'

'You're right.' I'm not just agreeing with him for the sake of it any more. He's right – he is. Suddenly a vision of me standing at my easel, paintbrush in my hand, comes into my mind's eye. Art really is my passion. Ironic, considering, but

I know now that, whatever happens, I'll be pursuing it in one way or another. Robert's right – life's too short not to follow your dream, and my dream is to paint. I'll probably never earn a penny from it, of course, so I'll have to find another job to pay the rent, but that doesn't mean I can't paint in my spare time, even if I'm no good. I've postponed it and buried the urge for far too long. I'm not going to put it off any longer.

'Of course, the other great thing about Maria is that she hates jelly-babies!' Robert jokes. We both burst into laughter and then he brakes suddenly. 'Look, Maggie,' he hisses, pointing out to the inky blackness, 'over there!'

'Where?' I can't see anything.

'Down the embankment – is that her? Is that Edward's daughter?'

I look to where he's pointing and I see Matilda, barely visible, sitting against a tree in the darkness. Is she hurt? It's impossible to tell – I have to get to her fast.

'Quick, let me get out!' I gasp.

'Hang on, I have to come with you,' he says. 'You can't go down there on your own.'

'Robert, I'll be fine,' I say, determined now. 'I have my torch, now let me out. She won't want lots of people making a fuss. Just call Edward and tell him we've found her – he'll be worried sick.'

'OK, then,' Robert agrees, as I scramble out. 'Be careful.'

'I will.' I turn to smile at him over my shoulder. Without his help, we might never have found her.

'Well done, Maggie,' he says.

'Well done?'

'Yeah, you've really got the hang of this country thing. I never thought you had it in you.'

'Neither did I! But I guess people really can change.' I close the passenger door behind me and creep down the embankment, trying not to skid as I go. Matilda hasn't moved a muscle – hasn't she heard me? It's as if she's in her own world. There's no sign of Drya – she must have bolted.

'Matilda,' I call softly as I get closer, 'are you OK?'

'Go away,' she says, her voice hollow. 'Just leave me alone.'

'Are you hurt?'

'No, I'm fine.'

My eyes adjust to the dark and I see her face, streaked with tears. 'Well, it's late and you're obviously upset – let's get you home.'

'No, just go away.'

'Please, Matilda. We've been so worried about you, please let's go home.'

'What's it to you?' she cries.

I'd like to say I want her to be safe but something tells me she might not believe me. After all, we haven't had the friendliest of relationships. I'm sure she blames me for being grounded – that may be why she ran away like this. 'You're right.' I shrug. 'It's nothing to me, really. I'm leaving Glacken tomorrow.'

Changing my tactic like this is a gamble, but maybe if I act disinterested she'll change her mind and come with me. Teenagers can do the unpredictable and I'm hoping a bit of reverse psychology will work.

'You're leaving?' Matilda snuffles.

'Yes.' My heart constricts as I confirm it. I have to leave – I have no other choice.

There's a silence as she absorbs this information. 'I see.'

'Yes, so you and your boyfriend can have the cottage back,' I say, trying to be light-hearted.

Maybe a little humour will do it – anything to get her back up the embankment and into Robert's jeep. But it doesn't work. She's not laughing, she's crying even harder. In fact, she's now wailing uncontrollably. What did I say? How have I made it even worse? I seem to have an uncanny ability to do that.

'He's not, he's not . . .' She dissolves into a sobbing heap and she can't go on.

'What is it, Matilda?'

The poor girl is in bits and suddenly my heart goes out to her – she looks so young and vulnerable, not at all like the sulky brat I've met before.

'Daniel broke up with me,' she chokes.

'I see.' I hunker down to her level. So that's what's wrong. Matilda has had her heart broken for the very first time. 'That's tough.' I reach out and hold her hand. She flinches but doesn't pull away. 'I remember when my first boyfriend broke up with me.'

She lifts her head and looks at me curiously, as if she can hardly believe I ever had a first boyfriend. I obviously look so haggard, these days, that she can't imagine I was ever young and wrinkle-free.

'Yup. I was about your age when it happened,' I go on.

'Don't tell me,' she says. 'It was no big deal and you got over it, right?'

'No. I was devastated, actually.'

'You were?' She pauses from sobbing.

'Yes. He snogged my best friend. Well, I thought she was my best friend – turned out she was a two-faced cow but, hey, you live and learn.'

'That's awful!' Matilda gasps.

'Yes. I got over it, though. Eventually.'

'Did you ever forgive her? Your friend?'

'Sure,' I say. 'It only took a few decades to do that.'

Matilda laughs and rubs her dripping nose on her sleeve.

'Do you want to tell me what happened?' I ask. 'You don't have to if you don't want to.'

Matilda looks warily at me, as if she's trying to decide whether to trust me or not. 'He wanted . . .' She clears her throat. 'He wanted us to have sex.'

'I see.' I try to keep my tone neutral, but inside I'm panicking. What am I going to say to this revelation? 'And how did you feel about that?' I try.

'I . . .' She snuffles again, but she's definitely sounding less hysterical now. 'I didn't want to.'

'OK.' Thank God for that – she's far too young even to be thinking about having sex.

'He said I was a frigid bitch.' She bursts into tears again.

Rage bubbles inside me. How dare that little upstart call Matilda such an awful name just because she wouldn't give in to his pressure? I've a good mind to march down to the village and tell his parents exactly how charming their son is. But then I see Matilda's face and I know that this would be exactly the wrong thing to do – it would completely humiliate her. 'Listen, Matilda,' I say. 'You did exactly the right thing.'

There are tears coursing down her cheeks. She looks so incredibly childlike I can't believe we're having this conversation. 'Do you think so?'

'Yes, I do. Having sex for the first time is a really special thing. It's not something you want to rush into. And it's definitely not something you want to be pressured into either.'

'He used to make me meet him in the cottage,' she sniffs.

'Rose Cottage?'

'Yeah. He said it was the perfect place to be alone. That's why we were there that day – you know, when you caught us.'

'I see.' Wow, the little shit had it all worked out.

'He's going to tell everyone I'm frigid. They're all going to laugh at me.'

'Matilda, I know it's hard not to give in to peer pressure,' I say, holding her hand even tighter, 'but you have to stand up for what you believe in. You wait until you're good and ready to have sex. There's nothing wrong with that. And I bet if you tell your friends how you feel, they might feel exactly the same way.'

'Yeah.' She considers this. 'Chloë said she was really nervous about it too.'

'Maybe she feels the same way you do, then.' Inside I'm appalled. Chloë? That puny girl with the freckles is thinking about having sex with her boyfriend? That's crazy! I fix a look on my face that hopefully says, 'You can talk to me about this,' instead of 'I'm calling everyone's parents, right now.'

'Maybe.' Matilda's face brightens.

'So talk to her about it. But even if she doesn't feel the same way, you have to trust your instincts. You'll know when you're ready. And you know what? You should try talking to your dad too – he's a good listener.' My heart constricts when I mention Edward.

'Some chance!' Matilda grunts.

'Why not try?' I say softly. 'He might surprise you.'

'He never listens to me. He hates me!' Matilda starts to cry hard again.

'That's not true, Matilda,' I say. 'How can you even think that?'

'I don't think it – I know it,' she sobs. 'It's my fault Mum died. That's why he hates me!' She buries her face in her arms.

'Matilda, it's not your fault your mum died – that was a tragic accident.'

'If it hadn't been for me, she wouldn't have gone out that day – she was cross with me because I wouldn't tidy my room.' Matilda's face is bleak.

'That's not why your mum went riding that day,' I whisper, 'and even if it was, it wouldn't make it your fault. You need to talk to your dad about this.'

My heart is breaking for her: she's been carrying this burden ever since the accident. She totally blames herself for what happened – just like Edward does. He thinks June died because of the argument they had about the estate agent. No wonder Matilda's been so angry and confused. All her acting up was because of this. The truth is, the accident was no one's fault: it was just that – an accident.

'I didn't want to burden him with all my stuff, you know. When Mum died he was so devastated. I didn't want to add to his worries.'

'He's your dad, Matilda,' I say. 'He loves you and I know he'd love to listen. Just give him a chance and trust him.'

'You think so?' She looks doubtful.

'Yes, I do.' I smile with encouragement.

'Thanks, Maggie.' She shoots me a watery smile.

'Feel better?'

'Yeah,' she says. 'I do a bit. Why are you leaving anyway?'

I pause before I answer this. I can't exactly say, 'I'm running away from Rose Cottage because I lied to everyone and now they all hate me, especially your father.' Matilda would think I was mad, and if she thought that, she might be less inclined to take my advice about the sex thing. 'I have to go back to the city,' I reply. That's not a lie, not technically. I do have to go, but not because I want to.

'Oh, right.' She rubs her tear-streaked face. 'When are you coming back?'

'Em, I may not be coming back.' I avoid her eye. 'Something's come up that I have to deal with. It's . . . complicated.'

'But what about the cottage? And the ponies?' She's confused. 'Who's going to help Dad?'

'I'm not exactly sure.' I look away from her. 'He'll cope without me.'

'You haven't told him, have you?'

Her voice is accusing. How come all these kids are so clued-in, these days? I can't get away with anything! 'Like I said, Matilda, it's complicated.'

'It wasn't that complicated a minute ago when you told me not to have sex with my boyfriend.'

Crap. Why is she interrogating me like this? I can see Polly being just like her in a few years' time.

Suddenly I make a decision. I have to tell her the truth. If I don't, she won't trust me, and if she doesn't trust me, she might give in to that creep Daniel. The thought of her being pressured into having sex when she doesn't want to makes me ache so badly to protect her I could cry. 'Matilda,' I look at her, 'I told a lie. Lots of lies, in fact. I'm not an artist. I'm an estate agent. Your dad never would have let me stay if he'd known the truth.'

'He doesn't like estate agents,' Matilda says solemnly.

'I know. I should have told him the truth. And I never should have got involved in the debate about the supermarket. I should have kept out of it.'

'But, Maggie, you were only trying to help! My dad said you were very supportive.'

'He did?' My stomach flips.

'Definitely. *And* he said you were super-smart.'

'Smart?'

'Yeah. I made up all that other stuff. I'm sorry. The truth is, Dad really likes you. That's why Granny doesn't.' Matilda giggles.

'I don't know what you mean.' Thank goodness it's dark — otherwise Matilda would see how my face is burning.

'Sure you do. Dad fancies you — anyone can see that. Granny doesn't like you because she doesn't want anyone to replace Mum. She was being nasty to you to drive you away.'

'Do you really think so?'

'Oh, yeah, it's textbook. I've seen stuff like this on *Oprah.*'

I can't help but laugh at this.

'Yeah, she feels threatened by you, it's classic.'

'Well, there's no need to be threatened by me,' I say. 'Edward doesn't like me in that way.'

'Oh, yes, he does,' Matilda argues. 'I've seen the way he looks at you, Maggie.'

'How does he look at me?' I'm almost afraid to ask.

'Like you're in some soppy romantic movie.'

I swallow, but say nothing. Was the way he looked at me for real, after all?

'Daniel never looked at me like that,' she says sadly. 'He only wanted to use me. Anyway, I don't know why Granny was being so mean – Mum would have liked you.'

I feel tears prick my eyes. I can't believe Matilda is saying all this. I can't bear it – if any of it is true, then the timing is terrible. The stupidity of what I've done hits me hard and I feel lightheaded – I've made such a twenty-four-carat mess of everything. 'But I *have* to go,' I wail. 'I have no choice. I've let your dad down, I've let everyone down. I'm so *stuuuupiiiid*!'

'Don't cry, Maggie.' Matilda drapes her skinny arm across my shoulders. Through my tears I see a tiny barcode tattoo on the upper inside of her wrist. I can bet Edward doesn't know about that. Then again, there seems to be a lot he doesn't know about his troubled daughter. If only I could help. I wish they could communicate better – Matilda is so warm and funny once you crack the tough-nut exterior. And she's a really good listener too.

'Sorry.' I snuffle. 'I'm not much use, am I?'

'Be quiet.' Matilda's voice is suddenly harsh.

'No, honestly, I'm *not* much use. I'm hopeless – here I am, trying to help you, and I end up sobbing on your shoulder . . .'

'Maggie. Shut up.'

'Eh?' That's out of order. I'm only trying to explain myself.

I lift my head to look at Matilda and see her staring over my shoulder, a terrified expression on her face.

'It's Drya,' she hisses.

'Drya?' Drya is back?

I twist my head to see the horse galloping wildly towards us, her eyes rolling in her head. If we don't jump aside she's going to plough right into us.

'Move, Matilda!' I shout, trying to push her away. But she's stuck, rigid with fear.

'Move!' I yell again, and with an enormous effort I shove her away. And suddenly I'm flying through the air.

Rule Twenty-seven: *Believe in happy endings*

'Is she going to die?' a small voice says.

'No, of course not,' another answers.

'She might,' the small voice replies.

'No, she won't – I promise.' The other voice softens a little.

'She'll be fine,' a third voice interrupts. 'She'll come round – the girl has grit.'

'I hope you're right, June,' a fourth voice says. He sounds worried.

June. Why does that name sound familiar? June . . . There's definitely a ring to it, but I just can't seem to put my finger on it somehow . . . But I won't think about it now, because all I want to do is drift back into the darkness and sleep.

'Dr Martin's on his way,' a fifth voice adds. 'He'll be here in a few minutes.'

'I have a Mars Bar,' someone adds. 'Would it help?'

'How would a Mars Bar help?' a woman says. 'She's unconscious – what are you going to do? Set up a drip and mainline chocolate through her veins?'

'Sorry,' the man says. 'I didn't think.'

'No, you didn't, you sausage-roll-eating traitor!' the woman snaps.

They sound familiar too. Why is that?

'That's enough. Out – all of you. She needs some peace and quiet.'

It's a man talking now. A man with a lovely deep voice. I can hear him, closer, whispering in my ear: 'Maggie,' he says softly. 'Maggie, can you hear me?'

I open one eye and try to concentrate. Who is he? I can't see very well. Maybe if I could get the other eye open . . . but I can't for some reason. It's as if the lashes are firmly glued together. Did I forget to take off my mascara again last night? I wish someone would invent a mascara that miraculously disappears while you sleep, just sort of dissolves into your skin, maybe. It's such a bummer to wake up with panda eyes. Now the gloop will have hardened and it'll take twice as long to get myself looking presentable for work. I hope I haven't run out of eye-makeup remover. The bottle was almost empty the last time I used it.

'Maggie,' the voice says again. 'Maggie, can you hear me?'

God, my head hurts – what did I do last night? I try to remember. First I forgot to take off my makeup; now my head is pounding like I have the worst hangover in history. Did I go out? My brain is fuzzy and, for the life of me, I just can't remember. Was I with Dom? Did he finally manage to get me to go clubbing? I'll kill him when I get my hands on him – what on earth did he make me drink? I've never had a hangover like this. Not ever.

I turn my face to the left, where the voice is coming from, and with one last effort I manage to wrench both eyes open.

There's a man kneeling by me – a stranger. A stranger who looks oddly familiar. Oh, my God. I've had a one-night stand. I've slept with a random guy. Is he someone I met in a night-club? I rack my brains, panic flooding through me. I must have been really, really drunk – that's why I ended up in this state, lying beside a total stranger. I can't believe I've done this. It's so not like me to hook up with someone I don't even know. Even if he is . . . gorgeous. God, he's gorgeous – even in my state I can see that. He has the most beautiful eyes, really smiley and crinkly and lovely.

'Are you OK?' he asks.

His voice is lovely too, really caring. It looks like I had a one-night stand with a really nice person. Not that this in any way absolves me of blame – I am a bad person, a very, very bad person. I should be ashamed of myself. I *am* ashamed of myself. If I could just sit up and get out of here . . .

'Are you feeling a bit muzzy? You hit your head pretty hard. The doctor's on the way.'

Doctor? What doctor? I hit my head? What's he talking about? I can't focus, because my skull is throbbing so much.

'Do you have a headache?' the stranger asks now, smiling kindly at me. Mmm . . . he's cute.

I try to nod, but even that hurts. But it seems the stranger knows what I'm saying. 'Here, take this.'

He lifts a glass of water to my lips and I drink thirstily. That'll be the hangover – that'll teach me to drink too much. I must be in a complete mess – what on earth did I get up to last night? I haven't had a shocking hangover like this in *years*.

'You'll feel better soon,' the stranger says. 'Are you comfortable?'

'Yes,' I hear myself say, even though my head feels like it's going to explode.

Who the hell is this guy and why does he look so familiar? And where exactly am I? I'm not in a bed – I seem to be lying on a sofa. Oh, God, it looks like we never even made it to the bedroom. I must have had wild-stranger sex in this guy's front room – right here on this chesterfield with the worn cushions. Come to think of it, the cushions look familiar – I'm sure I've seen them somewhere before. And that smell . . . it's sort of musky, almost outdoorsy. It smells like . . . horse manure.

And then it comes to me, like a blinding flash of light. This isn't some gorgeous guy I've had a one-night stand with after a drunken night out. This is Edward – my temporary landlord. I am in the country, not in some stranger's flat after drunken sex.

It all comes flooding back – Robert turning up at the meeting,

Ted having his heart-attack, Matilda going missing. And Edward. He knows the truth about me. Oh, God.

'Did I . . . did I faint?' I croak.

'No, you didn't. Drya ran into you and you fell and hit your head pretty hard,' Edward says.

Drya? That's right. Matilda took Drya – she ran away.

'Matilda?' I croak. 'Is she OK? Is she hurt?'

'She's fine.' Edward smiles. 'A bit shaky, but fine. Thanks to you. She told me everything about . . . about Daniel. We had a very long talk.'

'Good – that's good. She's a nice kid – she's just a confused teenager.'

'You're right. And I haven't been a very good listener. But that's going to change.'

I'm so proud of Matilda I could burst – she's taken my advice to heart and reconnected with her dad. She'll be OK now, even if she's heartbroken for a while.

'How's Drya?'

'Not so good – she fell too.'

'Oh, no, I'm so sorry.'

'Don't worry about that,' he says softly. 'You and Matilda are safe, that's all that matters. It could have been so much worse.'

'Yes, I suppose you're right.' I'm trying to make sense of it all.

'We have to get you checked out, though – you might have concussion. The doctor will be here in a minute.'

'How did I get here?' I ask.

'Robert drove you,' he replies. 'He's been a great help tonight.'

Robert. Of course. 'Can I maybe have some more water?' My throat feels like sandpaper.

'Sure.'

He holds the glass to my lips again and I take a sip – the cool liquid feels wonderful as it slips down my throat.

'Is Polly OK?' I ask. 'I hope she wasn't frightened.'

'She's fine,' Edward says. 'She was very concerned that you might die, but once we reassured her that you weren't going to she recovered pretty quickly.'

'Die? Why would she think I was going to die?'

'Well, I guess since her mum passed away she's had a heightened sense of fear that people she's fond of will do the same. The psychologist says it's perfectly natural – a sort of transference, I think.'

'Polly's fond of me?'

'Oh, yes,' he says. 'She's very fond of you. She says you're different from other people. You're not naff apparently.'

He fiddles uncomfortably with the blanket that's draped across me while I try to think of something to say. Everything is such a mess – there's no getting away from it.

'I'm not an artist,' I confess. 'But I think you know that already.' I may as well tackle the subject – there's no time like the present.

'Yes, I do.'

Edward's voice isn't angry. Why is that?

'I'm an estate agent.'

There. I've said it. If there was any doubt in his mind about what he overheard in the hall I've cleared it up for him. There can be no misunderstanding any more.

'An unemployed estate agent is what I understand,' he corrects me.

He still doesn't sound angry. Why? He hates estate agents – he blames them for his wife's death. He thinks they should all rot in hell.

'That's true,' I say. 'And I'm homeless too.' In for a penny in for a pound.

'That's why you agreed to stay in Rose Cottage? You had nowhere to live in the city?'

'Yes, that's right. I didn't mean to lie – it all just got out of control . . .' I struggle to sit up and explain it properly to him.

'Sssh, you need to rest.'

'*Maggie!*'

Before he can continue, Polly bursts into the room and flings herself at the chesterfield. Edward drops my hand. It's only now I realize he was holding it tightly as we talked.

'Hi, Polly!' I smile at her.

'Are you OK?' Her plump face is creased with worry.

'I'm fine.'

'Do you promise?'

'I promise.'

'Pinkie promise?' She holds out her baby finger to me and grabs mine with hers.

'Pinkie promise,' I repeat.

'I was really scared.'

'I'm sorry, Polly. I didn't mean to scare you.'

'Polly, you have to go,' Edward says kindly. 'Maggie needs her rest.'

'Can't I just sit here, Dad? I won't talk.'

I nod at Edward.

'OK, then,' he ruffles Polly's hair, 'but not a peep, OK?'

'OK. I swear.'

Polly hunkers down on the floor beside me and takes my hand. 'Can I just tell Maggie one thing?' she asks, after about two seconds of silence.

'Polly!'

'It's OK,' I say. 'Go on, Polly.'

'We all know you're not an artist,' she announces solemnly.

'You do?' Of course they do. Nothing stays secret in Glacken for very long, I know that.

'Yup. Odette told us. And then Peg and Ted told her she should mind her own business!'

'They did?'

'Yes – Peg said that everyone has secrets and we should forgive and forget. Then she and Ted got all mushy and kissed – it was naff! They're going on a second honeymoon to see the Taj Mahal. I know what that is – we did it in school.'

I can't believe it – not only has Peg forgiven Ted for the sausage-roll transgression but she's agreed to go on a holiday! Ted will be over the moon – this is the adventure he's been longing for. 'What happened next?' I ask.

'Well, then Granny told Odette she wasn't welcome here any more. She told her to leave.'

'Really?'

'Yup! And then Odette said that Granny was a withered old hag!'

'No way!' I gasp.

'And then Granny told Odette that everyone knew she wasn't really Dad's girlfriend and she never would be. Granny likes you now – she says you have gumption.'

'I didn't know that was what Odette was telling people.' Edward looks mortified. 'I couldn't believe it.'

'So, you were never in a relationship with her?' I ask, gobsmacked. Can it be that she fabricated the whole thing? Was it all in her mind?

'No!' Edward shakes his head furiously. 'Never! I was just being friendly – I never knew she thought it would lead to anything more.'

'You *see*, Maggie?' Polly is triumphant. 'I *told* you she was a wicked witch, didn't I?'

'Yes, I remember.' How could I forget?

'Guess what else she did?' Polly is on her feet now, hopping with excitement.

'What?'

'She wanted to put Drya down.'

'Oh, no!' This is terrible, Edward will be heartbroken.

'Yes, but Dad wouldn't let her — would you, Dad?'

'No.' Edward shakes his head. 'Drya needs extra love and attention now — it's time we gave it to her. We won't give up.'

'I'm so glad.' I beam at him. I'd always thought she was such a sad horse — maybe she can be helped after all. 'Anything else exciting happen?' I ask Polly.

'Well, Robert had to go back to the city, but he said to give you this.'

Polly leans across and kisses me on the forehead. Robert has sent me his love — he really is one of the good guys. Hopefully the adventurous Maria will see that too.

'So,' Polly continues, 'everything is just the way it should be.'

'What do you mean?'

'It's just like the movie, remember?'

'Ah, the movie, yes.'

Poor Polly is still living in Fantasy Land where boy meets girl and it all works out.

'So, all you have to do is kiss Dad and then it will be happily ever after.'

'Polly, I don't think . . .'

I'm stuck for words. The last person Edward will want to kiss is me — not now, not after everything.

'What do you say, Maggie?' Edward asks softly.

'About what?' I stare at him. Is he joking?

'Polly is looking for a happy-ever-after. It would be terrible to disappoint her — don't you think?'

'But, what about . . .?'

'Maggie, I don't care what you do for a living. I just want you in my life.'

'You do?' My head is spinning again, but not because I hit it – because of the way Edward is looking at me.

'Yes, I do. Besides, I think you *are* an artist at heart. Which is why you'll be the perfect curator for the new arts centre in Glacken.'

'The new arts centre?'

'Yes, I spoke to Robert about it – he thinks it's a brilliant idea. He's going to recommend it to Laurence. If Xanta agrees to provide funding, we'll get the green light.'

'And Peg and Ted?'

'I've explained it to them properly and they're all for it. They can see how it will benefit the village. Besides, it sounds like they're planning a lot of travel over the next few months. Ted's already been looking up destinations on his iPhone.'

I gaze at him, love filling my heart. He's worked it all out – it's amazing.

But then I remember: what about his wife? He's not over her – I saw him in the graveyard only days ago and he was grief-stricken. How can he ever move on?

'He's even told Mum about you – didn't you, Dad?' Polly says, as if she can read my mind. Maybe she does have a second eye, just like Theresa's twins.

'I did,' Edward agrees. 'I brought some of her favourite flowers to the church and told her all about you. I know she'd have liked you very much.'

Favourite flowers? They must have been the roses he laid on the grave. He was asking for her blessing.

'There's only one problem,' he says, frowning for a second.

'What's that?' I ask.

'Well, when Claire gets back from India you'll have nowhere to live.'

'That's true . . .' I say, suddenly feeling much, much better. 'What do you think I should do?'

'Well, I suppose you could stay with Peg and Ted,' he says seriously.

'In that love nest? I'm not sure,' I muse.

'I see what you mean,' he replies. 'Well . . . I guess you could stay with us. We could do with some help in the stables.'

'You could?'

'Yes. You'd need to have experience, though – we can't have just anyone mucking out.'

'I'm pretty nifty with a pitchfork, as it happens.'

'You are? Well, then. That could work.' He leans towards me, his eyes liquid with desire. 'I might have to draw up a new legally binding contract, of course,' he says.

'And I'll have to get my lawyers to take a look before I sign on the dotted line,' I reply.

'That's very satisfactory,' he mutters.

Then he lowers his head and his lips meet mine.

I hear Polly scream with delight in the background as I close my eyes and melt into Edward's arms. She's right, this *is* just like the movies – it's exactly as I always imagined it would be: absolutely perfect.

Six Months Later

'So, what would this holistic therapy do for me exactly?' Jimmy the guard asks Claire.

'It would relax you, Jimmy,' Claire explains, smiling easily. 'An aromatherapy massage could melt all your troubles away.'

'I have been feeling a bit stressed recently,' Jimmy confirms.

'Have you?'

'Yes, there have been some work-related issues . . .'

I cringe as I hear this – poor Jimmy never got his promotion, despite his prodigious note-taking. It's been the talk of the village for weeks now. That and Odette's sudden departure. Ever since she left under a cloud to start a small-animal practice in the city people have been talking about very little else.

'Well, then, a massage could help,' Claire says. 'I'm not fully qualified yet, of course, but I could still give you one if you like. I need the practice.'

'It won't hurt, will it?' Jimmy is momentarily alarmed.

'Of course not.' Claire is affronted at the suggestion.

'Not unless you want it to, Jimmy.' Ted sniggers.

'Ted!' Peg chastises him. 'Sorry, Claire,' she says. 'I think he's still a bit jet-lagged.'

'It's not jet-lagged I am, it's giddy – giddy with life!' Ted laughs.

Ted is bronzed and healthy-looking – losing all that weight really suits him, and shaving off his handlebar moustache has transformed his smiling face.

'Now, Ted, people don't want to know about you and your

giddy life.' Peg slaps his arm good-naturedly. She's tanned and happy too. Ever since they started globe-trotting, they've really blossomed – it's knocked years off them both.

'That's all right, Peg.' Claire grins. 'If I was just back from Brazil I think I'd be pretty giddy too.'

'We're going to the Norwegian fjords next,' Ted says, a gleam in his eye. 'Aren't we, Peg?'

'If you behave yourself,' Peg replies.

'You really love to travel, don't you?' Claire asks.

'We do, Claire, we do!' Ted enthuses. 'Sure you only live once, and you've got to make the most of it.'

'I have to admit,' Peg's voice is a whisper and I have to strain to hear her, 'I was never a fan of going out foreign, but I've been converted. Travel really does broaden your mind.'

'I totally agree,' Claire says. 'Going to India changed my life.'

'Ah, India!' Peg sighs dreamily.

'That's where we had our second honeymoon,' Ted explains.

'Are there Indians in India?' Polly pipes up.

'Well, yes,' Claire says.

'Cowboys?'

'No cowboys, sorry.'

Polly looks disappointed. 'Did you hear that, Granny?' she shouts. 'There are no cowboys in India.'

'Quite right.' June smiles as Matilda hands her a glass of wine. 'There are more than enough of those here.'

'Now, June,' Laurence tuts, 'when am I going to convince you that I'm no cowboy?'

'Maybe when you stop acting like one.' She arches a brow at him.

'But look what I've done for the village – this arts initiative was practically my idea, you know.'

'Hardly, Laurence.' June's tone is withering. 'None of this

would be happening if it wasn't for Maggie. She and Edward deserve all the credit.'

June smiles at me, real warmth in her eyes, and I smile back.

'Matilda, will you please tell your grandmother that I'm not the big bad wolf?' Laurence pleads.

'She won't listen to me.' Matilda laughs. 'Granny is her own woman. But you can keep trying.'

I feel my heart swell with pride: Matilda has been a much happier girl in the past few months. Helping Drya with her recuperation has really settled and matured her: the change has been astounding.

'What else can I do?' Laurence laments to Polly. 'I've tried every trick in the book to get your granny to go out with me – nothing works.'

'She likes hot chocolate,' Polly says. 'Have you tried that?'

'Who mentioned hot chocolate?' Edward calls, poking his head through the door.

'Daddy!' Polly squeals, bounding towards him.

'Look who I found outside,' Edward says, guiding in a group. There's Dermot and Yvonne, Robert and Maria, Mum and Dad, Theresa, Malcolm and the twins too. I can't believe they're all here – everyone I love is in the one room. All those untruths I told are long forgotten.

'Have we missed it?' Dermot asks anxiously.

'No, they haven't cut the ribbon yet,' Yvonne replies fondly, linking her arm through his.

From where I'm standing I can tell she's wearing high-street shoes – she told me she sold her designer collection of Louboutins and Jimmy Choos on eBay to help pay the bills. I seriously underestimated her – she's not the gold-digger I thought she was. The truth is she's stuck by Dermot through thick and thin, despite his troubles.

'Good!' Dermot grins. 'I need to get Dom on the phone

– he won't want to miss Maggie becoming a proper country bumpkin.'

'So, Maggie,' Edward looks to me, his gorgeous blue eyes dancing mischievously, 'are you ready to become a proper country bumpkin, then?'

'As ready as I'll ever be.' I smile at him, my heart filled with love.

'Then what are we waiting for? Let's cut the ribbon and get this party started.'

Together we grip the scissors and slice through the red ribbon as everyone cheers and the cameras flash.

'Glacken Arts Initiative is officially open for business!' Edward cries. Then he leans in to kiss me and, laughing through tears of happiness, I kiss him back.

Acknowledgements

Thank you to:

My dedicated editor Patricia Deevy and the fantastic team in Penguin Ireland – Michael McLoughlin, Cliona Lewis, Brian Walker and Patricia McVeigh; Tom Weldon, Naomi Fidler, Ana-Maria Rivera, Jonathan Parker, Tom Chicken, Keith Taylor, and the superb sales, marketing, publicity, editorial and creative teams in Penguin UK – without their hard work my books would never end up on shelves; Alison Walsh for her wise words and calm unflappability; Hazel Orme for her expert copyediting; lovely Simon Trewin, Ariella Feiner and the team at United Agents for the kind calls and hand-holding; all the Irish and UK booksellers who support my novels every year – I'm so grateful.

My great friends – you're not in this one either, I swear! My beloved Mam and Dad: thank you for everything, I love you more than words can ever say. Dearest Martina, Jean Christophe, Eoghan and Jessie, the best support crew in the world! Thank you so much, I love you all. Darling Caoimhe, Rory and Oliver: you three light up my life. I couldn't do any of this without you – I love you guys.

My readers: thank you for making my dreams come true. I hope you enjoy this read wherever you are.